She raised her eyes to find Lord John watching her. Did he resent her, this man who would be her master for days to come? She had exchanged father and guardian and mentor for his protection, and she would like to believe that he at least thought fondly of her.

His dark brown eyes seemed to soften. "Do you wish, without reservation," he asked, gentleness in his voice, "to become my servant?"

"I wish it." Her voice was shakier than she would have liked.

He bent forward then and pressed her hands between his own, then lowered his head until it hovered just above hers. "I seal your vow this day," he said, his own voice simmering with emotion, "with a kiss."

THE
SILVER
SWORD

ANGELA ELWELL HUNT

WATERBROOK
PRESS

COLORADO SPRINGS

THE SILVER SWORD
PUBLISHED BY WATERBROOK PRESS
5446 North Academy Boulevard, Suite 200
Colorado Springs, Colorado 80918
A division of Bantam Doubleday Dell Publishing Group, Inc.

Scriptures in this book, unless otherwise noted,
are from the King James Version.

Most of the characters and events in this book are fictional.

For further information on the historical basis of the book, see page 389.

ISBN 1-57856-012-8

Copyright © 1997 by Angela Elwell Hunt

Printed in the United States of America
January 1998—First Edition

1 3 5 7 9 10 8 6 4 2

All books are either dreams or swords . . .

Amy Lowell, *Sword Blades and Poppy Seed*

Contents

The
Heirs of Cahira O'Connor

——=◦(◐)◦=——

Book 1

Prologue

E ven from across the library I could feel the stranger's eyes upon me. "Just ignore him and he'll go away," I muttered to myself, clicking furiously at the computer keyboard. But from the corner of my eye, I could still see him—a soft little man of late middle age, his features delicately carved with lines of concern and a small round paunch bulging over the waistband of his trousers.

The screen before me flickered a moment, then brightened as the modem received its transmission. When in the world had the college installed this computer, anyway—1993?

With infuriating slowness, the ancient modem finally retrieved twenty-eight references to "piebaldism," the topic I'd chosen for my research project. Only *twenty-eight?* Just a few minutes earlier I had typed in my name, "Kathleen O'Connor," and the Internet search engine had pulled up over sixty-six *thousand* references to "O'Connor" and/or "Kathleen." It would be nothing short of a miracle if I managed to come up with enough information to keep my writing prof happy on just twenty-eight references.

"Excuse me. Miss O'Connor?" I looked up, struggling to contain my impatience. The strange man stood beside me now, his shoulders hunched in a touching sort of dignity, his wool hat in his hand. A thin, carefully clipped mustache rode his upper lip, and his face seemed firmly set in deep thought.

"Yes?" I forced a polite smile. No use in letting him know I was ready to scream for security if he turned out to be some kind of kook.

"I pray you will pardon what must certainly be an untimely

intrusion," the man said, a note of apology in his voice. "Let me introduce myself. I am Henry Howard, a professor of European history here at the college. And though you must pardon my inquisitiveness, I asked the librarian for your name. She said you come here often."

Didn't all English majors live in the library? I nodded. "Nice to meet you, Professor Howard," I said, glancing back toward the computer screen. "But I'm in the middle of researching my semester project, and there are others waiting to use the computer."

"I don't mean to interrupt." He tightened his hold on his hat. "But I couldn't help noticing your hair. It is quite lovely. And quite . . . unusual."

Was that some sort of pickup line? "Thank you." I turned back toward the computer and typed my name, hoping to convince him I had things to do. I've heard comments about my hair for most of my life, and if this man had some sort of hair fetish, I didn't want to encourage him. Most people either love my hair or hate it, depending upon whether they consider redheads temperamental or spirited.

Professor Howard had not taken the hint. "That streak near your temple—"

I cut my gaze back to him, ready to blast him with a withering stare.

With one hand he pointed toward my head in a tentative gesture. "I know this may be a bold question, but is that discoloration natural? It appears to be, and it is quite distinctive, but you never can tell with young girls these days. One of my nieces has painted a black stripe down the center of her head." He shrugged helplessly as his voice drifted away, but his gaze remained locked with mine. Didn't he have sense enough to be embarrassed by his bad manners?

"The streak is natural," I answered quickly, determined to be done with him. "I've had it since childhood."

"Did your mother . . . " The professor hesitated and gripped his hat again. Maybe he did realize he was being nosy. "Did either of your parents have such a discoloration? Or one of your grandparents?"

"I don't think so," I answered. In spite of my annoyance, my confounded curiosity—the character flaw my mother always predicted would get me into trouble—rose up like a kite. Did he want to interview me for some kind of genetics study? No, he had said he taught in the history department, not the college of sciences.

"I wondered." A smile found its way through the mask of uncertainty on his face. "You must think me terribly rude, badgering you with questions of such a personal nature, but I couldn't stop myself when the librarian told me your name. The O'Connor clan of Ireland has a bit of lore attached to it—mythological lore, really—but when I saw you and heard your name—well, I thought it would be lovely if the story were true."

I leaned back and crossed my arms, still studying his face. I had far too much to do to be listening to such nonsense, but this rambling professor had really intrigued me. I had always been interested in genealogy, but since returning to college I stayed so busy trying to juggle my part-time job with writing assignments that I scarcely had time to read a newspaper, much less research my family tree.

Maybe it wouldn't hurt to indulge the professor for a moment or two. "What lore?" I rested my elbow on the table and propped my chin on my hand. "I know very little about my family tree."

"Ah. If you'll permit me—" The professor pulled a chair from the empty carrel next to mine, then sat down, resting his hat on his knees. "The O'Connors ruled over medieval Ireland as warrior kings of Connacht. From the day the Normans first entered Ireland, the O'Connors served as faithful allies of the English sovereigns, but in 1235, treacherous Norman foot soldiers and archers crossed the Shannon River and killed the ruling O'Connors in their ancestral home. That much we know as fact. But it's what we don't know for certain that fascinates me."

He lowered his voice and leaned forward as if he were divulging a great secret. "It is said that Cahira, daughter of the great king Rory O'Connor, lay in childbirth as the attack began. She was delivered of a son on that fateful day, and as the murdering Normans entered the castle, a serving maid spirited the baby away. The men had been dispatched to the towers and defensive positions; most were dead or dying. Cahira, still weak from childbirth, chose to defend her home rather than flee with her child."

Slowly and deliberately, the professor removed his glasses and began to wipe them with a handkerchief from his jacket pocket. "According to legend, Cahira picked up a sword to defend the chamber in which she and her ladies had taken refuge," he said, critically examining the lenses of his glasses before returning them to the bridge of his nose. "They resisted in a valiant display of courage, but the women were no match for the professional knights. And as Cahira lay dying of a wound from a Norman blade, she lifted her hand toward heaven and besought God that others would follow after her—in her words, 'bright stars who would break forth from the courses to which they are bound and restore right in this murderous world of men.'"

The professor told the story in a smooth, almost soothing voice, but I felt my heart rate increasing with every word. Why did the story move me? And why was I sitting here listening to this fanciful and melodramatic professor when I had a project to begin? This warrior princess and I had the same last name, but surely we had about as much in common as an apple and an oyster.

"That's an interesting story." I smiled at Professor Howard and pointed toward the computer screen. "But I really need to get back to work."

Apparently not one to be easily dissuaded, Professor Howard straightened himself in his chair. "There is more to the tale, Miss O'Connor. Cahira had red hair, too. In fact, seeing you made me think of her." He gave me a slightly reproachful look. "I had hoped you might be acquainted with her story."

Did he think all redheads pledged themselves to some kind of secret club? "No, I don't know much about Irish history," I answered, fingering the mouse and hoping he'd take the hint. "I'm an English major. And I have this project to do—"

"Cahira also had a streak of white hair near her left temple." His eyes gleamed with a curious intensity. "I have seen an artist's rendering of the princess. If I believed in such possibilities, I would think you could be her sister."

The remark left me speechless. All my life I have been teased about the sprout of white hair that grows from my left temple. As a kid, I was called names ranging from "skunk head" to "Cruella De-Ville." As a teenager, I tried dying it, and once or twice even lightened the rest of my hair to match the streak, but that area of my scalp had a will of its own. Lately I'd learned to leave it alone. I could finally just roll my eyes at what the world thought of my looks; too many other things demanded my attention. Sometimes I almost forgot I had a freakish white sprout growing from the side of my head.

But people like Professor Howard were always reminding me. Now he wanted me to believe I might be related to some Irish princess who apparently cursed her descendants to roam in the stars or some such thing.

I shook my head and protectively tucked the strand of white hair behind my ear. "Thanks for sharing that story, Professor, but this streak is a result of piebaldism. That area of my scalp doesn't produce pigment. My situation isn't as pronounced as someone with albinism, but the condition is similar."

"I know," Professor Howard answered, a small, fixed smile on his face. "Piebaldism is inherited. And yet you say neither your parents nor your grandparents share this condition. Is there, perhaps, an aunt or an uncle, probably on your father's side—"

I held up my hand, cutting him off. "No one. But the gene could have come from some great aunt, for all I know. O'Connors are everywhere."

"As scattered as the Irish." He stared at me in silence for a moment, his eyes gleaming with interest, then pulled a card from his coat pocket. "I believe, my dear, that you may be directly descended from Cahira O'Connor. I know it sounds unlikely, but what's the harm in a little investigation? If you'd like some guidance, here's my office number. If I'm not in the office, one of my student aides will take a message." He leaned forward and clapped his hands to his knees. "Call me if you have any inclination to learn more, Miss O'Connor. I have several books which should interest you."

Not knowing what else to do, I took the card. Professor Howard stood, nodded regally, then threaded his way through the carrels until he disappeared from sight.

The card he had placed in my hand was simple and direct:

Henry Howard, Ph.D.
Professor of Medieval European History
New York City College
212-555-2947

I stared at it for a moment, then felt a blush burn my cheeks. If this was Professor Howard's technique for introducing himself to young women, I had to admit his approach was unique. Of course I had no intention of contacting him again, but in the space of a few moments he had spun a story that brought me from complete lack of interest to fascination.

"Excuse me, but are you about finished here? I need to use the computer."

A grungy-looking guy in a tee shirt and jeans spoke up behind me, and his question caught me off guard. "Um, I'm just starting," I said, glancing at my watch. "And I'm signed on for another fifteen minutes. Check the reservation sheet at the reference desk."

The guy snorted and moved away, but I knew he'd be back, circling like a vulture. I had to get to work.

I was about to crumple the professor's card and toss it toward the nearest trash can when a sudden thought struck me. Since I was researching piebaldism, why not focus my topic a little? What could it hurt? Almost without thinking, I entered the command for a new search. "Find piebaldism and O'Connor," I murmured as I typed. If the gene really did run in the O'Connor family, there might be some record of other O'Connors with piebaldism.

Searching . . .

I drummed my fingers on the desk, waiting for the glacial modem to search and report. The professor had made Cahira's story sound romantic and dashing, but her curse or prophecy or whatever you want to call it hadn't made a bit of sense. Bright stars in their courses? Total drivel. Poetic, yes, but drivel nonetheless. Maybe the professor had overdosed on his morning coffee and caffeine had kicked his imagination into high gear.

Search results . . . four.

I took a quick, sharp breath as the computer screen flashed again:

Piebaldism and O'Connor:

Rory O'Connor, the last king of Ireland, killed in the Norman Invasion in 1235 . . . Survivors in that bloody attack included a grandson, who was spirited away from his mother's arms as the Normans attacked. According to legend, the child's mother, Cahira O'Connor, rose up from her bed of travail to wield a sword against the enemy, but scholars believe this may be an anecdotal myth fabricated to ennoble the sufferings of a murdered Irish princess. Cahira was noted for her exceptional beauty and a bold white streak through her red hair, one of the earliest recorded instances of piebaldism. . . .

The Hussite Crusades: holy wars, against the followers of Bohemian reformer Jan Hus, launched by Pope Martin V, successor in 1417 to the antipope John XXIII (not to be confused with the modern pope who took the same name in 1958). Among Hus's more influential followers was Anika of Prague, a fifteenth-century woman who fought as a knight prior to the Hussite Crusades. Annals of that time record an unusual white streak through the hair over her left ear, probably the result of piebaldism. Several chroniclers report that she claimed to spring from the ancestral throne of the O'Connors, ancient kings of Ireland.

Explorers and Seafaring, women at sea: Aidan O'Connor, a seventeenth-century artist described by her contemporaries as a "spirited lass with flaming hair marked by spout of gold," undoubtedly a case of piebaldism. The apprentice of a cartographer, she disguised herself as a common sailor to go exploring. While sailing with the Dutch explorer Abel Tasman, Aidan O'Connor fought hostile natives, studied the flora and fauna of several Pacific islands, and later published a volume of engravings described by her contemporaries as "amazing."

Civil War, women in battle: Flanna O'Connor, a nineteenth-century Charleston woman who disguised herself as a soldier and fought in the Civil War at her brother's side. Commonly known as the Velvet Shadow, she was as well known for her ability to rescue wounded comrades from behind enemy lines as for the singular pale streak which ran through her red hair. See "piebaldism."

All my previous plans faded like a bad radio signal. Could Professor Howard's story be true? Could there really be a link between these O'Connor women and the unusual physical characteristic we all shared? What were the odds that three women—four, counting Cahira herself—would share the same physical characteristic and risk their lives pretending to be men.

The idea was extremely far-fetched, and yet there was a certain symmetry to it. What had the professor told me? A dying woman had begged God to allow bright stars to break forth from the courses to which they were bound and restore right in the murderous world of men—

My thoughts halted as abruptly as if they'd hit a brick wall. Of course! The bright stars were the women! Cahira had barricaded herself in that chamber with the women of the castle. And, knowing that the men had gone to defend the fortress, she had stepped out of her roles as mother and daughter and princess in order to pick up a sword and fight. In that hour of weakness and fear, she may have regretted her feebleness and femininity.

My imagination caught the image. I could almost see this woman, drenched in sweat, her limbs still trembling from the exertions of labor and childbirth, her husband's heavy sword in her hand. Her maidservants were doubtless around her, some crying, some cowering, a few helping the nurse and infant escape through a tunnel or window. And Cahira, knowing that her situation was hopeless, begging God to allow her descendants to live and grow strong in order to restore right in a savage world.

And they had! Or had they?

The back of my neck burned with excitement, and a curious, tingling shock numbed both my brain and my fingertips on the keyboard. Professor Howard had slipped his little story into my imagination, and now I was delirious with discovery, having validated his so-called myth.

But it was too easy, far too simple. Had I really stumbled onto something the professor did not know—or had I been set up?

I cleared the computer screen and reran the search through a different search engine, this time reversing the order. "Search for O'Connor and piebaldism," I muttered, typing. I hit the enter key and clicked my nails on the desk in a flood of anticipatory adrenaline.

There was no way Professor Howard could know that I would actually run a computer search to test his little story. And if I had searched only for O'Connors, I would have pulled up thousands of references, too many to fully investigate. Maybe the link of piebaldism had never occurred to anyone else. I did have a special interest in the subject, after all.

Searching . . .

The computer beeped as the screen filled with the same four references I had seen earlier. Cahira of the thirteenth century, Anika of the fifteenth, Aidan of the seventeenth, Flanna of the nineteenth. All warrior women descended from the O'Connors, and all similar in appearance.

The possibility of a link between them seemed crazy, absolutely fantastic, but what if my hypothesis were true? These four women had each lived two hundred years apart, in different countries, under vastly different conditions. None of them would have known the others existed. And yet they were all O'Connors. They had all fought as men, for at least a brief span of time. And all of them had red hair marked by a streak of white—

Just like me. My mouth flew open in numb astonishment. I was about to enter the twenty-first century, two hundred years after Cahira's last warrior descendant. Could I be . . . the next one?

The thought was too incredible to comprehend. My fingers began to tremble as fearful images took root in my imagination. Were the histories of these women somehow tied into my own future? I was a student, not a soldier, but did some global tragedy or struggle lie beyond tomorrow's sunset? The idea seemed ridiculous, totally implausible. Yet I would still be in my twenties at the turn of the century, young enough to bear the blessing—or curse—of Cahira O'Connor, if such a thing really existed.

My logic kicked in. *It has to be a coincidence,* I told myself. *You've read too many books, seen too many far-out movies. You asked the computer for entries with two terms in common. Out of thousands, no, millions of web pages on the Internet, you shouldn't be surprised that something surfaced. Professor Howard's odd devotion to that myth spooked you, that's all. And it's late. You're tired. And you're facing a deadline...*

I put my hand on the mouse and cleared the screen, but thoughts of Cahira and her descendants persisted. How could the strange timing—every two hundred years—be explained by mere chance? And how could four women have the piebald patch in exactly the same place? And I hadn't searched for links about women who lived as men; that fact had simply come out of nowhere.

I whipped open my spiral notebook and turned to a clean page. If I couldn't let it go, I could investigate. I'd change my topic for my semester project, and instead of researching piebaldism, I'd explore the histories of Anika of Prague, Aidan of the O'Connors, and Flanna the Velvet Shadow. And maybe, if I had time and my professor approved, I'd do a background check on Cahira herself.

And if by chance I discovered that Professor Howard was a lonely man pulling some sort of academic scam, I'd publish my findings in the college newspaper and expose the creep. But if he had told the truth, he might have just changed my life.

The first red-headed wonder was Anika of Prague, the woman who fought as a knight—in an actual suit of armor?—in Bohemia.

Bohemia? In my adolescent days, my mother had often accused me of being bohemian, but I don't think she meant it as a compliment.

I entered "Bohemia" into the computer's reference book program and pressed the enter key.

Thirty seconds later, there it was:

Bohemia (Bo-HEE-mee-ah), a historic region of 20,368 square miles bordered by Austria (SE), Germany (W, NW), Poland (N, NE), and Moravia (E). The traditional capital is Prague. With the dissolution of Czechoslovakia (1993), the region became part of the Czech Republic. In the 15th century Bohemia was the scene of the Hussite religious movement. . . .

Bingo. According to the other search, my girl Anika followed a man called Hus. I hit the "print" button and skimmed the entry again. I could look up "Hus" and do a bit of checking on this Hussite movement. And maybe there'd be something under "Czechoslovakia" about this Anika of Prague.

Was all of this a quirk of fate or a divine appointment? I wasn't sure. In that moment I only knew I had to find all I could about Anika . . . because in learning about her past, I just might learn something about my own future.

I typed her name into another search program and snapped the enter key.

Searching . . .

Ernan O'Connor

One

Mama?" Anika was six again, small and helpless, alone in the upstairs room of an inn outside Prague. Father had gone out to the stable to meet with a man who had promised to find them a horse. Anika moved through the musty chamber. It felt like pushing aside curtains of black velvet, perfumed with the odors of unwashed bodies and the scent of sour hay. In the silence of the darkened chamber she felt her mouth go dry as fear rushed in. "Mama?"

"Hush, love, I'm here." The straw mattress rustled in the dark, then Mother's warm hand found its way to Anika's elbow and pulled her down onto the mattress beside her. Anika curled against her mother and hugged her knees, blinking as her night eyes adjusted to the dim light. Two other women slept on the far side of the room, the heavy sounds of their breathing blending with the snores of the innkeeper's dogs. The two huge mastiffs slept near the door, alert to any newcomer.

Mother's own breathing deepened and slowed; she had fallen asleep again. But Anika was not tired; she had slept in her mother's arms on the long walk and awakened in this room. She was never tired these days; there was too much to see. Father was moving the family from a farm out in the mountains to Prague.

"The University is in Prague," he had told Anika, "and people from all over the world go there to learn. They will need books, and they will bring books, and we will be prosperous in our little house. Wait and see, me wee bird, wait and see."

Anika sat up and crinkled her nose at the odors in the room. The strong scent of hay that covered the floor and filled the mattresses. The warm, comforting smell of the dogs. Anika liked that smell. One of the mastiffs sensed her gaze and lifted his head, rewarding her with a calm, droopy smile. Anika raised her chubby hands and clapped them to keep the dog's attention, but the huge animal simply lowered its head back to its paws and sighed loudly.

Anika clapped again, then giggled when the animal abruptly lifted its head. But it did not look at her this time. The dog stared at the window, where the black sky had brightened to the color of sunrise.

Anika clapped once more, willing the dog to look at her. But instead it nudged its mate, who woke instantly and whimpered. Restless, the mastiffs stood and paced between the window and the doorway, then began to growl.

"What's wrong?" Anika swung her legs from the prickly mattress. "What's wrong, dogs?"

The biggest dog, the male, darted toward the staircase. The female whined for an instant, then gently took the hem of Anika's garment between her teeth and pulled her toward the dark hallway.

Anika laughed. What sort of game was this? She followed the dog, allowing the shuffling giant to gently lead her down the stairs.

In the big room below, wisps of gray smoke drifted over tables and chairs. A few red-eyed men slouched over a table in the corner while the innkeeper sat at his stool, his head propped on his hand, his eyes closed. As the whining dogs scratched at the door, Anika sat on the bottom step, content to wait on her father.

One of the men at the table suddenly lifted his head, like a cat scenting the breeze. "Is that smoke?" He stared out the window, then elbowed his companion. "Fire! There's fire outside! The barn!"

Anika shrank back against the wall, watching in confusion as the men leaped up from their tables. The innkeeper awoke and fumbled for a leather pouch inside his desk. Two of the men who had been sitting at the table ran toward the door, crashing into one another in an effort to reach it. The third man rushed for the stairs, nearly tripping over Anika in his headlong dash.

"Fire!" The cry echoed now from the courtyard outside, and the air vibrated with shouts, cries, and the sound of screaming horses. Some big person—Anika could not see clearly in the confusion—jerked her from her place, slung her over a shoulder, and carried her outside.

The barn and the inn were a mass of flame, their thatched roofs blazing like hay in a parched field. The sodden men who had been sitting inside now stumbled over themselves to fetch water and buckets, and through the noise Anika heard her father's voice: "Let me pass, you eejits; me wife and child are inside!"

"Papa!" Anika turned, throwing herself into her father's arms, but his eager embrace was entirely too brief. "Where's your mother, lass?" He bent down to look her in the eye, his hands tight on her arms. "Came your mama downstairs with you?"

Anika put her finger in her mouth and shook her head. "The doggie brought me," she said simply, pointing toward the mastiff that stood howling outside the flaming barn.

Her father rushed toward the building, but a line of men threw up their arms and held him back. "Too late, man," one of them said. "You can't go in there now. 'Tis a tinderbox."

And then, like a sound from heaven, Anika heard Mother's voice and looked up. With the two other women, Anika's mother leaned out the window toward safety and the rescuers below.

"Help them!" Ernan O'Connor shouted, pointing to the women. He ran up to the burly innkeeper and clapped his hand on the man's shoulder, whirling him around. "By all the saints, lend a hand, man! Have you a ladder?"

"Look yonder." The innkeeper pointed to the far end of the house. And there, in the devilish glow of the fire, Anika saw two black-robed men steadying a ladder for a plump, balding man in red who moved slowly and carefully downward, as if he had all the time in the world.

Ernan O'Connor rushed forward, and Anika ran to keep up.

"Let me use this ladder." Anika's father grabbed one of the black-robed men and tugged on his sleeve. "There are women still in the building, at the south end."

"Would you take the ladder while the cardinal is still upon it?" The man's eyes went wide with surprise. "Patience, fellow. He is nearly down, thank God."

The man in the red robe landed heavily on the ground, and the two men in black sighed in relief. Anika's father grabbed the ladder, but the man in red shook his head and pointed up toward the window he had just vacated. "My vestments," he said simply, staring at one of the black-robed ones. "You must get my vestments and the satchel with the parchments."

"But, Your Eminence—" one of the men protested.

"What sort of amadons and eejits are you?" Anika heard her father roar. With the strength of two men he laid hold of the ladder and pulled it from the window, but the black-robed ones stopped him.

"I'll go." After tossing a single guilty glance toward Anika's father, the tallest man sprinted up the ladder. As black smoke billowed overhead, he crawled through the window, then a moment later a pair of bundles flew out the opening and landed at Anika's feet.

The man in red nodded soberly and turned away, not even waiting to see if his servant would return. Other men had gathered about now. Pushing Anika back, they pounded on the ladder, urging the man upstairs to hurry down while at the far end of the building the women wept and screamed and tore their hair.

"Papa!" Anika stood on tiptoe, but she could no longer see her father. She slipped away from the crowd and found him beneath the window where the women waited. Dense clouds of black smoke rolled out the window above the women's heads, and Anika could hear a whispering, crackling noise, as though the fire contained a horde of gremlins who laughed and cackled to themselves.

"Jump, me darling, and I'll catch you." Father's voice broke with terrible sadness as he lifted his arms to Mother. "Don't wait a minute more; just jump!"

Anika watched her mother move out onto the edge of the window ledge, ready to leap into Father's arms. A cloud of smoke rolled out the window and hugged Mother like an old friend. Anika felt the heat slap her face; it was like the rare days when her father had money enough for two logs in the fireplace and set them to burning at once.

"Jump, love!" Mother nodded and leaned forward, but in the instant before she could slip off her perch, the roof roared like the sea and rushed downward. Amid a flood of flames and cinders and sparks the other waiting women flung themselves toward the open window.

For a moment Anika thought it had begun to rain bodies, timber, and ashes. Father was knocked off his feet as a falling beam hit him on the head. He lay sprawled on the ground, his hands extended in front of him, his eyes closed as if he slept.

As Anika whimpered softly, the innkeeper and his friends began to untangle the other bodies. Of the three women, the first was scarcely hurt at all, and the second suffered only a broken leg and some singed hair.

But Mother lay quiet and still, her head bent to the side as if she were laughing. She wasn't burnt at all; she lay asleep on the ground. "Mama, wake up," Anika urged. She squatted low to whisper in her mother's ear and could smell smoke on her mother's skin. She reached out and shook Mother's arm; the skin was still warm and soft as a rose petal. "Mama! Why won't you wake up?"

"Come away, child." The innkeeper's wife, a matronly woman with an ample bosom and lap, pulled Anika up and moved her away from the heat of the burning building. "Your mama has gone to heaven."

Anika shook her head. "My mama is asleep."

"No, child, her neck's broke." The woman dashed a tear from her soot-streaked cheek, then knelt and clasped Anika's hands in her own. Her eyes darkened and shone with an unpleasant light as her sweaty hands squeezed Anika's knuckles. "Your mama's dead, child, and it's all that cardinal's fault. Don't you ever forget it, you hear? As

God is my witness, the Roman church and her meddling priests will be the death of us all."

Anika did not understand, but she nodded obediently until the woman released her hands. Not knowing what else to do, she stood silent as the woman rose to watch her home burn to the ground. From somewhere in the distance Anika heard the hoarse cry of her father's weeping.

And when the man in the red robe gathered his bundles and turned from the ghastly scene, Anika clamped her eyes shut, afraid to look upon the man who would not give her mother the ladder.

"Go away," she murmured, afraid to open her eyes lest he still be there, mocking her with his smug little smile. "Go away, please." The words hurt her throat, as though she'd swallowed some sharp and jagged object. "Go away, go away, *go away!*"

"Anika! Open your eyes, wake up!"

Her eyes flew open even as her heart congealed into a small lump of terror. But the face staring at her was not the cardinal's. Her father sat on the edge of her bed; his hands gripping her arms and the corners of his mouth tight with distress.

"Papa?" The word was hoarse, forced through her constricted throat.

"Anika, you're having a nightmare." His eyes searched her face. "Are you all right?"

She took a quick, wincing breath. She was home, safe in bed. Not six anymore, but sixteen.

"Are you all right then, or shall I be having to leave a light burning for such a big lass as you?" Her father smiled at her now, but she saw the dark memories at the back of his eyes, under the mocking humor. He knew what she'd dreamed—she'd had these dreams off and on for years. He probably dreamed of the fire, too, but he wouldn't want her to worry about him. He was an unselfish man, Ernan O'Connor.

"Thank you, Papa," she whispered, slipping her arms around his neck. Relaxing in his embrace, she closed her eyes, but the vague shadows of her dream still drifted across her eyelids. She snapped her eyes open again and stared over his shoulder at the flickering candle's light as her father rocked her slowly and crooned an Irish lullaby.

A beautiful figure wins love with very little effort, especially when the lover who is sought is simple, for a simple lover thinks that there is nothing to look for in one's beloved besides a beautiful figure and face and a body well cared for. I do not particularly blame the love of such people, but neither do I have much approval for it, because love—

"Anika!"

More surprised than frightened, Anika looked up from the book she kept hidden under her parchments. Her father stood in front of the door, his face pressed to the tiny shuttered opening.

"Quickly, me girl! Hide Hus's tablet and the parchments! The archbishop comes."

The worried tone in her father's voice sparked Anika's fear. She slammed her book shut and, with the ease that comes from long practice, dropped Master Hus's wax tablet to her lap and shuffled the uppermost sheet of parchment beneath the others on her writing board. Archbishop Albik was not her favorite clergyman—if truth be told, Anika liked him little. But as the archbishop of Prague, in Bohemia his influential voice was second only to that of King Wenceslas.

Her father opened the door, and the archbishop's coolly impersonal tone broke the stillness of the copyist's shop: "Grace and peace to all who dwell herein." Anika took one quick look downward to be certain Master Hus's tablet *and* her book were safely hidden, then pasted on an innocent smile as her father stepped aside and bid the archbishop enter.

Anika fought inward revulsion every time she saw the stiff and starched Archbishop Albik in her father's bookshop. Some high personage in Rome had appointed him to serve the city of Prague, and, like his predecessor, Albik seemed more intent upon solidifying his position and power than serving God's people. Lately, in fact, he had proved himself a devout enemy of all who loved and sought the truth of the gospel.

"Good day to you, my children," Albik said, regally inclining his tonsured head as he entered the room. He extended his bulky gold ring for her father's kiss, and Anika glanced down at her desk so she wouldn't have to watch her father kneel and genuflect. Why wouldn't the archbishop leave them alone? Weren't there other copyists in the city for him to harass? But none of the others were close to Jan Hus.

The archbishop glanced about the small work space as her father stood and politely clasped his hands before him. "To what happy occasion do we owe this honor, Your Grace?"

"What use would I be if I did not see to the welfare of the souls in my care?" the archbishop answered, his countenance completely immobile. His eyes flashed over the room, taking note of the rolled parchments, the bottles of ink, the precious books safely stored in chests at the back of the small shop. "I see you are busy." The holy hand lifted in a limp gesture and indicated the collection of wax tablets in a basket near Anika's writing table. "I did not know our fair city housed so many writers. Of all the copyists on this street, your shop is by far the busiest."

"Well, naturally, the students and teachers at the university keep us occupied, thank God," her father answered, bowing his head in respect. "And me daughter is skilled with a pen and ink. By the grace of God and with her help, we are quick, and we are pleased to present our customers with fine work. They bring us their books and lessons, don't you see, and we are also able to rent out several of the books we keep in our library—"

"What are you inscribing here, Ernan O'Connor?" The archbishop walked over to the writing board where Anika's father had been working. His quill lay on the desk, the ink-filled ox horn remained uncovered. A large parchment lay flat on the board, a pumice stone holding it in place.

"Ah, I was readying this parchment for writing," her father explained, a gleam of relief in his eye. "I had not yet begun to copy anything."

"But you were ready to begin." Archbishop Albik gestured toward the wax tablet near the edge of her father's writing table. "What will you copy today? More scribblings from students at the university? Or perhaps one of the masters' lessons." He casually stroked his chin. "None of these tablets would contain a sermon from the preacher at Bethlehem Chapel, would they? Or the words of the heretic Wyclif?"

"I would not allow heresy over the threshold of me house." Anika's father straightened his shoulders. "I am ever mindful of me daughter, Your Grace, and would not endanger her immortal soul by allowing heresy to enter her thoughts. We are a God-fearing household; haven't I said so?"

Albik gave him a brief nod. "See that you remain so, Ernan O'Connor." When the archbishop lifted his hand, Anika lowered her head, more to duck the blessing than to humbly receive it. She felt no love and little tolerance for Prague's newest prelate. She and her father had dutifully attended several services at his church and left spiritually dissatisfied. The archbishop led the service in a manner so dull and dry the words seemed to be coming from him after a lengthy journey through a barren wilderness. His words, moreover, were Latin, and though Anika understood the tongue, not many of her fellow Bohemians did.

Fortunately, the archbishop seemed more intent today upon spying out the bookshop than in gauging the depth of reverence in her glance. Albik looked around the shop one final time, then turned on his heel and moved with stiff dignity through the doorway. One by one, the archbishop's attendants—an odd assortment of priests, scribes, and other clerics—momentarily peered into the bookshop as if checking to see if their master had left some ray of holiness behind, then whirled and hurried after His Grace.

Without speaking, her father sank into his chair. When she was certain the archbishop and his cronies had gone, Anika retrieved the wax tablet she had dropped into her lap. "He would never suspect that you would allow me to copy such important work, Father," she murmured in a low voice, her eyes intent upon the doorway lest some spying monk suddenly materialize. "He would never believe I am copying Master Hus's sermons."

"He fears more than the copying, me wee dove," her father answered, spreading his ink-stained hands over the blank parchment on the board before him. "He fears the words that you copy. Certain men, armed with naught but a pen, have successfully stormed bulwarks others could not take with either sword or excommunication." He sat very still, his eyes narrowing. "Truth to tell, I think Albik and those like him fear for the Church itself. Their positions, their power, perhaps even their immortal souls are at stake. For if Jan Hus is true, and everything I read in Holy Scripture tells me he is, then the priests and bishops will be wanting to be rid of him . . . and anyone who has aught to do with him."

Fear clamped down on Anika's throat. She had heard rumors in the street, rumors of war that would surely come, a holy crusade to wipe out words like those she penned every day.

Her father's eyes met hers then, and he smiled, chasing her apprehensions away. "But now, Daughter, I'm perishing with the hunger of a dozen men. Why don't you see if there's any bread and cheese in the larder?"

"Yes, Father," she whispered. As she slid out of her chair, *The Art of Courtly Love* slipped from beneath her apron and fell to the floor with a thud. With a surge of guilt Anika gathered it up, ashamed at having taken advantage of her father's trusting nature and more than a little embarrassed by the book itself.

But her father had turned his attention to marking the blank parchment before him. Anika held the book to her pounding heart, ready to explain that she was only dreaming, that she wasn't ready to fall in love and marry just yet, but her father seemed blissfully unaware of what had happened behind him.

Anika paused a moment, then found it impossible not to grin at her father's broad back. He knew what she was reading; he knew everything that went on in their tiny house.

She slid *The Art of Courtly Love* back into the wooden chest from which she'd taken it, then climbed the stairs, humming as she went.

———o———

"Aye, Ernan, I'll expect you'll be showing the likes of me to the street, after such august company as you've had this morning."

Anika felt a rush of pleasure as she recognized the voice. She hurried down the stairs with her tray and turned the corner in time to see Sir Petrov, her father's best friend and their closest neighbor, momentarily dwarf the doorway with his massive height. Though he had undoubtedly seen more than sixty summers, age had not diminished the man's size or the strength of his voice. His shoulders had shed the corded muscles he wore when he carried arms for Lord Honza of Chlum, but his presence was still imposing. Upon his forehead a swath of wavy white hair fell in a series of commas over skin toughened like a dry hide, and his eyes were startlingly dark against his tanned skin and white hair.

Petrov's thin mouth quirked with a cynical twist when he saw Anika. "Having your dinner, are you, and not offering an old friend a bite?"

"'Tis a bit strange, don't you think, Anika," her father said, winking at her, "that Sir Petrov comes always at dinner?" He wiped his hands on a scrap of linen and stood to greet his friend. "Petrov, welcome, and partake of whatever you please. We have only bread and cheese today, nothing grand, but you are always welcome at our table—"

"I thank you, but I am not hungry." Petrov shut the door behind him, stomped his boots on the floor, and shook his dusty mantle from his shoulders. Without ceremony, he hung his cloak on a peg near the door, then propped his lanky frame upon a stool and clasped his hands. "So tell me." His seamed face tilted from Anika to Ernan. "What auspicious occasion brought the archbishop of Prague to your house this morning? Yours was the only shop blessed with his presence, you know. The entire street has done nothing but buzz about it, and I'm only sorry I wasn't here to greet His Pompousness myself."

"In truth, it was nothing," the copyist answered, sitting again at his worktable while Anika spread a napkin before him. "A cordial visit at best, and a fruitless spy mission at worst. He asked how our business was and wondered why we had so many tablets to copy. I assured him that our proximity to the university and me daughter's skilled hand account for our busy shop."

The older man lifted a bushy brow. "He said nothing of Master Hus?"

Humor sparkled in Ernan's eyes. "Ah, sure, he asked if we ever copied heresy, and I assured him that we did not. And I still stand before God as an honest man."

Petrov tilted back his head and laughed. "You are, Ernan, until the archbishop brings you one of *his* sermons to publish. What will you do then? Refuse him, or declare yourself a hypocrite?"

"If the archbishop should ever bring me a tablet to be copied," Ernan answered, the beginning of a smile twisting the corners of his mouth, "I fear I shall be too busy to serve him. Look around, you see that we have more than our share of work."

Anika gave her father a generous portion of bread and cheese, then settled back at her worktable. Breaking off a bite of bread, she shot the old knight a shy smile. "Have you nothing to do today, Sir Petrov? No ladies to rescue? No dragons to slay?"

"Ah," the knight said, loosening the button at his high collar, "I can tell you are your father's daughter, Anika. Wit alone would not put such a cynical tongue in your head."

"But I'm not being cynical, dear Petrov," Anika answered, clasping her hands as she looked up at him. She really did adore the aged knight and knew he liked nothing better than sharing tales of his adventures. The few knights who reached Petrov's age usually retired in quiet houses on their masters' estates, but Petrov's beloved master had died before bestowing such an award upon his loyal captain. He could have remained in service to the nobleman's son, but Petrov had chosen to retreat to the city rather than spend his remaining lifetime again proving himself in a vocation more suited for young men. Now he lived in the small house across the street from Ernan O'Connor's bookshop and earned his daily bread delivering books and occasionally sharpening the dueling skills of the sons of great lords who were too embarrassed to display their incompetence before their own households.

Anika suspected that beneath Petrov's bluster and booming voice lay a very lonely man. Now she gave him her most charming smile. "If you have time, Sir Petrov, I would like to hear about the day you escorted your lady to church and the jealous suitor tried to kidnap her. I never tire of that tale."

"I do," her father objected good-naturedly, but he crossed his arms and settled back to listen. Both of them knew Petrov couldn't be stopped once he launched into a story.

Anika nibbled at her cheese and bread, momentarily forgetting about her waiting work as Petrov told of a bold attempt to snatch a noblewoman and his valiant assault upon her pursuer. He had almost reached the point where the lady fell off the horse and into a stream when the bookshop door creaked again. A different priest entered, and at the sight of this man Petrov halted his story in midsentence.

"Master Hus!" Anika's father uncrossed his arms and immediately stood to greet his visitor. "Faith, it's good to see you. How are you faring today?"

In appearance and manner, Jan Hus differed from the archbishop as much as a lamb differs from a wolf. Shunning the trappings and robes of a learned clergyman, Hus preferred a simple brown cassock like those of the lowliest monks. He wore a priest's tonsure cut into the crown of his thick brown hair, and a severely pointed beard jutted forth from his chin with the impertinence of a scolding finger. He was an important man—a master at the University of Prague and Father Confessor to Queen Sophia—but he welcomed everyone he met with disarming friendliness. Touches of humor lined his mouth and edged his eyes, which shone with merriment, a hint of mischief, and a quick intellect. In his dress and posture, Jan Hus seemed a simple monk, but the eyes, Anika thought, revealed the rich complexity of the man beneath the cowled robe.

Even Petrov stood to acknowledge the worth of the bookshop's most recent visitor. "Master Hus, I am honored." The old knight doffed the shapeless sugar-bag hat he wore and greeted the priest with a ceremonial bow. "If ever you have need of a willing heart or a sharp sword, you have but to call on me."

"Thank you, Sir Petrov." Hus acknowledged the knight's offer with touching dignity, then turned to Anika's father and eased into a smile. "Well met, Ernan! I hope I have not come at an inconvenient time, but I thought I would check on the progress of my sermon against the selling of indulgences. Brother William has just informed me that a papal legate is on his way to Prague. Unless I am mistaken, the pope has taken action against us."

"Has he published a bull?" Ernan's brows knitted in a frown.

Anika watched her father and took note of the worried tone in his voice. The neglect and indifference of the church might have been indirectly responsible for her mother's death, but her father had responded to the church with an equal indifference of his own until he began writing for Jan Hus. Now papal decisions and the abuses of power that Hus preached against seemed to affect her father personally.

The master glanced back at Petrov. "I'm certain my friend the knight will understand the implications. Ever since the Great Schism, when the church ended up with three popes, all claiming to be God's anointed head of the church, the papacy has been in chaos. No one of them would relinquish power to any of the others. And now Pope John is intent upon consolidating his empire and broadening his base of support. Ladislas, king of Naples, has threatened Rome, so our Pope John has decided to proclaim a holy crusade against him. To any who will take part in his war the pope will grant plenary indulgence and the forgiveness of sins."

A glaze seemed to come down over Hus's eyes. "The bull says those who contribute toward the expenses of the campaign are guaranteed a place in heaven. The bull is to be read every Sunday in every church, but I have not obeyed the order. How can I read a declaration of war when I am trying to lead men to peace?"

"We will not tolerate this illegitimate pope!" Petrov's voice slammed into the conversation. "We are Bohemians, and we are wise enough to see through this pope's selfish schemes. We will not be drawn into his little vengeances and petty wars—"

"Unfortunately, my brave friend, there are many who believe the pope has these powers, even the authority to forgive sin before it is committed," Jan Hus interrupted. "And I fear they will be drawn into his trap."

"Now I understand why the archbishop was so interested in me work today," Ernan said, stroking his beard. "Are you saying, Master Hus, that Pope John is *not* the representative of Christ on earth? Are you prepared to publish this statement? There would be dire consequences—"

"I'll say it privately here, and I will even proclaim it before my classes at the university," Master Hus answered, his cheeks brightening with color. "But I have learned, Ernan, that discretion and mercy must be intertwined. I cannot proclaim the truth to people not ready to receive it. If they lose faith in the pope, how am I to be certain they will not lose faith in the Church? In Christ himself? They must know in whom they have believed, and too many of them are yet strangers to the gospel."

Even in the shadowed light of the room, Anika saw the preacher's face heat to red. "But know this, my friends—this Pope John has nothing to do with Christ. Before he took that name he was known as Baldasarre Cossa, a murderer, pirate, and soldier, not an honorable knight like you, friend Petrov. He holds nothing but contempt for good while he cleaves to that which is evil. I have heard it reported, on good authority, that he is given to almost every form of vice. His vile character is no secret, but by shrewdness, audacity, and treachery he has risen from lowly thief to sovereign head of the Church."

Master Hus stopped suddenly and threw a guilty glance in Anika's direction. As a blush burned her cheek, she lowered her eyes.

"Do not fear to speak plainly around me, Master Hus," she said simply. "My father has withheld nothing that is truthful from me, and I have read of the many evils that occupy the world. There is little you could describe that I have not read about."

"The lass speaks the truth," her father asserted, nodding vigorously. "She is not like any other sixteen-year-old girl you would meet in Prague. Anika is far wiser than her years."

"Would that I had learned so much at her age." The minister's eyes clouded with some sort of misgiving for a moment as he looked toward Anika, then he returned his gaze to her father. "I fear I have forgotten the point of my story."

"The pope," Petrov provided helpfully. "You said he was a knave and a cutthroat."

"Ah, yes." A rueful smile flickered across the priest's face. "Well, God works in ways we cannot fathom. In any case, Ernan, I shall need as many copies of my sermon as possible. My students will be pressed to compare my stand on the selling of indulgences against the pope's bull. And the papal emissary will soon be among us."

"I have completed the first copy." Anika's father shuffled among the rolled parchments on the table behind him. "And Anika will soon be hard at work on the second. We could have ten copies within two days, if that pleases you."

Her father's words pierced Anika's conscience. She *should* have been hard at work on Master Hus's sermon, but she had been enthralled with *The Art of Courtly Love.* Not that she expected to be courted by a nobleman, but she enjoyed reading about a way of life she would never experience.

A thoughtful smile curved the priest's mouth. "Ah, you are too good to me, Ernan O'Connor. I know you will work hard on my sermon while other work goes begging, and I cannot pay what you need to provide for your daughter—"

"God smiles upon us, and we have not gone hungry," Ernan answered, pushing sweat from his forehead up into his mop of auburn hair. "And if the truth is to be told in this troubled time, a book is far more willing to speak than many a man."

"Well said." Hus lifted a hand toward Anika, then turned to her father and lowered his voice. "In fact, Ernan, I have also come today to speak a private word in your ear. If there is some errand your daughter could run—"

Anika felt a blush run like a shadow over her cheeks. When would they stop treating her like some sort of fragile flower? Only a moment ago the preacher had noted her sophistication, yet now he was willing to send her away as if she were only a simple child. What news could he bring that she could not understand or imagine?

"Sure, and I was just wanting to send Anika out with these books," her father said, pointing to a wrapped parcel on a stand near her desk. He turned to her and gestured toward the door. "Anika, me wee bird, those books are to be delivered to the new rector at the university." Standing, her father laced his fingers behind his neck. "Be sure to place the books directly into the rector's hands. They are too valuable to be entrusted to anyone else."

"Yes, Father," she murmured, hoping the discontent in her voice would not spoil the preacher's opinion of her.

Hus winked at her as she stood and tied her cloak around her neck. "I apologize for sending you away," he said, his mahogany-colored eyes softening.

"I understand," she said, trying to force a smile. "You have something to discuss that has nothing to do with me, so it is best that I am out of the room."

"On the contrary, my dear, the news I bring has everything to do with you," Jan Hus answered, the smile suddenly leaving his eyes. "And for your safety, I think you should allow our friend Sir Petrov to escort you to the university. I will see you later, perhaps when you have returned."

Petrov rose stiffly from his stool and gathered the bundled books into his arms. "I will finish the story I began for you," he said, opening the door for her with one hand as he balanced the books with the other. "As I recall, the lady had just tumbled into the stream, and I stood there with only a broadsword to protect her honor."

Anika gave Petrov a fleeting smile, then turned and curtseyed to

Master Hus. She lingered near the doorway as long as she dared, hoping to catch some clue of what he intended to discuss with her father, but he picked up one of the wax tablets and pretended to read it, clearly indicating that he would not speak until she was well away.

With a heart burdened by care and curiosity, she reluctantly moved through the doorway, allowing Petrov to take her arm and lead her along the slanting streets of Prague.

Though he was happy to serve as Anika's escort, Petrov had no inclination to wait with her for the rector. Naturally impatient and burning to know what matter had compelled Master Hus to seek privacy, Petrov asked the rector's housekeeper to send the girl home with a trusted chaperone, then took his leave of the two women. He quickly retraced his steps and entered the bookshop without knocking. Ernan O'Connor and Jan Hus were deep in conversation over the copyist's worktable, and neither man even seemed to notice that Petrov had reentered the room.

"So you see how it is, then," Hus was saying, all traces of humor gone from his eyes. "Your daughter is old enough to marry, and more than a few men have noticed that she is pleasant and comely. You have done well to raise her alone, Ernan, but what plans have you made for her future?"

"Why shouldn't she spend her future here with me?" Ernan's face brightened to a tomato hue. "I've taught her to read and write four different languages. There's not a lass within a hundred miles of Prague who has read as many books! And she can quote the Scriptures in Bohemian, French, or even English. I would have taught her Gaelic as well, but there's not much call for me mother tongue around these parts. I had planned that we should continue together in the business—"

"You have done a fine job, and I'm not disputing her virtues," Hus interrupted, putting out a soothing hand. "But the idea of a woman in trade is absurd. She will need to marry, and what womanly skills have you taught her? The bread you ate for lunch today—

did she bake it? Does she know the least bit of what a woman should know in order to become a wife?"

Twin stains of scarlet appeared on the copyist's cheeks. "She can read a book as well as you, Master Hus, and translate it, too."

"Be honest, Ernan." The preacher looked up and shot Petrov a glance that clearly said, *Help me out.* Uncertain which end of the debate he should support, Petrov lowered himself to the corner stool and crossed his arms, waiting to see whose was the stronger argument.

"Anika will work with me." Ernan gave the minister a forced smile and a tense nod. "She has no need to marry. Together we make a good income, and no scribe in Prague does a better job of book copying. The university students pay her by the column—sixteen columns of sixty-two lines for a penny, what an income! And Anika handles the book rentals—soon the rentals will bring in as much as the copying. As long as me daughter has her books, she will not starve."

"What if she *wants* to marry?" the preacher countered.

The copyist's steel-blue eyes widened with astonishment. "Why would she? She has a home here, and a father to provide for her."

"She may want a home of her own. She reads the romances; your daughter may even yearn for a husband . . . and love."

Surprise siphoned the blood from Ernan O'Connor's face. Petrov sat still, his heart contracting in pity for a loving father who had suddenly realized that his daughter was no longer a child. In truth, Petrov himself had been dreading the day when Anika would leave them, but he had not dared think that time might be fast approaching.

"I respect you, Master Hus," Ernan said, his voice trembling with suppressed emotion, "but I cannot thank you for bringing this notion to me house. Anika has no need to marry; she needs nothing. She has been provided for—each book in those chests yonder is worth its weight in silver. I spent fifteen months copying the Scriptures in the engraved chest; the book is mounted on wood and overlaid with gold leaf—"

"Ernan, I can see that I've upset you, and it was not my intent to do so." Hus paused to look at Petrov. "And I am glad that you have returned, my chivalrous friend. Though you no longer use your sword, your knowledge of the nobility may help us in certain days ahead."

Petrov nodded silently, aware that his pulse had quickened.

Hus squared his shoulders, then turned to face Ernan again. "I did not come to you about Anika, Ernan, because I want you to find her a husband. If you want to enjoy her sweet presence in your home for a few more months, who am I to tell you that you should not? But do not let your eyes deceive you. You may see your daughter as a child, but others see her as a grown woman, and a most lovely one."

"Priests—" Ernan spat out the word, "are not supposed to notice such things."

The preacher's mouth twitched with amusement. "Priests are men, too, Ernan. But I did not come today to warn you of a priest. I came to tell you that unless you consider marriage for your daughter and see her safely betrothed to a husband, other men may be inclined to consider her for less honorable purposes. I have overheard—how, I cannot say—that a certain youth of Bohemia has noticed your daughter's beauty. He has even taken to following her in the streets."

"What?" Petrov's pensive mood veered sharply to anger. "By the hounds of hell, I will discover this youth and pull out his spying eyes!"

The preacher lifted his hand. "That would not do, brave Petrov, though we appreciate your courage and devotion to our Anika. No, what is needed here is not violence, but knowledge. Ernan, you must make a plan for your daughter. If she is willing to be wed, you should set about finding her a suitable husband of whom you approve. The knave I spoke of is of noble birth, and while he would not be likely to take your daughter as his wife, he would not hesitate . . ." the preacher's eyes slid down to the table top, "to use her in an ignoble fashion."

Petrov glanced at his friend; Ernan's face had become a glowering mask of rage. "Who is this who dares to think of me daughter in such a way?"

"You do not have the power to control young men's thoughts, Ernan, any more than our fathers could control ours when we were young and unsettled." Hus pressed his slender fingertips to the table. "But you must do your part to keep your daughter safe. Make it known that she is betrothed, even if the marriage is two or three years hence. Make it clear to any who would ask that she lacks neither purpose nor protection. Men are less likely to steal an innocent lamb if they know both the herdsman and the owner are standing guard."

Comprehension broke upon Ernan's face like a spring breaking forth from under a sheet of ice. "I will heed your words," he said simply, gripping the edge of his worktable. "I will begin—tomorrow—to find a suitable match. But this must not be rushed. Anika herself must be consulted." He pushed himself up from the table, his muscular arms trembling. "I love my daughter, gentlemen, and won't be marrying her off to just anyone. And if you will excuse me, I must fetch a cup of water from the bucket upstairs. There is much I need to consider."

"We will leave you to your thoughts," Hus answered, rising. As Ernan turned toward the back staircase, Master Hus looked at Petrov and gestured toward the doorway. Without speaking, Petrov stood and turned to follow the minister.

"Grace be with you until we meet again, Ernan, my friend," Hus called, opening the door. "Do not hesitate to send word if you need me."

The copyist waved a hand and muttered as he moved up the stairs, but Petrov did not hear his reply. With surprising force for so slender a man, the preacher propelled Petrov through the doorway.

When they were safely within the camouflaging noise of the bustling street, Hus took Petrov's elbow and pulled him away from the copyist's shop.

"Where did you leave the girl?"

Petrov blanched. "With the rector's housekeeper. I did not know she was being followed."

"Go there at once, and personally escort Anika home." Lines of concentration deepened along the preacher's brows and under his eyes.

Petrov felt his pulse quicken. Was the threat really so great?

"If she is truly in danger," he said, one hand automatically going to the silver sword hanging at his waist, "will you tell me who this wayward lout is? A hunter warned is a hunter forearmed."

The minister's eyes clouded with hazy sadness. "I did not want to tell Ernan, lest he confront the youth or the youth's father at an inopportune time." Hus lowered his voice to a confidential whisper. "And you know fathers, Sir Petrov. Wisdom often flies out the window when a daughter's safety and honor are concerned."

Petrov did not know much about fathers, having never been one or known his own, but he warmed to the implied compliment in the preacher's words. "You can tell me the lad's name," he answered, nodding. "And I will guard Anika and her father with my life, if necessary. The loyalty I once swore to Lord Honza I yield now to you. May God strike me if I fail in my duties to either the girl or Ernan O'Connor."

The preacher clapped his hand on Petrov's shoulder. "You are a good man, Sir Knight, and I knew I could confide in you. The youth who concerns me is Miloslav, son to Lord Laco of Lidice."

"Lord Laco?" Petrov's breath caught in his throat. The previous Lord of Lidice had been a foe of Lord Honza's, and the name still made Petrov's heart pound. The present Lord of Lidice had to be descended from Petrov's old enemy, and apparently this Miloslav was cut from the same traitorous cloth.

"I have heard it suggested," Hus went on, his brows drawing downward in a frown, "that the youth fancies our Anika. He has been told that Ernan has no great fortune, therefore the daughter might be compelled to seek employment as a serving maid." His eyes caught and held Petrov's. "I do not need to tell you what sort of service Miloslav has in mind. Unfortunately, the nobility think that lesser folk have neither brains nor morals, and they are not above taking whatever they desire."

"Do not fear." Petrov spread his feet and stood before the minister with the solidity of a fortress. "Anika will not be harmed. I will not let the young man within twenty paces of her."

"But we must guard against Anika, too," Hus warned, lifting his hand. "She is a romantic. She yearns for the love she reads about in books, and Miloslav may know the words to win a girl's heart. He is a handsome lad, and if she were won with lies and flattery, even so virtuous a girl as Anika might be brought to ruin and despair."

"I would die before I would allow her to be hurt, Master Hus." Petrov placed one hand across his chest and rested the other upon the priest's arm. "I have known the girl since she was a wee child of six or seven, and upon my oath as a knight, I promise both you and God that I shall protect our Anika."

"Do not forget to guard your tongue," Hus warned, nodding. "Do not reveal to Ernan O'Connor the names of either Lord Laco or Miloslav. Members of the nobility often visit his shop, and with one slip of the tongue he might place his life and his daughter's virtue in danger. If he were to erupt in anger . . ." Hus let the sentence trail off.

"Ernan O'Connor shall never know the lad's identity," Petrov answered, his heart swelling with a feeling of purpose he had thought long dead. "As you trust in God, Jan Hus, you may trust in me."

Two

Unrest moved like an ill wind over Prague as the papal legate arrived in the city. Citizens who attended the Roman churches knew about the papal bull and Pope John's awful curse against Ladislas. Those who attended Hus's Bethlehem Chapel had heard enough to realize that the pope's messenger would stir the smoldering fires of controversy and distrust. Rumors of a coming confrontation between the pope's prelates and the Bohemian preacher spread through the city like a wind-whipped grass fire.

Tucked away in the bookshop, Anika heard the rumors, too, but paid them little attention. Jan Hus had been in trouble with church authorities before, and his quick intellect won every debate. On the first Sunday in May, she rose with the sun, then slipped into her best dress, an emerald, floor-length gown with an empire waist and a simple white collar. Long flared sleeves with dagged edges extended to the floor, accenting her slender waistline.

Frowning at her reflection in her mirror, Anika brushed her mane of long red locks, then separated the stubborn strand of white hair and quickly plaited it into a delicate braid. She pulled it up and over, then pinned it beneath her hairline on the opposite side of her head. She had been troubled by this unusual white streak for years but lately had begun to arrange her hair in this braided fashion. Worn like this, under a veil of crispinette, the discolored braid appeared to be a false hairpiece cunningly tied into her own hair. No one had ever commented on it when she wore her hair this way, and when she worked in the shop she tucked the offending streak up inside her cap so no one could see it.

Finally ready, she pulled back the curtain that separated her sleeping compartment from the rest of the family quarters. Her father sat on a chair by the table, already dressed for church. Apparently his thoughts were not fixed on worship, though, for his eyes were directed at a pamphlet in his hands, and his face had gone brick red.

Anika lifted a brow as she approached. "Good morrow, Papa. I trust your dreams were more pleasant than your present thoughts."

"By all the saints, Daughter, Cardinal D'Ailly plans to attend services at Bethlehem Chapel today!"

Kneeling by the hearth, Anika reached for an iron poker and shoved the charred remains of last night's log onto the still-glowing coals. Despite the advent of spring, the morning air still snapped with cold.

"Perhaps nothing will come of it," she told her father. "Our good Master Hus will not want to make trouble. He yearns to make peace with those who oppose him."

"Hrumph!" was her father's only reply.

Later that morning, as Anika sat next to her father in the large hall known as Bethlehem Chapel, she blinked in amazement to see that her father had heard correctly. A red-robed cardinal, one of the virtual rulers of the Roman Catholic Church, sat in a front pew to the left of the pulpit. Beside him sat a richly dressed nobleman Anika did not recognize, and beside the nobleman fidgeted a young man probably only three or four years older than Anika herself.

Jan Hus seemed not to notice that his congregation included more illustrious company than usual. He mounted to the lectern and led his congregation in rousing song, into which Anika joined with her customary jubilation. The uplifting song, one Hus himself had written, inspired her worship, but her thoughts were distracted from their heavenly plane when her eyes fell upon the youth seated on the cardinal's pew at the front of the church. He was attractive, she supposed, with clear blue eyes, classically handsome features, and a secretive expression. Reflected light from the chapel windows glimmered over his blond hair like beams of icy radiance, and indomitable pride shone through the eyes that caught and held her gaze.

For a moment he looked at her with an interested and somewhat surprised expression, then his mouth took on an unpleasant twist. As Anika went mute with surprise, his lips puckered—and he sent her an undeniable kiss, in front of her father, the entire church, even Holy God Himself!

Anika lowered her head, coloring fiercely. What was he doing? What if someone saw him? What if someone thought she had *invited* such a greeting? They would think her the lowest kind of wench. No honorable woman would offer her attention to a man while her thoughts ought to be turned toward God!

As the congregation sang on around her, Anika took a deep breath and forced herself to calm her feelings. Her father had not commented; maybe he had not noticed. The couple seated in front of her had not turned around in surprise or revulsion; perhaps they had not seen. Perhaps no one had noted it. If Anika could ignore the forward youth surely nothing else would happen.

She lifted her eyes to the preacher, the image of the young man blurring her peripheral vision. She could feel heat in her face, and she knew he was still looking in her direction—probably grinning. Mocking her. Why? What on earth had she ever done to him?

The song ended, and Master Hus bowed his head for prayer. Anika followed suit, but the top of her head burned with the touch of the man's eyes upon her. She bit down hard on her lower lip. Surely she was imagining things! A perfect stranger had no cause to smile at her; perhaps he was smiling at someone seated in the pew beyond. Perhaps his betrothed, or even his mother or a dear aunt sat right behind Anika, and she had misinterpreted his affectionate greeting.

She sighed in relief. What a fool she was, how overwrought her imagination! She had spent too much time reading *The Art of Courtly*

Love; all that prattle about stolen glances and displays of public affection had addled her brain. She had imagined everything, including the young man's continued glances in her direction. After all, she hadn't actually looked up at him again, and he probably wasn't looking toward her at all. She could check now, just to be sure.

In the midst of her pastor's prayer, she sneaked one disobedient look upward. The young man *was* still staring at her, openly flouting everything right and holy. His blue eyes glinted with mischief as he grinned and gave her a conspiratorial wink.

No. She had to be mistaken. Quickly, quietly, she lowered her head and turned slightly so she could look behind her. Surely another young woman sat there, the object of this man's unseemly affection—but no one sat behind her but the miller and his wife, a blowzy woman with many chins and many children.

Anika lowered her head, her stomach churning in disgust. She leaned closer to her father's protecting arm and closed her eyes tightly, blocking out all thoughts and sights of the froward youth who had no business behaving so rudely in God's own church.

"Papa," she whispered when the preacher's prayer had concluded, "who are the men seated in the pews next to the pulpit?"

Her father's face hardened into a marble effigy of contempt as he looked up. "That, Daughter," he answered, barely troubling to lower his voice, "is the Cardinal D'Ailly and Lord Laco of Lidice. I don't know who the younger man is, but I'd guess we're looking at Lord Laco's son."

Anika looked down again, her flush deepening to crimson. A nobleman's son! At least her worries were unfounded. Once he learned she was only a merchant's daughter, he would take his attentions elsewhere. Even *The Art of Courtly Love* admitted that love between upper- and middle-class folk was a poor idea.

Jan Hus stepped slowly to the lectern, well aware of the forbidding presence on the front pew at his right hand. Cardinal D'Ailly had not wandered into Prague and into this church by mere happenstance, but Jan could not say with a clear conscience that God had led the cardinal to this church for spiritual edification. No, D'Ailly's presence had less to do with the plans of God than the plots of men, and those plots were yet to be revealed.

"Friends," Hus began, placing his copy of the Scriptures on the lectern before him. "I would like to read to you from the gospel according to Saint Matthew."

"Stop."

Like an echo from an empty tomb, the cardinal's voice echoed through the large sanctuary.

"Your Eminence?" Jan obediently turned and lifted an eyebrow. "Do you wish to address the congregation?"

Slowly, as if weighted down by his own self-importance, Cardinal D'Ailly rose to his feet. A short, plump polyp of a man, the cardinal gave Hus a fixed and meaningless smile, then took a deep breath, swelled his chest, and faced the startled congregation. "Pope John has sent his representative, bearing the sacred pallium as a token of authority, to publish a bull throughout the kingdom of Christ. Yet I have heard that the bull has not been published or posted upon the doors of this church."

Jan bit his lip, resisting the urge to rebel. *Blessed are the peacemakers, for they shall be called the children of God . . .*

The cardinal extended a hand toward a cowled priest seated in the front row. As the man stood to his feet, D'Ailly made a simple introduction: "This man, Master Hus, is the holy father's legate."

Conscious that two thousand pairs of curious eyes watched from the pews, Jan bowed in respect. "Grace and peace unto you, from our Lord and Savior Jesus Christ."

The emissary's eyes gleamed like glassy volcanic rock, his emotions and intents impossible to read. "Will you, Jan Hus," the priest called, his thin voice cutting through the silence of the chamber, "obey the apostolic mandates?"

Hus did not hesitate to fill his role in what was obviously a scripted drama. "I am ready with all my heart to obey the apostolic mandates."

The surprised messenger's shoulders dropped slightly, then he smiled. "Did you hear?" he said, glancing up at D'Ailly in what looked like relief. "The master is quite ready to obey the apostolic mandates."

Jan resisted the impulse to shake his head in utter disbelief. Another trap—this one sprung in his own church. Well, the hunter could be snared as easily as the prey, if God so willed.

"Your Eminence," Jan stepped forward a half-step and turned toward the cardinal, "understand me well. I said I am ready with all my heart to obey the doctrines of the apostles of Christ. If the papal mandates agree with these, I will obey them most willingly. But if I see any papal mandate at variance with the doctrines of Christ, I shall not obey, even though the executioner's stake were staring me in the face."

The roar of absolute silence filled the church. The papal legate gaped at Hus; D'Ailly's displeasure was palpable. But from the people in the pews, *his* people, Hus felt silent support.

Standing before the congregation of Bethlehem Chapel, Jan Hus felt his heart swell with holy pride. His church had been founded by two laymen who desired to provide a house of worship suited for the preaching of God's Word in the people's language. In all other churches of Prague, the encumbrance of Roman rites and ceremonies left no opportunity for preaching the gospel, yet the charter of Bethlehem Chapel required its preacher to reside in the city and preach in the Bohemian tongue twice a day on all Sundays and feast days. The job was a duty and honor Jan Hus was pleased to fulfill.

Now he glanced down at the stunned papal legate and decided to speak plainly. "Many of our people are farmers, my brother; we know the value of grain. What is the law of God? Good grain. What is the command of men? Mere chaff."

Leaning over the pulpit, Jan looked Pope John's emissary directly in the eye: "Note that down, cowled monk, and carry it to the other side."

He straightened and returned to his lectern in silence. His words still vibrated in the air, as if hanging overhead for inspection, and in the resonating silence Jan felt a new sensation descend upon him, the eerie sense of detachment that accompanied an awareness of impending disaster.

In one breath, in the space of a few seconds, he had questioned papal authority and refuted papal direction. If given an opportunity, he would expose papal corruption and the personal sin of the one who called himself Pope John. In the past Jan had appealed to this pope, shown him the reverence due his position, and tried to address him in respectful language. But he could no longer pay homage to a corrupt system led and managed by the most corrupt of men.

He gripped the edges of the pulpit and stared out across his congregation. These people were the reason he entered the fray and kept up the fight. They were starving for spiritual truth, and there were too few priests willing to provide it.

Pope John, who promised heavenly immortality for a price, could not be allowed to toy with immortal souls in order to broaden his personal power base in Italy. Jan Hus could not and would not sit idly by while thousands of men paid an eternal price to slake one man's ambition.

———

For weeks Prague's dinner tables buzzed with various versions of Master Hus's encounter with the cardinal. Anika, her father, and Petrov had a most spirited discussion; Ernan declared that the growing movement toward nationalism would eventually lead to war; the old knight insisted that war would never come to Bohemia.

"Sure, and don't I know there will be war?" Ernan said, his eyes shining like cobalt. "Patriotism is a kind of religion—'tis the egg from which wars are hatched. All this talk about Bohemia this and Bohemia that—'tis certain to come to fighting. Men will carry swords until they learn to carry the cross, and that day is not yet come."

"No war," Petrov persisted, rapping his bony knuckles upon the table. "We are a nation of Christians, and Christians should not fight each other. In disarming Peter, Christ disarmed every warrior. Except for self-defense against evil, we should all hang up our swords."

"Well, naturally, it is not a bad thing to love peace," Ernan countered. "But there comes a time when people can't bear the burdens placed on them. Master Hus is helping people see those burdens, things they've never seen before. And if it isn't right, it won't be borne. Haven't I said so before?"

Anika rested her chin on her hand and let their words wash over her. If war did erupt, she felt certain Master Hus would have nothing to do with it. Despite his outspokenness from the pulpit, he was not foolishly reckless. He spoke the truth when pressed, defended the Scriptures, and attacked the papacy's wrongs whenever confronted directly, but he seemed to realize that outright revolt would arouse a sleeping dragon. His comments to the cardinal had been his most blunt in a long time.

"What will happen now?" she asked. She crossed her arms and looked from her father to Petrov. "Will the interdict be imposed again?"

"No one can say," Petrov admitted, "but I have heard that some of Hus's younger followers have laid extreme plans. On the morrow they intend to visit every church and publicly contradict any priest who preaches the indulgences. The people will certainly join in their protests."

"I'll be wanting to pray for them," Ernan interrupted. "For their safety and that God would grant them wisdom. For this undertaking will not come easily, and I fear it may cost these brave souls a high price."

How high a price? Anika wondered, but something cautioned her not to ask.

Jan Hus walked outside his small house, his hands behind his back, his head lifted to the star-thick sky above. Prague slept now; nearly every candle and lamp had been extinguished along the street. It was during these moments of silence that Jan was best able to think . . . and God was best able to penetrate the crowded confusion in Jan's mind.

"I've tried, Father," he whispered, stopping to rest in the black velvet shadow of a stately spruce. "I've tried to warn Jerome and the others to go more softly, to advance cautiously for the sake of those who still carry your gospel in their hearts. I know there are priests and cardinals who have not been snared by the lust of the eyes, the lust of the flesh, and the pride of life, but . . ."

He paused, marshaling his memories. So many unfortunate things had happened over the past few months; he could not blame Jerome and his friends for growing impatient with the cardinals in Rome.

He folded his arms and leaned back against the broad trunk of the tree, revisiting small memories clipped out of time and perfectly preserved in his mind. The most recent memory was also the most troubling. One week after the sermon in which Jan declared that he would not condone the pope's selling of indulgences so that Christians might sin with a clear conscience, Jerome organized a group of university students in an open protest against the papal proclamation. In a mock procession one student dressed as a harlot and rode through the cobbled streets of Prague with a chain of silver bells around his neck. In his hands he held a large sheet of paper, clearly intended to represent the papal bull. A great crowd of students and townsfolk carrying sticks and swords followed the "harlot" as the chariot procession wound its way through Prague's main streets. As they walked, the leaders of the parade proclaimed, "We are carrying the writings of a heretic to the stake." In Charles Square, amid thunderous applause, the rebels placed the false document under a makeshift gallows and set it afire.

"We did it," Jerome gaily reported the next day, "to remind the people of the archbishop's burning of books."

Jan saw fire in his disciple's eye and felt himself shudder. During the previous year, in an effort to explain his positions on the church and scriptural truth, Jan and several other gospel preachers had loaned their precious copies of Wyclif's writings and other theology books to the archbishop. In a bold countermove, Archbishop Zbynek, predecessor to the current archbishop, took advantage of King Wenceslas's absence from the city and brought the valuable books out into the palace courtyard. Over two hundred volumes, many of them beautifully embossed and splendidly bound, crumbled to ashes in a fire fueled by spite, while bells tolled from the city tower and the priests sang the funeral chant "Te Deum."

The archbishop had meant to end his troubles by this gesture, but his book burning only poured fuel on the flames of strife. When King Wenceslas learned of the archbishop's rash act, he stormed and cursed while Queen Sophia wept. The freedom-loving citizens of Prague were enraged. Riots broke out in churchyards. And then, sooner than Jan would have believed possible, fresh copies of Wyclif's writings and his own sermons spread like gossip through the city, inscribed by hands as fast as Anika O'Connor's. Copies of the Holy Scriptures, which the priests did not have the nerve to burn, began for the first time to appear in homes of the common folk.

Jan smiled ruefully, recalling the way he had begun his sermon the next Sunday: "Fire does not consume truth. It is always a mark of a little mind to vent anger on inanimate and uninjurious objects."

Even that simple statement was reported to the church hierarchy. And in retaliation for Hus's opposition, Pope John XXIII issued an order demanding that Jan appear in Rome and give an account of his actions.

The memory of his own reaction to the pope's summons passed through Jan like an unwelcome chill. Upon hearing the news, he had simply refused to go. He held little personal respect for a pope he knew to be the worst sort of scoundrel, and he did not wish to desert his congregation in a time of great unrest. Furthermore, Jan had little money and no desire to ask his wealthy friends to loan him funds to provision an extended journey.

His refusal to appear in Rome was the beginning of troubles for Prague. When Jan refused the command, Pope John issued a decree excommunicating Jan and commanded that it be published in all the churches of Prague.

His tight expression relaxed into a smile when he recalled Prague's reaction to his excommunication. The severe maneuver, formally banishing Hus's soul to hell, meant little to Jan personally, and shortly thereafter crowds filled Bethlehem Chapel to capacity whenever he spoke. People who would never have ventured out to hear Hus the scholar now crowded about the church doors to hear Hus the excommunicated heretic. Sir Petrov, a devoted doorkeeper and assistant at services, estimated one Sunday that at least ten thousand people had gathered to hear the hell-bound preacher proclaim Jesus Christ and God's great salvation.

Jan's smile faded when he recalled what happened next. When excommunication only broadened Hus's influence, Archbishop Zbynek proclaimed an interdict over the city of Prague and its neighboring villages. While the interdict lasted, no person other than a priest, beggar, or child under twelve could receive a Christian burial or be taken to another diocese for burial. There could be no public services in the churches, no weddings, no ringing of church bells. Mass could be said only behind closed doors, and communion could be administered only to the dying. As long as the interdict remained in effect, the entire city's population had to assume a general appearance of mourning and fasting.

No matter how much he had secretly enjoyed goading the dour and selfish archbishop, Jan Hus sincerely regretted the interdict. The excommunication did not hurt, for it was useless and directed only at him, and he was certain of his salvation. But the interdict affected the entire city, particularly those who were deep in bondage to the Roman system and had not seen the light of true salvation.

But God would not allow them to suffer more than they could bear, and relief came when Archbishop Zbynek died in September 1411. The new archbishop, not wanting to live in a cursed city, wisely lifted the interdict. And a few months of uneasy and fragile peace had existed between the pope and the Bohemian reformers until Pope John published his bull announcing the sale of indulgences. Now, to Jan's horror, his position had led to open rebellion in the city streets. If Jerome and the other students were not more discreet, Archbishop Albik might be forced to take harsh action to underscore his authority.

"Father God, you will look after them, no?" Hus asked, lifting his eyes to the sky again. The sky was still thick black, but the stars were less brilliant than before. Morning would soon dawn, and he had not yet slept.

But there would be time for that later. Hus shook off his mantle of memories and vigorously rubbed his face, reminding himself of the tasks ahead. He had two sick parishioners, a dispute to settle among three laymen, and a lecture to prepare for his university students.

"Sufficient to the day is the evil thereof," he quipped, smiling at his own joke as he moved toward his house.

Three

Ernan O'Connor's words proved to be prophetic—the price of rebellion was high. Three days later Anika and her father were hard at work in the shop when Petrov appeared again, his white hair disheveled and his eyes blazing.

"They have captured those who led the rebellion," he announced, panting as he came through the door. "Three students were arrested this morning and taken to the town hall. The magistrates sided with the pope's men and have already sentenced the young men to death."

"Surely not!" Anika's father rose from his seat as if propelled by an explosive force. "The magistrates should not act alone. The king must be consulted."

"The king is away." Petrov's expression was tight with strain. "Runners went at once to Master Hus, of course, and I expect he will appeal the council's decision. But rumors are flying as thick as flies through the streets, and if they are not stanched—"

"We will see a bloodbath," Ernan finished in a flat voice. In one swift gesture he threw a light piece of linen over his parchments, then moved toward the door.

"Father." Anika placed the lid on her ink horn with a light tap. "Surely you don't expect me to stay here? I could help you."

"The streets are no place for a young woman if trouble is afoot."

"But Master Hus needs help. And you often tell me that a man who will not go to the aid of a friend is no man at all."

"You forget, wee bird, that you are not a man."

Anika sighed, thinking she had lost her bid for freedom, but then her father looked at Petrov. "Things are quiet now?"

The older man nodded. "Master Hus has begged his people to remain calm. For now, at least, the streets are at peace."

The copyist turned to his daughter. "Hurry then, lass, and don your cloak. Master Hus will need cool heads and supportive voices around him now."

A mob of university masters and students had clogged the street outside the town hall by the time Anika, her father, and Petrov arrived. The guards allowed them into the building solely because Petrov insisted that Ernan O'Connor was Master Hus's personal scribe. With Petrov behind her, Anika followed her father through a crowded chamber that smelled as if the air inside had been breathed too many times. As the three of them slid into a tiny space at a far corner of the room, they heard Jan Hus giving an impassioned defense of the three young men who had led the rebellion against the sale of indulgences.

"I do not approve of their course of action," Hus was saying as Anika stood on tiptoe to watch the proceedings, "but their actions are the outgrowth of my teachings, so I alone must bear the blame. Do not hold the rashness and boldness of youth against them, magistrates, but free them under my authority. I will meet with you later, and we will discuss what must be done to repair any damage. But do not carry out this sentence of execution, I beg you. By all that is holy and true, look to the light of God in your heart and reconsider your sentence."

A guard at the door shouldered his way to the front of the room, then whispered in the chief magistrate's ear. After a moment, the magistrate's face reddened, then his mouth spread into a thin-lipped, anxious smile. "I hear there are more than two thousand of your people outside," he told Hus, his dark eyes widening in accusation. "You cannot expect us to make an unbiased and sound judgment in such a situation. If we do not rescind our verdict according to your wishes, the mob outside could tear this place apart."

"My esteemed friends," Hus answered, tenting his slender hands beneath his chin, "I am opposed to violence. The peaceful people outside are concerned for truth and goodness, so you have no reason to fear them. I ask only for your word that you will forestall the execution until a committee can reconsider this action and consult King Wenceslas when he returns."

A silence fell upon the gathering. Then the quartet of magistrates murmured to one another. Anika felt a trickle of sweat run down her forehead; the heat of the crowded room was stifling.

"We agree, Master Hus," the chief magistrate finally said. "We will postpone our judgment. Go outside, tell your people to disperse. They must depart to their homes at once."

Sunshine broke across the preacher's face. Smiling his thanks, Hus lifted his hands to heaven for a moment, then turned and nodded toward familiar faces in the crowd. Anika saw him smile at her father and Petrov, then the striking preacher's gaze caught hers.

What compassion filled Jan Hus's eyes! No wonder he had been able to charm the magistrates out of a death sentence! With her heart overflowing in awe and wonder, Anika followed her father out of the town hall and joined the others in praise and thanksgiving. A tragedy had been averted.

The distant sounds of wailing broke the gray stillness of the next morning. Dropping her quill pen, Anika rushed to open the door, then beheld a gruesome parade: a dozen women holding blood-stained aprons and scarves to their weeping eyes, several men carrying broken bodies upon makeshift litters, others bearing woven baskets covered with crimson-stained cloths.

"What has happened?" The cry echoed up and down the street from late risers and merchants opening for business. "Who has died?"

"The three students," came the reply from a score of voices. "Beheaded!"

One woman, seeing Anika's startled gaze, stopped to tell the tale. "At sunset, scarcely an hour after the magistrates' promise to Master

Hus, they killed them. The council mocks us and would have concealed their crime, but the washerwomen found the bodies in the courtyard."

Anika felt a hand on her shoulder and looked back to see her father standing behind her, his hat on his head, ready to join the procession. Without speaking, she gathered her scarf from a basket by the door and slipped it over her hair, then followed her father.

Plodding forward in the spontaneous procession, Anika tied the scarf under her chin, her vision still colored with the memory of Jan Hus's victorious smile and the concern in his eyes. He had believed the magistrates, the church's pawns, and they had utterly betrayed him.

Behind her, someone began to chant the mass for the martyrs, and Anika lifted her voice, joining in. At one fine house a noblewoman with a basket of expensive linen rushed out to shroud the bodies; other women along the way dipped their handkerchiefs into the bloody baskets, creating a holy relic of blood and linen.

Anika watched silently, knowing she needed no relic to remind her of this dark day. The heaviness in her chest felt like a millstone she would carry with her always. Her shoulders drooped, her pace slowed. For a bewildering moment she felt that she was mourning her own death, for something in her, some fragile element of trust and faith, was gasping in a dying breath, and she could do nothing to save it.

The magistrates had lied and murdered. They had flagrantly deceived Jan Hus. If they would lie to a man of God, what prevented them from lying to the common people?

The women's keening wails rose and fell, cycling through cries of sorrow into screams of horrified anguish. And through the roaring din, Anika held her hand over her heart and wondered what sort of evil would next visit her city.

All of Prague waited to see what Jan Hus would do to retaliate. "He will take his case before the king," Petrov predicted, while Anika's father thought Hus might finally urge his followers to armed action. But the preacher did nothing. Overcome with grief for the three young men, he retreated into his small house for several days, then appeared to preach a funeral sermon in the students' memory.

On the Sunday following the martyrdom, Hus preached as usual in Bethlehem Chapel but did not mention the tragic events of the past week. Hus's enemies, Petrov whispered during a lull in the service, were saying that he had been frightened into silence.

But Anika had copied thousands of the preacher's words, and she knew him better than either Petrov or her father did. She suspected Master Hus entertained neither fear nor anger, but he realized hundreds of soldiers now patrolled the streets of Prague, alert to any sign of trouble. If Hus uttered one word of vengeance or even hinted that retaliation might be a proper course of action, more innocent blood would stain the stones of the city streets.

And so he said nothing but led the service as usual.

"Do you think the king will continue to side with Jan Hus, or will he be forced to support his magistrates?" Petrov asked as the three walked home from church.

Anika turned to study her father's reaction. She had wondered the same thing. "There is no way we can know," Ernan answered, clasping his hands behind his back in a thoughtful pose. "The king loves Jan Hus, but Wenceslas is a temperamental man, subject to moments of fury. And Master Hus has never been afraid to make enemies of those who stand against Christ. Do you remember his friend Palec? I heard he and Hus recently held a debate over the sale of indulgences. Palec thought the sales ought to be allowed under the pope's authority, but Hus stands firmly against them. At the end of their confrontation, Palec left the hall, his face set in anger, and Hus said, 'Palec is my friend, truth is my friend: Of the two it is only right to honor truth most.'"

A scowl flitted across Petrov's lined face. "Master Hus had better be careful. Palec is not without influence."

"Neither is truth," Ernan remarked gamely. "And I find I must agree with the preacher. For how can a man receive pardon of his sins from a pope, a bishop, or a priest? Scripture says that God alone can forgive sins through Christ, and he pardons the penitent only."

Anika brightened, recognizing words she had recently penned. "Master Hus has asked us to set forth his convictions on placards for church doors," she explained, glancing up at Petrov, "for he intends to debate anyone who would say it is permissible for the Holy Father to sell permission to sin."

"Anika, you must be fair," her father remonstrated, lifting his hand. "The Church does not regard indulgences as giving a soul permission to sin. In theory, indulgences are to be granted only to the repentant and are to cover only the element of penance which requires good works."

"But people do not make such fine distinctions," Anika argued. "They see the indulgences as covering all the elements of repentance and penance. They want to give their money to the church, then live like the devil and experience no consequences for their behavior."

"Your daughter's tongue and mind are as sharp as my sword," Petrov remarked, a gleam in his faded eyes. "She looks like a woman but talks like a monstrosity, Ernan O'Connor. Women should not debate such matters! Did Hus not tell you the girl would be better served by learning to cook and sew than by reading and writing?"

"A friend does not gloat," Ernan answered gruffly, slipping his arm around Anika. "Especially when he is right."

"Father!" Anika cried, feigning disdain.

Bending down, her father planted a loud kiss on her cheek. "And though I may have erred, I'll take a bright and literate daughter in place of an idle and foolish one any day. I would place odds on Anika in a debate against the archbishop, for she has learned all that Master Hus teaches, having copied most of his books and sermons herself—"

At that moment the sound of galloping hooves and a shouted warning cut through the hubbub of the street. A carriage barreled through the narrow boulevard, scattering women and children, men and servants. Petrov flung out his arm to shield Anika, nearly knocking her from her feet. A few paces beyond her the carriage lurched into a puddle in the road, throwing up a mud shower. Much of the grime, Anika noticed in dismay, flew into her father's face.

Anika had often been impressed by the power of her father's temper; in him dwelt a white-hot rage that harmlessly expended itself after a few blustery moments and then vanished without leaving a trace or bearing a grudge. His temper erupted now, flaring toward the occupants of the offending carriage. Later, looking back, she would think that if a hundred carriages had passed them, ninety-and-nine would have continued without stopping, heedless of the cries and calls of the common folk in the street. But this was an unusual carriage and its owner a most notorious nobleman.

The vehicle had not gone twenty paces past them when the groom pulled the horses to a halt. The restless team pawed the ground, unable to understand why they had been halted during what should have been a routine trip through a street of tradesmen, a small row of shops shuttered to observe a holy Sunday.

Anika shivered, but not from the cold. A window blind in the carriage rose and a pair of dark eyes peered forth.

"Ernan," Petrov warned in a dark voice as he wiped mud from his sleeve, "perhaps we should return home by another street."

"I'll not be backing down when I've done nothing wrong." Ernan said, lifting his chin. He strutted forward a few steps. "'Tis a bit odd, don't you think, that a man and his daughter can't even walk down their own street without nearly getting run over?"

"Father," Anika called, her adrenaline level rising. "Sir Petrov is right. A book I want to read is waiting at home. Let's be away now."

Oblivious to their cries, Ernan O'Connor strode forward like David to meet Goliath. With mud still clinging to his face, he stalked to the side of the carriage and planted himself by the doorway, his hands on his hips, his eyes snapping with righteous indignation.

"Never fear, child," Petrov murmured, placing his hand on Anika's shoulder. "Your father can handle himself."

To Anika's horror, the carriage door creaked and opened. At once Lord Laco's imposing figure filled the opening, while in the two windows Anika recognized the faces of Cardinal D'Ailly and the obstinate youth she had seen weeks ago at Bethlehem Chapel.

She felt a sudden chill. Surely the bloody events of the past week had conspired against them. These men, especially the cardinal, would be in no mood to hear protests from a man known to be Jan Hus's ally.

"Have you something to say to me, sirrah?" Lord Laco's stentorian voice echoed through the street. "Why stand you gaping up at my carriage?"

"I should think you have something to say to *me*, sir," Ernan answered. Despite her fear, Anika felt her heart swell with pride. What Ernan O'Connor lacked in stature and wealth, he more than made up in boldness and courage.

"You have urged your groom to drive the horses at a dangerous pace through the city," Ernan went on, pounding the air with his broad fist. "Last week two children were struck by a reckless carriage just like this one. Now my face bears witness to the proximity of your carriage wheels. How could I be bathed in mud if your driver wasn't reckless? You must caution him—there are ladies and children on this street."

"Ladies?" Lord Laco's thick lips twisted into a cynical smile. Pointedly, he looked directly at Anika, then returned his gaze to her father. "I see no ladies. I see only an ignorant peasant girl, a broken-down old man, and a heap of Irish scum. So if you take care to remain out of my way, we shall not impede your progress any longer."

"Father—" The youth who had humiliated Anika in church tugged on the nobleman's sleeve. Lord Laco retreated into the coach for a moment, then returned to the doorway. When he spoke again, his tone was almost contrite. "I beg your pardon, Ernan O'Connor. My son has just reminded me that I have good reason not to be harsh with you."

"Me, sir?" Ernan frowned.

"Yes." Lord Laco's tone became as smooth and sweet as butter. "You have a comely daughter, sir, who seems old enough for proper employment. My son would like to hire her as a chambermaid. She will be well treated, of course, and housed on my estate."

"Me daughter," Ernan answered, drawing himself up to his full height, "will serve no man but her husband. She will remain with me until she is married."

Lord Laco smiled benignly, as if dealing with an ignorant and temperamental child. "Better a chambermaid in a castle than wife to a peasant, my friend. I believe you are underestimating the honor I would like to bestow upon you. Half the fathers in Prague would surrender their daughters to me in an instant—"

"Then I'll be wanting you to count me among the half who would resist you," Ernan interrupted, frowning with cold fury. "Me daughter will remain with me."

Lord Laco shrugged slightly, then turned to the cardinal, who had watched the entire episode with an impatient frown upon his face. "Your Eminence," Laco said, his smile oddly out of place on a countenance like his, "we seem to have reached an impasse. Since this is the Lord's holy day, I submit this situation for you to resolve."

"I see here," D'Ailly replied in a bored tone, his fat fingers curving under his chin, "a stubborn and rebellious father who would defy not only God, but his earthly masters as well. In this hour he has stolen your lordship's time, your energy, and your attention. He has also openly defied your authority . . ." the cardinal's eyes flitted toward the open windows where residents were watching with undisguised curiosity, "before a large section of the populace."

Laco drew his lips in thoughtfully. "Have you a verdict, then?"

"Yes."

For the first time, Anika felt the cardinal's eyes fall upon her, and at the touch of his gaze she felt an instinctive stab of fear.

"We know this girl's father associates with Jan Hus. You would be committing an act of mercy to take her from his polluting influence. In your house, she would be safeguarded by the true Church."

Icy fear twisted around her heart as the cardinal's dark eyes smiled at her.

"My verdict is that you have every right, even a duty, to take the girl."

"No," Anika whispered in a small, frightened voice. Surely this was a dream, it could not be happening—

"So be it." Lord Laco turned toward a pair of knights who rode behind his carriage. "Take the girl from her father, and bring her to the castle. If you encounter resistance . . ." at this he looked directly at Anika's father, "use your swords."

"You can't do this!" Anika heard her father roar.

Laco eased himself back into the carriage, then leaned across his son and gave Anika a dry, one-sided smile through the window. "If you find the cardinal's judgment unfair, call a magistrate."

Laughing, he fell back into his seat as the carriage lurched away.

Four

Laco's words seemed to come to Petrov through strangely thickened air.

Use your swords.

His sword! It hung by his belt as always, a symbol of his knighthood and his skills in warfare, but how many years had passed since he unsheathed it for anything but training or an empty bluff?

The sound of dear Anika's cry propelled him forward; his hand reached for the instrument that years ago had completed him, made him whole. The hilt felt cold and foreign in his hand, and when had the blade become so heavy?

There was no time to wonder. The two knights riding behind the carriage had spurred their stallions at their master's command; the closest was already closing in upon Anika, his arm extended to sweep her up across his saddle.

"You shall not do this!" Petrov's blade sliced through the air, striking the knight squarely on the forearm, right at the point where the heavy leather gauntlet joined the metal vambrace that protected the arm. The blow did little more than startle the knight, but it gave Anika time to whirl away.

"Run, Ernan, take Anika!" Petrov yelled, turning to brace himself for the second man's attack.

"I will not run," Ernan answered, pulling a dagger from his belt. "I am within me rights to resist."

Petrov shook his head, his blood rising in a jet. "Can you not see that they intend to have us? This is no debate, Ernan—it is war!"

The first knight, cursing his injured arm, wheeled his mount around and trotted slowly toward a hitching post. The second slipped from the saddle and drew his sword, advancing steadily toward Ernan.

Petrov glanced behind him. In his younger days he would have taken on two men without hesitation, but he had seen sixty-five summers and was no longer the warrior he had once been. Ernan was a man of books, not the blade, and might prove to be worse than useless in a fight. Behind them lay the winding streets and alleys of Prague, a veritable maze if they should choose to escape. But they would have to run *now*, for the knights were coming closer, as confident as cats intent upon a pair of sag-bellied rats.

"Ernan, listen to me," Petrov commanded. "Take your daughter and run through the alleys! I will meet you later."

"No! I am not willing to let this lord take me daughter or me honor, and both must be defended. If Lord Laco wants a fight, by heaven above, I'll give him one!"

Like a fool running for gold, Ernan let out a yell and charged the knight Petrov had wounded. The knight, grinning as his quarry sprinted forward, waited calmly until the last possible moment, then drew his sword. With a quick parry and thrust, he ran Ernan O'Connor through.

Staring in horror, Petrov watched his dearest friend clutch the raw edges of the knight's blade with both hands, then spin in a half-turn. He caught Petrov's eye and offered the older man a trembling smile. "'Twas not the fight I hoped for," he whispered, glancing down to see blood on his hands. His eyes lifted to Petrov's for a moment, a look of intense and clear longing filling his gaze. "I've been a wee bit unwise today. Take care of Anika, Petrov. Live—and take care of me daughter."

Petrov scarcely had time to nod before the second knight commanded his attention. Half-blinded by hot tears, he managed a reasonable defense of himself before tripping backward over a planter some well-meaning housewife had set out to beautify the street. Laco's knight, chuckling at his helpless quarry, stood ready to dispatch Petrov's soul to heaven, but a summons from his comrade broke the silence.

"Leave the old man, Oswald; he's nothing. The master wants the girl, and she's vanished."

Still grinning, Petrov's assailant lowered his blade. "I'll not do you the honor, old man," he whispered, his eyes glinting with malicious glee. "Old men should die in their beds, not flat on their bums in the middle of the street."

Furious at his helplessness and vulnerability, Petrov pushed himself up, ready to charge the retreating knight's back, not caring if he was struck down. But Ernan's dying charge rang in his ears. Anika was still in danger, an orphan now and in need of his help.

Biting back his pride and anger, Petrov took one last look at Ernan's motionless body, then furtively shadowed his way into the alleys, searching for Anika and whatever remained of his wounded pride.

"Now she will never come willingly!"

Feeling restless and irritable, Cardinal D'Ailly turned from the impetuous youth's face and stared out the carriage window, bracing himself for yet another of Miloslav's temper tantrums. He had been Lord Laco's guest for only a month, but already he longed for the peace and quiet splendor of his apartments in Rome. No amount of gold or influence could compensate for having to endure this youth's constant yammering for attention.

"Shut your mouth, Son." Lord Laco pressed his lips together in anger. "She would never have come with you; the girl has pride—a great deal more than you, from what I can tell."

"Father!" The son recoiled from his father's hot eyes and tried on a smile that seemed a size too small. "I'm sure I don't know what you're talking about."

"Don't you?" For a moment Laco's eyes met D'Ailly's, and he smiled in apology. "Forgive us, Your Eminence, while we participate in a small family squabble. My son has no patience and no sense."

"Father, you can't ruin this for me. I've wanted her ever since I saw her in the marketplace, so you'll have to get her. There's not another girl as pretty within miles of Lidice, and if she won't come willingly, you'll have to send someone to fetch her."

Laco closed his eyes, opened his mouth—his signal that Miloslav had transgressed the bounds of human understanding. "I have heard, Son, about the knights you sent to follow the girl. And I myself saw her blushing in church that Sunday we went to Bethlehem Chapel. I can only imagine what you did to embarrass her so."

The self-centered youth lifted a brow. "Nothing. I only smiled at her."

"Nothing less than a glimpse of the devil himself could have put such fear and loathing into her eyes," Laco answered, propping one of his heavy boots on his knee. "I warned you to stay away from her, but you would not."

"You said I could have her."

"I said you could *inquire* after her. But you approached her yourself and scared the maiden away. So now her father would rather die than allow her to come to us."

"Is he dead, do you think?" Miloslav turned slightly in the seat and looked out the window as if he could look back down the road and see into Prague.

D'Ailly crossed his legs, wearying of the conversation. "I cannot imagine your father's knights letting him live," he dryly inserted, offering his host a small smile of acknowledgment. "Nor can I imagine a father allowing his daughter to be spirited away. Yes, I would imagine he is dead, and probably the old knight, too." He lifted his arm and rested it in the window frame. "The old knights are doggedly stubborn about such things as virtue and honor."

"Then can I have the girl?"

D'Ailly looked at Miloslav and felt his stomach churn. He had seen many faces as hard, cruel, and pitiless, but rarely upon men so young. In the past month he had observed that the younger nobleman would commit almost any act to gain his father's attention; this was probably just another ploy to earn Laco's notice.

The Lord of Lidice wasn't watching even now; his cold eyes were fastened to the window and the passing scenery.

"Wait and see, Miloslav," D'Ailly suggested, turning his gaze to the mountains outside. "Patience is a godly virtue, remember?"

Running, stumbling, sobbing, Anika ran through the alleys and streets, purposely taking a circuitous route to confuse anyone who might attempt to follow her. What had they done to her father? And what had they intended to do with her? She would have gone willingly with the loathsome lord's men if she had known her father's life would be at risk if she did not, but she had not been given a chance to negotiate. And now her father—a harmless *copyist*, for heaven's sake—remained behind, battling for her life and honor. Only God knew what would become of him and Petrov.

"Are you all right, miss?" A tall and richly dressed nobleman suddenly stepped out of a doorway, and Anika shrank from him as if she had seen a ghost. *One of them.* Trembling in every sinew, she turned and darted down another alley, confusing her already muddled sense of direction.

She walked quickly, her head down, not knowing or caring where she went. At least an hour passed before her heart steadied to a beat that allowed her to breathe normally. Crouching on the ground, she braced her back against a building and forced herself to think. Lord Laco had recognized her father, so he would know where the bookshop was located. She dared not return home, so she would have to go to Petrov's small house. The old knight lived alone, and she would be safe there. Her father *(God, I pray he still lives!)* would seek help immediately, taking his case before the magistrates *(Can they be trusted?)* or even King Wenceslas, and thus the matter would be resolved. Both the king and queen admired Jan Hus, so the preacher would eloquently plead her father's case in the royal court. In a matter of days the issue would be settled, and Lord Laco's vile threats would cease.

But what if Father has been hurt? What if Sir Petrov is captured? What if my father is wounded, lying unconscious somewhere, unable to

*care for himself? Or, if Father has escaped and gone home, will he be
safe, or will Lord Laco send others to look for me?*

Her face burned as she remembered the keen probing eyes and
mocking expression of the younger man. All of this trouble could be
laid firmly at his feet, she decided, though she had no idea why he
had chosen to turn his depraved attention upon her. Surely a nobleman's son could have his pick of Bohemia's beautiful maidens. If he
truly wanted a chambermaid, he had only to visit the nearest inn,
where women aplenty brazenly advertised the services they offered.
And if he wanted more than a maid . . .

She shuddered, thinking of some of the stories she had read. At
sixteen she was untried and inexperienced in the ways of the world,
but she had read enough to understand that an amazing variety of
people lived in it. She knew about liars, thieves, and murderers, cutpurses and cutthroats, pirates and pillagers. She knew what harlots
sold and lechers bought; she understood the scriptural references
against all sorts of fornication.

She did not consider herself a blushing maiden, and yet she had
never done anything to spoil her own innocence. As a motherless
child, she had traveled the world through the pages of the books she
copied. In her vicarious adventures she had memorized poetry,
thrilled to war songs, and giggled at ribald satires from the Monk of
Montaudon who had regaled the king of Aragon one hundred years
before. She had studied books of law and medicine. She had explored
and questioned the philosophies of ancient Greeks and Romans.

But what good would any of that knowledge do her now? Grief
welled in her, black and cold, and she huddled against the wall and
pulled her knees to her chest, waiting for the sunset. When the cloak
of darkness fell upon the street, she would venture to Petrov's house
and pray that two precious people would be waiting there to greet
her.

Alone in her misery and weariness, Anika lowered her head to
her knees and slid into a fitful sleep.

Five

"Your mama has gone to heaven."

Anika stubbornly shook her head. "My mama is asleep."

"No, child, her neck's broke." The innkeeper's wife dashed a tear from her soot-streaked cheek, then knelt and clasped Anika's hands. Her eyes darkened and shone with an eerie light as her damp hands squeezed Anika's fingers. "Your mama's dead, child, and it's all that cardinal's fault. Don't you ever forget it, you hear? As God is my witness, the Roman church and her meddling priests will be the death of us all."

Anika did not understand, but she nodded until the woman released her. Not knowing what else to do, she stood silently as the woman rose to watch her home burn. In the distance she heard the ragged cry of her father's weeping.

The man in the red robe gathered his bundles and turned from the ghastly scene. Anika clamped her eyes shut, afraid to look upon the selfish man who would not surrender the ladder to her mother.

"Go away," she murmured, afraid to open her eyes. "Go away, please." She felt a tremor run down her throat and heard the gulp as she swallowed her fear. "Go away, go away, go away!"

"Anika! Open your eyes!"

Her eyes flew open, eager to see her father's broad face, but another face loomed before her, a face with eyes as wide and blank as black window panes, as though the soul they mirrored had long since flown.

The face belonged to Cardinal D'Ailly.

"No!"

Horror snaked down her backbone and coiled in her belly as Anika woke and stared into the darkness, trying to see the face that had slashed her sleep like a knife. In a rush of remembrance the features formed again in her memory, and her stomach churned and tightened into a knot as fear brushed the edge of her mind. A cold sweat prickled on her forehead, and she could feel her heart beating like bat wings.

Had Cardinal D'Ailly truly been at the fire where her mother died, or had the horrific events of the past day superimposed his face on the clergyman in her recurrent nightmare?

She clenched her hand into a fist and pressed it to her mouth, unable to make sense of the terror locked inside her dreams. She was as defenseless now as she had been on the night her mother died. Again she was alone in the dark, but she was no longer a child. Though an enemy might lie in wait for her, she could elude him.

Now that darkness had fallen, she would find her father. She rose to her unsteady feet, stretched her cramped muscles, then slipped through the alleys until she recognized Broad Street. Her father's shop was not far away, but she moved slowly and cautiously, lingering in the shadows, darting forward in silence. The curfew bells had already rung. She knew she would be questioned if the king's soldiers discovered her, but maybe her pursuers had withdrawn, not wanting to violate the king's curfew.

Or would they care? How powerful *was* Lord Laco?

After dodging splashes of moonlight and torchlight for nearly an hour, she crept into the doorway of Petrov's house and turned to study her father's bookshop across the street. No candle burned in the window; nothing appeared to move within. The window blinds had not been lowered for nighttime's approach.

Her father was not home.

She whirled around to study Petrov's house. There! Through the shutters she did see a light burning inside, though 'twas only a small candle, not a proper lamp. Still, that single flame was a sign of life, and life meant hope.

Holding her breath, she knocked on the door. After a long moment she heard Petrov's husky voice. "Who goes there?"

"Anika," she whispered, surprised that her lips had the power to speak at all.

A latch clicked, the hinges protested, then the door swung open. Petrov opened his arms to her, and Anika fell into his embrace with joy and relief. "Sir Petrov! I am so glad to see you! I was so frightened!" With her arms locked around his waist, she looked up. "Where is my father?"

"Hush, little bird." The old knight's spidery hand rested on her head for a moment. Then he hurried her inside and bolted the door.

An odd coldness settled upon Anika, a fearful and darkly textured sensation, heavy and threatening. "Sir Petrov," she asked, an unusual note of command filling her voice, "I must know. Where is my father?"

The old man's features went dead white. "With Master Hus."

Anika closed her eyes and sighed. "Good. You are clever, my friend! Lord Laco would never dare to search for him at the church. Can you take me to him now, or must we wait until morning?"

The old man gave her a quick, denying glance, then lowered his bony hands to her shoulders. "Anika, dear one, your father truly is in heaven, for a more godly man I never knew." His face seemed to crack; pain and sadness and regret poured forth from his eyes, his voice, even his quivering nose. "His body alone is with Master Hus; his spirit is with the Lord. And you cannot be with him now."

Anika clamped her jaw shut and stared at nothing as the old feelings of abandonment tugged at her soul like a powerful undertow. Death had visited her again, and again it was somehow her fault. She had left her mother's side before the fire; today she had abandoned her father . . . and now he was dead, too.

She felt as though devilish hot hands gripped her heart, slowly twisting the life from it. The gypsies would say she was cursed, born under an unlucky star, destined to lose both parents through her own inattention . . .

"Anika, listen to me." Petrov's voice still scraped terribly, but the words began to come faster. "You cannot go back to your father's shop. It is not a safe place for you."

"Why not?" she answered thickly, her sense of loss beyond tears. "What does it matter?"

"He died defending you, little bird. Lord Laco's son insulted you, and your father certainly knew enough of young men to see malice in the youth's eyes. If you return to your home tomorrow, Laco is certain to send someone to fetch you. And now you have no defender, save me."

Defender. She looked up at the old knight, suddenly not caring whether or not she hurt him. "Why didn't you save him?" Her breath burned in her throat. "You're a knight, Sir Petrov. You know how to fight. My father is not a fighter. He couldn't have prevailed against those men without your help."

"I tried." Trembling with sorrow, Petrov's hands fell from her shoulders. His gentle brown eyes overflowed with tears as he sank to a chair and lifted his eyes toward heaven. "God above knows I tried. Would that I had my youth, my strength, my ardor! But I am not what I was, Anika. I could not prevail. I would have been run through with the sword, too, but—"

"But what?"

Petrov hung his head, and his lips went as pale as his cheeks. His voice was low and controlled, but Anika could hear the undertone of desolation. "I was not fit to kill. There was no glory in it, so my opponent let me live."

His misery was so overwhelming, so palpable, it was like another body in the room—a laboring, grieving presence. Anika sank to a low stool in the small and sparely furnished chamber. Why was she hurting the friend her father loved best? Petrov was staggering under a load of shame she could only begin to comprehend.

"Your father," he went on, his voice fainter than air, "bade me live to look after you. And I am afraid I will not even be able to do that, for I cannot defend you against Lord Laco's knights. They will come looking for you on the morrow, for Laco is a determined man."

"He is a brute." She spat the words, choking on her anger. "He deserves to die the death he decreed for my father. And that son with him. And that loathsome Cardinal D'Ailly."

Petrov lifted his head, surprise written on his features. "Anika, you should not say such things. Perhaps you can be forgiven for saying them to me, but if you repeat those words and the report reaches Laco's ears, you will be in worse straits than now." His brows drew together in an agonized expression. "I will take you tomorrow to Jan Hus. You can say your farewells to your father, and we will tell Master Hus all that happened today. Maybe he can find employment for you with a family in the city."

"No." She swallowed hard, lifted her chin, and boldly met his gaze. "The evil ones must pay for what they have done, Sir Petrov. And I intend to see that they do." She looked away and studied the single candle burning on Petrov's table. "I had a dream tonight—a familiar dream, for it has visited my sleep many times. In my dream I revisited the place where my mother died, and Cardinal D'Ailly was there."

"You cannot believe what you see in dreams," Petrov countered, shaking his head. "The devil plants false ideas and feelings while we sleep."

"If it was not D'Ailly, it was a cardinal like him; they are much the same."

Petrov blinked at her in bewilderment, then loosely crossed his arms. "The cardinals are not *all* evil, little one. There are some who love God more than power or the pleasures of this world. Yet they wear the robes of cardinals, too."

"Still—" She drew a long, quivering breath, barely mastering the passion that shook her. "I will not suffer them. No more. Not any longer."

"And what will you do?" he asked, managing a half-laugh. "We all suffer them, little bird. There are some like Master Hus who dare to try to change things, but he is working from within the church. We do not know enough to challenge the churchmen. We are un-educated—"

"I am not uneducated," she interrupted, cutting him off with a glance. "And I do not know what I will do. But we will sleep on our problem, and if God is good, perhaps he will provide an answer."

Petrov's answer, when morning came, was simple and direct. "We should work within the civil law as Master Hus works within the church," he told Anika. And though she had her doubts about the wisdom of his plan, she washed her tears from her face, then took Petrov's arm and went to the town hall to meet with the council of magistrates. In the same council chamber where Anika had heard the magistrates falsely promise a fair trial for the three students, she and Petrov reported the events that led up to Ernan O'Connor's death.

The chief magistrate, a haughty man with craggy features, stared at Anika from across the table. "You are aware, of course, that Lord Laco and his son will have to be summoned to give their account of the incident," he said, his mouth pulling into a sour grin. "If their stories do not mesh with yours, Cardinal D'Ailly himself might have to be consulted. And we have heard on good authority that the cardinal is en route to Rome."

"Consult with whomever you have to," Petrov answered gruffly. "Anika and I do not fear the truth. Master Hus will account for our characters. The girl, her father, and I have had many dealings with him."

At the mention of Hus's name, Anika saw the chief magistrate's eyebrows slant together in a frown. *It was a reasonable idea, Sir Petrov*, she thought, silently following the knight from the council chamber. *But the chief magistrate's hatred for Jan Hus is a living thing, and it will consume us if we are not careful.*

Before the day ended they received a summons to appear before the council the next morning. Anika felt her skin crawl with revulsion when she walked through the chamber doorway on Tuesday morning and saw Lord Laco, his son, and the two knights who had been in attendance on the day of her father's murder. One of the knights wore a thick bandage around his forearm, and bluish green bruises mottled the other's face.

"Sir Petrov, did you cause so much damage?" Anika whispered, staring at the other knight's puffy face.

"I only wish I had," Petrov answered, a muscle quivering in his jaw. "The brute has been in a yard fight, or else he has deliberately punished himself to elicit mercy from those who will judge us."

With a thickly beating heart Anika wound her way through the crowd of observers. Master Hus had volunteered to face the magistrates with Anika and Petrov, but all three of them knew his presence might only muddy the waters. And so Anika and Petrov stood alone before the magistrates and waited to hear the result of the council's investigation of their complaint.

The head magistrate glanced up at Anika and Petrov, then nodded grimly toward the bench where Lord Laco and his men sat. "We have spoken to this nobleman, his son, and his knights," the chief magistrate said, eyeing Anika with a taut and derisive expression. "And their stories, told separately, agree in form and detail. According to them, their carriage was progressing through the streets when a shout from your father stopped the vehicle. When his lordship looked out and apologized for splashing mud on . . ."—he glanced down at his notes for a moment— "Ernan O'Connor, the copyist hurled curses and insults at Lord Laco. In an effort to further demonstrate his goodwill, the noble lord then offered employment to the daughter." The magistrate looked up and studied Anika for a moment. "But this offer was proudly and scornfully refused. The lord and his party then departed, their business done, but the copyist and his companion savagely attacked two of the lord's knights. A fight ensued, and the knights of Lidice defended themselves and their master's honor."

The magistrate nodded toward the wounded knights with a taut jerk of his head. "You see the injuries before you. In the attack, Ernan O'Connor was struck and killed, and the knight called Petrov fled away through the city streets, as did the girl."

The magistrate and Lord Laco exchanged a subtle look of amusement. "Have I forgotten any detail, my lord?" the magistrate asked.

"No," Laco answered in a tense, clipped voice that forbade any argument. "That is the entire truth."

The magistrate nodded. "Then the council finds you, Sir Petrov, guilty of criminal mischief and fined a week's wages." The magistrate's voice was stern with no vestige of sympathy. "And you, Anika of Prague, since you lack parents and a fit guardian, are charged with finding gainful employment so you will not join the other beggars in the street. If you cannot find a suitable place by sunset one week from today, you must accept employment from Lord Laco, if that nobleman is still of a mind to offer it."

Anika's gaze met Lord Laco's for the first time. "I am still willing," he said, his granite eyes locked on her. "As long as she pleases my son." The smile in his eyes contained a sensuous flame. "As a chambermaid, of course."

The magistrate wagged his head. "We are agreed, then. If you find no other employer willing to take you, you will report to the steward of the lord's estate at Lidice seven days hence, ready to begin service to your new master."

Anika muffled her tears as a flash of wild grief ripped through her. Turning to hide from her enemies, she buried her burning face against Petrov's shoulder as the knight led her from the room. He shielded her as best he could, but as they passed through the vestibule, where a crowd of citizens stood silent and still, a tall man with dark hair and even darker eyes stopped them by slipping his hand under Anika's chin.

"I overheard your case," he said, a strange, faintly eager look flashing in his eye as he turned from Anika to Petrov. "Is there anything I can do?"

Anika's eyes flooded with tears at this unexpected show of compassion. To her relief, Petrov answered for her. "Is there work for her in your house, my lord?"

"I do not know," the man answered, his voice rich with warmth and concern. "But my steward may be able to find something if you bring her to us."

"Thank you, my lord," Petrov answered. He nodded a farewell, then led Anika through the curious onlookers.

"Who was that man?" she asked when she finally found her voice.

"A noble and godly man, Lord John of Chlum," Petrov answered, his own voice thick and unsteady. "The son of my old master."

Jan Hus buried Ernan O'Connor in a subdued ceremony at noon the day following the council's ruling. Anika herself had asked for the quiet funeral. It seemed the only decent thing she could do for her father, the only good opportunity that remained in her life. In six days, unless God worked a miracle, she would be on the road to Lidice, ready to offer herself in the hellish service of Lord Laco.

Standing beside her father's open grave, she took a deep breath and tried to swallow the lump that lingered in her throat. Her mother, her father, even God had apparently deserted her. Justice had vanished from Bohemia, a kingdom that once prided itself on its love for freedom and truth.

The afternoon seemed to sleep under a heavy, dove-colored sky. Weariness enveloped her as she tried to concentrate on the words of the funeral service, but too many scattered thoughts assailed her brain. She had found no employment in Prague. Lord Laco must have published the news that he wanted her at Lidice, for jobs that should have flourished like weeds for a strong and willing girl had vanished overnight. No one wanted to hire the daughter of a murdered man, especially when a powerful nobleman expressed a keen desire that she fail in her quest for work. At the end of the week she would have to submit to the council's decree and travel to Lidice— what else could she do?

"Dominus vobiscum," Master Hus concluded, his hands gently cradling his prayer book. "The Lord be with you."

"Et cum spiritui tui." Anika gave the response in a dull, flat voice. "And with your spirit."

No great crowd had appeared to mourn the copyist, only Petrov,

Anika, and Master Hus, who now knew the entire story of the ridiculous mock trial. At the conclusion of the service, Petrov remained behind to help the gravediggers complete their work while Master Hus took Anika's arm and gently led her away from the open grave.

"I am concerned, Daughter, about your health and safety," he said, giving her a careful smile. "What will you do when the appointed day arrives? You cannot submit and go to Lidice, but I could argue your case before the king."

Anika stubbornly shook her head. The magistrates were the king's men, and ever since the martyrdom of the three students she had trusted neither the king nor his subordinates. She and Petrov had presented their case, they had appealed for justice, and those who represented authority had turned a deaf ear and a blind eye to the truth.

"Thank you, Master Hus, but no." She covered his hand with her own and breathed an exasperated sigh. "My father is gone, and nothing can bring him back. As you were silent after the students' execution, so I will be silent in the face of my father's murder. If God is just, he will work vengeance for me. Do not the Scriptures say that God will avenge?"

"Anika, I did not remain silent in hope that God would punish the evildoers." Hus's brown eyes darkened with emotion. "The Scriptures are quite clear—we are not to pray for our enemies' destruction. We are to bless them that spitefully use us, to pray for them—"

"Pray for murderers?" She swallowed hard, trying not to reveal her anger. "Master Hus, can you honestly tell me you did not beg God to punish the guilty when those three men were beheaded? You went into seclusion—what were you doing in your house, praying that God would *bless* traitors?"

The preacher's gentle smile vanished, wiped away by astonishment. "Anika," he said slowly, as if carefully choosing his words, "forgive me for again underestimating you. I forget that you are an unusual girl."

"I'm not a girl. I'm sixteen, well beyond the age of marriage."

"Yea, that you are." His expression softened into one of fond reminiscence. "I tend to think of you as Ernan's wee girl, though you have been copying books as well as he for six or seven years. But you cannot consider yourself an independent woman, Anika. Such an idea is a contradiction in terms. You are alone now, and you will need a benefactor. If you will not let me take your case before the king, let me find a suitable guardian until this trouble with Lord Laco has passed. If we can find a protector for you, I am certain we can convince the council you do not need to work for Lord Laco. Maybe I can find a woman who needs a seamstress or a noble family who requires a tutor for their daughters."

"Thank you, Master Hus, but those things don't interest me," she answered in a rush of words. "I am not skilled with a needle, and I have no interest in caring for children."

The preacher abruptly stopped and turned to face her, still holding her hand. A mischievous look came into his eyes. "Of course! You ought to marry! Would you be happy as a wife? I believe your father had begun to make inquiries for a suitable husband, and it is time you thought of beginning a family of your own."

Anika listened despite a vague sense of unreality. "I have no dowry and will not be married to some peasant I don't even know. No, Master Hus, I will not marry. Not now."

The preacher's smile faded. "Forgive me. You are right; it is too soon. A convent then. You could get to a nunnery until your heart has time to heal from this grief. Later, if the idea pleases you, you could become a tutor or a bride—"

"No nunnery." She spoke with quiet but desperate firmness and pulled her hand away. She would never bury herself within the bowels of a religious system she had come to despise. She had been exposed to truth as she copied Hus's sermons and the Holy Scriptures. How could he even suggest that she closet herself away in a place where women beat themselves in penance for sins and begged their way into heaven? She had embraced the truth and been set free; she could not forsake it now.

"Anika." Disconcerted or disappointed—Anika couldn't tell which—Master Hus crossed his arms and pointedly looked back toward the graveyard. "You cannot refuse every idea I offer. You must choose one of them. Your father would want you to follow my counsel, and there are only so many paths an honorable young woman may follow."

Her brows lifted with annoyance. "Don't worry, Master Hus, I am not likely to choose the things a *dishonorable* wench might do."

He stared at her, baffled, and Anika hastened to explain. "I don't know what I will do when the time comes, but I will pray tonight and seek Petrov's counsel. But I will not go to Lord Laco's house, of that you may be certain." She looked away, avoiding his eyes. "I may run away."

Hus opened his mouth, about to protest, but she silenced him with an uplifted glance. Swallowing the sob that rose in her throat, she looked up and gave him a smile. "You may be sure I will take what I have learned from you wherever I go. I will not do anything to disappoint my heavenly Father or my earthly father—who is also in heaven—nor will I give you cause to be ashamed of me. But I cannot be a tutor or a wife or a postulant, Master Hus. I am none of those things. My heart is too heavy to be a bride, too angry to be a postulant, too impatient to teach children."

Assailed by a tumult of confused thoughts and feelings, she fell silent, waiting for her emotions to subside. "Truth to tell, I don't know what I am," she whispered, not willing to look up and face Hus's gentle, loving look. "But I will survive. And you need not worry about me. I will remain with Sir Petrov until I know what I should do."

"This storm will not last forever." Hus reached out and placed his hand on her shoulder. "Will you send word to me if you need help of any kind? I cannot imagine you alone. I will not sleep if my friend's daughter is wandering in the darkness—"

"I could never be in darkness," she answered, bringing her gaze up to study his beloved face. Next to her father and Petrov, this was the man she loved most in all the world. He had taught her, molded her, shown her the light . . . largely without even knowing it. "I promise I will be careful."

"Then go with God." He gave her shoulder a squeeze and let his hand fall back to his side. "And know that whatever path you choose, I will pray for your success."

"Thank you, Master Hus." Before he could retreat, she stepped forward, embraced him lightly, then withdrew through the gathering night.

Six

A rainstorm hovered over Prague that summer afternoon. The skies themselves seemed to open and weep with Anika as she mourned her father's death and considered the injustice of life. She had grown up with a father who loved the beauty of books, a knight who loved chivalry and honor, and a preacher who loved righteousness, yet none of those ideals brought her comfort now.

What good were books when her eyes were too full to read? Where was chivalry when those with power abused the innocent? And what kind of righteousness urged common folk to turn the other cheek while God's representatives corrupted the kingdom?

Anika sat at the tiny window in the front of her father's shop, having dared at last to enter and take stock of what had been her old life. She now possessed parchments, books, and chests, a table, a lantern, five candlesticks, two woolen cloaks, two dresses, six sleeves, and two chemises—one of silk, a birthday gift from her father. In addition, she owned an assortment of tools from their work: several razors, two pumice stones, two awls, two narrow parchment rulers, and a single boar's tooth for polishing the final page.

What pitiful possessions. With a moan of distress, she turned away from the sight of so many bits and pieces of her old life. If she married, all these things would have to suffice for a dowry; she had nothing else. And if she were taken by Lord Laco, he would undoubtedly seize the bookshop, filling his role as her "guardian."

A suffocating sensation tightened her throat. She would not allow his vile hands to touch a single precious parchment her father had inscribed. No matter where she went, she would be sure to protect her father's beloved books.

Of all her belongings, the books were the most valuable, but how could she take them with her? She supposed she could leave them with a merchant for rental, but few merchants took a woman seriously, and once the books left her hands they would probably be lost to her forever. She had no time to arrange a private sale, no time to call for the books currently rented to students, no time to organize her father's house or his affairs.

What a sudden thing death was! In one moment she and her father had been no more concerned for their earthly possessions than for what they might eat for lunch; scarcely four days later she was assessing her future in light of the value of a few books, tools, and scribbled parchments. The house would be snatched up by someone else with money enough to pay the rent, and whatever Anika couldn't carry with her would be confiscated or stolen while the landlord wasn't looking.

Outside the window, bolts of lightning chased each other across the sky, white and jagged like running skeletons. The subsequent blast of thunder rattled the shutters and Anika's bones. She pressed her hand over her face in a convulsion of sorrow, her throat aching with regret.

If only she hadn't run when the knight attacked. Her father died defending her, a helpless girl.

If only she hadn't been born female.

If only she were a man.

Things would be different.

———

"Sir Petrov!"

The old knight felt his body stiffen in shock as Anika flew through the doorway, her hair dripping with rain, a strange light of excitement in her eyes. By all the saints, he had never thought to see her face alight like that again!

"I know, Sir Petrov, what I must do! I know where to find a position!"

Despite his sorrow, a surge of relief flowed through him. If she had found work in Prague they would not have to escape the city. Though he would have gone to Hades and back in order to help his friend's beloved daughter, he had been hoping to avoid a trek across mountain miles and a series of table-scrap meals.

He turned in his chair and leaned toward her in a gentle, inquiring fashion. "Whom have you talked to?"

"No one, Sir Petrov, and that is the beauty of it!" She sank onto the bench by his table, and the urgent vibrancy of her voice caught him off guard.

His nerves immediately tensed. "The beauty of what?"

"My idea." She gazed at him in satisfaction. "Or perhaps it is your idea. I never would have considered it if not for your stories."

Petrov held up a trembling hand. "Slow down, Anika. What stories? What are you talking about?"

"The stories about your days as a squire. You were just a young boy of twelve when you became a squire at Lord Honza's manor. You learned to serve, you learned to read, and the knights taught you how to fight."

Petrov hesitated, blinking with bafflement. "'Tis what every squire learns. What of it?"

Clasping her hands together, Anika leaned toward him and lowered her voice. "I will be a squire. No one will think to look for me among the men and boys in a garrison. You will cut off my hair and dress me as a boy, and then you will take me to Chlum Castle. And while I am there, safely hidden away, you will safeguard my father's books and advertise them for rent. Thus you will have a shop, I will have a safe place, and I will learn how to defend myself from people like Lord Laco's son."

"No, no, and no," Petrov answered, barely able to keep the laughter from his voice. What had happened to the levelheaded young woman he knew yesterday? Surely Ernan's death had made her take leave of her senses, for not a word of her speech made sense.

"What do you mean 'no'?" She leaned back, a nervous and slightly puzzled look on her pretty face. "My plan makes perfect sense, Sir Petrov. You need money, and I haven't forgotten that the council fined you for coming to my father's aid. Now you can pay your fine and earn a decent wage, too. If you do not help me manage Father's books, his works will fall into others' hands. They might even be burned if the wrong people take possession of them. And in five days I will face Lord Laco unless I find suitable employment. So why shouldn't I be a squire, Sir Petrov? Do you not remember teaching me how to hold a sword?"

He shook his head, dazed. "You were just a child."

"But I learned well! Parry and slash, parry and stab, feint and lunge, I remember it all!"

"Anika." Petrov lowered his head onto his hand, sensing the onslaught of a murderous headache. She would never know how deeply she had just honored him, but the idea was foolish. If they attempted such a ruse and were discovered, the knights of Chlum would say that Petrov had dishonored the ideals of chivalry, the virtues of truth, loyalty, and honor. But who better personified those ideals than Anika?

"You said Lord John of Chlum was a kind and gentle master," she continued, scarcely giving Petrov time to think. "Why wouldn't I be safe among his men?"

"Knights are trained to fight, Anika, and men are not kind in war," Petrov murmured, rubbing his temples. "Nor are knights gentle when they are alone. God put women in the world to keep us tolerable."

"Why do you speak of war?" Anika pushed her lower lip forward in a pout. "There is no war. Bohemia has not known war since before I was born. You were always telling my father that war would not come here again, for Christians should not fight each other."

"Anika," he said, feeling suddenly limp with weariness, "I am a man, not God; I could be wrong. Who can say whether or not war will come? I will not gamble with your life. Besides . . ." he flung his hand out, hoping to distract her, "I cannot believe God would bless such an endeavor if you deny your womanhood. It is a precious and God-given gift."

"Deborah did not deny her womanhood, yet she led the Israelites to war," Anika countered. "And God used Mary to bring the greatest warrior of all into the world. Do not argue with me, Sir Petrov. I shall deny nothing of myself, but if it is necessary to *hide* what I am, then so be it. As a squire I will be in the service of a good man, I will be safe and well fed, provided for, taught, clothed, put to good use—"

"Hold, Anika." Petrov held up a hand. "Let us consider this idea of yours on the morrow. Perhaps it will make more sense in the clear light of morning."

And perhaps, he thought, rising to bolt the door and shutter the window, *you will realize what a truly foolish notion it is.*

In the morning, Petrov was chagrined to realize that Anika's determination had only increased during the night. Apparently she hadn't slept at all but had lain awake plotting and planning how such a deception might be accomplished. She had a boyish figure, she reminded him more than once, she was reasonably tall and as slender as a reed. She was quick and agile and spoke with an educated accent, as a nobleman's son would. She read and wrote with a fine hand, as a learned man's son should, and she had no relatives to interfere with her plans.

"But, Anika! If you were to go to Chlum as a maid I could agree—"

She silenced him by tossing her hair across her shoulders in a gesture of defiance. "My father did not teach me to read and write so I could empty chamber pots," she reminded him. "Besides, Laco's spies could find me at Chlum if I remain a maid. But I will be safe in disguise. Of all the nobles in Bohemia, Lord John of Chlum is reputed to be one of the most honorable. If you were to present me as a squire to be trained at Chlum, what could Lord John do but accept me?"

Strangely enough, Petrov did not now find the idea as abhorrent as he had the night before. Though he hated to admit it, Anika's plan did bring him a trace of hope. If she were hidden away at Chlum for a few months, Lord Laco might grow weary and stop searching for her. And in the meantime, as her father's friend, he would oversee Ernan's bookshop, thereby ending his worries about how he would manage to keep meat on his bones and wood on the fire.

"With the income from the bookshop you could present me to Lord John with a small tribute," Anika was saying now, her eyes artless and serene. "And you could say that I am your ward, which is not a lie at all. I am your ward now, and you are my guardian."

Petrov held up a finger and paused a moment, letting the silence stretch between them. "I must be very clear on one point—I will not lie to my master's son. A knight is sworn to be true to his master above all else," he told Anika, his voice firm and final. "I will not lie to Lord John, not even for you, little bird."

"You can't be calling me 'little bird' if we are to do this," Anika reminded him, her green eyes bright and bemused. "You shall have to think of another name."

"What would we call you?"

"Kafka," she said suddenly.

And before her appealing smile, his defenses melted away. Kafka meant "bird," and she knew he could use that name without feeling guilty of deception. "My little Kafka," he said, rewarding her with a larger smile of his own. "I have much to teach you, and you have only a few days in which to learn. If Lord Laco comes looking for you before the day you are to join his household—"

"You shall tell him quite truthfully that you have found me an appointment in the country," Anika answered, rising lightly to her feet. "And he may search for me all he likes, but he shall never find me."

Petrov watched her go and began to wonder just how long they could maintain this façade. Anika was sixteen, and soon she would tire of these foolish games. Until then, at least, she would be safe from Lord Laco. As soon as that danger had passed, Petrov would return to Chlum and bring his ward back to Prague.

It was a good idea, as long as the charade was only temporary.

———

With money Anika found in Ernan's moneybag, Petrov ventured into a sword smith's shop and eyed the array of gleaming weapons upon the wall. Anika would need a light, flexible sword, something more for show and practice than for actual use, but he would not let her go defenseless into a knights' garrison. He loved the girl too dearly to risk either her virtue or her life.

"Goin' into battle, are you, eh, knight?" the sword smith asked, squinting up at Petrov with shifting eyes. "Why does such an old man need a new sword?"

"For the same reason he needs a bed and bread," Petrov answered smoothly, shifting the silver coins in his fist. "A man must eat and sleep and defend himself if he is to survive."

The smith grunted. "The heavier, two-handed swords are more popular now," he said, pointing Petrov toward a gleaming sword which would probably cost twice as much as the shorter single-edged sword Petrov had been examining.

"Look at me," Petrov said, stepping backward and lifting his hands. "I am sixty and five years old, how am I to lift such a heavy blade? Let the young ones carry those iron weights. I will stick to something light and quick."

A flash of humor crossed the man's dour face. "All right. Let me see your silver, and I'll let you know what I have to suit you."

Petrov dropped the two silver coins on the man's table, then tensed when the sword smith threw back his head and roared with laughter. "You're jesting, right? Is this a joke? Did the magistrates send you down to test my prices?"

"No." Petrov's embarrassment turned quickly to annoyance. "That is good silver, enough to buy a sword."

"Enough to buy a sword twenty years ago maybe." The man's features twisted into a maddening leer. "Now add more silver to those coins there, or be on your way and stop cluttering up my shop with your clattering bones. I haven't time to spend with the likes of you, old man."

Something inside Petrov shriveled a little at the man's harsh expression, but he pointed instead to a collection of daggers in a wooden case. "How much for those?" he asked, aware that his hand trembled like the last leaf of autumn.

The man's eyes narrowed as he eyed the silver coins again. "You might have enough for a blade. A little one, small enough to fit inside a boot."

"Fine," Petrov answered, lifting his chin. "Make it very, very sharp."

———

Anika could not sleep the night before her appointed day of departure. Petrov had spent five hectic days preparing her for life in a garrison, and some part of her still reeled in wonder that she was pursuing such an unconventional course. Her father, God rest him, would not approve, nor would Master Hus. But her father had left her alone, and the preacher had wanted to send her off as a wife or seamstress. Anika would not have felt comfortable filling those roles even before her father's death.

She couldn't imagine life without a pen in her hand. She loved the feel of a slender quill and the process of making words flow and blossom to life on parchment. As she moved her hand over the blank pages, watching words and pictures and borders combine in a work of art, she rejoiced, knowing that the words represented concepts and emotions that would touch hearts and stir souls. She would have been content to live each day of her life at her writing desk, copying the words of Master Hus and other great professors.

A month ago she would have been happy to live her life in the company of her books, her father, and her father's friends. Strange how she had always spent her time in the company of men. She actually knew very few women; she had only passing acquaintances with women at the market and the landlady who came to collect the rent once a month. She did not dislike others of her own sex, but she had not been taught the code that unlocked female simpers and sighs, and she could not fathom the rationale behind the affected speech and behaviors of noblewomen who wandered into the book-shop. *The Art of Courtly Love* and other books like it had raised far more questions than they had answered.

Her father and Petrov had always treated her with kindness, consideration, and honesty. She had never been given reason to believe she was less than a man because she had been created female, and the men in her life made her feel cherished, revered. Her father had always called her his "secret weapon," for her skill with languages and her deft hand had enabled him to produce beautifully copied books in half the time of his competitors. When most other fathers set their daughters to work in the kitchen, Ernan O'Connor had propped Anika up beside a writing table and placed a quill in her hand. While other girls pounded bread, Anika smoothed parchment with a pumice stone; while other young ladies sewed and embroidered, Anika mixed inks and drew word pictures. By the age of twelve she became an equal partner in her father's business, and she had never believed that she might not be able to accomplish anything she set her mind to do.

Outside Petrov's house, the moon sailed across a sky of deepest sapphire, casting bars of silver across the floor of the chamber. From the other side of the room, the old knight snored loudly, his back to her.

Dear Petrov. What would she do without him? Her hand crept to her forehead, where a neat row of bangs lay just above her eyebrows. Just before sunset, while there remained enough daylight to see, Petrov had taken the small dagger he bought for Anika and shorn her waist-length hair. He cut her hair in the short-cropped style preferred by all noblemen, but when he came to the small plait of white hair, he paused and lifted his brows in a quizzical expression.

"What about this?" he asked, frowning as though he had never noticed the white braid before.

"Cut the white streak out," she said firmly, gripping her chair with both hands. "Down to the scalp, Sir Petrov. No one must see it."

Her head felt curiously light without the weight of her coppery locks, but one glance in her small mirror convinced her that she made a strikingly plain boy.

By the time blue-veiled twilight crept into the house, Petrov had burned the remnants of her hair in the fireplace. As the stench of burning hair filled her nostrils, Anika gathered up her chemises, gowns, sleeves, and collars, then locked them into a chest. Petrov pointed toward a pile of garments on the table. From a widow whose son had just died from fever, he had purchased a pair of soft leather boots with deep cuffs, a pair of thick hose, a short tunic, and an open-sided tabard of rich brocade.

"They will think I am a nobleman's son for certain when they see me in this," Anika exclaimed as Petrov modestly turned his back so she could slip into the outfit. "What if Lord John asks who my father is?"

"If he does, tell him the truth about your father's Irish roots," Petrov answered, chuckling. "Tell him you are descended from the great kings. The O'Connors were a powerful clan in Ireland, and I'm not certain they still aren't."

And so, lying in the dark, Anika had composed her story. She was the child (she couldn't in good faith declare herself a *son*) of an Irishman, O'Connor by clan, and honorable by birth. Her father had been killed in battle (hadn't he?), and Sir Petrov was her father's dearest friend and her guardian. She wished for asylum and instruction in the chivalric arts of knighthood; she wanted to serve an honorable lord and defend God's enemies from injustice and falseness. The charade would work. She would pass as a boy and be safe until the danger was over.

"If I learn my lessons well," she whispered, watching the play of moonlit shadows outside, "I will be prepared if Lord Laco or his son should ever come after me again. And when the time is right, I shall have my vengeance against Cardinal D'Ailly."

Novak

———✦———

The sun had not yet risen when Petrov shook Anika awake. "Wake up, Kafka," he murmured, a note of pride in his voice. "Today we journey to Chlum."

Anika sat up, ran her fingers through the fuzzy ends of her shorn hair, then stepped into her boots, remembering to hide the dagger beneath the cuff as Petrov had taught her. Within five minutes she was dressed and ready to go, her gunnysack packed with a comb, her pen, and two small books: a copy of Paul's letter to the Ephesians (her favorite epistle of late because Paul wrote of putting on the whole armor of God) and *The Art of Courtly Love.*

She stood in the doorway and held out her hands, inviting Petrov's inspection, but frowned when his brow furrowed. "What is wrong?" she asked, glancing down to make certain she had not forgotten some necessary article of clothing.

"You are missing one thing every squire needs," the old man answered, his hands moving toward his own belt. Slowly, lovingly, he unbuckled the silver sword that hung at his waist, then proffered it to Anika like a king granting gifts.

"Your sword," she breathed, awed by the significance of his gesture. "It is yours, Sir Petrov. I cannot take something your master gave you."

"You cannot train at Chlum Castle with a stick, Squire Kafka." He gave her a rare, intimate smile, beautifully bright, and his voice was uncompromising, yet oddly gentle. "Take it. My master gave it to me, and so I give it to you. Use it well, but only in the defense of truth."

Anika extended her hand and took the hilt, her body vibrating with new energy and purpose. "Thank you, Sir Petrov." She inclined her head in a deep gesture of thanks. "I pray I will honor you with it."

As devoutly religious as he was proud, Petrov refused to escort Anika to Chlum until they had stopped by the church to pray. "But what if Master Hus sees us?" Anika protested, horrified. "He may recognize me and will not approve, Sir Petrov. He thinks I am fit only to become a governess or kitchen maid."

"I've heard that the preacher has been detained at the archbishop's house for at least two days." Uncertainty crept into his expression as he paused by the door. For the first time that morning she heard doubt in his voice. "I will not do this unless we have the Lord's blessing, little bird. I must know that God approves. 'Tis a strange and dangerous thing we are doing."

"Let us go to the church, then," she answered, gathering her cloak from the peg on the wall. "I would not have you going soft on me now, Sir Petrov. 'Tis too late to turn back; my hair is all shorn off, and my dresses are locked away."

Outside, the eastern sky blazed in shades of copper and sapphire as the glowing rim of the sun pushed its way over the rooftops of Prague. A lighted window of the church spilled a golden glimmer onto the stone pathway as Anika and Petrov walked up to Bethlehem Chapel, but Anika was relieved to see that Master Hus's small house was dark. Petrov walked with long, purposeful strides—probably eager to be rid of his obligation, Anika thought—and they found the large chapel empty. A half-dozen torches and lamps illuminated the altar, but shadows canopied the far-off ceiling while darkness shrouded the side walls. Anika had never been inside a deserted church. She felt almost as though she had stumbled upon God himself and disturbed his privacy.

A wave of apprehension and last-minute doubt swept through her as she and Petrov approached the altar. Was her plan a sin? Was she being presumptuous to ask God's blessing on this expressly duplicitous venture?

Petrov's knees cracked through the silence as he knelt on the stone floor. "In nomine Patri, et Filii, et Spiritui Sancti," he said, lifting his eyes to the huge wooden crucifix behind the altar. "In the name of the Father, and of the Son, and of the Holy Spirit."

As Anika slipped down beside him, she saw a priest enter from a side doorway. Seeing them, he stopped and folded his hands, allowing a pair of spiritual seekers a moment of private colloquy. Anika thanked God that she had thought to lift the hood of her cloak over her head.

She raised her hand to make the sign of the cross. With three fingers to symbolize the Trinity, she began her prayer. "I touch my forehead in recognition of the Deity in Heaven," she said, turning her eyes toward the floor, "I touch my belly to show that Jesus descended into Hades, I touch my right shoulder because the Son is seated on the right hand of the Father, I touch my left shoulder to expel Satan from my heart."

"Forget the formalities, say what is on your heart," Petrov whispered, nudging her with his elbow. "We have a visitor. Master Jerome."

Anika pressed her lips together, thinking. The idea of hiding herself among knights had sprung from her imagination, but had the seed been planted by God himself? She knew that many in Prague would think her the worst sort of sinner for denying her gender and playing a squire's part. Undoubtedly they would quote the Old Testament scripture that spoke of the sin of a woman putting on that which pertains to a man.

But those same people would enjoy a nice pork roast on Sunday. They would wear garments of mixed fabrics, and none of them would send their women to dwell outside the city walls when they began their monthly issue. They kept only the Old Testament rules they found convenient, and Anika had a particularly convenient reason for hiding herself away.

"Father God, holy and true, I don't know if what I intend to do is right," she muttered hastily. "But I promise to do my best to honor you. The chivalric ideals of knighthood are holy and true to your Word, and I will do my best to keep them. Guide me, Holy God, and lead me in the way I should go—"

"Hurry." Petrov spoke in a broken whisper. "Jerome comes."

"Adjutorium nostrum in nomine Domini, qui fecit coelum et terram," she finished quickly. "Our help is in the Name of the Lord who made heaven and earth. Amen."

She bowed her head in time to see the shadow of a robed priest fall upon the stone floor beside her.

"May Almighty God have mercy on you, forgive you all your sins, and bring you to everlasting life," Jerome said, his voice low and smooth in the nearly empty church. "Is there something I can do for you, my children?"

"No, Master Jerome." Placing his hand on Anika's shoulder for support, Petrov looked up at the priest and slowly rose to his feet. "My ward will today join the knights at Chlum Castle. We came to ask God's blessing before we depart for Lord John's estate."

"Then let me add my blessing as well."

Anika froze, keeping her eyes lowered, as the priest stepped closer. Jerome stared at her in silence while her heart raced and her fingers fluttered with fear. Then his patrician thumb firmly traced the sign of the cross upon her forehead.

"Go with God," he said in a formal voice, then added, "and may our blessed Jesus Christ calm your nerves, my son. Your hands are trembling like a frightened girl's."

Panic rose in Anika's throat and threatened to choke her, but Petrov merely laughed and patted her shoulder. "After a month at the castle, nothing will frighten this one," he said, practically pulling Anika up from the floor. "Keep us in your prayers, Master Jerome. This young squire will need courage, and I will need comfort, for I shall be terribly lonesome when my house is again empty."

"Your name, my son?" Jerome asked.

Anika looked up, finally daring to meet the priest's gaze. She had not known Jerome nearly as well as she had known Master Hus, but she knew he was an honest man and an ardent defender of Hus's efforts to expose and reform what had become a corrupt church.

The priest's mouth was curled as if on the edge of laughter. Was he smiling at her cowardice? Or because he knew he had just blessed a girl in a man's hood and tunic?

"Kafka," she whispered in the deepest voice she could manage. "Please remember to pray for Kafka, Master Jerome."

"I will." The priest gave her a warm smile. "If you will pray for me and our Master Hus. This is a difficult time for all."

"We will," Petrov answered, tugging on Anika's sleeve. "Excuse us now, Master Jerome, but the sun has risen, and we have a journey to begin."

Since neither Petrov nor Anika owned a horse, they walked on the road leading toward Chlum until a farmer with an empty wagon passed by. Petrov offered the man a coin if he and Anika could ride in the back of the wagon, and the man grudgingly agreed.

With her hose-clad legs dangling off the back of the hay wagon, Anika sat in silence beside Petrov and watched her world gradually slide into the distance. With a sudden pang, she realized that she had underestimated her attachment to the city. She had been so intent on preparing for the future that she had given very little thought to what would become her past. She might not see the bustling streets of Prague again for weeks, even months! And though most squires were taught to read and write, she was bidding farewell to her book collection, her writing, the stream of interesting students who brought her their essays and stayed to argue the finer points of apologetics. These encounters had enriched her life and sharpened her mind. Would she know anything like them out in the quiet countryside?

"Sir Petrov," she cried, suddenly squeezing his arm with both hands, "you will take good care of my books, won't you? You'll need to hire another copyist so the students will continue to come to the bookshop. And make sure the renters take good care of the books. Do not allow them to scratch grooves in the margin with their fingernails or use straws from the lecture room floor as place marks—"

"I will mind the shop as if you were looking over my shoulder," Petrov answered, firmly removing her hand from his arm. "And you must learn this, little Kafka. When one man wishes to gain the attention of another man, he does not grab his arm and threaten to pull it from its socket. He might nudge him with an elbow, or tap him on the shoulder, but he would never squeal and cling to his companion. Do you understand?"

Petrov's aged eyes squinted toward her with tenderness, and Anika wanted to fling her arms around him in gratitude. But instead she meekly lowered her head and murmured, "Yes, Sir Knight. I understand."

"Good."

For a long while they rode in silence through a verdant countryside. The kiss of sunrise had cast a rosy flush upon the western mountains, and an emerald ribbon of fields and summer foliage bordered the rutted road. The small mud-and-timber houses that had dotted the fields outlying Prague disappeared altogether, and Anika knew they were now entering the vast tracts of lands managed by the nobility. Many different lords owned most of the estates that composed the kingdom of Bohemia, and their lands extended over fields and mountains and plains.

In the drowsy summer heat, Anika lay back on a pile of hay and fell into a shallow doze. When she awoke, the sun stood high in the sky. To her left she saw jagged mountains rising like armed warriors safeguarding Bohemia against the raging world beyond. To her right shimmered a vista of silver water and endless cobalt sky.

"It is lovely here," she whispered to Petrov, sighing deeply. "I had forgotten that the mountains were so beautiful."

"We don't see many sights like this in the city," Petrov admitted. "Prague has its pleasures, to be sure, but this sort of beauty is not one of them."

"Where are we?"

"Chlum Manor." Petrov extended his freckled hand, and Anika noticed that it trembled slightly, either from age or repressed emotion. "Lord John owns the land as far as you can see in any direction."

Anika stared at the horizon, letting the import of those words sink into her soul. Lord John was not only honorable, he was wealthy. "And this is where you grew up?"

"Yes." Petrov nodded. "I was twelve when my father left me with Lord Honza, Lord John's father. I was a squire first, then became a knight. My master and I served in many battles together, including a winter in Livonia." Raw hurt glittered in his faded eyes as he continued. "We were obeying the orders of an archbishop, but it was not what I thought a crusade for Christ should be. We set fire to everything, driving men, women, and children away from their villages in the cruelest month of winter. But nothing like that has happened in a long time."

"And then?"

Petrov shrugged. "Lord John was only a boy when his father died. I had to choose between remaining at Chlum or returning to Prague to see what could be found of my old life. I chose the latter, and though I never found any trace of my family, I have not regretted my return to the city. I fear that knighthood—the chivalric code and the occupation—is not what it was when I served Lord Honza. And though I hear wonderful and noteworthy things about Lord John, I am too old to mount a horse and wield a sword again." He flashed her a gap-toothed grin. "That shall be your duty, Kafka."

She was about to offer a spirited rejoinder when she realized they were passing through the gates of a small settlement. Rising to her knees, she turned and saw that the hay wagon had entered a village that seemed nearly insignificant when she compared it to Prague. From the center of the village a church steeple jutted from the rooflines, dragging up a cluster of wattle-and-daub houses that lay scattered around the edge of the churchyard. Next to the creek, the mill's waterwheel lazily paddled the current. Even from this distance she could smell ale from the centrally located brewhouse and bread from the adjacent bakehouse. At the farthest point from the creek, a small pen held the commonly owned animals: a pair of cows, a half-dozen sheep, and, in a separate pen, a bull. Chickens had free rein—they scratched and clucked and roamed freely through the street and screeched from the villagers' open windows. Anika gaped in surprise to see the mud-encrusted face of a pig peering at her from an open doorway. The pig looked for all the world like a stout peasant woman watching the world pass by.

"Where is everyone?" Anika asked, noticing that no people watched from the small buildings. "Have they had plague here?"

"They are all at work in the lord's fields," Petrov answered, picking his teeth with a hay straw. "The miller is in his mill, no doubt, and the ale maker is probably at his brew pot. But everyone else will work until setting sun forces them to stop weeding."

Anika lifted her head to feel the warmth of the sun on her face. "I thought Lord John would have more tenants than these," she remarked idly. "These are not so many to serve such a great lord."

Petrov's mouth quirked with humor. "This is but one village, little bird. There are at least two dozen others like it outlying the master's fields. Lord John is one of the wealthiest lords in Bohemia, probably second only to Lord Laco and the king."

Anika felt a flicker of apprehension course through her at the mention of her enemy's name. Would Laco try to find her when she did not show up at his estate today? How determined was his vile son?

"Sir Petrov, you must keep a quiet tongue and never say that name again," she murmured, studying the road behind them as if at any moment a cavalcade of horses might suddenly appear in full pursuit. "Do not mention my name in the bookshop, and never speak of that lord or of my failure to appear at his house. It may be that he will forget all about me. Or he may petition the city council to discover my whereabouts—"

"Have no fear," Petrov answered, a look of implacable determination on his lined face. "No word of you or of that depraved man shall cross my lips unless I am asked directly. And then I shall do all in my power to safeguard your secret."

"I know you will, my friend," Anika answered. Carefully, teasingly, she nudged him with her elbow in a properly masculine gesture. "I know you will."

Setting her trepidation and nervousness aside, she straightened her back and tried to concentrate on the task ahead. She simply had to be accepted as a squire. Lord John might be willing to grant her refuge if she approached as a woman and in her own name, but some spy from Lidice would be certain to find her in time. Any nobleman who could bribe magistrates and get away with murder would have no trouble passing a few silver coins and learning the whereabouts of a frightened young woman.

Anika remembered the look of steely determination in Miloslav's cold blue eyes, then shivered. A man like that did not give up easily.

Petrov felt his pulse quicken when the hay cart turned onto a smoother, wider road. Within half an hour he would be in the courtyard of Chlum Castle itself, and he had not set foot inside that place in—how many years? At least twenty. Lord John had been a boy of thirteen when Petrov left; he was now a respected nobleman with two fine sons of his own. He would have few memories of Petrov, if he retained any at all, but perhaps he would honor his father's old captain and grant Petrov the boon he sought.

They had passed through four villages like the one Anika first noticed, each larger and more prosperous than the last. Shifting in his seat, Petrov glanced at the road ahead and saw the tower of the castle looming over the trees ahead—almost home! Odd that he should automatically consider this place his home. But it was, and if all went well, it would be Anika's, too . . . for a little while.

He heard Anika gasp when the tall walls of the castle chemise moved into view. The castle, built by the first lords of Chlum in the mid-thirteenth century, rose with loftiness, majesty, and grandeur from the summit of a hill. The girl—now the *squire*, he corrected himself firmly—had probably never seen a structure quite like it.

"It is so—big!" she whispered, turning wide eyes upon him.

"Such walls! Why does a peace-loving man need a house with such tall walls around it?"

"Because not all men love peace as he does," Petrov answered dryly. He gave her a gentle rebuking smile. "You must not let your face reveal your surprise and naiveté, Kafka. Guard your emotions. Weigh every word before you speak. You may be yourself around me, but let no one else see into your heart, or your secret will be as obvious as the sun above our heads."

She nodded, mutely accepting his advice. Grateful that for once she had not argued with him, he turned toward the walls and pointed out several aspects of their construction: "Listen carefully, for you will need to know these things. The overhanging projections you see are machicolations, from which missiles and boiling liquids can be dropped through openings at the top. Those holes you see below the battlements are flared to the inside; they give an archer room to move from right to left and cover a broad field of fire while presenting only the narrow slit as a target. The outworks of the castle are strong, but the main lines of defense are centered around the castle inside."

"There's another castle inside?" Anika murmured, staring ahead. "I can't see anything but the wall."

Petrov shook his head. "It is good you cannot. Behind the wall in front of us are two additional walls, one inside the other, with a stout tower at each corner of the innermost wall. Two powerful gatehouses guard the gates to the east and west. Within the inner walls stands the castle in which the lord and his family reside. A cross wall divides the castle into two baileys: the outer containing the great hall and offices of the garrison and steward, the inner holding the family's apartments and private offices."

"His family?" A gleam of interest lit her eyes.

"His sons. Lord John has two small boys, I forget their names. But I remember that three years ago Master Hus said a funeral mass for the Lady of Chlum. So you will have to deal with a master, his two sons, their tutors, the chaplain, the steward, the captain of the knights—"

"It all sounds very confusing," Anika whispered, her eyes shadowed with doubt. "What if I offend one of those people or venture into the wrong place? I do not belong in a castle, Sir Petrov. I fear I shall never succeed. Perhaps we have made a mistake—"

"Enough!" For the first time in his recollection, Petrov felt irritated with the girl. She could not show fear. Anika had chosen this path herself, and even if he had not fully supported her at first, he did now. For years she had embodied all the virtues and ideals of knighthood, and in just a few days she had progressed remarkably in the basics of swordplay. She was prepared in dress and weapons, with his silver sword swinging from her hip and a sharp dagger in her boot, and she had received a blessing from the priest.

Petrov smiled as he recognized his emotion: pride. He had never fathered a son, but if he had, he would have wanted the boy to have the same bold heart that beat in this girl's breast.

He fumbled for her hand, then held it between his own. "Anika, do not fear. When you are at a disadvantage, forget your weakness and find your strengths." An indefinable feeling of rightness filled his soul, and he struggled to share his sense of conviction. "Trust in God, trust in me, trust in the training I have given you." He gave her a grin. "I think you will live to see the morrow."

Eight

Anika bit her tongue to keep from crying out as her boots clumped loudly over the wooden floor in Chlum Castle's great hall. Lord John's residence was all Petrov had said it would be, but in sheer size and vastness it overwhelmed every castle of Anika's book-fed imagination.

The castle's collective life obviously revolved around this spacious hall. Several different hubs of activity filled the chamber, and the sounds of people talking, laughing, even singing vibrated around her as she accompanied Petrov through the hall. She thought for a moment or two that her legs would fail her, but miraculously she kept going.

To her left, a group of knights loitered around tables, the remains of the day's dinner strewn over the rough-hewn surfaces. To her right, several richly dressed ladies were seated in a tight knot, their heads bobbing like the villagers' chickens as they clucked and chirped and clicked their embroidery needles against hoops in their laps. Directly before Anika a yawning fireplace, as wide and tall as a man, occupied center stage. Before it another cluster of people gathered around elaborately cushioned chairs, and it was toward this group that Petrov advanced.

Anika clung to him like a shadow, averting her eyes from the inquisitive glances lifting in their direction.

"Look there," Petrov whispered as they walked, pitching his voice to reach Anika's ear and not a step further. "The man in the red chair is Lord John. We will speak to him when he has finished talking with his guests."

Anika blinked and glanced up for a moment, then lowered her eyes again to the dusty floor. The handsome man in the high-backed chair looked vaguely familiar. Then she remembered—he had spoken to her that ghastly morning she and Petrov appeared before the town council. She had been so flustered and upset that she had barely looked at him, and she fervently hoped that he had been equally distracted and would not remember her face.

Petrov halted a discreet distance from the master, and Anika dared to lift her eyes again. Two people stood before the lord of the manor: a pale woman in a silken gown and a grizzled knight exuding masculinity and anger.

But it was Lord John who caught and held her attention. Even seated, his was a compelling, self-confident presence. He wore an elegant pleated tunic with narrow fur cuffs, soft leather boots with fashionably pointed toes, and a simple gold band upon a finger of his right hand. A long fabric belt emphasized the narrow line of his waist, and a high stand-up collar accentuated his strong jaw. His glossy brown hair was cut short, and his patrician features gleamed in the light from two narrow windows on opposite sides of the fireplace.

All in all, Anika decided, he was a pleasure to look upon. But the expression on his face as he studied the knight before him indicated that he was mightily displeased with something.

With a discreet little servant's cough, Petrov warned Anika to be silent while the knight endured his interrogation. Anika took a half-step back, behind Petrov, so she could study the trio without being observed. The woman stood opposite both the lord and the knight, the third point in a triangle that clearly pitted her against one man or the other—or perhaps both. With her hands on her slender hips, she gazed at both men in a silent fury that spoke louder than words.

"Tell me, Lady Zelenka," Lord John said, turning his gaze

toward the young woman, "exactly what Sir Novak has done to cause you such distress."

"Well!" The young woman, wearing a fashionable and expensive double-horned headdress over a wealth of blond hair, tossed her head. "If I must explain myself to you, my lord, perhaps you have no regard for my feelings at all. I said this man is impertinent, and I expect you to act on my behalf."

"I am not unaware of your feelings," the master answered smoothly, turning to his knight, "but Sir Novak has served this household for nigh on fifteen years, and I have regard for his feelings as well as yours. So if you could explain the cause for his impertinence, perchance I can discern where the problem lies. For I know Novak, and though patience is not his greatest virtue, I believe he would sell his soul before intentionally displeasing me."

"He . . ." The lady lifted her chin and met the knight's icy gaze straight on. "He called me an insolent cat."

Lord John looked away and pressed his lips together. For the briefest instant, Anika thought he was biting back the need to laugh.

"Did you, Sir Novak," he said after a moment, his voice now heavy with rebuke, "refer to Lady Zelenka in such a way?"

"My lord," the knight met the noblewoman's accusing eyes without flinching, "if I did, 'tis no more than she deserved. I was trying to help her into the carriage, and she wouldn't budge unless I carried her over a puddle betwixt the carriage and her threshold. Well, my lord, I've faced the Saracens in the Holy Land, and I've fought with vagrants and scoundrels in the woods, but I've never willingly taken a she-cat in my arms, and I was not about to start this morning. You command my honor and my life, Lord John, but you'll not command me to carry a wench in ladies' clothing—"

"I have heard enough," John answered, cutting his knight off with an abrupt nod. He averted his eyes from both parties to the dispute and stared at the floor, then folded his hands. When he spoke at last, he lifted his eyes to the lady. "My dear Lady Zelenka, I offer a thousand apologies for my man's behavior. Sir Novak has not spent much time in the pleasant company of the softer sex, and his manners are apt to be a bit brutish. Indeed, I should have sent a far more genteel knight to escort you. I pray you will forgive me for my short-sightedness."

Still bristling, the lady shot a glance toward the unrepentant knight. "You speak very softly, Lord John, but what about this knave? Is he to go unpunished for this insolence? If you do nothing, how am I to know that the next knight you send me will not commit some worse effrontery? Are my sorrow and grief never to be assuaged? There is a price to be paid here, sir, and I think it best that you promise to pay it."

The master studied her thoughtfully for a moment. "You have my word upon it," he said simply, his eyes dark and unfathomable. "Sir Novak shall not leave this room until I have meted out his judgment."

"A harsh judgment?" the lady snapped.

"A suitable judgment," he amended, his eyes trained on her.

Partially satisfied, the lady turned toward the other women, her jaw tightening as she glided away. Lord John said nothing until she had been seated and enfolded by the ladies' conversation. Then he offered his knight a forgiving smile. "I'm afraid you must wait here, Novak, until I think of a suitable judgment for you," he said, his voice dry as he peered around the vast chamber. A trace of laughter echoed in his tone. "Maybe I should have you escort the lady home."

"Too harsh!" Novak protested, a smile in his voice.

Then Anika felt Lord John capture her eyes with his.

She looked quickly away, helpless to halt her embarrassment as Petrov's hand fell on her shoulder and prodded her forward.

"My Lord John of Chlum, grace and peace to you!" Petrov's age-crackled voice broke the silence that rang in her ears. "I, Sir Petrov of Prague, have a boon to ask of you. If, in token of the years I gave in sincere and loyal service to your father, you would but hear me—"

"Weren't you my father's captain?" Lord John straightened and motioned them forward, an arched eyebrow indicating his surprise. He gave Anika a bright-eyed glance, full of shrewdness.

"Yes." Petrov bowed deeply from the waist. "By the grace of God,

I served your father from the time of my youth until his death. Since that time I have been affiliated with a book merchant and copyist in Prague, but I am ever true to the Almighty God and to the ideals I swore to defend in my vow of knighthood."

Something in Petrov's words caused a warning cloud to settle on Lord John's features. "Which bookseller," he asked, folding his hands, "did you serve?"

Petrov hung his head in a pose of sorrow. "Ernan O'Connor, who departed this life barely one week ago."

"I know of the man," John answered, nodding soberly. "He worked for Master Jan Hus. And he had a daughter . . ." his eyes flicked at Anika, then returned to Petrov, "about the age of this youth."

"Aye, that he did," Petrov answered, nodding again. "The girl has been set to work in the country. Another matter, Lord John, brings me to you today. The youth you see before you . . ." Anika felt the pressure of Lord John's eyes upon her, and she blushed, "is sixteen, and my ward. As you can see, your lordship, I am in no condition to foster a youth. And so I have taught the child what I know, and am quite certain that the heart beating in this young breast is as loyal and forthright as any on earth."

Petrov stepped back and fell to one knee in a surprisingly graceful movement for a man of his advanced years. "If you hold any regard for me or for your departed sire, Lord John, I would beg you to consider taking this youth as a squire at Chlum Castle. Kafka is an orphan, without parents or fortune, but skilled in reading, writing, and languages. The heart you see before you is true, the eye sure, and the soul marked by the grace of Almighty God."

Lord John closed his eyes for a moment, then pinched the bridge of his nose. "What say you, Sir Novak?" he asked, not opening his eyes. "Have we room for another squire?"

Anika shifted uneasily from foot to foot, staring at the floor as the brusque knight studied her.

"He'll need a bit of fattening up. He scarcely looks strong enough to lift a saddle."

"That's what I thought." Lord John lowered his hand, then opened his eyes and looked directly at Anika.

"What do you say to this, young man?" he asked, a look of faint amusement in his eyes. "Are you as loyal, true, and God-fearing as Sir Petrov suggests?"

Anika struggled to find her tongue. "I hope to please you, sir," she answered, grateful that her voice came out in a roughened rasp. "I will do all in my power to make a good knight."

"I see." Lord John drew his lips in thoughtfully, then glanced up at his knight. "Well, Novak? Shall we take him under our protection and into our service?"

Novak, doubtless still stewing over his reprimand, gave Anika another cursory glance. "If it pleases you." He lifted one burly shoulder in a shrug. "You can set him to mucking out the stables. Perhaps, my lord, you could assign him to cater to Lady Zelenka." He lowered his voice, lest the women across the room overhear. " 'Tis obvious that she hates me, and you know I cannot abide women. Their endless chatter, their idle threats, their vapid games and coquetries are enough to drive a man to drink—"

"Know you much of women, lad?"

Anika's stomach dropped like a hanged man when she realized Lord John intended the question for her. *He knows! He knows, and the ruse is over before it is begun—*

"I'm sorry—give me your name again, young man."

She stammered before the sheen of purpose in his eyes. "Ka . . . Kafka."

Lord John rested his chin on his hand, a bemused smile on his lips. "Kafka, have you spent much time around women? Is there anything you could teach Sir Novak? He is a fine captain, my best man, but I cannot have him offending every woman in the kingdom."

Relief, tentative but true, coursed through Anika's body. "Yes, my lord. I know much of women. I . . . lived with one."

"Oh? Did you dwell in a convent, then?"

A momentary panic set upon Anika until she looked up and saw his teasing smile. "No, my lord. But I had a mother. And I have read many books, including *The Art of Courtly Love*. You may trust me, sir."

"Very well, then." Lord John crossed his arms and looked at Petrov. "To you, Sir Knight, I am pleased to grant this boon. Your ward, Kafka, shall join my household as a squire and take his vows of knighthood when he is willing and ready to withstand his test. And you, squire," he shifted his gaze to Anika, "shall have Sir Novak as your tutor. He will train you in all you need to know. In return, you shall serve him with all your energy." His mouth twisted into a wry smile. "And when you have a spare moment, I beg you—please teach Sir Novak how to be more diplomatic with women."

"Sir!" The sole voice of protest rose from the frustrated knight. "I have no need of a squire; I am too old to be training a young one—"

"I believe Lady Zelenka demanded that I grant you a suitable judgment," Lord John answered with mock severity. "Thank God that you did not merit a harsher one than this. Gentlemen,"—he rose to his feet—"I give you good day."

Without a backward glance, Lord John of Chlum turned and left the hall.

———•———

John smiled as he made his way up the narrow winding staircase that led to his bedchamber and private office. He had found it difficult to keep a straight face in that last interview, for Novak's irritation and frustration with women like the fiery Lady Zelenka were legendary. The knight frequently complimented John's wisdom in not remarrying, but Novak had never known how pleasant marriage could be. The knight had no young sons who needed a mother, and he had never tasted the sweetness of lying in a godly marriage bed with his wife's hair entwined about his neck . . .

John abruptly slammed the door on his memories. The only things left of his marriage were his sons and the raw sores of an aching heart. He had, in idle moments, wondered if he would ever find happiness in love, but though a succession of titled, beautiful young ladies routinely attended dinners and festivals at Chlum

Castle, not one of them had been able to hold his attention as well as his heart. After his arranged marriage, he had developed a fondness for his wife, but if he married again, he hoped love would come naturally, without force.

He had met countless beauties, women who could sing like nightingales and crochet as skillfully as spiders. His friends had introduced him to women with quick wits, sharp tongues, and brains that could tally the castle expenditures more rapidly than his steward. If he had wanted a soft, attractive woman, one to pleasure and soothe and bear many children, he could have plucked one from any house in Bohemia.

But this was not an age for softness. Trouble roamed the land in the guise of godliness, and corruption had already begun to erode the foundation stones of his beloved Bohemia. These were days when strength and courage mattered most, in women as well as men. And while John wasn't exactly certain what his soul yearned for, he knew he had not yet found it.

Unless Zelenka's fiery anger could qualify as courage.

He paused in the stairwell, gathering his thoughts. Perhaps he would ask her to remain at Chlum for another week.

In the wide courtyard between the thick chemise walls and the castle itself, Anika unleashed her tongue. "Sir Petrov, why didn't you say something?" she hissed, her body as tight as a bowstring as she followed the old knight through the blinding sun. "Why did you stand idly by while Lord John assigned me to that man? He hates women, Petrov, and he will hate me without even knowing why. For though I may disguise my body, it is more difficult to disguise my nature, and a woman is what I am!"

"The idea was Lord John's; who am I to dissuade him?" Petrov answered, nodding complacently. "And I don't think I could have arranged it better myself. You will be in good hands, little bird, for Sir Novak is a noble knight. I have heard many reports of his valor and loyalty. He is honest, even if he is rough. He is skilled. He is loyal to a fault. He supports his master, his master supports Jan Hus, and we are aligned in the same cause. I see the hand of Almighty God in this, and you should sleep well tonight."

"Sleep well?" She stopped abruptly in the sand. "Sir Petrov, how can I sleep at all with that ogre at my side?"

"The Lord who keeps you neither slumbers nor sleeps," Petrov answered, grinning over his shoulder. He slowed his steps but did not stop. "Have you forgotten? The Lord is your keeper: the Lord is your shade upon your right hand. The sun shall not smite you by day, nor the moon by night. The Lord shall preserve you from all evil, he shall preserve your soul. The Lord shall preserve your going out and your coming in from this time forth, and even for evermore."

The words of Scripture acted as a salve; the anger and fear that had been building inside Anika slowly dissipated. "The One Hundred Twenty-first Psalm," she whispered, feeling a stab of guilt. That psalm had been her father's favorite, and in her childhood he had made her recite it whenever the old nightmare woke her.

"You will be blessed," Petrov answered, turning so that he stood directly before her. "God holds you in his hand, and I have no worries about what will happen on the morrow. You have a bright heart, little bird, and you carry my silver sword. They will keep you safe until we meet again." He looked briefly over his shoulder, then returned his gaze to her and smiled tenderly. "If you were wearing a woman's gown I'd embrace you now," he said simply. "But as you're not, and because there are eyes upon us, I'll just say farewell."

He reached out and grasped her hand as a man would take leave of his friend, but he held her hand a moment longer than necessary, his eyes brimming with affection and concern.

Staring at him, Anika floundered in an agonizing maelstrom of emotion. She *wanted* to become a squire, she *wanted* to learn to defend herself. She had no choice but to leave Petrov and Prague and Master Hus, for Lord Laco was as determined as a bulldog; he would not leave her alone until he found her or wearied of the chase. And above all, she yearned to learn the ways of war, so when she at last stood before Cardinal D'Ailly—and she knew she would one day—

she would know how to exact vengeance for the sake of her mother and father.

Why, then, did she feel such an acute sense of loss?

"Take care of the books," she told Petrov for what felt like the hundredth time. *Take care of my old life. Keep it safe so I can return to it one day soon.*

Petrov understood her unspoken message. "I will take care of everything, Kafka," he answered, smiling at her as if she were a small child. "And I will see you again in yet a little while."

And then, as tears sprang to her eyes, he turned smartly and walked away, a majestic, sword-thin figure retreating into the gathering dusk.

Nine

For an hour after Petrov left, Anika wandered through the court-yard, her gunnysack in her hand, her head lowered, her step quick. She figured no one would suspect she had no idea what to do as long as she appeared to know where she was going.

"You! Squire! Over here!"

Anika turned toward the sound of the voice and saw her new master, Sir Novak, lounging in the doorway of a large stone chamber built into one of the inner defensive walls.

"Are you coming in at all? Or are you going to circle the court-yard until midnight?"

His sarcastic tone made her flush with humiliation, but she lifted her chin and walked quickly in his direction, swinging her sack up and over her shoulder. "I didn't know if you wanted me to bed down in the garrison or the stable," she mumbled as she approached.

"In here, boy," Novak answered, pressing his broad hand to the back of his neck. "This is the garrison, and all the lord's men sleep in here. Come in, put your stuff away, and let me have a look at you."

Taking a deep, unsteady breath, she followed him into the room. Ignoring a knot of knights playing cards in a corner, Novak sat down at a table cluttered with several half-empty tankards and the remains of dinner. Her boots crunched over layers of dried bread crumbs and chicken bones littering the floor. Not knowing what else to do, she lowered her gunnysack to the ground in front of her, then paused by the table and turned to face her new master.

His gray eyes narrowed and hardened as he studied her. Emboldened by his scrutiny, Anika studied him in return. Her father would have said that Novak was a man's man, a model of masculinity. His neck was so thick that his head appeared to rest directly on his massive shoulders, and even sprawled in a chair he looked taller than any man in the room. Bulging muscles outlined the hauberk, or coat of mail, that he wore, and even though his face had the craggy look of an unfinished sculpture, an air of command flowed from him. She would have known that Novak was the captain of the knights even if Lord John had not told her.

"How may I serve you, sir?" she asked, dipping her head slightly in a sign of respect.

"Who said I wanted you to serve me?" he snapped, venom in his voice. "Heaven knows I need a brat at my ankles like I need a hole in my boot. But since Lord John has commanded it . . ." he thrust his fingers through the fringe of graying hair above his ears, "I suppose I will have to tolerate you. But I will have you know—"

He lowered his eyes, dark and hard as cannon balls, upon her.

"What, sir?" Anika lifted her chin, determined not to let him cow her into submission. If she cringed before her master today, she'd be cringing for weeks to come. She'd never be successful as a squire.

He gave her a black look, irritation evident on his face. "First, boy, you will never interrupt me again. Second, you will not become a knight in a week. Too many cocky youths think they can move into a garrison one day and ride with our knights on the morrow. You have much to learn before you'll even set foot in a stirrup."

"I am ready to learn," Anika answered, waving aside his doubts.

"A squire must learn to serve before he learns to fight," Novak answered, gazing at her speculatively. "You are not here to serve Lord John. From this day forward you will be my personal servant. You will clean and care for my armor, my weapons, my possessions, and my horse. If we are called away, you will accompany me as a camp servant. And you will not—" his lips thinned with anger, "speak to me about women. Keep your books and your thoughts about that cursed race to yourself."

Anika forced her lips to part in a rigid smile. "I am ready to serve, sir."

"Good." Novak paused and took a long swig from a tankard, then wiped his mouth with his sleeve and looked at her again. "After you know how to serve, then you will learn how to be a knight. Until then you will hunt with me, and we will test your courage as we hone your riding and weapons skills. You will practice with the sword; you will strengthen your body to carry the weight of armor. At dinner you will attend me at the lord's table, you will listen and not speak, you will learn how a knight conducts himself. You will learn how to wrestle—"

"To wrestle?" For a moment Anika lost custody of her tongue. She had not imagined herself stripped down to her chemise, circling in the blazing sun, grappling with men more powerful than she—she could not do it! Her secret would be revealed.

"Have you a problem with wrestling?" The corner of Novak's mouth twisted with exasperation. "Honestly, boy, are you already a coward? How do you expect to fight an enemy if you will not grapple with your comrades?"

She lifted her chin. "I am not afraid, sir." Pride kept her from arguing. She would find a way to prove herself, and she'd face whatever challenges lay ahead as they surfaced. If Novak forced her to wrestle, she'd just find a way to make certain her opponent never laid a hand on her.

"I will do whatever needs to be done," she continued, stiffening at the challenge in his eyes. "And I can offer my skills to help you. I am a good scribe and reader—"

"A knight must learn to fight, not write," Novak groused, fingering his graying beard in a gesture that signaled his irritation. "He is not fit for battle who has never seen his own blood flow, who has not heard his teeth crunch under the blow of an opponent or felt the full weight of his adversary upon him. If you are to train with me, young man, you must do all these things and whatever else I ask of you. If I am pleased, I shall present you to Lord John. If he accepts you, you shall take the vows of knighthood before God and all this company."

He lifted his hand in a gesture which encompassed the entire garrison, and for a moment Anika felt her resolve falter. Perhaps she had been too optimistic in thinking she could hide here. She had thought herself agile and quick, and maybe she was, but the men loitering in this chamber were giants who had undoubtedly survived tournaments and armed conflicts and jousting. The knights of Chlum had faced encounters in which they either defended themselves or accepted disgrace, and none of the men around her looked as if they accepted disgrace easily.

She closed her eyes and clenched her hands, aware that Novak watched her with a speculative expression. She could not let him see her doubts. She must not give in to fear, or she would find herself at Lord Laco's manor, a slave to his treacherous son—

"I am not afraid," she repeated, opening her eyes. She leaned her head back and met his gaze, then folded her arms as tight as a gate.

"Aren't you?" Before she had time to answer, Novak's arm jerked in a sudden movement, and Anika was dimly aware that he had pulled something shiny from his sleeve. Something sharp and swift whirled past her head, then struck the wall behind her with a faintly metallic clink.

She turned and saw a blade vibrating in the mortar of the stone wall. His dagger had missed her head by inches. And, thanks be to God, she had been too surprised to even flinch.

Novak's left eyebrow rose a fraction. "Very good," he said, his voice cool. "Very good indeed, Kafka. Perhaps you shall make a knight after all."

Anika struggled to maintain her fragile control. Courage had not kept her still; she had merely been too startled to react. But even this could work in her favor. "I certainly hope," she managed to say, her stomach clenching in a delayed reaction to the danger she had just faced, "that you will teach me to throw like that, Sir Novak."

His face split into a wide grin. "I will, lad, if you please me."

Anika shifted her weight. "What would you like me to do first, sir?"

Novak jerked his head toward a darkened chamber beyond another doorway. "You'll find my bunk in the farthest corner. There's hay in the storeroom, so make yourself a place to sleep under my bed. That will be your place from this night until the day you become a knight, Squire Kafka."

The corners of his mouth twisted upward as he lifted his tankard in her direction. "Welcome to Chlum Castle."

An hour later, Novak reclined on his burlap mattress and folded his hands beneath his head, watching the lad who was now his charge. His temper had flared when Lord John proposed the arrangement, for Novak had already trained his share of squires, and he looked forward to a time of relative ease. But this lad seemed bright and willing, and he hadn't retreated under Novak's lashing tongue or wet himself when tested by Novak's blade.

Thus far, the lad had represented himself well. He had the makings, too, of becoming a favorite at court, for the ladies would like this handsome youth. His fair skin magnified the inky shadows in his green eyes, though the set of his chin suggested a stubborn streak. His features were so perfect, so symmetrical, that any more delicacy would have made him too beautiful for a boy, but that obstinate chin saved the face from perfection.

Novak grinned. God help the woman who had a chin like that. And God help the man who married her.

The knight turned slightly on his mattress, pretending to sleep but not quite ready to quit the day. The boy was fumbling now with the discarded pieces of Novak's armor, trying to hang them properly while still treating them with due respect. The heavy hauberk lay on the floor like a molten pool of fabric; the greaves that had covered Novak's legs and the vambraces for his arms were scattered like discarded limbs. Novak had shed his armor with a simple command, "See to it," and 'twas obvious that the boy had little or no experience with dismantling and storing a valuable suit of armor. But he would learn, and he had already proved himself adaptable. His hands, though small, were stained with work, and that was good. He possessed an unflappable temperament; the exercise with the dagger had proved that point. And though his tongue was sharp, it might prove to be as valuable as a sword in days to come.

The boy bent to lift the heavy breastplate, then managed to fumble and send it clanging to the floor.

"Mount the breastplate on the pole yonder, and hang the other pieces from it," Novak offered in a sleepy voice, closing his eyes. "One piece hangs upon another."

"Thank you, sir." The boy's whisper was as light as a woman's, and Novak nodded, grateful that his sleeping companions would not be disturbed.

All in all, Novak supposed, this judgment of Lord John's was not so harsh. The boy was not as fragile as he appeared, and it might be nice to have someone to polish his armor and tend to his horse. For a while, at least, it might not be too arduous a task.

Ten

W ell?" Lord Laco of Lidice lowered his glass to the table and glared at the two knights who crept furtively into the room. "Where is the wench?"

"Not there," his captain answered, loosely crossing his arms. "We went to the bookshop, then to the church, then to the preacher's house. They say she's been set to work for a family in the country—"

"Impossible!" Laco hissed, flashing them a look of disdain. "The girl was a nobody; she had no connections. No one in Prague would have dared take her in, and she couldn't even *know* any of the nobility!"

"Nonetheless, my lord," the second knight offered, "she is gone."

"Father!" From his place at the end of the table, Miloslav's features contorted with shock and anger. "You promised you'd get her for me!"

"I will."

"But when?" His son's cold eyes sniped at him. "Some powerful man you are, Father! You cannot even convince a wench that your grand castle is preferable to scrubbing floors in some lord's kitchen. She was just a common girl, no lady, nothing special—"

"Then why," Laco choked on his own words, "do you want her? Take any girl you want, Miloslav. Go out into the fields, find any farmer's daughter, and do what you like with her! But forget this red-haired wench!"

"I can't forget her." Miloslav's voice was cloyingly sweet now, like a spoiled woman's. "I saw her, I want her, she interests me. Her eyes were like green ice, Father—she would be a challenge! And so," he leaned back in his chair and studied his nails, "I must have her. Search all of Prague, send messengers and spies to every castle in Bohemia. But find her for me, Father. Just because I want her—and because I'm your son. And no one ever says *no* to you, do they, Father?"

Laco leaned back in his chair and rested his chin on his hand. "No," he repeated with contempt, "no one *ever* says no to me."

Eleven

Looking back, Anika realized that her life as a squire began when Novak flung his dagger toward her head. In that moment she understood she could not let her guard down for an instant, not while she lived in this masculine world where knights of power, brawn, and strength jostled continually for position.

After wrestling with Novak's armor for an hour that first night, she slipped out of her tabard and slept fitfully on her bed of straw. During the night she awoke several times, scratching at her arms and legs as some variety of minute creatures crept from the straw to warm themselves between her leggings and her skin. How did the knights live with fleas and bugs? She had been no expert in the art of housekeeping, but she knew that alder leaves spread around the room would draw the fleas and imprison them in sticky sap. She made a mental note to ask one of Lord John's servants about the possibility of cleaning up the knights' garrison. The floor needed sweeping, the straw cried out for freshening, and half the tankards were coated inside with fuzzy growths.

In the days that followed, she silently shadowed Novak and did his bidding without question or complaint. The day began with the sunrise, and she rose quickly, slipped her tabard over her leggings and undershirt, then helped the knight into his hauberk and embroidered surcoat. Novak, like the other knights of Chlum, wore the heraldic colors and symbol of Lord John's family. Two hundred years before, the first Earl of Chlum had chosen a gold cross as his family emblem and embroidered it upon a field of blue, the color representing heavenly trust. All of the knights wore the emblem proudly, Anika noticed. Their shields, lance pennons, and even their horses' regalia were all emblazoned with a gold cross upon a vibrant blue background.

With a quiet sigh of relief, Anika noticed that the knights never bathed—at least not in an organized fashion. They routinely washed their hands in small finger bowls at the dinner table, but though hands were to be kept as clean as possible, no knight seemed to care what sort of stains the rest of his body bore.

After helping her mentor dress in his suit of mail and surcoat each morning, Anika quietly fell into step behind Novak and followed him to the great hall. There the knights entertained themselves with games or conversation until Lord John appeared. The master of the household liked nothing better than to begin the day with a rousing hunt, and Anika frequently found herself with the other squires, trotting on foot behind their mounted masters as the hunting party pursued a stag or wild boar through the woods outside the castle.

If the hunt was successful, the task of skinning the beast and carting home the bloody meat fell to the squires. The first time Anika was instructed to slit the throat of a stag she felt her gorge rise in horror. But the animal was already dead, she reminded herself, and this bloodletting was necessary in order that the meat might be properly drained and fit to eat. And so, gritting her teeth, she withdrew her dagger from her boot and brought it across the animal's neck in a swift, sure stroke.

When she and the other squires returned to the castle, they invariably found that preparations for dinner were well under way. Dinner was the high point of the castle day, and any important guests were treated to the best Chlum Manor had to offer. The squires and lower servants were employed to attend the guests at dinner. While her stomach rumbled and her mouth watered, Anika carried pitchers of perfumed water to the guests who wanted to wash their hands, then stood behind the diners, dispensing towels, baskets of bread, or whatever the guests needed.

The magnificent bounty of the lord's dinner table always amazed her. She and her father had enjoyed a great variety of foods in Prague, but she had never seen a dinner to rival those served in Lord John's hall. On any given day, the tables would sag beneath bowls of black puddings, sausages, platters of clove-flavored venison and pepper-seasoned beef, eels and herrings and freshwater fish. On the "lower" tables—those situated farthest from the master—guests helped themselves to huge bowls of spiced pottage, roasts, pastries, and bowls filled with sauces made of vinegar, verjuice, and wine.

The food began arriving from the kitchen and pantry as soon as the lord and his party returned from their morning adventure, and the knights had always filled the hall by the time the squires returned from the woods. Rows of tables lined the great hall, and at these were seated all the members of Lord John's household: the military personnel, including the knights, guards, men-at-arms, and watchmen; clerks; high-ranking servants; and Lord John's secretary. Visiting vassals from other manors under Lord John's authority filtered among the household members, and every day Anika saw new faces in the dinner crowd.

At the front of the spacious hall stood a raised platform upon which Lord John sat at his table with his steward, Demetr, and any honored guests. From time to time the master called for the assembly's attention in order to introduce his guests—the imperious Lady Zelenka one week, a lovely Lady Ludmila the next—and always, Demetr watched the dinner proceedings with hawkish eyes, as if he measured and calculated exactly how many bites of the lord's bounty went into each mouth present.

During her first week at the castle Anika had assumed that Lady Zelenka was soon to become Lord John's wife, and she was stunned when one of the other squires told her that Lord John did not want to marry again. "Why not?" she blurted out, too surprised to phrase the question more tactfully.

Her informant, a thin, wiry twelve-year-old called Lev, shrugged and lifted a basket of bread into his arms. "Some say he is too busy to woo a bride. Others say he hasn't found one to please him. I've even heard it said that he still mourns for his wife in heaven."

Anika frowned as she followed Lev from the kitchen. Though her master did live a busy life, beautiful young women regularly visited the castle. Surely one of them would catch his eye, unless Lev was right about Lord John's mourning. She did not doubt that he would please any woman, for among all the knights and important visitors to the castle, she had not seen another man half as imposing or attractive.

She paused for a moment and wondered if his sons had inherited his charm. She had not yet seen any sign of the noble children; she assumed they were safely tucked away in the castle with their tutor and a nursemaid. She resolved one day to befriend one of the servants and try to learn more about her mysterious master.

There was little time in her day for idle gossip or speculation. After dinner and its subsequent entertainment—either music from a traveling troubadour, jokes from a jester, or carols and dancing—the knights returned to the garrison to pursue their individual interests while the lord met with his steward and various overseers of his estates. More than ready to rest, Anika joined the other squires in the noisy kitchen, an outbuilding situated well away from the castle. Amid the lowing of cattle and the bleat of sheep in their pens outside, she forced herself to eat with fingers too tired to hold a knife and spoon.

After her brief meal came her time of training, and Novak proved to be a stern taskmaster. To build her endurance and strength, he set her to cleaning out the stables. To help her become unafraid around the huge stallions that served as the knights' war-horses, he commanded her to curry the beasts. In order that she might be familiar with each piece of armor, Novak had her clean and polish his armor until it gleamed. Everything she did, Novak assured her, including serving at dinner, raking the sand in the courtyard, and butchering wild game, was designed to shape a squire into a knight. And, little by little, ache by ache, Anika realized that he spoke the truth.

She would have passed her first four months at Chlum Castle in relative obscurity if Lord John had not loved poetry. After the labors of the day, most noblemen called for a small supper which they ate with their wives and children. Since Lord John had no wife and seemed intent upon hiding his children, he called for his best men: Novak, his captain; Demetr, his steward; and Vasek, his chaplain. In the company of these three—and a host of servants, including Anika—Lord John ate a light supper and relaxed with the men he loved best and trusted most.

After dinner, when the torches were lit and night had drawn down like a black cowl over his estate, Lord John yearned for peace and reflection. He customarily asked his chaplain to bring a book to dinner until he discovered that Novak's squire was a gifted and eager reader.

Anika wasn't sure why she spoke up that night. During dinner Lord John had asked the chaplain to fetch a copy of *Roman de Renard,* a book of verse tales which were popular in France and Germany. Anika felt a thrill shiver through her senses at her master's request; the collection of tales about Renard the fox, Ysengrin the wolf, Tybert the cat, and King Noble the lion had been one of her favorite books since childhood. She had made several copies for noblemen in Prague and had committed certain melodic verses to memory.

But Vasek flatly refused to read it. "The book is frivolous and vain," he protested, slapping his hand on the table in a rare display of temper. "It is bad enough that you spend your time with that troublemaking Hus, Lord John, but to request such inane entertainment at supper is far beneath a man of your character."

The silence that ensued after the priest's outburst was like the hush after a tempest when the leaves hang limp in the quiet and nature seems to catch her breath. Anika paused behind the lord's table, her water jug on her hip, her mouth open in surprise. The chaplain was a dour old man, rarely smiling and speaking only when spoken to, but never had she seen him give any sign that he disapproved of his master's actions or affiliations.

Still, he was a priest. And in the instant when he spoke against Jan Hus, Anika's brow lifted. Could he be one of those who supported the corrupt pope?

Before she knew what her tongue intended, spiteful words poured from her mouth: "That book is neither profane nor frivolous. It is a celebration of life. If Vasek will not read, I will read it for you, Lord John."

The servants at the back of the room gasped in delighted horror, and Anika bit her lip, paling at the enormity of her blunder. Squires and servants were to be seen, not heard. They were to serve and learn meekness through humiliation. They were to listen and observe their betters until they could unconsciously ape the manners and tongue of the nobility. Never *ever* were they to speak out and draw attention to themselves.

"Kafka!" Novak's angry rebuke hardened his features, and Anika felt her face grow hot with humiliation. Of all the squires in the castle, she had the most reason to be quiet and inconspicuous, and yet in one thoughtless moment she had drawn the attention of the master himself.

She lowered her head but looked up through her lashes. Lord John was staring at her, but his quick brown eyes were humorous and tender, not reproachful.

"I am glad you can read, Kafka," he said, his tone mild and curious. "But these verses are written in French."

"If it please you, my lord," she whispered, keeping her eyes low, "forgive me for speaking out of turn. I misspoke myself." She paused, torn between wanting to fade back into the tapestries upon the wall and sharing the joys of a good book. She glanced upward and took a wincing little breath. "But I speak French. I read it, too."

"Well." The master's voice echoed with surprise and delight. "The pleasure shall be ours, then. Vasek, if it pleases you not to hear verse during your supper, you may take yourself away." He glanced at Demetr and Novak. "Do either of you have any objections to hearing the story of Renard the fox?"

Demetr shook his head quickly, and though Anika thought she saw disapproval in Novak's eye, he shook his head as well. "Then, Kafka, take the book from the chest yonder and begin reading wherever you like. What a delightful evening we shall pass tonight!" A wry smile curled his lips as Vasek scuttled away. "After a trying day, there is nothing better than frivolous entertainment to put the mind at rest."

And so Anika found the book and lost herself in the story she read, laughing at the fox's jokes and weeping during the woeful episodes. When she had finished, Lord John declared that he had never spent a more agreeable evening and that from that night forward Kafka the squire should be free from his serving duties in order to read and entertain the master and his men.

Anika clutched the book to her chest and lowered her eyes as a feeling of glorious happiness sprang up in her heart. She was safe, she was content, and, truth be told, she was thoroughly enjoying the danger and excitement of her disguise.

All in all, life at Chlum Castle was very satisfying.

Twelve

"Help!" Anika cried, feeling as hollow as her voice sounded. The muscles in her arms and legs screamed from strain, and she was quite certain that on the morrow she would find bruises on her back and rear. Novak had just given her leave to make her first practice run to tilt at the quintain, and Anika had found the exercise completely beyond her ability. 'Twas bad enough they'd placed her upon a moving mountain of restless horseflesh, but then she had been handed a heavy shield for her left arm and a lance for her right. She was *supposed* to ride at a breakneck pace toward the quintain, a cross-shaped target with a shield on one arm of the swiveling crosspiece and a punching bag on the other, but right now that goal seemed as impossible as scratching her ear with her elbow.

All morning long she'd watched her fellow squires hit the shield with their lances, then duck before the swinging weight came round to unseat the unwary. Only one boy, a small page called Svec, had been too slow and was knocked from his horse. Anika had felt certain she could manage the quintain. 'Twas a child's exercise, after all, as elementary as learning to tie a knot or parry a sword blow.

But then they had placed her upon her mount, and Anika immediately wished she had been more honest about her lack of riding experience. All boys from the country practically grew up on horseback; they could tell a stallion from a mare and an Arabian from a Percheron at thirty paces.

Anika knew absolutely nothing about the beasts, but her fellow squires made riding look easy. And for weeks she had been grooming, feeding, and harnessing the creatures. How difficult could riding be?

She soon found out. The stallion she mounted was a Percheron called Midnight, a war-horse from Normandy. Midnight was an elegant, heavy animal whose head towered above hers when she cleaned his stall. He eyed her with undisguised curiosity when she climbed upon his broad back, and she hugged her knees tight to his side, feeling like a flea on a dog's neck. The shield hung heavily upon her left arm, but she reminded herself to keep it high, protecting her face and chest. A series of tattered flags hung from the end of the ten-foot lance she clung to with her right hand, and for a moment she wished they would disappear. It was all she could do to hold the lance—how was she supposed to control the animal, aim the flags, hit the target, and then remember to *duck*?

"Ready?" Squire Lev stood at her side holding the reins. When she nodded, he draped the strips of leather over the pommel of her wooden saddle.

The stallion tossed his great head and bounced in agitation. Anika placed her weight on the stirrups, which suddenly felt dangerously insubstantial. Seeing no way out, she nodded. Lev smacked the stallion across the rear, sending the animal bolting across the field.

Mercifully, Midnight had faced the quintain many times before; he knew where he was expected to run. For fifty paces or so, Anika actually thought she might at least partly succeed. But gravity and the impact of Midnight's drumming hooves inched the lance from her hand as if a relentless ghost tugged it away from her. As she lost her grip on the lance, her feet lost their place in the bouncing stirrups, and her body began inexorably to shift, bit by bit, out of the saddle.

She knew she was going to fall before she ever reached the quintain. Fortunately she had the presence of mind to drop the lance (which she had nearly lost anyway), and when she hit the ground, she remembered that she should roll away from the stallion's dangerous hooves. But she landed on the bulky shield still strapped to her arm and found that she could not move. The war-horse's pounding gait had reduced her muscles to jelly, and the impact of the fall knocked the breath from her lungs.

"Help!" she managed to gasp. For a few seconds she heard nothing. Lev, Novak, and the other squires were still down field, mercifully away from her humiliation and pain. But in a moment they would be here at her side, and they would undoubtedly chide her. Perhaps Novak would be sorry that he had sent her off so ill-prepared. Maybe he would blame himself, but he would certainly want to know why she hadn't learned to ride—and why she hadn't told him she couldn't. How could she answer him?

She lifted her head. The stallion, finding himself free of rider and rein, had stopped to browse the new grass on the field. The quintain stood stiffly in the distance, mocking her. Her lance lay in the grass a few feet away like a toothpick some giant had discarded. And her comrades—she squinted and looked down the field. Her comrades were laughing!

No one was coming to check on her; not one of them had even ventured away from the others. Lev was bent over, slapping his hands on his knees, and Novak stood apart with his arms crossed, a bemused smile on his face.

With renewed humiliation, she looked away and struggled to push herself up. Why had she ever imagined they might actually *care* what happened to her? Depending upon his mood, Novak saw her either as his slave or his burden; the other squires probably thought her weak and unworthy competition.

"You are behaving like a girl," she sternly told herself. She shook the shield from her arm and stood to her unsteady feet, then quickly ran her hands over her body. Everything still worked. She was not hurt, and they knew it. But she had been perilously close to tears, too close to revealing herself.

She drew a deep breath and forbade herself to tremble. She would face them, and she would learn to ride that mountainous horse. She would practice alone, all night if necessary, and if they found her at sunrise with her neck broken, well—

"They will know who I really am," she whispered, fighting against tears she refused to let fall. "And they will know that a woman would not give up."

"Now, canter!" Lev's voice rang out over the dull clomping sounds of the horse's hooves on the road, and Anika kicked the stallion and leaned forward, pressing her lips together so no sound would burst out. The horse broke from the jerky, bone-crunching trot into a smooth canter, and Anika wanted to whoop in gladness. She was learning!

Lev had agreed to teach her to ride in stolen moments throughout the day. "I don't know why you can't sit a horse," he told her as they cleaned the supper dishes the night after her disastrous tumble, "but I'll help you learn, if you like."

She gave him a smile of pure relief. Lev had proved to be a good friend, something she had not expected to find behind the castle walls. At twelve, he was already tall and straight, with a sensible, practical nature. As they worked together in the kitchen, Anika learned that Lev had been serving in Lord John's household since he became a page at the age of seven.

"I can't imagine your mother letting you go so young," Anika said, spilling a tray of tankards into a huge barrel of water. "Seven is a very tender age."

"My mother did not miss me," he answered, an easy smile playing at the corners of his mouth. "And my service was my father's idea. He wanted his son to learn as other men's sons did."

Anika turned, bewildered. "Your father? Is he a nobleman?"

"Umm." Lev's face closed, as if guarding a secret. "I thought you knew. I thought Novak would tell you."

"Tell me what?"

Lev dumped another tray of tankards into the dish barrel, then a smile played at his mouth. "Lord John is my father."

Anika was too surprised to do more than nod. No wonder she

had never seen Lord John's sons! One of them had been by her side all along! And the other—

"Don't you have a brother?" she asked.

Lev lifted a shoulder in a shrug. "Svec. He's still a page. He won't be allowed to become a squire until he can tilt at the quintain without falling off."

Anika stood silently, shocked by a sudden elusive thought she could not quite fathom. So she wasn't the only one in the garrison trying to prove something! Svec, bless his heart, and even Lev felt the same pressure she endured. No wonder Lord John did not single his sons out! He was trying to give them a normal life, one free from constant examination and discussion.

"Who knows?" she asked when she finally found her voice. "The steward? The servants?"

Lev shrugged again. "I expect most people from the castle know. But none of the visitors or my father's guests." His dark, earnest eyes sought hers. "I wouldn't want you to think my father doesn't love me. He does. He just wants me to learn like other boys."

"I understand," she whispered, plunging her hand into the warm water to pull up one of the tankards. "And I think I can see the wisdom in his decision."

"As I can see the wisdom in teaching you to ride," Lev went on. "And as a knight must demonstrate courtesy and largess to his companions, I would be happy to help you learn."

"Squire Lev," she had answered, handing him a dripping tankard, "I would be happy to accept your offer."

A blush of pleasure rose to her cheeks now as Anika grasped the reins. After several days of practice, one lesson had sunk into her brain—riding was a matter of blending into the horse. She had been too frightened before, too stiff and afraid of falling off. But if she kept her eyes on the goal and did not stop to worry about how she got there—

"Slow him, Kafka!" Lev called, gesturing toward the place where the main gate and barbican met the road. "Here comes a rider!"

Anika obediently pulled back on the reins and brought the horse to a jerky stop, then dismounted and led the stallion back toward the gate. A rider would bring guards pouring out of the tower to hear his news, and she did not want to explain these private riding lessons. Maybe, she thought, pulling the stallion off the road, the rider brought a message from Petrov, telling her she could return home.

A sweat-streaked horse, gray as a thundercloud, came trotting up to the entrance to the castle barbican. The rider, who wore a black surcoat and dusty boots, tossed the reins of his exhausted mount toward Lev, then dismounted and pulled a parchment from a leather bag at his belt. "Lord John of Chlum," he said simply, one brow raised in inquiry.

Anika was about to reply that the lord was in the great hall when at least a half-dozen knights appeared in the passageway, their hands hovering suspiciously above the hilts of their swords.

The visitor inclined his head. "Grace and peace to you, friends. I bring a message from a friend in Prague, a letter for Lord John of Chlum."

"Who is your friend in Prague?" Novak asked gruffly, his thumbs tucked into his belt. "And what is your name?"

The man smiled but shook his head in disapproval. "My name is not important. And I am sworn to secrecy about this errand, Sir Knight. But I can tell you that I obey a lady who fears for her safety and the good of all Bohemians. The letter I bear is of dire import, and I have been urged to see it safely and directly into Lord John's hand."

Novak gave the stranger a grudging nod. "Enter, then," he said, stepping aside to make way for the messenger. "But know that we are watching. With one word from our master or one ill-intentioned action from you, this day shall be your last."

"Never fear, I mean you no harm." A shadow of annoyance crossed the messenger's face as Novak motioned for other knights to surround the stranger. "Just lead me to your master."

Lev and Anika watched silently until the men passed into the castle. Then Lev tugged on Anika's sleeve. "Let's follow, Kafka," he said, turning toward the kitchens. "We'll sneak in through the back entrance."

"Should we?" she asked, searching anxiously for the meaning behind the messenger's words. The messenger had said the important letter came from a lady. Lady Zelenka? Lady Ludmila? Or some other titled beauty who sought Lord John as a husband? She really had no business in the hall, but since Novak and Lord John were involved in this mystery, it might not be unseemly for two squires to go see if their masters required anything.

Lev turned toward her, sensing her hesitation, but she tucked the stallion's reins under her arm and grabbed his sleeve. "What are you waiting for? Let's tie the horse and go."

The parchment lay in Lord John's hand when Anika and Lev crept into the hall, and Anika saw that a rigid, congested expression had settled on her master's face. She felt a thin, cold blade of foreboding slice into her heart. This news, whatever it was, could not be good.

After a long moment Lord John looked up at Novak. "Our friend in Prague writes that Michael of Deutschbrod has been appointed by the pope as procurator de causis fidei in the case against Jan Hus. And our friend," he added in a lower, huskier tone, "fears that Hus will not fare well. She writes that people in Prague are already calling this devil Michael de Causis."

"What is that?" Lev whispered, turning to Anika. "I don't understand Latin."

"This Michael is the pope's advocate in matters of faith," Anika answered, her eyes searching Lord John's face as he reread the missive. "Apparently he intends to prosecute Jan Hus."

Lord John refolded the letter, then sat in silence for another moment, staring at the floor. Finally he lifted his eyes and gave his attention to Novak. "Sir Novak, my most faithful and sure knight, you must take a message to Jan Hus. He must come here for dinner tomorrow and stay for weeks, if necessary. His enemies are restless, and

I worry about his safety if he chooses to remain in Prague. The streets are crowded—some cutpurse is altogether too likely to slice his throat instead of his purse strings." He glanced next at his steward. "Demetr, prepare a chamber for our friend, and make whatever provisions necessary for his needs. He is a stubborn man, and if we must hold him here by force to save his life, we will."

Finally he looked again at the messenger. "You must take this verbal message to our friend; I dare not send it in writing. Tell her she is a blessing from heaven and a most gracious lady. Tell her I am honored by her trust in me, and I will do all I can to ensure the safety of our mutual friend Master Hus."

The stranger received this message in silence, then bowed deeply.

"If there is anything else you need, please speak now," Lord John added.

"A fresh horse," the man answered, folding his hands. "Nothing else. Unless, perhaps, the knight you are sending to Prague might escort me as far as the outskirts of the city. My lady thought it best for me to ride out alone, but I would prefer to have an armed man at my side for the return journey."

"Shall we send a company, my lord?" Novak asked. "We could send a dozen knights—"

"No," John answered with staid calmness. "Sir Novak, you will ride with him, and your squire, too. An armed company would rouse our enemies like a bugle, but no one will notice two men and a boy on the road."

Anika took a quick breath of utter astonishment. *She* would be riding to fetch Jan Hus? She couldn't! He might recognize her. She ought to see if Novak would take Lev instead.

But in spite of her worries, tender thoughts of Petrov rose in her consciousness. Why shouldn't she return to Prague? She could stop at the bookshop and visit her father's friend. In visiting as Kafka, she might discover if Anika could safely return home. She missed the old knight more than she had dreamed possible, and Petrov would know if Lord Laco had stopped searching for her.

Lord John stood in farewell; Novak and the messenger left the chamber through the main hallway.

"You've got to go!" Lev whispered, sending her off with a shove. "Novak won't wait!"

"God in heaven," she murmured a heartfelt prayer as she turned to hurry out the back entrance, "give me wisdom. And blind Master Hus so he will not see me."

She looked up to find Lev at her side, his eyes wide with curiosity. She had foolishly spoken the prayer aloud, and he was certainly wondering why she had to hide from the famous preacher of Prague.

"I once committed a sin and confessed it to the preacher," she said simply. It was the truth, for he had heard enough of her confessions to fill an ocean. "I am embarrassed lest he recognize me."

Lev smiled and slapped her on the back. "Then take my hooded cloak," he answered, pushing her toward the garrison. "And remain silent. Haven't you noticed that men with much on their minds do not notice a boy who says nothing?"

Thirteen

A nika and Novak left the unnamed messenger at an intersection of roads outside Prague. *Where does he go from here?* Anika wondered, watching him trot away. *To the home of Lady Zelenka or Lady Ludmila?* Once the taciturn stranger had disappeared on the road, Anika began to beg her master for leave to visit Petrov.

"You know Sir Petrov. You met him the day I came to the castle," she said, knowing that she walked a thin line between winning his permission and rousing his anger. "The old knight and I are close. If I do not see him today and tell him I am well, I may not see him for months. Surely God has sent this opportunity for me to go."

"All right, be off with you," Novak answered, waving her away as if she were an annoying mosquito. "But you must report to the preacher's house before sunset. I will urge Master Hus to make haste, for we should begin our return to Chlum before dark."

"I will hurry," Anika promised, spurring her horse. The animal snorted at the unexpected touch of metal upon his flank and took off so abruptly that Anika's head snapped back and she nearly lost her seat. She heard Novak laughing behind her, but she hung on tenaciously, taking grim satisfaction in the fact that she had not fallen. Novak thought her a clumsy rider, but she had come a long way in a short time. She would impress him yet.

The city was so crowded that once she passed the city walls, Anika had to dismount and lead her horse through the streets. Hordes of pedestrians clogged the roads; wagons and oxcarts and carriages jammed the alleys. Why had she never noticed this congestion before?

Her heart sang with delight when she turned onto the narrow street where her father's bookshop lay. The building was just as she remembered it, although a little smaller than the place in her memory. Two students stood in the doorway, wax tablets in their hands and precious books tucked under their arms. Anika quickly tied the horse to a post and threaded her way through the students until she stood before Petrov.

He was studying a parchment upon which someone had written a line of figures that looked more like chicken scratches than proper writing. Anika waited for him to lift his eyes, and when he did not, she murmured a low greeting. "Grace and peace to you, Sir Knight."

He raised his head, and his dark eyes flew open. "Little bird!" She saw that he wanted to embrace her, but thankfully, the table stood between them. She reached out and clasped his hand in both of hers.

"Sir Petrov, it is good to see you."

His seamed face lit up like sunshine bursting out of the clouds. "What brings you to Prague? Is all well?" He leaned back in his chair, a frown puckering the skin between his eyes into deep wrinkles. "Is anything amiss?"

"I am fine. Nothing is amiss at Chlum Castle," she leaned forward and lowered her voice, "but something is afoot in Prague, I fear. Lord John has sent me with Sir Novak to escort Master Hus to Chlum."

Petrov leaned upon the desk and tapped his finger against the side of his head, thinking. "I have heard rumors but paid them no mind. Master Hus has not changed his behavior in church, so I am not surprised there is trouble." His brows pulled into a brooding knot over his eyes. "'Tis a pity your father is not here to help me sort through these things! He always knew the state of affairs around our unfortunate preacher."

"What rumors have you heard?" Anika spied her old chair behind a desk and slid into it.

A student in the doorway called for Petrov's attention, but the knight waved the man away, then turned toward Anika and leaned forward, propping his elbows on his knees. "The preacher's enemies have sent letters of complaint to the pope. Of course they have done this for years, but lately these letters have mentioned Hus's condemnation of the pope's fondness for granting indulgences. Though many of Hus's fellow priests are forsaking his friendship, every day he gains new supporters among the nobility and common people. He has lit a candle in their hearts and minds, little bird. The truth of the gospel has shined in a dark place, and they will not go back to their old ways."

"Tell me, Sir Petrov, is one of these noble friends a woman?"

The old man shrugged. "Surely he has many women friends, as well as men. But his enemies are the ones to be feared. They say that the cursed Michael of Deutschbrod has been appointed to bring Hus to Rome. They want Hus to pay with his life for his actions against the pope."

"I have heard of this Michael of Deutschbrod," Anika answered. "But only that he is the pope's advocate."

"He is a total knave, the worst sort of scoundrel," Petrov answered, scowling. "If he were a knight, we would have turned him out and not allowed him to live. But he did not take the vows of knighthood—he swore instead to honor God. He was a parish priest who neglected his duties in favor of obtaining money by fair means or foul, it mattered not. For King Wenceslas he devised some method of working the royal mines, then absconded with the money entrusted to him. With his ill-gotten gold, he has offered his influence and unsavory skills to Pope John, and the devil himself could not use him more foully!"

"What will this Michael do?" Anika asked, an uneasiness rising from the bottom of her heart. "Is Master Hus safe in Bohemia? Surely he is, for unless he goes to Rome—"

"I cannot answer that," Petrov answered. "Danger lurks everywhere, little bird." For an instant a wistfulness stole into his expression. "We can only pray and wait for God's will to be done—just as I am waiting for a sign that you are safe and can return to me."

Anika lifted her head, distracted from her thoughts of Jan Hus. "That I am safe? Surely you know I am."

"I pray that you are." Petrov lowered his head into his hands and kneaded his forehead as though it ached. "The day after I took you to Chlum, a pair of Lord Laco's knights appeared here, demanding to know why you had not presented yourself to serve that nobleman."

Anika's heart thumped against her rib cage. "What did you tell them?"

Petrov lifted his eyes and looked at her, his mouth tight and grim. "I told them you had found employment elsewhere. They cursed me and left but went next to Master Hus's house. The preacher told them exactly what I had told him—that you had found a position with a family in the country. But the preacher couldn't tell them which family, and I wouldn't tell them, so Lord Laco's suspicions are not assuaged."

"Why does he trouble himself on my account?" Anika asked, dismayed to hear a faint thread of panic in her voice. "Why won't he leave me alone?"

"Because you are the one thing young Miloslav has desired and cannot obtain," Petrov answered, a faint light gleaming in the depths of his dark eyes. "Be patient, Anika, and remain where you are. Be strong and well."

"I will, Sir Petrov," Anika promised, realizing that she found the thought of remaining at Chlum infinitely satisfying. She loved Petrov and wanted to be with him, but if she returned to Prague, she would miss Novak and Lev and Svec and those quiet hours after supper when she read to Lord John.

In penance for her disloyal thoughts, she glanced around to be sure no students or townsfolk lingered in the doorway, then leaned forward and gave the old knight a kiss on the cheek. As Petrov stammered a farewell, she hurried out to meet Novak and Master Hus.

By the time Master Hus had attended to his duties and said his farewells to friends in Prague, the molten orb of the sun hovered low over the western mountains. A cold wind rushed out of the mountains, urging travelers to hurry and find shelter.

Anika discovered that Lev was right. With her face safely hidden within the cowl of the hooded cloak and the additional cover of gathering darkness, Hus did not recognize her. He rode beside Novak, eager to refute Lord John's concerns for his safety, his eloquent hands fluttering left and right as his mount's ears flickered back and forth in a crazy pattern of annoyance.

Huddled within the heavy cloak, Anika remained silent on the journey. The preacher might well recognize her voice even before recalling her face. And as she bobbed up and down in the placid pace of the animals, she listened to the men's conversation and learned a great deal about the preacher's situation.

"The council in Rome has reaffirmed my excommunication," Hus said, lifting his eyes to the first bright star that shone from the cobalt vault of the heavens. "They have pronounced the great curse upon me. No man is to associate with me, no man is to give me food or drink, no man is to grant me a place where I might rest my head. Wherever I sojourn, religious services are to cease, and if I die on this journey, you are not to give me a Christian burial."

"Well, we'd better pray you don't die then," Novak joked, laughing gently. "I would hate to tell my master I was forced to leave your body by the side of the road."

Anika stiffened at Novak's ungracious humor, but the preacher's next words put her mind at ease. "It is a good thing I place my faith in the Lord of heaven and not the lords of the Church." Hus dropped his hand to the pommel of his saddle. "My God is unchangeable and all knowing. He knows I could do nothing to merit his grace, and yet he has accepted me as one of his own. But these men in Rome expect me to submit to them before I can belong to the family of God. They proclaim that I am barred forever from entering heaven, but they would quickly change their opinions if I were to recant my beliefs. And so I will keep my eyes upon the One who changes not."

"Even so, I am stunned by the severity of their sentence," Novak said, turning sideways in the saddle to look at the preacher. "And I grieve for you."

Hus smiled with beautiful candor. "Don't grieve for me, Sir Knight. I am confident in my Lord." The smile suddenly faded. "But I do worry about those who have no understanding of the truth. The most recent papal bull published against me is not directed at me alone. In order to punish all those who stand with me, the pope has decreed that Bethlehem Chapel—which he describes as a nest of heretics—should be torn down to its foundations. And as long as I reside in Prague, another interdict is proclaimed against the city. Again, there are to be no marriages, no Christian burials. Communion is available only to the dying. The people of Prague, I fear, will suffer terribly. For their sakes alone I have consented to accept your gracious master's kind invitation and leave the city."

"Why do you endure it?" Novak asked. "Why don't you just leave the Roman church? You are confident in God, and your reputation is spotless. There are many who would follow you if you began your own church. Lord John would build you a chapel in Chlum, and you could do God's work without intervention from those red-robed devils in Rome—"

Hus held up a quieting hand. "There have been enough divisions in the body of Christ," he answered, shaking his head. "Even now there are three who would be pope—Gregory, John, and Benedict—each claiming to be the head of the church. The common people do not know whom to believe. They cannot read the Bible for themselves; they can only trust the parish priest who speaks to them on Sunday. Would it not be better to reform the church from within than to establish a new one to compete with the old?"

"If a bottle is cracked, is it not better to pour wine into an entirely new bottle?" Novak countered, smiling blandly. "A bottle held together by glue and gum will still leak."

"I am not the only one who weeps for the Church," Hus

murmured in a tone of deep conviction. "There are others, even a few cardinals, who see what sin has done to the establishment of Christ's blessed church." He sighed, and in the gentle light of the rising moon Anika saw that pain had carved merciless lines on his face. "But, Sir Novak, we are only men. Until he who is complete and holy comes to rule over us himself, no institution we establish will achieve perfection. Who is to say that the church I establish would not in ten years be as corrupt as the one we strive to reform? Men are imperfect, and power corrupts. It is only through humility that we learn to lead, and through knowledge of our ignorance that we learn to seek the truth."

Night had completely fallen by the time Hus finished speaking, and a million sparks of diamond light brightened the dark canopy overhead. The trio of riders continued on in silence, each lost in thought.

Jan Hus repeated his convictions and concerns before Lord John the next day at dinner. Twice Anika nearly spilled water upon the enthralled guests so intent was she upon listening to the courageous preacher's exploits. Had so much happened in the four months since she left Prague?

"Last month a group of Romanist citizens attacked the chapel while I was leading prayers," Hus said, folding his hands on the table as he addressed Lord John's household at dinner. "Fortunately, several of our men were keeping watch and repelled them. I thank God that our people, though determined, are peaceful. Even when a group of German fanatics attempted to seize me while I spoke from the pulpit, our men subdued the invaders without injury. God has been good to us."

"How have you responded to these violent overtures?" Lord John asked, stroking his chin. Anika noticed that he had not touched the food on the trencher before him. "Surely it is not wise, Master Hus, to allow this sort of thing to continue. You should make an offensive move, keep your enemy off balance."

The preacher's mouth curved in a smile. "I know nothing about military matters, but I have made one special effort to end this strife. Since Pope John is not willing to hear my defense of my positions, I have lifted my appeal from the pope to the Lord Jesus Christ himself, the Judge who is neither influenced by gifts nor deceived by false witnesses. Last week I read my formal appeal from the pulpit and posted copies in Prague's public places." His face fell for a moment. "I must admit, such an action brings me bittersweet pleasure. Every time I handle a published piece of my work, I am reminded that my favorite copyist has been most foully murdered. Ernan O'Connor was a friend and scribe unequaled in Prague, and I miss him most sincerely."

Hus paused to stir the bowl of porridge before him, while Anika swallowed hard and bit back tears, comforted by the knowledge that she did not mourn her father alone.

"Surely there are other copyists in the city, Master Hus," Lord John offered, lifting his glass from the table.

"Yea, but not like Ernan O'Connor," the preacher answered. "He had a daughter who wrote and spoke French, Latin, English, and Bohemian with equal ease. She was more fluent and a faster copyist than Ernan himself." He chuckled. "And she was much more pleasant to look upon."

"What happened to the girl?" Novak asked, a polite smile on his lips. "Surely she could still work for you."

"Alas, she is lost to me now. Lord Laco of Lidice took a dishonorable interest in her, and I'm afraid the girl was forced to hide herself on one of the estates in the country."

"Laco," Novak interrupted, lifting his hand in an emphatic gesture, "is a rogue. I beg your pardon, Lord John, for I know he is a nobleman, but I would not trust him any more than I would spit in holy water."

"I hate to judge a man before God has finished with him, but I must agree with you," Hus answered. "He said his son wanted to employ the girl as a chambermaid, but I saw the way the youth looked at her. He would have used her most cruelly, I am certain, and cast her out when he had finished taking his pleasure from her. I am not certain where the girl has found a home, but I thank God that she managed to circumvent Lord Laco's purposes."

Having heard enough, Anika turned quickly away, grateful that her duties allowed her to scuttle away to fetch a fresh pitcher of water. She had been fortunate that no one had required her to speak to Master Hus directly, for surely he would recognize her voice or her smile if she confronted him.

As she moved away, one sudden, cold, lucid thought struck her: With these men Jan Hus had been brutally honest about Lord Laco's intentions. Why hadn't he been as forthright with her? Did he think it necessary to shield a maiden from the harshness of life?

If you thought to protect me from evil, she thought, shivering as the cold November air outside hit her in the face, *you are too late, my friend.*

Anika couldn't sleep. The old nightmare had awakened her and now the steady, deep breathing of exhausted men filled the silence around her, punctuated occasionally by an abrupt eruption of baritone snoring. Before going to sleep, she had mulled the preacher's words for a long while, and with each passing moment her aversion to Lord Laco and his son grew deeper and her alarm more disquieting. She had some knowledge of the way men and women were supposed to interact in love, for she had read the romances of Chrétien de Troyes and Marie de France. But she had never considered that a man might actually want her for purposes less than holy marriage in the sight of God. She had never kissed a man's lips; she had never even *embraced* anyone but her father, Petrov, and Master Hus. While reading romances she had thrilled at the idea of a lover's kiss, but the thought of Lord Laco's blue-eyed son pressing his cold lips to her flesh made the hair of her head tingle with revulsion.

What drove a woman into a man's arms? Love, certainly, but how did love grow between ordinary people? In romances a handsome knight always performed some great feat of valor to prove his love to a lady in distress, but knights did not line up to rescue the daughters of humble book copyists. And even though Anika had needed rescuing a few months before, no one but Petrov had risen to lend her aid.

She turned onto her side and pressed her hand over her ear, trying to block out the sound of so many snoring men. If her father had not died, she supposed that he would have eventually negotiated with a suitable and similar family with an eligible son. She would have been betrothed and finally married. Perhaps she would have learned to love her intended husband during the time of betrothal. She might even have welcomed his kiss. But such things took time. How, then, could Lord Laco's son have seen her and desired her without even knowing her? Surely what he felt was not love.

She sat up and silently slid out from under Novak's bunk, not willing to wake any of her companions. If her father were still alive, she would have asked him what made a man desire a woman, but she did not think she could ask any of the men of Chlum without revealing her ignorance and her true nature. For all men thought alike—she now understood that truth clearly. More than once she had stumbled upon the knights telling a crude story involving women. The men had all roared with laughter at the conclusion of the tale while she blinked in dazed exasperation, understanding nothing. There were some aspects of women they found irresistible, but it wasn't a woman's tongue, brain, or wit. These things men tended to criticize.

Anika crouched by the fireplace, hugging her knees to her. Why did men praise hair, breasts, and slender backs when those attributes counted for almost nothing? Long hair only blinded one's eyes on the dueling field, breasts were only useful for feeding infants, and slender backs were apt to break under heavy loads.

Understanding men, she decided, was as impossible as cutting your straight hair short and willing it to grow out curly. But though she could not understand her companions' motivations, she had found it easy to mimic their behavior and actions. She did not have the strength of other boys her age, but she more than made up for her weakness with her quick tongue and breadth of knowledge. She had yet to successfully tilt at the quintain, but she had outpaced her fellow squires in music, poetry, and dancing. Though Sir Novak pretended merely to tolerate her, she knew her mentor took pride in certain of her accomplishments.

She glanced over at her sleeping master. His arm hung limply from his bunk, its dark hairs vibrating softly with the sound of his breathing. Fire shadows danced on the walls of the garrison, lighting the other knights' bearded faces with an orange-red glow. She bit her thumbnail, transfixed by the sight of square faces, round faces, pale faces, flushed faces, scarred faces, bearded faces, rutted faces—

Manly faces. There was not a feminine face in the room, save hers.

The air suddenly seemed thick and heavy, filled with the smells of hay, leather, and sweat. Yearning for the bracing bite of the night-cold air, she pulled a woolen cloak from a peg near the door, slipped it over her shoulders, and stepped outside, her boots crunching on the rock-strewn sand of the courtyard. A guard pacing along the top of the castle wall stopped for a moment and stared, but she waved him off and pointed toward the lavatory in the tower. He nodded and turned away, dismissing her.

She did not stop at the lavatory, though, but moved on toward the small pool the servants used for watering the animals. This area was quiet once the servants had gone to bed, and she liked to retreat from the others and sit on the wide lip of the stone wall edging the water. The garrison often seemed too loud, too male, for her to sort her thoughts effectively, and this round reflecting pool was lovely in the dark.

She hopped up on the stone wall, then turned and tucked her knees under her chin. The bright pepper of the stars spangled the dark sky above, and she hugged her knees to her and drew in a deep breath, enjoying the solitude and the quiet. The wide courtyard gleamed like silver under the full moon. At her left hand the castle keep rose strong and solid; the barbican and gate stood like sentinels in the distance at her right.

Living with fifty men was more mentally taxing than she had

imagined possible. It felt good to get away and remind herself, if even for a few moments, who and what she was: Anika of Prague, a middle-class sparrow living among the partridges, cranes, and pheasants of the nobility. The bird analogy had come from the pages of *The Art of Courtly Love,* and that author continually reminded Anika that no matter who caught her eye or captured her heart, she could never belong among the nobility. *You can only hide and learn, in the hope that soon you will be free to return to Petrov and Prague.*

From far outside the castle walls came the mournful call of a wolf, as lonely as the cry of a lost and wandering spirit. One guard upon the wall called to another, "Lo, did you hear that?" Then silence prevailed again.

Anika rested her chin on her knees, feeling her eyelids grow heavy. Snug in the warmth of her cloak, she would not mind passing the night out here under the stars—

"Would that I had your peace of mind, Kafka."

Lord John's resonant voice brought her instantly awake. As her eyes flew open she threw out her right hand, ready to push herself off the stone ledge and retreat—

There was no stone beneath her hand—she had overestimated the width of the ledge. Tumbling over like a tenpin, she felt the waters of the pool rise up to meet her. Surprised by the darkness, she kicked and thrashed in the shallow water, disoriented and unable to see moonlight above.

A strong arm caught her and pulled her upward. Gasping for breath, she scrambled to place her legs beneath her, then abruptly stood up, embarrassed at her humiliating clumsiness.

Upset from his place on the ledge by her sudden upward motion, Lord John pitched forward with a cry and an oath.

At the sound of a thunderous splash, Anika wiped her eyes and backed away in horror. The water was barely up to her knees, but she suddenly wished that she had drowned. Dying in Lord John's watering trough would be vastly preferable to soaking the master in the middle of a cold November night.

Through her haze of panic, she heard the sound of slapping

footsteps along the ramparts. Then the glow of two torches appeared above the wall. "Lord John! Is trouble afoot?"

Anika wiped her arm across her nose and retreated into the shadows as Lord John rose to his feet and vigorously shook his head. She cringed beneath the spray, hoping he would choose to go away and quietly bemoan the fact that he had accepted the world's most uncoordinated squire.

"All is well, have no fear," her master called to the guards, lifting his hands in emphasis. "I merely decided to cool off in the pool."

"But, my lord, it is freezing out here." One of the guards moved closer, and Anika crouched down, hiding herself in the shadows. 'Twas bad enough that Lord John knew which of his squires had pulled him into the pool, but she'd be the laughingstock of the entire garrison if the guards discovered her identity.

"Go back to your post," Lord John commanded, placing his hands on his hips. In three steps he crossed the pool and mounted the ledge, his garments streaming water. As Anika's heart trembled within her breast, he waited until the reluctant guards retreated, then turned and extended his hand. "Come out, Kafka. You'll catch the ague if you remain in there all night," he said, the warmth of his smile echoing in his voice.

Still trembling with fear and the cold, she reached out and accepted his help, then let him pull her onto the ledge. She released his hand quickly, then jumped to the ground and stood before him with bent shoulders. Lowering her head, she braced herself for a rebuke.

"I thought, when I saw you sitting there, that it must be wonderful to be young and free from worry," he began, his voice surprisingly gentle. "And I'm afraid I owe you an apology for startling you. 'Tis my own fault that we are wet and freezing out here."

"No, my lord!" As their eyes met, she felt a shock run through her. By all the saints, this was an unusual man!

"I shouldn't have left the garrison," she said, lowering her eyes. She could feel her cheeks blushing hotly against the cool night air. "But I couldn't sleep."

"Does Novak still snore?" he asked, his profile dark against the moonlight. "I have traveled with him, and I remember most distinctly that his snore could wake the dead."

"Yes." She struggled to stop the chattering of her teeth. "Yes, my lord, he does. Usually it does not bother me, but tonight—" She wanted to explain the concerns that had driven her outside, but she couldn't. Here stood an honest man who would probably be willing to listen and offer advice, but by her very presence in his home she was being dishonest with him.

"I had a nightmare and couldn't sleep," she answered, hugging herself again. She steeled herself against the cold and commanded her body not to shiver.

"Perhaps you are not as free from worry as I thought," he answered, locking his hands behind his back. He stared at the ground for a moment, then moved a mound of dirt with the toe of his shoe. "I am much distressed about my friend, Master Hus. He will not be returning to Prague, I'm afraid, for his conscience will not allow the city to suffer for his sake. The interdict is hard upon the common people, so the preacher is consigning himself to exile. He fears he will not be happy away from his work, but I have tried to convince the goose that he can work here just as well as in Prague."

"The goose, my lord?" Anika frowned in bewilderment. Lord John was usually not so disrespectful.

"A joke." Lord John's eyes shone in the pale light of the moon. "The Latin word *auca* can be translated 'Hus' and means 'goose.' You may not believe it, but Master Hus can actually be a merry man. He is not always a serious scholar."

Anika pressed her lips together, smothering a smile. She had seen Master Hus's mischievous side many times in her father's bookshop, but she could not explain *that*. "He will not suffer as long as he has friends like you," Anika offered, feeling a surge of gratitude and loyalty toward her master. "He will sojourn here for a while, and then he will take the gospel out to the people."

"You speak as if you know him." Lord John's dark, silky brows rose a trifle.

"I—have read his works, my lord," Anika stammered, nearly at a loss for words. "I know the fire of evangelism burns so steadily in his breast that he will be compelled to carry his work out into the villages."

"You are right. Already he has asked me to give him leave to visit the villages of this estate." He drew his arms across his chest and rubbed his wet sleeves, fighting the cold. "Would you, Kafka, be interested in joining my expedition to escort the preacher?"

Anika hesitated, torn between wanting to please her master and not wanting to expose her identity. Jan Hus might recognize her if she accompanied him into the countryside, but she had been successful at hiding herself thus far. And if she went . . . she would be near Lord John.

"Yes, my lord," she said, bowing her head. "I would be pleased to join such a cavalcade. I will serve you in any way I can."

"If you don't freeze to death first." Amusement still lurked in his eyes. "Well, get you into the garrison and dry those clothes by the fire. We will speak more of this on the morrow. And the next time you venture out to sit by the pool, Kafka, I promise not to disturb you."

With a parting smile he turned and walked toward the castle. Watching him go, Anika shivered again and shook her head, suddenly regretting her disguise.

Fourteen

J an Hus's absence from Bethlehem Chapel did little to dispel the
enthusiasm of the crowds who gathered there the Sunday after he
disappeared into exile. All of Prague had heard of the preacher's decision to leave the city so the interdict might be lifted. Peasants and
nobles alike flocked to the chapel to hear Hus's chief disciple, Jerome,
expound the Word of God.

Petrov went to the church early, in part to find a front row seat
where his aging ears could hear above the crying of babies and the
shushing of their mothers, and in part because he wanted to discern
which way the political wind would soon be blowing.

"Let me repeat what Jan Hus has told you," Jerome proclaimed
to the crowd of over three thousand Sunday worshipers. "So long as
there is no difference between the teachings of Scripture and doctrines of the Church, we do not antagonize or find fault with the latter. But whenever any disagreement is plain, we ought to follow the
Scriptures instead of the mandates of men."

Petrov looked around him. Most of his fellow citizens were nodding in agreement; this was a logical and sound conclusion. Genera-
tions ago, Bohemia had been evangelized by two priests who
translated the Scriptures into the common language and invited any
believer, clergy or laity, to participate in Holy Communion. Theirs
had been a participatory faith from the beginning; their forefathers
had never needed priests to interpret Scripture or act as intermedi-
aries before the throne of God.

"Our friend Jan Hus, whose great love for you compels him to be absent today," Jerome went on, "investigated the writings of the Englishman Wyclif, the one condemned as a heretic. At first he was horrified by several of Wyclif's beliefs, but as Master Hus continued to acquire knowledge of the Holy Scriptures, he found that Wyclif's ideas are consistent with God's Word. Christ, not Peter, is the rock upon which the Church was founded."

Jerome churned the soul-bed of the congregation with a voice like measured thunder, drawing cries of agreement from the anxious, upturned faces.

"We seek only God's truth," he said, his dark eyes shifting from one person in the crowd to another. "And perhaps God has sent our beloved pastor away from us in the same way He allowed persecution's sword to scatter the early Christians from Jerusalem. For we know this: Wherever he goes, our friend and brother Hus will continue to preach God's love for all and the need for all to come to repentance. Though he has been accused of making the clergy odious to the people, how can the sinner criticize the prophet? Violence and anarchy mark many clergymen today; turbulence, crime, lawlessness, profligacy, and corruption have tainted the highest leaders of Christ's church. Church positions are bartered and sold. Priestly avarice is unblushing. The three rival popes, instead of attempting to lead us to God, use the power of excommunication as a political tool while they tax the faithful to support armies needed to vanquish their enemies. They promise to forgive sins if a person contributes money to advance their ungodly ambition, and yet the Scriptures tell us only God has the power to forgive sins."

The ferocity of Jerome's passion was both frightening and exhilarating. This was exactly the kind of sermon Petrov feared. Jan Hus was an excellent and persuasive speaker, but he tended to awake the *intellect* of his hearers while Jerome baptized his listeners with the fire of holy enthusiasm. Members of the congregation left Hus's sermons ready to live peaceably with all men, but today they might leave ready to pick up their swords and fight.

As if it had a mind of its own, Petrov's hand moved to the place where his own sword had hung from his belt. Since giving it to Anika he carried only a dagger, as any prudent man would. But if Jerome kept preaching like this, Prague might soon boil with blood. Every man would need a blade, if only for self-defense.

"The possession of power has begotten the love of it, and the fingers which grasp the holy scepter will not loose their hold upon it," Jerome went on. "Will we allow this to continue? Will we allow the archbishop and the pope's prelates to tell us we cannot bury our dead or share in the cup of the Lord's suffering? No! We are Christians, we are Bohemians! We will not be ordered and commanded by the impostor in Rome!"

The congregation responded with cheering as Petrov's mind whirled with a crazed mixture of hope and fear. With the others he tentatively lifted his hands, carried away on the wave of rising enthusiasm. The rafters above echoed with the roaring shout, and Petrov smiled, savoring this small but satisfying victory. Perhaps they would not have to defeat the Romanists with swords. Perhaps God's truth would prevail through the sheer force of righteousness.

He shifted in his seat and lowered his hands, studying the cheering people around him. A sort of passionate beauty kindled each face, a desire to search out and strive for truth, for right, for the glory of God.

This feeling was what he had lost when he surrendered his calling as a knight! When his old master died, Petrov had allowed his zeal for the cause of Christ to die as well. But God was good. He would allow Petrov to find the fervor he had lost. No longer would the knight look back with longing on his yesterdays, because *tomorrow* would require men of purpose and conviction, passion and courage!

A quick and unexpected movement caught his attention, a shifting of shadows near the pulpit. Petrov leaned forward. On the other side of the lectern, in the vaguest of movements, a man in a brown robe had leaned into the empty space in front of the pulpit. It could have been an innocent gesture, but Petrov did not recognize the man's face. Dark shadows surrounded the stranger's eyes but did not quite disguise the murderous passion in his gaze.

Around Petrov, the enthusiastic cries faded to the soft strains of prayer. As the man in the brown robe inched toward the pulpit, a shining blade poised in his hand, Petrov wrapped his palm around the handle of his dagger and inched toward the edge of his pew. Jerome, who had closed his eyes and lifted his hands in prayer, did not see the enemy.

Rising to his feet in one fluid movement, Petrov moved toward the assassin. Today he had no maidens to protect, no doubts to conquer. He was a sworn knight, born and bred to battle, ready to defend the cause of Christ.

Fifteen

A pox on him!" Zelenka murmured under her breath as the door to her chamber opened. She had hoped that Lord John stood outside, but the loathsome toad that passed for a captain stood in the hallway, his hand at his sword, his mouth curved in a mirthless smile. By all the saints, did John purposely intend to annoy her by sending this creature to escort her to dinner? The humorless gray-bearded knight fairly exuded dour disapproval every time she crossed his path.

No matter. She would ignore him today as she had ignored him yesterday and the day before, and she would tolerate him for as long as it took her to win Lord John's heart. She had already outlasted the feeble attempts of that frail hothouse flower, Lady Ludmila, and Zelenka was certain she would eventually be mistress of Chlum Castle. After all, if John was as uninterested as he pretended, why did he continue to allow her visits?

She waved her hand, dismissing her two maids. "One moment," she called to the knight in the doorway, then bent low over a looking glass to check her reflection. At fifteen, she was older than most marriageable girls, but she had convinced her father that nothing less than her marriage to the Earl of Chlum would enhance his own position. And so to that end she had applied herself, lightly anointing her head with olive oil until her tresses shone like gold, tinting herself pink and white through the delicate application of sheep fat and rouge, and propping herself up to sleep so her maids could work through the night to complete the intricate braids said to capture a man's fancy.

Today she had chosen to wear her second-best gown of silver brocade woven with red roses and trimmed with fur at the sleeve. The myriad of delicate braids had been caught up in a headpiece of fine mesh crispinette topped with an embroidered and beaded roll that sat atop her head like a crown. A jaunty short veil hung from the back of the headpiece, a bit of frippery intended to catch a man's eye as a lady moved away.

Zelenka stepped back and sighed deeply, expanding the bodice of her fitted gown. All in all, she made a pleasing picture. And best of all, now that Lady Ludmila had been recalled by her father to accept betrothal to a more willing suitor, no competition remained on the horizon. Handsome, wealthy, aristocratic and melancholy Lord John was Zelenka's for the winning . . . and the wedding.

"Consider now, my lady," the arrogant captain's voice broke into her thoughts, "the possibility that your face has not changed since you gazed at it two moments ago."

Zelenka lowered the mirror, fury almost choking her. She would love to upbraid this knight before his master again, but she'd been fool enough to do that once and saw that it accomplished little. 'Twas obvious Lord John was fond of this rapscallion, though only heaven above knew why. If she voiced another complaint, she ran the risk of proving the knight's contention that she was a harridan and a shrew.

Better to handle this one on her own.

"God save you, knight," she called, permitting herself a withering glance in his direction. "I had hoped you would be called away today. Isn't there a war in the Holy Land to which you must repair? Or perhaps King Wenceslas needs your able assistance."

"My place is with Lord John." He glared at her, frowning. "And if I may speak frankly—"

"By all means, do." Turning, she shot a commanding look at him from lowered lids. "Let what is said here remain between you and me, for we need have no secrets from one another. You despise me, I abhor you. I see no reason for us to cover our mutual antipathy with pleasant smiles and good graces."

At this he raised his eyes to her face in an oddly keen, appreciative look. "Very well said, my lady. But to my point—you would not be happy as mistress of Chlum Castle, and perhaps it is best that someone tell you so. Your intentions are obvious for the world to see."

"Are they?" She clasped her hands tightly together and lifted a brow. "Tell me then, does your master know the desires of my heart? Does the chaplain? The steward? Of course not. They believe I am here merely to spend time with my father's beloved friend. Our families are close, and it is only natural that I should go a-visiting near Christmastime. And since your lord has no mistress to help him celebrate St. Nicholas's Day," she cast him a coy smile, "I am willing to remain here and help where I can."

He did not answer but gave her a look of disbelief, rage, and frustration. She lifted her skirt and flicked an imaginary speck of dirt from her gown, completely pleased with herself. She'd won the point. Though this man hated her, the other men around Lord John thought her an angel from heaven. The steward believed her a thorough and talented overseer. Due to her regular attendance at daily mass in the castle's chapel and a series of heartfelt confessions, the chaplain believed her to be one step away from saintliness. Now, if only she could convince Lord John to see her as a woman who needed marrying.

"Come, Sir Knight," she said, moving past him with her head held high, "we should not keep our master waiting."

———

Zelenka smiled in secret pleasure when Lord John led her to his table and waited behind her chair until she had seated herself. 'Twas a small gesture, in truth, but one that a husband routinely performed for his wife. After a few more days and a few stolen moments under the mistletoe, surely she could win his heart and take this seat permanently.

The steward clapped his hands, and at his cue the servants and squires began to bring in heaping platters of food. Zelenka nodded graciously to Jan Hus, who had been seated by her left hand, then inclined her head toward the chaplain who sat beside Hus. Once she had given those perfunctory acknowledgments, she turned her attention back to Lord John.

"My lord, how fared your hunt this morning?" she asked, folding her hands in a pose of tranquil gentility.

"Ah, Lady Zelenka." His arresting face creased into a sudden smile. "I fear we have neglected you. We have no other women guests at Chlum, and I'm afraid we have not entertained you very graciously."

Tilting her head to one side, she stole a slanted look at him. "I understand that you have been busy, my lord. I, too, have been occupied, for I spent a great part of the morning giving confession to your chaplain."

"Aye, my lord, she did," Vasek interrupted, beaming his approval.

"But I asked about your hunt." Zelenka placed her elbows on the table and laced her fingertips, giving Lord John the fullness of her attention. "Tell me all about it. You speak to these other men throughout the day, but if I do not capture your attention at dinner, I am at an unfortunate loss—"

"We did not hunt, Lady Zelenka, so I am sorry to disappoint you," John answered, tucking the edge of the tablecloth into his belt to serve as a napkin. As a squire approached and lowered a heaping bowl of pottage to the table, Zelenka frowned. John's attention had wandered again. His gaze rested on the face of the squire who served him.

"Are you well, Kafka?" Lord John asked. Zelenka detected a certain thawing in his tone. "You did not catch the ague after your swim the other night?"

"I am well." The boy ducked slightly as a blush burned his neck.

"Then what do you say to an excursion on the morrow? My friend Master Hus wishes to ride to Husinec, his birthplace. He plans on preaching to his own people before venturing farther, much as Christ himself did."

The squire's emerald eyes met the master's for a mere second, then he returned his gaze to the pottage as if a world of fascinating information lay within. "If my lord wishes me to go, I will," he said, his voice low and soft. His slender hands trembled upon the bowl he placed on the table, and as he straightened, he nervously wiped his delicate fingers upon his tabard.

Puzzled, Zelenka narrowed her eyes to study the boy's face. The face was well modeled and feminine, the skin glowing with pale gold undertones, the nose exquisitely dainty. A musk-rose flush, more appealing than the color Zelenka had applied to her own skin, adorned the boy's high cheekbones and deepened as the master continued to speak—

Zelenka's mouth dropped open. By all the saints, this squire was no boy! A girl stood before them, a young woman clothed in a man's tunic and leggings, her red hair cropped short, but a woman nonetheless. Could none of the others see it?

Zelenka twisted her head and gaped at her dining companions. Lord John was conversing with the lad in an offhand manner, the hungry chaplain had given his full attention to his trencher, and Master Hus seemed to be staring into heaven itself, his gaze distracted and focused on some distant calling.

Zelenka turned again to the disguised girl. The impostor's breath had quickened under her master's gaze, her cheeks colored in a still deeper hue, and her head had fallen so low that a shock of coppery hair hid her eyes. Why did she hide? And, more important, why did Lord John's attention make her blush?

Quickly Zelenka averted her own eyes, waiting until the squire routinely ladled a mess of pottage onto the trencher before her. Lord John might not have time for her today, but she would make this squire take time for her. This Kafka held a delightful mystery too irresistible to ignore. And where one found secrets, one usually found advantages.

Zelenka was determined to find and uncover them. Until she and Lord John were betrothed, no other woman, not even one in hiding, could be allowed to distract him from Zelenka's ambitions.

———

"You, squire." An hour after dinner, Zelenka ventured out into the courtyard where she found the squire called Kafka involved in a fencing match. The deceiver lowered her sword, then cast a questioning glance toward Zelenka. "Yes, *boy*, I am speaking to you," Zelenka called, gesturing for the girl to come forward. "Pray give me a moment of your time. Sheathe your sword and come at once."

The squire murmured a word of apology to her fencing partner, then stepped aside and approached. "Now," Zelenka commanded, lifting the hem of her gown as she began to walk. "Say nothing, but accompany me through the courtyard. I have a few questions to ask and would have you answer me truthfully."

The squire nodded wordlessly, and Zelenka lifted a brow, impressed with the girl's ability to bridle her tongue. What sort of creature was this? Intelligence was etched into this sensitive face, lightly flushed now with exertion, but the effect was not unbecoming. The blush upon that cheek now was like the flush of sunset on snow, a natural beauty any fool ought to recognize.

Zelenka took a deep breath, striving to keep her tone as natural and friendly as possible. "I have been visiting Chlum for many years, and I do not remember your face. How came you, squire, to be in the service of my Lord John?"

The girl stared for a moment at the ground. "A friend of my family once served Lord John's father. When my father died a few months ago, my guardian brought me here."

Zelenka smiled, slowly considering this information. "So you *are* new. Do you like this life?"

"Yes, very much."

"I see. Better than your old life?"

The girl lifted a shoulder in an elegant shrug. Zelenka laughed. "Come now, you may loosen your tongue with me! I see that the charmless Sir Novak is your master. Do you like him?"

"Yes." There was no hesitation in her answer. Though Zelenka did not see how any woman could like the surly knight, apparently the girl spoke the truth. But Novak was not Zelenka's chief concern.

"What of the nobleman you serve?" she whispered softly, her eyes narrowing. "What think you of Lord John?"

The girl stopped abruptly and looked up, her green eyes wide and frightened. Zelenka smiled with warm spontaneity. "Come now, boy, don't think I intend to spy out your loyalty! I ask only because you are new here, and . . ." she lifted her chin and assumed all the dignity she could muster, "because it is very likely that I shall become your mistress within a few months."

Was that a flicker of pain in the girl's eyes?

"Yes, in truth," Zelenka went on, keeping her voice light as she began to walk again. "I shall be your mistress, and I would like to have the love of all the knights who serve my lord. So if you intend to remain and take vows of loyalty to Lord John, I will want your loyalty as well."

She stopped on the path and turned, staring directly into the false squire's eyes. "I want to know," she went on, her eyes blazing into the other girl's, "that I can count on you. All who love Lord John must love me as well. And if you cannot vow fealty to both the master and mistress, perhaps you should reconsider your decision to remain here."

The girl's lids slipped down over her eyes, and she turned, her hands twisting at her waist. "Of course you have my loyalty." She spoke slowly in her falsely deep voice, as if she were carefully rehearsing each word before pronouncing it. "As God is my witness, if the master marries, I will serve whomever he takes as his wife. You need not fear disloyalty from me."

"Very well," Zelenka answered. "Thank you for your company, Squire Kafka. I am sure we shall talk again." She inclined her head in a deep bow as the pretender hurried away, then murmured, "Either Lord John or I will talk to you again very soon."

Sixteen

"Hitherto I have preached in towns and marketplaces," Jan Hus announced as the guests gathered at John's small supper table that night. "Now I shall preach behind hedges, in villages, castles, fields, and woods, wherever there is opportunity. There is a little lime tree near Kozi which will make a delightful pulpit."

With a nod of his head, John motioned the preacher to the chair beside him. "We shall begin as soon as we are certain of your safety." He gave his enthusiastic guest a reassuring smile. "But you cannot go venturing off into the woods until we are certain the Romanists have not set traps."

"I do not fear what man may do to me," Hus answered, the light of conviction filling his brown eyes. "Our Lord preached along the waysides and hillsides of Palestine, and I shall do the same along the Pyrenees Mountains."

John was about to reply when a movement at the door caught his eye.

"Master." A guard bowed deeply. "There is a messenger outside who bears a letter from Jerome of Prague. He says the message carries important news for both you and Master Hus."

John looked at his supper companions. Only Hus, Vasek, and Novak were present at the table, and he was confident all three could be trusted. He nodded to the guard. "By all means, bring him in." He gestured to Kafka, who stood along the wall with Lev and Svec, waiting to be put to service. "Kafka, you read so well. Since the news concerns two of us, would you read so we may hear it at the same time?"

The sensitive squire stepped forward with embarrassed dignity, then bowed and hurried to receive the letter. Once he had taken it from the guard and broken the seal, he moved to stand under one of the rush lamps on the wall. In a hushed, muffled voice, the boy began.

"To Lord John, Earl of Chlum, and Master Jan Hus, greetings," he read in his strangely soft voice. "Grace and peace be with you all on this most sorrowful of occasions. It grieves my heart to tell you that during services yesterday, one of the devil's own attended our service and rushed the pulpit before I had finished speaking. The Lord graciously preserved my life; however, for our mutual friend, Sir Petrov of Prague—"

Kafka stopped, his eyes darting over the page, his face pale in the glow of the rush light.

"Continue," John urged. "Why do you stop?" He shot the squire a penetrating look, then remembered. Kafka had been close to Petrov; grief and shock had undoubtedly caused the words to wedge in the young man's throat.

"Sir Petrov of Prague, lately a bookseller—" the boy's voice dropped to a suffocated whisper—"stood forward and bore in his body the blade intended for me. It was by the grace of God that Sir Petrov felled the murderous priest before dying upon the altar himself."

"Terrible news," John murmured, stealing a quick glance at his startled dinner guests. Jan Hus said nothing but stared at the squire, a look of stunned surprise on his face. John turned back to Kafka. "Is there anything more, squire?"

Clearly upset, the boy lifted the parchment with trembling hands. "It is not my intent to alarm either of you, my friends," he read, his voice fragile and shaking, "but you should know that our enemies have grown in boldness and insolence. Last night, in retribution, a group of cowards burned the bookseller's shop where the knight had kept a collection of Bibles and books for rental."

Though tears gathered in the corners of Kafka's eyes and slowly spilled from his long lashes, he kept reading. "Included, I regret, were several of your own books, Master Hus. The perpetrators of this act cried 'Death to the Hussites' as they laid on their torches."

The squire paused again, swallowing thickly. John let the silence stretch, knowing the boy would continue when he was able.

"I am writing not only to tell you about the demise of our godly friend but to warn you, Master Hus and Lord John, that our enemies are not satisfied with your departure from Prague. Take care, my friends. Be cautious. And remain at peace, knowing as I do that God will preserve you to accomplish his will."

Kafka stared at the message for a moment more, then dropped his arms to his side. "It is signed, 'Jerome,'" he said flatly. His expression was pained; the old knight's death must have wounded him deeply.

John turned his eyes away, strangely moved by the boy's sorrow. He himself had tasted heartbreak and not so many years ago . . . but all men had to face grief at one time or another. Novak should tell his charge that a man will never know his own strength until he has grappled with adversity.

"I am sorry to hear this," Novak said, breaking the silence. "But my knights are well trained, Master Hus. Do not fear; we will not let you come to harm."

"Perhaps tomorrow's journey should be postponed," Vasek interjected. "Why teach the holy truths of God under a cloud? People may flock to hear an outcast bold enough to defy the edict of excommunication, but do you want to lure them with the bait of sensationalism? Should they not be drawn instead by the sweet urgings of the Holy Spirit? Though I know you regret this most foul murder, notoriety will surely draw the crowds."

John frowned at his chaplain. "Notoriety may draw them, but it will not convict them," he said flatly. "If they heed the message of Jan Hus, it is because the power of God lies behind his teachings. And he is no outcast; his blameless life shames his persecutors. The fact that they cannot prove his wrongdoing gives lie to the interdict and their decree of excommunication. How can they justify their persecution of a man who has done no wrong? He is blameless in his teaching and willing to be corrected if fault can be found—"

"Friends!" Hus interrupted by holding up his hands. "I appreciate your spirited defense of me, John, but I am unworthy of it. I am as much a sinner as the vilest man on earth, but the grace of God has brought me to salvation. And it is this salvation that I must preach to those who are captive." An almost imperceptible expression of pleading shone from his eyes. "I would like to begin on the morrow."

"In a few days." John transferred his gaze to Novak. "When we know the roads are safe. I have men going out now, searching to be sure there are no strangers waiting at the inns in the area. And we will send a full complement of knights, to be certain there are no knaves waiting with mischievous daggers."

"In a few days, then," Hus agreed, his eyes gentle. "Whatever you say, my friend."

Anika slipped out of the lord's chamber and flattened herself against the stone of the hallway. The tears that filled her eyes now were not like those that had blinded her as she tried to read Jerome's letter. Those tears for Petrov were hot; they burned. These were silent and steady, and all they did was remind her that her only link with the past, with her *life,* had been obliterated—by a priest. One of Hus's enemies, one of those corrupt, misguided clerics who cared more for power and position than the truth of the Scriptures.

She needed to be alone with her thoughts. With a choking cry she tore herself away from the solidity of the stone wall and hurried into the stairwell, leaping over the slanting steps until she reached the silent upstairs chapel. A shaft of light from the fading sun angled down from one of the windows, trapping slow convections of dust in the space above the altar.

Anika stared at the dust, her memory flitting back to a night when fine black ashes, backlit by a raging fire, had fluttered down upon her face. The voice of the innkeeper's wife, thick and clotted, echoed in some distant compartment of her mind: *"The Roman* church and her meddling priests will be the death of us all. Don't you ever forget it, you hear?"

The old woman was right. The corruption of certain leaders in Rome had reached out to take yet another innocent life. Petrov had no business dying in church, in a sanctuary. She moved toward the altar. What on earth had possessed him? Why had he stepped forward? His time of glory had passed; Petrov should have been content to spend the rest of his days renting books and telling stories of chivalry and the crusades.

But even as she raised her questions, she realized the answers. Petrov was a sworn knight, faithful and true. No power in the world could have stopped him from using his sword in the defense of a holy man of God.

She had been living with knights for nearly five months; she had come to understand the holy pride and passion fueling their endeavors. Petrov's light had gone out of the world, but he had shared his light with her, even placing her as a squire, a knight-in-training.

She caught her breath as an idea formed in her mind. Why couldn't she continue at Chlum and actually become a knight? Nothing remained for her in Prague, no bookshop, no friends, no family. She felt more at home in the garrison at Chlum than she would in any other place. With the stern-faced Novak standing guard as her mentor, no one would dare harass her. And under Novak's tutelage she just might master the skills required of a knight. If God would give her strength, she could meet any challenge, and she would do anything to protect Jan Hus and avenge Petrov.

Anika fell to her knees at the front of the chapel and rested her forehead against the altar. "Father God, forgive me for being distracted," she whispered, anger and alarm rippling along her spine as she clutched the edge of the altar table. "I thought more about my master and my safety than in finding vengeance for those I love. Now Sir Petrov is a knight no more, so I shall take his place. And he shall be avenged. My father shall be avenged. My mother shall be avenged. And I will do all I can to defend Master Hus."

She fumbled at her waist for a moment, then unsheathed Petrov's silver sword. Holding the hilt, she lifted the point of the blade toward heaven. "As You, God, are my Lord and King, I swear I shall do everything in my power to grow strong enough to strike a blow against the evil churchmen who have spawned this murderous corruption. I take a holy oath before you, Lord. Give me strength. Give me skill. Give me courage."

Silence sifted down like a snowfall, but Anika knew God had heard her vow.

Zelenka sighed with exasperation. She had been waiting outside Lord John's chamber long enough to recite four "Our Fathers." The men lingered over supper far longer than usual, but in the past five minutes servants had carried out the empty bowls and a guard had escorted Master Hus to his chamber. In a moment she would be able to steal Lord John's attention—

She smiled as his long, lean form finally filled the doorway. "Lord John."

"Yes, Lady Zelenka?" His eyes seemed burdened with some troubling concern, but he broke into an open friendly smile at the sight of her. Zelenka folded her hands, congratulating herself on another small victory. "My lord, if I might borrow your ear for a moment—"

"I am sorry," he interrupted, leaning against the doorframe. "I know the routine here must bore you. I suppose you expected parties in this season of merriment, but we are so caught up with Master Hus—"

"I am not bored."

A wry but indulgent glint appeared in his eyes. "I suppose you will be wanting me to send you home on the morrow. I don't blame you. Now that Hus has left Prague, gaiety can return to the city. And you, dear child, are the gayest of them all. I hate to see you marooned out here away from all your young friends."

"I can be merry anywhere," she answered, trying to still the wild pounding of her heart. The man was perceptive; surely he knew why she sought his company. "And I would not leave you so soon, especially not now."

"Not now?" He quirked his eyebrow teasingly. "Why not now, pray tell. Is there some suitor in Prague you are seeking to escape? Is that why you have hidden yourself out here?"

"Nothing in Prague concerns me a whit," she answered, looking down at her hands. "Just you . . . and your household, of course. In the faint hope that I might be of some service to you, I have been trying to learn about your estate. Demetr runs an orderly household, but he does not know everything. In my endeavors I have discovered—" She lifted her hands in a helpless shrug. "I scarcely know where to begin. You are being deceived, my lord."

"Deceived? How so?" His smile faded slightly, but still he looked at her as if she were ten years old.

She felt a lurch of excitement within her as she boldly met his gaze. "A trickster has infiltrated your household. I am not certain, but I wonder if the pretender could be a spy for your enemies, which, I understand, are legion."

Zelenka rejoiced when his jaw muscle clenched angrily. Finally she had managed to pierce that complacency and indifference! "Surely you are mistaken." His eyes became somber again. "My people are loyal."

"But this one, I fear," she looked down, idly smoothing her fingernails with her thumb, "has escaped your suspicion. For who would suspect a mere squire of being a spy?"

"A squire?" He pulled back his shoulders and lifted his granite chin. "Which squire could you mean? There is only one new boy, Kafka, and he came directly from my father's old captain of the guard. And since he has come, he has done nothing amiss."

She leaned forward, every curve of her body speaking defiance. "His very presence here is a lie, a pretense. For the one you call Kafka is no boy." She paused, watching her words take hold. "Kafka is a girl."

Intense astonishment touched his face. "A girl?" he repeated dully, a grayish pallor blooming beneath his skin.

She parted her lips in a secretive smile. "A woman, in fact."

"Impossible! Such a thing would be impossible to hide. I would have seen the truth!"

"Perhaps, my lord," she remarked, pleased at how nonchalant she sounded, "we see only what we want to see."

Her words were playful, but he understood that her meaning was not. Two deep lines of worry appeared between Lord John's dark eyes. "How do you know this?"

"My lord," Zelenka let the words roll slowly off her tongue, "just as you can spot a hip-splayed hound from forty paces, so one woman can recognize another. One has but to look at her with open eyes. The truth is written there for anyone willing to see it."

He did not dispute her but leaned back against the wall, staring into space. "Why would a girl spy on us?" he finally murmured, more to himself than to Zelenka. "If he—she—was sent to harm Master Hus, she has had opportunity already, and yet she has done nothing."

"Yet Kafka has volunteered to ride with you on the preacher's excursions, has she not?" Zelenka let the question fall into the silence. "And who can say what opportunities this false squire will have in the days to come?"

"Kafka *is* exceedingly well versed for a squire," John murmured again, still staring into space. He turned slowly until his gaze met Zelenka's. "I ought to have suspected something. How many squires enter a castle speaking four languages? She must have come from a noble family, but what father would send his daughter on such a dangerous mission? If she were discovered by the knights in the garrison—"

His voice trailed off as he turned his eyes away, and Zelenka knew he had stumbled onto a subject not fit for a gentlewoman's ears. She stepped back, disappointed. This was not the reaction she had hoped for. He was expressing compassion and wonder, while she had expected anger and hostility.

"My lord, whatever her reasons, you should dismiss her at once," she said, daring to reach out and place a hand on his arm. "And you should consider the possibility that your man Novak knows about this spy, as well. Is Kafka not Novak's shadow night and day? If so, surely your captain knows. And if he knows, he has deceived you, his sworn master. Far be it from me to advise you, but perhaps Kafka and Novak should both be sent away."

"Thank you, Lady Zelenka," Lord John said, his hand abruptly falling over hers. She thrilled to his touch, but when she lifted her gaze, she found no trace of warmth in his eyes. "Thank you," he repeated, firmly lifting her hand from his arm. "But I should consider the matter and lift my thoughts in prayer before taking any action. You must excuse me now."

Without a further word, he turned and left her alone in the empty hallway.

John was not surprised when Lady Zelenka decided to return home the next day. After sending Demetr to convey best wishes for a safe journey and a merry St. Nicholas's Day, John watched from the balcony of his chamber as the chariot and armed escort trotted through the barbican and down the road that would return Lady Zelenka to her father's estate. The poor girl would make someone a fine wife, but she had cast her bread upon the waters one time too many at Chlum Castle. John wasn't certain why she had been so intent upon pursuing *him*, but she had shown stubborn persistence and resolute strength of character.

And, in a strange way, Zelenka may have been useful. He pulled his eyes from the departing carriage and looked toward the circle where a group of squires and knights were training for an upcoming Christmas tournament. Novak stood outside the ring, his hands on his broad hips, a scowl upon his bearded face. Before the grizzled knight, in the ring, Kafka and Lev circled one another, blunt wooden swords in their right hands, unlit lanterns in their left.

In a surge of interest, John leaned forward upon the balcony railing. If Lady Zelenka spoke truly, his son was dueling with a girl. Surely Lev would have noticed something.

"En garde!" Novak called, and the two squires assumed their positions: lanterns held up in back, right hands pointing the blunted swords toward the opponent's chin.

John crossed his arms and squinted toward the dueling pair. He had spent many sleepless hours considering Zelenka's charge and had decided to investigate himself before confronting either Novak or Kafka about the lady's supposition. He suspected Zelenka's story was a lie born out of a vindictive desire to strike at Novak.

Was the squire in the courtyard below a woman? Surely not. With an adventurous toss of his head, Kafka urged Lev to lunge, then swiftly parried the blow. The dubious squire moved with a quick agility unlike that of the other boys, but his quickness was off-set by a lack of power.

John lowered his chin into his hand and frowned. In the belted robe that swirled around Kafka's slender legs, John thought he could discern the hourglass shape of a tiny waist and wider hips. That full-ness around the bosom could easily be explained by padding and ar-mor, but Kafka's figure was certainly more rounded than Lev's. But then again, the youth was older.

Squire Kafka lunged and leaped back, twirled and parried a blow, then moved a second too late. Lev's sword struck Kafka's padded jacket.

"Score one for Lev!" Novak roared.

John pressed his fingers over his lips, still watching and wonder-ing. Kafka turned toward him, and beneath the ridiculously boyish haircut John saw an oval face with a daintily pointed chin, wind-whipped color in the cheeks, and sweetly curled lips of soft pink. At another cry from Novak the duel began again, and this time Kafka rushed forward with surprising aggressiveness, startling Lev. Kafka's sword struck home, winning the point.

"One for Kafka!" Novak roared. Delighted, the squire threw back his head and let out a great peal of girlish laughter.

The truth crashed into John's consciousness like surf hurling against a rocky cliff. This Kafka was no pre-adolescent boy. Zelenka spoke truly—this squire was a woman.

John stood as still as stone as the shock of discovery hit him.

During the night he had been able to convince himself that the spoiled Zelenka hated Novak and his charge enough to mistake a gentle and sensitive boy for a girl, thus casting doubt upon the knight's loyalty. But this was not of Zelenka's doing.

Kafka's voice floated up to him from the courtyard. "Sir Novak, do not leave us! Another round, please!"

That voice would *never* deepen.

How could they have been so easily deceived? And why would Petrov, who had proved his righteous character even in his death, attempt to deceive his former master's household? During the months Kafka—or whatever her true name was—had been at Chlum, she had conducted herself wisely and with great discretion. John was reasonably certain no one else knew her secret. Even Demetr, who saw and knew everything, had been thoroughly duped.

We see only what we want to see.

Pensively John stared across the courtyard to the horizon, where a gray winter haze veiled the sun. Could the girl have been planted by Hus's enemies? It did not seem likely. Her guardian had died in Hus's cause. The girl had journeyed with Novak to escort Hus from Prague, so if she had meant him harm, she could have already committed it. And when Kafka spoke of Hus the night John found the squire by the pool, her eyes had shone with admiration and conviction. Traitors did not wear such faithful faces.

So why was she here?

John's mind reeled with uncertainties, but quick questions needed slow and thoughtful answers. Straightening himself, he returned to his chamber, determined to wait . . . and watch.

Lord John of Chlum

Seventeen

For the remainder of November and most of December, John carefully negotiated a fine line between wariness and indulgence. Jan Hus was eager to carry the gospel into the countryside, but John preferred to err on the side of caution. He did not want Novak to lead Hus into the villages until the way was safe, and he could not guarantee the preacher's safety until he had determined the sources of danger.

A few enemies were obvious. Churches affiliated with Archbishop Albik openly opposed Hus, placarding him on their church posts and condemning him from their pulpits. Any priest who wished to advance in Rome's ecclesiastical hierarchy stood firmly against Hus, for how could a man advance in the church if he had set himself apart from it?

King Wenceslas, though a friend to Hus, could not openly support the preacher for fear of upsetting the delicate balance of power in his kingdom. A number of teachers at the university who had once firmly aligned themselves with Hus had gone over to the other camp as soon as it became clear that Hus intended to defy the pope's summons to Rome. And though many noblemen privately agreed with Hus, most were silent on the subject of his support, self-consciously protecting their inherited influence and positions. They were not willing to risk war, or even censure, by supporting the wrong side of a political and theological controversy, and so they kept their opinions to themselves.

John knew that differing opinions could be found even in his own household. His chaplain, Vasek, did not agree with Hus's actions. Though John suspected that Vasek might actually agree with Master Hus's theology if the two would only sit down and rationally discuss their beliefs, the older man was scandalized by the trouble Hus had attracted in Prague. Vasek wanted nothing to do with the crusades into the countryside. He spoke little when Hus sat at John's dinner table, and he did not invite the preacher to offer mass in the castle chapel. When the two happened to meet in the hallway, Vasek often stared right through his fellow priest, his face revealing no more recognition than if Master Hus had been thin air.

But at least Vasek was predictable. The masquerading squire, on the other hand, was an unknown and dangerous risk. Under the guise of spreading Christmas cheer, John had sent runners into Prague and the surrounding countryside to discover if one of his fellow noblemen had an unmarried daughter who had recently gone on a pilgrimage, but his scouts had returned with no news.

After trying on every conceivable explanation and finding none that fit, John was almost convinced that Hus himself had sent the girl to spy out John's loyalty. In a private moment at supper, John rested his elbows on the holiday table bedecked with holly, ivy, and evergreen, then turned to his friend. "Do you trust me, Jan?"

The preacher was momentarily speechless with surprise. "Trust you? Of course, John. Completely."

And so clear was Hus's countenance that John knew he spoke the truth. When the preacher smiled and asked what had possessed John to ask such a question, he merely shook his head. "Perhaps we both should be careful whom we trust," he said, his eyes following Kafka as she stood with a book at the front of the room, reading.

After the huge Christmas banquet, when the doors of the castle were thrown open to the villagers of Chlum, John decided to force the impostor's hand. Novak was the squire's mentor, and the burly captain could provide the perfect opportunity to unmask the girl and her motivations.

John waited until Christmas morning. During the gathering in which he dispensed his knights' annual gifts, he presented Novak with a stunning white stallion. Later, suspecting that his captain might be eager to ride out and put the animal through his paces, John suggested that he and Novak take a ride through the country-side.

"A ride, my lord?" Novak asked, shooting him a twisted smile. "Instead of a hunt? I thought you would want to give the dogs a run."

"Not today," John answered, heading down the circular staircase that led to the main hallway and then out to the courtyard. "I want to speak to you privately, and I fear these walls may have ears."

"Shall I bring a guard, my lord?"

John paused a moment. He might as well keep an eye on the girl, too. "No guard will be necessary, Sir Novak, but you may invite your squire. Lev and Svec would probably enjoy a ride on a morning as fine as this."

The day was an intriguing combination of a brisk wind and a warm sun. The snow had melted away, and a warming zephyr rushed up the hill as the riders' horses picked their way through the wet leaves and debris of winter. Lev, Svec, and Kafka led the way, the two younger boys whooping in youthful exuberance, Kafka following be-hind them in a slow and protective pace. The scenery passing by was dreary, but John felt his heart lift as he watched the three young people ahead of him. If Kafka was an enemy, she seemed a particu-larly agreeable one.

They reached a barren field of whispering gray chaff. As the squires set their mounts to thundering over the dried grass, John reined in his stallion and waited until Novak's mount halted at his side.

"Your squire rides well," he remarked idly, his eyes following the slender figure on the tall roan. "Kafka has more than distinguished himself in his time here. Surely it is time to consider knighting him."

Novak's bushy brows shot up in surprise. "Knight him? You think he is ready?"

John shrugged. "He rides well, he is light on his feet, and he can wield a sword as well as Lev."

"He is not strong." Novak pushed his lower lip forward in thought. "He never wins at wrestling, but he is so quick he has yet to be pinned." His smile deepened into laughter. "The other boys can hardly catch him."

"He is old enough," John went on, testing the depth of his captain's knowledge. "I would have thought him about sixteen, but upon that cheek I see no sign of whiskers yet."

"No." Novak frowned. "Neither do I."

"'Tis of no import. Bearded or not, we will need every knight we have to ride with Master Hus. There may be trouble we do not expect."

"Still—" Novak ran his hand through his hair in a detached motion. "I hate to disagree with you, my lord, but the boy is not . . . in the mold. There is something about him that does not feel right. I have wondered if he might not be better suited for the clergy than for knighthood, for he is soft-spoken and seems to have a heart for helping others."

John looked away, his lips trembling with a repressed smile. Novak had not seen the truth, either. He had sensed something, to be sure, but he was as blind to the squire's true gender as John had been. Whoever the girl was, she had fooled even her mentor. Perhaps such an accomplishment deserved a reward.

"I wish," he said, chuckling with a dry and cynical sound, "for your squire to become my man. Kafka is old enough. And his weaknesses will certainly come to light in the days ahead."

A muscle clenched along Novak's jaw, but he inclined his head in a formal salute. "As you wish, my lord," he said, pulling back on his reins. The stallion pranced in anxious anticipation, and Novak jerked his head toward the squires racing in the winter-dried field. "By your leave, my lord, I will go and give Kafka the news. He will need to prepare for his test."

"Tell him," John answered simply. Novak gave his stallion a kick and galloped away, but John remained behind, soothing his anxious mount with quiet clucking sounds. "Now we will see what happens," he murmured to no one in particular, "when the girl undergoes the test of manhood."

"A test?" Panic like Anika had never known before welled in her throat. Petrov had never said anything about a test; in all his glorious accounts there had been no reports of testing.

Novak nodded and rested his hands behind him on the cantle of his saddle. With an air of resignation he looked toward the horizon. "I told Lord John I didn't think you were ready, but he insisted that you are." Novak's tone was coolly disapproving. "You seem to have caught his eye, Kafka. Now you must live up to his expectations."

"I don't think I can," she whispered, her heart beating painfully in her chest. "Sir Novak, you must ask him to delay this test. I want to become a knight and fight in the cause, but I am not ready."

"Lord John thinks you are." The glitter in his half-closed eyes was now both possessive and slightly accusing. "And so you shall be. We shall train you today and tomorrow. Then you will take up the stones."

"The stones?"

"Aye. Each knight marks a stone with his emblem, and the stones are put into a helmet. The squire ready to be knighted must remove a stone and then joust with the knight whose stone he has drawn. If he is felled from his horse during the joust, he must then face his adversary in hand-to-hand fighting with whatever weapons he still carries. The fight is not to the death but to the victory. The test ends when one knight concedes."

Anika's mind raced through the faces and forms of the proud knights in Lord John's garrison. She had spent most of her time training with Lev, Svec, and Novak; she had never even *dreamed* of facing one of the other knights in a duel. They were *men,* walking tree trunks with brawny arms and thirty-pound lances. She had watched them hack at wooden stumps for hours on end without wearying. Their arms were iron; hers were noodles. Though she had practiced swordplay with Novak, he was her teacher, and she always suspected that he had restrained his strength when dueling with her. Clearly he was not in favor of her undergoing this test now.

He didn't know she could never win a competition against one of the other knights. Not in ten thousand years, not with constant practice. She would never grow muscles like theirs; she would never have a man's stamina.

"What if I refuse to take this test?" She stared at Novak with wide eyes. "Will I be sent away?"

"Yes. The test is designed to measure your courage as well as your strength," Novak answered, his eyes cold and proud. "If you cannot face your comrade, you cannot face an enemy. There is no shame in failure—a squire can always be tested again. But a coward who refuses to undergo his test has no place at Chlum Castle."

She looked away, rounding up her scattered emotions. He was right, of course. The idea of a test was rational and clever. It kept ill-prepared youths from doing dangerous men's work. But it might also keep her from fulfilling her vow of vengeance.

She bit her thumbnail, thinking. By desperate and quick evasion she had managed to thwart those who would pin her in the wrestling matches. She had won many a duel because she *thought* before she struck. And she regularly beat the other squires and even a few of the knights in the verbal gymnastics that passed for entertainment after dinner.

A strange numbed comfort calmed her fears. She might not be able to pass a test through conventional means, but there were always unconventional opportunities. And she had sworn to become a knight. If this was the door God had opened, she would have to walk through it.

Imposing an iron control on herself, she looked her teacher in the eye. "I will be ready," she said, girding herself with resolve. "Teach me whatever tricks you have to teach, Sir Novak, and then pray that I will do my best. For I would not shame you or Lord John in my quest to become a knight of Chlum Castle."

"Good for you," he answered simply, his eyes brightening with pleasure.

"Your armor," Novak told her the next day as he helped fasten the brass buckles which linked one molded piece to another, "will prove to be a mixed blessing. Always remember that it can prevent you from doing damage as much as from being damaged."

"I have always heard," Anika answered, holding her arm out so Novak could fit the guard of vambrace over her elbow, "that the chief danger in battle is being trampled or smothered if unhorsed." She laughed. "So I have decided to tie myself to my stallion, so I will not fall off."

"Do not laugh, my young friend," Novak answered roughly, dropping her arm. It clanked against the brass plates that covered her chest and abdomen. "I almost think it is better to wear only a suit of mail than all these armored plates. I have heard of many a wounded man who had to be carried into the garrison and carved out of his harness before being put to bed."

"Then why am I wearing all this?" she asked, stiffly turning to face him. "Why am I trussed up like a banquet-table turkey?"

"Because even in a practice exercise when the blunted arms of courtesy are used," Novak said, lifting her heavy, open-faced helmet, or basinet, "a knight can be killed. A headless spear can pierce a suit of mail; a blunted sword can break a bone. You will wear this armor, Kafka, and be grateful for it."

Anika stifled her protests and accepted the helmet, knowing it was no use to argue with a man as set in his ways as Novak. In many respects he had been a blessing to her. Like Petrov, Novak clung to the old ideals. Bravery, loyalty, and faithfulness to God meant far more to him than financial rewards and political power.

But his rigidity and traditionalism could prove to be her undoing. She had already stopped and corrected herself a thousand times in his presence, adjusting her speech, her mannerisms, the way she talked and moved and sighed. Certainly he would have no patience or understanding for a woman who had dared to cross the threshold of the knights' garrison. Though he seemed to respect her as a student, she feared he would feel nothing but contempt for her as a woman.

But today her secret lay closer to the surface than ever. She'd begun the cycle of her monthly bleeding and had been having cramps since morning. She had stoically denied the pain and discomfort, turning away so he would not read the worry and annoyance in her eyes. At least once an hour she excused herself to go to the lavatory, where she covered fresh straw in a long strip of cloth. A narrow band of leather around her waist held the straw and cloth in place, yet she worried that Novak might yet guess her secret. Once bound up in her armor she could barely move, much less attend to her feminine needs. And his presence, as he hovered near to attach her armor, was nerve-racking.

"We shall not practice the actual joust today," Novak said, eyeing her critically as he stepped back to survey his work. The armor he had put on her was the smallest to be found in the castle, and still she felt like a child parading in her father's clothes. "But I want you to get used to the armor's weight." He moved toward the door and pushed it open, letting a stream of crystal cold air into the chamber. "Come, let's go outside and attempt a bit of swordplay. You must learn to move in the armor as the grasshopper moves in his hard shell, to accept it as your second skin."

"No grasshopper ever carried a shell this heavy," Anika grumbled, slowly clanking her way out of the garrison. The helmet under her arm weighed ten pounds alone, and the breastplate was at least that heavy. Added to the vambraces for her arms, the gauntlets on her hands, the fauld and culet which covered her abdomen and hindquarters, and the heavy mail shirt underneath it all, and Anika had easily doubled her weight.

How was she supposed to fight encumbered like this? She could barely move. Only one thought gave her the courage to keep moving. In her fencing trials with her fellow squires, she had learned that her chief advantage lay in a rapid and aggressive advance. She had not won every contest, but she had always scored the first point. The other squires now knew her approach, but none of the other knights would expect so small an opponent to come at them without warning.

"Are you ready, then?" Wearing his armor as comfortably as an old slipper, Novak picked up his blunted sword and moved to stand across from her.

"One moment." Anika unceremoniously dropped her sword to the dusty ground, then lifted the heavy helmet and lowered it onto her head.

She felt as if the world had suddenly gone silent and dark. The conical helmet completely enclosed the sides of her face and neck, leaving only a T-shaped opening. Her eyes peered through the horizontal bar of the "T", while the two-inch vertical opening ran from the bottom of her eyes to her chin, allowing her to breathe . . . and pray.

Holy God, if you would see me through this . . .

She lowered her bulky arms and turned to face Novak.

"Your sword," he said, flicking his own blade toward her impatiently. "You cannot fight without a weapon, Kafka."

She bent forward, careful not to let gravity pull her off balance, until her heavily meshed hands finally found the hilt of her sword. She had chosen to fight with her own lightweight weapon instead of a blunted blade, and Novak had voiced no objection. He was probably certain she would not do him any harm.

She gripped the silver sword in her right hand and placed her left hand up behind her, bending her knees until she found her center of gravity. In her heavy hauberk and armor, she felt ponderous and lifeless, barely able to move.

Anika bounced on her legs, testing their strength under this additional weight. Though she had been practicing in her coat of mail for weeks, she had never worn full armor until today. The unexpected lunge forward was her best move, and Novak knew it, but she was not sure she could manage a lunge in this clattering collection of metal.

Novak peered at her down the length of his blade and began circling slowly. "Ready," he said, his eyes snapping with challenge. As confident as a terrier, he wore no helmet at all, only his hauberk, a breastplate, and gauntlets, the least a knight could wear and still feel properly protected.

She lifted her sword and drew the handle in close to her breast, matching Novak's movements around the circle, knowing he would not make the first move. This practice session was intended to ready her for her final test, the coming day when she would prove to all of Chlum Castle and the unseen heavenly host that she was capable of fighting for God, that she could strike a blow against those who had killed her parents and Petrov, those who would take God's truth and subvert it, turning it into a lie.

Lord John's two mastiffs ran by, woofing at some imagined danger, and Novak's eyes flicked toward the dogs. Seizing the moment, Anika lunged forward, straining with all her might, aiming her blade toward the spot where his breastplate should have joined the gardbrace, the vulnerable spot over his heart.

With one sure stroke, Novak parried the blow and stepped away. With another blow his weapon caught her sword and sent it whirling end over end, out of reach. And then, like the trained warrior he was, he reflexively stuck out his foot and tripped her, sending her sprawling in the dirt.

Facedown in the courtyard, Anika tasted defeat and dust in the same moment. She felt like a turtle kicked over a cliff—sore, jostled, and very, very heavy. She tried to push herself up, but a rivet on the gauntlet of her right hand had tangled itself in her hauberk, effectively hobbling her.

"Get up, you imbecile!" Novak's voice hardened ruthlessly. "Do you think you are fit for the test? For knighthood? I will shame you into readiness; rise up and come at me again!"

"I can't," she whispered, her voice breaking miserably.

"Never say 'can't'!" Novak continued to roar, his voice turning every head within earshot. Anika gritted her teeth, understanding his intention. He wanted to rouse her fighting spirit, to prod her into rising, to whip her into a determined frenzy so she could prove to *herself* that she had learned her lessons.

He couldn't know that her motivations ran far deeper than a need to prove herself. But at the moment she had no fight in her soul, nothing but a vast heaviness and a dull, persistent ache in her belly. The shock of defeat held her immobile, and though she knew this one fall was nothing to be ashamed of, a sensation of sickness and desolation swept over her.

What was wrong with her? Why was she suddenly exhausted, drained of all will and thought?

Novak came to her rescue before she could humiliate herself with weeping.

"Get up when I command you," he whispered in a gruff voice, lifting her by the shoulders as if she weighed no more than a sack of feathers. He pulled her up and spun her around until she gazed into his eyes. In his expression she saw anger, but also hurt, disappointment, and something that looked like bewilderment.

Wrenching out of his grasp, Anika staggered forward on heavy feet and ran toward the shadowed safety of the stable, freeing her hands from the confining gauntlets, then shedding other scraps of armor along the way. She ran past the startled grooms, then fell into a hay bed in an empty stall. The sweetly mingled scents of horses, manure, oats, and hay comforted her as her eyes welled with hurt and her fingers trembled as she fumbled with the buckles and clasps that linked the remaining pieces of her armor together.

She would have to take it all off and leave it with Novak. Then she'd have to leave the garrison and throw herself upon Lord John's mercy.

Why had she ever been so foolish? Serving in Lord Laco's house couldn't be this humiliating or painful.

"God save you, boy, why didn't you tell me you were hurt?"

Anika looked up, startled, and saw Novak standing over her, his dark eyes brimming with compassion. "There's no shame in being cut, even if by a piece of your own armor. Did one of the edges slip and pierce your hauberk?"

Her mind spun with bewilderment. "What?"

"You are hurt." The knight crouched before her in the straw, his eyes bemused. "Everyone is cut sooner or later, boy, but a knight gets up and keeps going. So show me your wound and I'll dress it."

"My wound?" She fought to control her swirling emotions.

Though her body was numb with weariness, she had felt no cut. The tiny hairs at the back of her neck rose with premonition.

"I saw the blood on the ground where you fell, boy, and I see it now on the straw where you sit. And a man does not bleed unless he is—"

"A woman," she responded sharply, abandoning all pretense. Her charade was over. Some things even a woman's wit and cleverness could not conceal.

Eighteen

Novak halted, shocked. Surely his ears had deceived him. The boy could not have surprised him more if he had claimed to be emperor of the world.

"I am a woman," Kafka repeated, her tear-filled eyes shifting like stars above. A tremor passed over her face, and a sudden spasm of grief knit her brows. "And I am sorry, Sir Novak."

Novak fell back into the hay, too startled for words. Surely such a thing was impossible. He, Novak, could not be wrong, and he knew the lad for a slight but sturdy boy of sixteen, one who was about to be sworn into service for Lord John and Chlum Castle.

"I am Anika, the daughter of Ernan O'Connor," Kafka was saying, an aura of melancholy radiating from the pale and delicate features like some dark nebula. "After my father was killed by Lord Laco's knights, Sir Petrov took me into his care. He had told me stories of knighthood since my childhood days, and so we thought it best that I go into hiding here." The squire gulped hard, hot tears slipping down his—*her*—cheeks. "Lord Laco was intent on having me for his son, you see, and I had no defender save Sir Petrov. And I have always wanted to know how to fight, for someday, somehow, I will take vengeance upon the evil churchman who killed my mother."

Still speechless, Novak leaned back upon the wooden wall. He closed his eyes, rubbed them, and opened them again, expecting to find a different squire before him, one somewhat altered from the boy he had trained. But Kafka sat there, unchanged, with the same delicate features, the same sad smile.

A girl. A female. A young woman.

Novak shook his head, slowly weighing the structure of events that had brought him and his squire together. Had he missed some clue along the way? Some bold suggestion, some hint, some giveaway word or deed? He could not recall anything. Either the girl was an extremely careful deceiver, or Novak had completely lost touch with his senses.

"You are a liar, then." He glared at the girl with burning, reproachful eyes. "You have lied to the master, to me, and to every man in the garrison. We ought to turn you out of the castle gate clad only in a chemise, for you have disgraced your own sex and the calling of knighthood."

"No." Somehow the sound of tears in her voice stunned him. "I never lied. Sir Petrov and I were careful not to speak any untruth. Never did he introduce me as a boy. He only said I was the *child* of a friend, not the son."

"Kafka is a man's name."

"The word means 'little bird.' It was my father's pet name for me."

A hot tear rolled down her cheek, and Novak looked away. Tears were the gelding weapons of women. She wanted him to pity her— and what else?

"The other knights will be furious." He crossed and then uncrossed his legs. "You have heard things not fit for a woman's ears."

"If the things I heard were not fit for a woman's ears, why are they fit for anyone at all?" she demanded, a flash of temper sparking through her tears. "I have done nothing to disgrace the knights at this castle. I have worked hard, harder than the lot of them, to prove myself. You have to admit that, Sir Novak!"

She threw the words at him like stones, and something in her attitude tempered his anger with amusement. By all the saints, what a knight this one would have made if she were a man! The heart of a lion resided in that small frame, and the persistence of a mosquito.

But she was female, and females had no place in a garrison. They belonged in the castle or the kitchen, or in the merchant shops or a convent.

"This sorts not," he finally said, gathering his thoughts. "You cannot remain here." He lowered his voice, fearing that others might hear. "Consider now, my girl, what might become of you if you were to persist in this! Why will you not consider a life in trade or tutoring? You have been well educated. But you cannot become a knight. Absolutely not."

"Why not?" She tossed her head and eyed him with cold triumph. "I have already become a squire."

"But not a knight. And you won't, for I'll not deceive my master. I won't lie to Lord John; I can't do that."

"I'm not asking you to lie to him." She crossed her legs and rested her arms on her bent knees, sighing. "But do you have to tell him what you have discovered? Why can't I go on as I am? There remains only my test—"

"You will be discovered. And if the master finds out that I have known, my loyalty will be called into question. And that—" he stiffened, "must never happen."

She sat in silence for a moment, her sea-green eyes darkening like angry thunderclouds. Novak marveled at her ability to sheathe her tears. "We cannot leave this place," she said finally, flushing to the roots of her fiery hair, "until we settle this."

"You are right," he agreed, casually picking up a piece of straw. He whirled it between his palms, then thrust it between his teeth. He had never liked women, but this girl, at least, had earned a measure of his respect. She was young and ignorant, though, so he might as well explain the facts of life.

"Your disguise is not good," he began. "Woman was made of Adam's flesh and bone, so she was made of more precious things than man, who was made of clay. Do you doubt me? There is proof. Man, made of clay, is more tranquil than woman, who is of bone, for bones are always rattling. If you take a man and woman and tell them to wash as well as they can, then take clean water and bid them wash again, which water bucket will be fouler? The man's, of course. For if you wash clay you make mud, and if you wash a bone, you make no such thing."

He looked at her, expecting some sign of acquiescence, but she only gave him a hostile glare. "If women are made of more precious things, then why are they expected to do all the work? Women travail in childbirth, they travail to suckle the child, to rear it, to wash and clean by day and night while the man goes singing on his way."

"So you hate women's work?"

"No!" Her jaw clenched as she rejected his words. "I liked keeping house for my father, but I enjoyed working for him far more. I was his scribe, a copyist, and I wanted nothing more than to write."

Stroking his beard, he regarded her carefully. "Then why can't you write for Lord John? He could put you to work as a scribe."

She shook her head, dismissing his idea. "I have a vow to fulfill before I will settle down to work for a man," she whispered, her voice choked with sincerity.

Novak paused, considering his situation. He could understand why an orphaned girl might hide from Lord Laco, for that nobleman's villainy and lecherous nature were well-known in Prague. And Sir Petrov had been a gentle and noble knight, so Novak couldn't fault her for thinking the garrison a comfortable and convenient refuge. But she simply couldn't continue as a knight, any more than Novak could become the Queen of Bohemia.

"Suppose you tell me why it is so all-important that you become a knight," he said, his voice cracking with weariness. "God made you a woman. Why can you not consider a role fit for women?"

"God gave me a mother and father, too, but evil men took them away," she snapped, the muscles in her face tightening into a mask of rage. "*Church men,* Novak. Cardinal D'Ailly was with Lord Laco when the order was given to kill my father. My mother died because a cardinal was too worried about his money purse to surrender a ladder to a woman trapped in a burning inn."

Novak slowly uncrossed his arms, taken aback by the fire in her gaze. She had been a determined squire, a tough opponent, but he had never seen this energy in her eyes. What other surprises lay inside her?

"Bohemia has its share of orphaned girls," he said quietly, stretching his long legs into the straw before him. "Yet none of the others have stooped to pick up a sword."

"None of them have Lord Laco searching for them, either," she said, tossing her head in disdain. "Becoming a squire seemed a useful and practical idea. Sir Petrov was dear to me, you see, and had filled my childhood days with stories of knights and lords and their ladies. He taught me how to hold a sword before I learned to write, and once I began to read, I devoured stories of the gallant knights of yesteryear—stories of men like you." The fringe of her lashes cast subtle shadows on her cheeks as she looked down at her hands. "I know it has never been done, Novak, but does that mean it cannot be done? Perhaps I can be of service to you and Lord John in the days ahead. I could spy for you in a woman's garb. I am small enough to slip through narrow openings, and I have learned to ride as well as any knight in your garrison. But please, do not make me leave Chlum. I have learned too much and come too far."

Her eyes, liquid pools of appeal, lifted to his, and Novak felt his heart constrict. 'Twas no wonder he hated women. He was helpless in their hands, and they knew it.

"I will keep your secret tonight," he answered, slowly pushing himself up from the ground. "But I cannot keep this truth from my master. Lord John must be told."

"Then promise me this, upon your honor as a knight." Across her pale and pointed face a dim flush raced like a fever. "Tell him *after* my testing. Give me the chance to prove myself."

"The test will change nothing." He leaned back, measuring her determination and her motives. "You will never be a man."

"But I will be a knight. And I will be sworn to serve Lord John." She straightened herself with dignity, a curious deep longing in her eyes. "You cannot begrudge me this desire, Sir Novak, since it is one you share."

She stood before him not as a mischievous impostor, but as a woman who had tested the depth of her commitment. In the light of her strength, Novak decided that she deserved a chance. Even though God had created her female, she was a fire eater, iron-willed and strong. History spoke of queens who donned armor and rode to battle with their armies—why couldn't a bookseller's daughter do the same?

"So be it," he said, holding up his hand. "You will undertake your test on the morrow. But if you pass the test, you must tell Lord John the truth before he administers the vows of fealty." Novak smiled as the fiery animation in her face dimmed. "Have faith, my squire. If you express yourself as eloquently before the master, it may be he will show mercy to you. But whatever you do, say your prayers and cleanse your heart. Your fate will be decided on the morrow."

Before she could weaken his resolve further, Novak turned and left her alone in the stable.

Seeking solitude, Novak climbed the winding tower staircase to the top of the castle walls, then spent the better part of an hour pacing along the ramparts, his hands behind his back, his head lowered in thought. Mixed feelings surged through him, emotions that grew more tangled and complex by the moment.

When Kafka had first revealed her deception, he had been angry enough to throw her to the wolves in the woods. Before he left her, however, he had not only agreed to keep her secret, but had promised to allow a mere slip of a woman to participate in a test that might result in her joining an exclusive and vaunted company of men—*his* men. It *was* true that several queens had worn armor and led armies into battle, but he had never heard of a queen taking the vows of knighthood. And though he had heard songs and poems extolling the valor of noblewomen who poured boiling oil over the heads of enemies who attempted to scale their castle walls, never had he heard of a woman who permeated the ranks of men in order to fight beside them.

His anger had evaporated, leaving only confusion. An inner voice reminded him that Kafka's ruse was a sin, probably a mortal one, for she had forsaken the role God had assigned her at birth. But she had never lied to him, Novak realized. In all his recollection, she had never claimed to be a man. She had given straight, simple answers to his queries about her background, and they had all rung with truth. And Sir Petrov had been her earliest teacher, and that aged knight had acquitted himself as honorably in his death as in life. For Petrov's sake alone, Novak thought he should give Kafka a chance.

But what if that chance resulted in the girl's death? She had failed miserably today in their practice duel. She was unused to wearing heavy armor, and a womanly frame would never fit into it properly. She had learned to ride well enough, but if her opponent unseated her and confronted her on the field, she might be wounded by even a blunted blow. Now, knowing the truth, Novak did not want to be responsible if she were hurt. Lord John would be furious when he discovered the ruse, and Novak would be disgraced for sending a helpless girl out onto the tourney field.

A helpless girl—by Saint Agnes above, that was a joke! Kafka—Anika—whatever her name, she would always be 'Kafka' to him—was anything but helpless. She had the courage of a bull, charging in where no woman had gone before.

A guard on the tower called a greeting, interrupting Novak's thoughts. The captain wordlessly lifted his hand to signal that all was well.

Maybe you should marry the girl and be done with it. The thought came from out of nowhere, stunning him with its clarity and incomprehensible logic. Marry her? An hour ago he'd wanted to fling her to the far side of the moon! But she had endeared herself to him as a boy, and surely she would prove to be a charming wife. She was of age, and maybe she could take satisfaction in knowing she was the wife of a knight instead of trying to fill out a suit of armor herself. Lord John would surely grant permission for Novak to marry and would likely give them a little house on the manor, much like the cozy cottage Demetr and his wife enjoyed.

Novak walked to the parapet and spread his palms over the

railing, enjoying the solid reality of the stone beneath his broad hands. He closed his eyes and studied the memory of Kafka's face, flushed with resolution and hope. Marry him? She wouldn't. She would be embarrassed at the suggestion, for he was old enough to be her father. She wanted to *carry* arms, not marry them, and that bright spirit would not go willingly into the dim and demure gowns of a married woman.

He sighed heavily, abandoning his foolish notion. There was only one thing he could do. He had promised to let her joust, but he could at least make certain of her opponent. Tomorrow when Kafka put her hand into the helmet and drew forth a stone, Novak would make sure the stone she drew was his.

———

As the first pale hint of sunrise touched the eastern sky, Anika awoke and braced herself for her day of testing. Novak had returned to the garrison late last night, and had self-consciously turned his back on her as he unbuckled his armor and removed his surcoat. He lay down to sleep in his shirt and rested in unnatural silence as she slipped into the straw beneath his bunk.

He was still snoring as she rose, visited the lavatory, then returned to slip her heavy hauberk over her own shirt. She could manage the heavy shoes, the breastplate, and the other body pieces but would need help with the arm and shoulder plates. By the time she was ready, she hoped Novak would be awake and in an amiable mood.

She owed him a great deal. Yesterday she had been at the brink of discouragement and despair, and his anger had pulled her back. The necessity of defending her decisions had strengthened and fortified them. She smiled gently as she fastened the breastplate buckles. Though she had suspected he was more fond of her than his gruff voice and actions would indicate, his willingness to keep her secret for a few more hours had proved her suspicions.

"So you are still determined to go through with this?"

She looked up to find Novak's gaze upon her, his dark eyes reflecting glimmers of light from the high garrison windows.

"Yes," she answered, mindful of the other sleeping knights around her. She could not say more, for any one of them might be awake and listening.

"Then say your prayers, squire," Novak answered, sitting up. He rested his hands on the edge of his bunk, a melancholy frown flitting across his features. "I will help you with the armor, and then I want you to find a place to pray for wisdom."

"And for strength," she added, extending the vambrace for him to strap onto her elbow. "I will need it for the test to come."

"Pray for wisdom," he repeated gruffly. He stood up and stretched the stiffness from his shoulders, then turned and took the vambrace she offered. "You will need wisdom most of all."

Nineteen

Two hours later Anika heard the trumpet call to summon her out of the chapel. With her composure like a fragile shell around her, she rose stiffly to her feet and moved down the winding staircase, through the hallway, and onto the porch that extended into the courtyard.

The morning sun was as bright as crystal on this clear winter day. The armored knights of Chlum, more than forty strong, stood in a circle around the imposing entryway. Lord John, wearing a surcoat of blazing blue, stood on the porch to oversee her test. Anika sighed in relief at the sight of her master. Her secret still held. Novak had not broken his word.

She looked for Novak and saw him not ten feet away. Silently, awaiting her attention, he stepped forward, Lord John's own crested helmet in his hand.

Silence loomed between them like a heavy mist. Anika breathed in shallow, quick gasps, then leaned forward to glance into the bottom of the helmet. At least forty small stones lay within.

"Squire Kafka," Lord John said, his eyes flickering with some emotion she couldn't decipher, "welcome to your day of testing." He paused for a moment, his steady gaze boring into her in silent expectation. "Do you still wish to become my man?"

Anika faltered. Lord John's *man*. A common phrase, but one which rang in her ears with deafening irony. She was not, and would never be, Lord John's *man*. But she might, God willing, become his *knight.* "More than anything on earth," she whispered, "I wish to become a knight of Chlum."

He exchanged a smile with her, then nodded and gestured toward the helmet. "Make your choice."

Half in anticipation, half in dread, Anika lifted her eyes toward the distant sky and thrust her hand into the helmet. Her fingertips kissed the stones—*Please, Father God, let me choose the right one*—then she pulled one into her palm and lifted it out.

Her fingers slowly unclenched; the stone was unmarked. She lifted puzzled eyes to Novak, then saw his lips move in barely audible words: "Turn it over."

With a trembling hand, she flipped the rock upon her palm. It was marked with a single "N," painted in a bright, bold stroke.

"Me," Novak said, letting out a long, audible breath. "You will joust against me." He shifted Lord John's helmet to his hip, then pointed toward the gate. "Take your mount to the east end of the field. The sun will be at your back."

Anika frowned at this bit of fatherly advice. Why was he determined to make it easy for her? This was supposed to be a *test,* not a demonstration.

An intriguing, unsettling thought whipped into her mind. "Wait," she called, stepping forward. Before the alert eyes of the entire company, she held Novak's stone aloft with her left hand while her right hand reached again into the helmet.

"It is decided; you will joust against me," Novak said, unsuccessfully trying to sidestep and turn away.

"It is *not* decided," she replied sharply, lifting another stone from the basinet. She lifted the second rock to her eyes, then held it high for all to see. "Another stone marked with an 'N,'" she called, bridled anger in her voice. "Who could this belong to? Have we a Nefen among the knights? Or perhaps a Nelek? A Neon, Neptune, or Neville? Perchance Lord John has a knight named Notus, Noble, or Nunzio."

"Kafka—" Novak began, flushing miserably.

"Sir Novak," Lord John broke into the uncomfortable situation. "Have you a particular reason for wishing to joust with your own squire?" He lowered his voice. "You are not intending to teach him a hard lesson during this test? For if you were, it would be an abuse of your power as teacher."

"No, my lord," Novak answered, his eyes large, glittering ovals of repudiation. "I did not intend to hurt the—my charge. I thought to protect him."

"Is there some reason why he should not take the test today?"

Anika held her breath as a thrill of frightened anticipation touched her spine. With one word now Novak could destroy her dreams. Not only would she not become a knight, but she would be publicly humiliated and censured before Lord John, his household, and his knights—

She could bear anything but Lord John's scorn.

"If you feel that he is not ready—" the master continued.

"Kafka is ready, my lord," Novak answered, his voice resigned.

Lord John turned to Anika, his brown eyes wide with concern. "Are you, Squire Kafka, truly ready to do this?" he asked, lowering his voice so that only she and Novak could hear. "It is no disgrace if you wish to delay the test. Indeed, we could wait another year—"

"I am ready, my lord," she said, clinging to her courage, praying she would not betray her inner agitation.

Lord John gave her a look that was compassionate, troubled, and still. "Then you must choose your opponent." He placed one hand on her shoulder and with the other gestured in a sweeping motion toward the waiting knights.

Anika felt her mouth go dry. She had not expected this. In truth, she would have been happy to fight Novak had he not intended to mock her, for she knew how he fought and could at least anticipate his movements. But the other knights were a mystery, and therefore dangerous.

She clenched her jaw to kill the sob in her throat and turned to face them. She had taken a vow, and she would do this. Though no one on earth understood the fires of vengeance that burned in her heart, she would keep her word. To be a knight and fight in the cause to which she had sworn her life, she would have to face worse enemies than these friendly foes.

"I choose . . ." Her eyes swept her audience with a piercing glance, then came to rest on the tallest, bulkiest knight in the garrison, a giant known as Sir Manville. She knew very little about him, for he kept to himself, but if she defeated him, Novak would know once and for all that she was capable of handling whatever enemy might come her way.

She straightened and placed her hands on her hips. "I choose Sir Manville."

"Kafka," Novak warned, but she ignored him, stepping down from the porch to meet her opponent.

Manville stepped forward, offering her the smile he used to freeze other men's blood. His head had been recently shaved, and the morning sunlight made his stubbled gray hair shine like a dead saint's halo. He came closer, nodding with respect to Lord John, then pulled his sword from its sheath and pressed the hilt to his lips, a ceremonial pose for readiness to do his lord's will.

Anika stared at the knight's huge hands. Veins squirmed across the skin like fat blue worms, and tufts of grayish-red hair decorated his fingers.

Father God, let me faint before he knocks me from my horse. If I am unconscious, he will not have reason to bruise me.

"Sir Manville," there was an edge to Lord John's voice now, "do you accept Kafka's challenge? Are you willing to participate in this test, or would you rather the squire choose another?"

Anika thought she heard a faint note of pleading in her master's voice. She boldly met the giant's eyes, determined that he not refuse her.

He didn't. "I am honored to be singled out," Manville said simply, lifting his heavy helmet. After sliding it onto his head, he stared at Anika through the slitted eye openings, and she thought she saw a spark of mischief—or malice—in those eyes. He lifted his sword in another formal salute, then turned on his heel and strode purposefully toward the stable.

"Lord John—" Novak called, his jaw tensing. "A word, please."

"Indeed, I was about to ask you for the same favor," the master answered, staring at Anika.

She felt the pressure of disapproval in his eyes but defiantly lifted her chin. "Excuse me, my lord," she said simply, lifting her own helmet to her hip. "But I have a horse to prepare."

Leaving her masters alone on the portico, she threaded her way through the milling knights and hurried toward the paddock.

"My lord," Novak said, twisting his hands in his belt as they walked into the castle, "if a man has promised not to reveal a secret, does he sin if he does so before the permitted time?"

"You have a secret?" John lifted a brow, then turned to face his captain. "But you are not to withhold secrets from me, Novak. You have sworn your allegiance. Apart from your allegiance to our God and the king, surely you have none higher."

"In truth, that's how I see it." Novak removed his hands from his belt and placed them squarely on his hips. "It's about Kafka, my lord. Would that I had spoken earlier! I have learned something, you see, about that squire. And once you understand what it is, you'll understand why I marked all the stones with my initial."

"Trying to protect him, eh, Novak?" John pushed open the doors of his chamber and gestured to a pair of chairs near the balcony. His own mind was congested with doubts and fears about how he should manage Kafka. He had hoped the test would provoke the girl into either running away or confessing her deception and her reason for infiltrating Chlum, but even now she seemed determined to endure the experience. Why?

As casually as he could, he gestured for Novak to sit down. "Please, take a moment and explain your actions this morning. But be quick, for our squire is now preparing his horse for the joust."

"Quite right." Novak sank heavily into the chair. "Kafka can't joust with Manville, my lord. If Manville even sneezes, he'll blow Kafka right out of the saddle. No, my lord, you must stop this test. Only you mustn't say why you're stopping it, for then she'll know."

John ran his hand through his hair, grimacing with good humor. His captain was struggling to reveal what John already knew, but at least Novak was trying to share the truth.

John settled into his chair, resting his arms on the sturdy wooden armrests. "You're trying to tell me," he said, parking his chin in the palm of one hand, "that our squire Kafka is a woman."

Novak's jaw dropped. "Twice welcome, my lord, for sparing me the words! How did you know?"

John felt the corner of his mouth lift in a half-smile. "I've known for some time. I was only surprised that *you* didn't know."

"Well," Novak averted his eyes, "of course I knew. But I was sworn not to tell. She's had a hard time of it, this young girl, and she says she had to come here in order to hide from Lord Laco. She grew up with Petrov, your late father's captain, God rest both their souls, and she says she's been handling a broadsword since she was ten. And I saw no harm in letting her continue with the other fellows, because she is quick, and a hard worker—"

A memory edged John's teeth. He held up a hand, cutting Novak off. "Lord Laco? She was hiding from Laco?"

Novak nodded. "Aye, my lord."

John closed his eyes, deliberately letting his mind run backwards. Jan Hus had said something at dinner about a bookseller's daughter who disappeared, an educated girl who had to hide from Laco's son—

He opened his eyes and stared at his startled captain. "She told you her name?"

"Aye. Anika. She said her father and mother were both dead."

Relief washed over him. John leaned back in his chair, at ease for the first time in weeks. The girl wasn't spying, she was *hiding*. And with good reason.

He turned his attention back to his flustered captain. "Truthfully, Novak, when did you discover her secret? This morning?"

The knight's face fell. "Yesterday." His eyes displayed with the tortured dullness of disbelief. "I should have seen it earlier, but I never dreamed such a thing would be possible."

"Nor did I," John answered, lowering his arms to the chair. "And if it makes you feel any better, Novak, I was blind, too, until Lady Zelenka pointed the girl out. It seems that one woman can flush another out of hiding better than a bloodhound."

A flicker of a smile rose at the edges of Novak's mouth, then died out. "What do we do about the joust?" His voice drifted into a hushed whisper. "You cannot let a woman joust against Manville."

"No, but I cannot openly shame the other knights by revealing her, either," John answered, leaning his elbow upon the armrest of his chair. "They will not take kindly to the news that a woman has been hearing their secrets and sleeping in their garrison. You will have to go out to the field of contest and quietly pull her aside. Maybe we can take her to the village and house her with a peasant family until we decide her future."

"That is well spoken." Novak pushed himself up. "I will see to it now."

Slouching down, John lowered his chin to his palm again and grinned at his captain. "She did do well, though, didn't she? She might have made a knight, after all."

Anika mechanically played the test over and over in her mind, trying to forecast Manville's probable moves. The joust would take place on a long rectangular field outside the castle walls. As soon as Lord John had taken his seat upon his balcony, a trumpeter would blow, and two fluttering blue pennons, one at each end of the field, would fall. She and Manville would spur their horses and charge toward each other from a distance of one hundred yards. The tilt, a wooden barrier that reached to her horse's flank, would separate the two opponents, and Anika would aim her lance across the tilt, directly toward Sir Manville's breastplate, until the point of impact . . . unless she was unseated first.

No. She blocked the thought; the contemplation of failure

would be anathema. Moving into the weapons room, she selected the lightest wooden tilting lance from the wall, then checked to be sure Midnight, now her favorite mount, was properly saddled. The grooms, always eager to view a competition, hurried to dress the horse in his jousting armor, a breastplate and a metal headpiece known as the chanfron. Anika eyed the metal spike protruding from the chanfron like a gleaming horn and hoped that Midnight's size and strength would intimidate Sir Manville . . . because her slight figure certainly wouldn't.

She checked the girth strap, then slipped her left foot into the stirrup and threw herself over the horse's broad back. Manville, she noticed as she glanced toward the far side of the stable, had already mounted his favorite steed. A servant held his horse's reins and was leading him toward the castle barbican.

"Hurry," she told the groom in a low voice.

The stableboy attending her grinned foolishly, then gave the horse's flank a slap. "In a hurry to get yourself killed, are you, Kafka?" He grinned and handed her the reins. "You are as ready as you will ever be."

She straightened, then made a quick clucking sound with her tongue, turning the stallion toward the doorway. Nervous flutterings pricked her chest as the huge animal moved out of the stable, through the barbican, and onto the tournament field. Averting her eyes from the crowd of onlookers gathering behind a rope, she faced the opposite end of the jousting field and forced her riotous emotions to settle down. In a few moments she would have completed her test. If she acquitted herself well, she would earn the right to be dubbed a knight. Of course Novak would feel compelled to tell Lord John her secret, and the Lord of Chlum might not agree to knight her.

But it wouldn't matter. In the eyes of her fellow knights, she would have proven herself. Her parents and Sir Petrov, watching from heaven, would see and know that she had not failed them. And if Lord John cast her out of Chlum Castle, she would take her new-found skills to another manor and continue her quest of vengeance.

For she had begun to believe her father was right—war did lie just over the horizon, and she was sworn to be involved in the battle.

She gave the stallion a slack rein and cantered slowly across the field toward her position. Midnight's speed and power exhilarated her, and her blood raced in response. Let the test begin. She had no intention of permitting herself to fail.

———

The air outside Chlum Castle rang with the uncontrolled sounds of a holiday crowd anticipating fine entertainment, for a host of servants, knights, and villagers had gathered around the outer barriers to watch the midday joust. The noise and anticipation made Midnight nervous; he danced in place, his head high and his tail arched. Biting her lip, Anika glanced up at Lord John's balcony. He had not yet appeared, nor had the trumpeter.

Anika shivered. A frosty wind blew over the field, knifing her lungs and tingling the exposed skin of her nose. Impatient to charge, Midnight blew gustily and then lowered his great head to graze the grassy border. "No," Anika commanded, jerking back on the reins to bring the animal to attention. The stallion could not relax; neither could she.

What was keeping Lord John?

On the opposite side of the field, Sir Manville waited, too, a pair of grooms at his side. Lev alone had followed Anika to the starting gate, and he stood silently beside her horse, nervously cracking his knuckles.

A meowing wail from one of the villagers' children rose from the crowd and raked across Anika's tense nerves. Beneath that sound she could hear her heart battering against her ears. Why was Lord John making her wait?

"Lo, look there." Lev pointed toward movement in the crowd. "Novak comes."

Lev's voice was curiously flat, and the sound of it chilled her. This was not customary. As her mentor, Novak should have been on the balcony with Lord John, awaiting her fate and praying for her success—

Unless he had revealed her secret.

And Lord John had forbidden her test.

"No." She uttered the word between clenched teeth and tightened the reins in her left hand.

"What?" Lev lifted his face toward her.

"Lift the bar," she ordered in a voice of authority.

"But Novak comes—"

"Lift the cursed bar!" she snapped, pretending not to understand his warning look.

Lev slid the restraining bar from its place and stepped back, nervously wiping his hands on his robe. Anika gripped the lance in her right hand and lowered herself behind her shield, willing herself to be as small as possible, a tiny target for the enemy.

"Kafka!" Novak's voice rose above the crowd now, demanding her attention.

With a slight smile of defiance, she gripped the reins again and leaned forward, spurring the horse.

The nervous stallion was more than willing to respond. As the spur raked his flank, he reared back, pawing the air with his front hooves. With Novak's bellow ringing in her ears, Anika urged her stallion forward to meet her opponent.

Twenty

A plague on him!" Manville gripped his reins and kicked the meddlesome grooms away. Somehow he had missed the trumpet. That cocky little Kafka was already advancing, his stallion throwing up great clods of earth behind those thundering hooves.

Manville tucked his lance under his arm and leaned forward, violently thrusting his spurs into the animal's tender flank. The great war-horse lunged from the gate, bellowing in rage, and Manville gripped the animal with his knees, balancing the lance easily along his muscled right arm. This boy would be easy to unseat, and once the lad lay on the ground, Manville would dismount, vault over the tilt, and press his sword to the lad's breastplate, confirming his defeat. Today this arrogant squire would be humbled before the entire manor.

Manville's mouth curved into an unconscious smile as his stallion shot forward.

From inside his chamber, John heard the crowd roar. Flying from his chair, he strode to the balcony and stared out at the jousting field. Squire Kafka, dressed in that ridiculously large armor, had prematurely charged out of the gate. And Manville, not one to let a challenge go unanswered, had raced forward to joust with a girl.

John clenched his fist as sheer black fright swept through him. He should not have been silent; he should have stopped this charade as soon as he discovered it. This foolish girl would die on yonder grass unless—

"Novak!" he called over the balcony, spying his captain in the crowd. "Stop them!"

He could not tell if Novak heard, for his voice was swallowed up in the clamor of the cheering mob.

Manville heard the crowd boil to life. He had the fleeting impression of someone shouting, the throng cheering, neckerchiefs waving in excitement. And before him Kafka drove relentlessly forward, his tilting lance alive and carving wobbly patterns in the air before his onrushing stallion.

Manville lowered his head and held his own lance steady, aiming it across the tilt toward the squire. His arms were stronger, his lance longer than the squire's lightweight weapon, and he was not surprised when his lance hit the squire's shield. The sharp and brittle crack of wood tore the air, and Kafka's shield flew away like a kite in a gale. Manville brought his own shield to his chest reflexively, but there was no answering blow—

Before he knew what had happened, his horse went down on its knees, flinging Manville aside like a discarded cloak. A gasp from the crowd spiraled down as Manville fought to control his balance, then the earth rose to meet him. Dirt and soft grass pillowed his hands and cheek; the sweet and salty taste of blood touched his tongue.

Manville looked up, disoriented. Twenty paces away, his stallion scrambled in undignified haste to his knees, then tossed his great head and moved away, apparently interested only in browsing the lush grass at the edge of the field.

Across the tilt, the squire turned his horse and trotted back, his lance still in his hand. Riding like a triumphant peanut atop an elephant, Kafka looked out from the slit in his visor. "God save you, Sir Knight," he called, pitching his voice low so the crowd could not hear. "Are you hurt?"

Manville shook out his heavy arms and legs to be certain nothing was broken. Age had not lessened his strength, but his bones did not take as kindly to bouncing off horses as they once had.

He rose to his feet with stiff and brittle dignity, leaning hard upon his lance. "I am not hurt," he called. He looked again at his horse. Though the animal had fallen, he seemed no worse off for his mishap.

"I do beg and pray you, squire—tell me what sort of curse you put on my horse," Manville drawled with distinct mockery. "He used to be a surefooted beast."

"I pointed my lance at his breastplate," Kafka answered, his voice slick with satisfaction. "I knew you would take my shield, so I decided to let you have it. And while you waited for me to fall, I struck your horse. I knew he would not be hurt."

Manville bit back an oath, then spat the blood from his mouth. "So be it." He moved his hand toward his sword. "Dismount then, and prepare to face me. This test is not yet finished. I am still on my feet, so I am not defeated."

Through the narrow aperture of the helmet, Manville saw a shadow of alarm flicker in the squire's eyes. Surely the boy hadn't thought a mere fall would break Manville's spirit! Slowly, reluctantly, the young man dropped his lance, then stood in the stirrups and dismounted.

"Kafka!" Novak's abrupt shout cut through the murmurs of the crowd. The captain vaulted easily over the fenced barrier and charged toward his squire. "You will report to Lord John. Now! This test is forfeited. It should never have begun!"

Manville thought the boy slumped slightly in relief. "Wait, squire," he barked, unsheathing his sword.

"The captain calls me." Kafka pointed toward Novak.

"Indeed," Manville remarked dryly, lifting his sword as if to inspect the gleaming blade. Eyeing Kafka over the hilt of his sword, he watched the squire take his horse's reins and lead the animal from the field behind his blustering teacher.

Manville lowered his blade, swiped a grass stain from his breastplate, and smiled beneath his helmet. To be sure, Kafka was an unusual youth. He'd broken several unwritten rules today, spoiling Manville's victory and angering Novak.

But on a field of battle a knight would want someone like Kafka by his side. Someone who wasn't afraid to be unconventional or take a chance. Someone who dared to act.

"Congratulations, Kafka," Manville murmured as he turned to tend to his own stallion. "If anyone would ask my opinion, I'd say you passed your test today."

———

John sat in a cushioned chair and stared at his captain and his female squire, both of whom stood before him with faces as set in fury as his own. His shock at the girl's actions had yielded quickly to anger—and then a defeating sense of impotence. What was he supposed to do? He had planned to send the girl away after telling her she could never pass a test of knighthood, but with one sure stroke she had unseated his best horseman.

He decided to dispense with the usual formalities and meet fire with fire. "I never intended for things to go this far," he said, glaring at Novak. "You, Sir Knight, should have had better control of your squire."

A momentary look of discomfort crossed the captain's face, then his lower lip pushed forward in something akin to a childish pout. "Consider now, my lord, the situation. Was I supposed to tie her hand and foot?" Novak spoke in a choking voice, as if he were strangling on repressed epithets. "You said, my lord, that we might let her continue—"

"I said you should quietly pull her out of the test," John answered, grinding the words between his teeth.

"My lord."

John jerked his head toward the girl. Her face was flushed, but an air of calm and self-confidence shone from her like a halo. "My lord, I think we can say that I passed your test."

"The test was halted. You did not defeat Manville. You had no chance to complete the duel."

She set her chin in a stubborn line. "How do you know I could not have defeated him in a duel? You did not expect me to unseat him in the joust, but I did. Other knights have not performed as well as I, and yet they wear your emblem." She looked up at him with eyes glittering in restless passion. "May I, my lord, take my vows and become a knight in your service? All who saw me today on the field will support your decision to make me a knight."

"No," John snapped, his voice hoarse with frustration. He opened his hands, trying to disguise his annoyance. "You are a woman, and knights are men. Can a rose become a tulip? No. Though it may share the same color, though it may even smell as sweet—"

"Tulips," she interrupted, seeming very pleased with herself, "do not smell."

John flung his hand upward, thrusting her objection away. "You cannot be a knight, and that is final. King Wenceslas would think I had lost my good sense were I to knight a woman."

"The king," she whispered, lifting a brow, "does not have to know. No one has to know, only you and my mentor Novak. I have kept my gender a secret until now; I can keep it forever, if need be."

"Lady Zelenka saw through your disguise," John retorted, irked by the girl's cool, aloof manner. "She told me your secret weeks ago."

The delicate brow—too delicate for a boy's he now realized—lifted again. "Weeks ago? And yet you said nothing."

"I was curious," he insisted with returning impatience. "I wanted to see how committed you were—and if my captain could be as blind as I."

"My lord!" Novak burst out, shocked.

"I am very committed, and Novak has found no fault with my labors," the girl answered, taking charge with quiet assurance. "I have worked without complaint, fought until my arms ached, mounted every horse I fell off. I have shared no secrets, spread no rumors, and drunk none of your wine. In respect to my moral behavior," her green eyes narrowed slightly, "I have behaved better than the men in your service. The chambermaids and village girls are safe in my company, and that is more than you could say for half the men in yonder garrison—"

"Enough." John folded his hands, determined to try another approach with this stubborn young woman. "Why do you want to be a knight? I understand that you are an orphan and destitute since the burning of your father's shop, and I have heard that you seek refuge from Lord Laco. But you could be safe and yet genteel as a lady's maid or a companion to some gentlewoman. You could enter one of the convents in the countryside."

Her expression clouded in anger. "I would not enter a Romanist convent if the gates of heaven lay therein," she retorted, rancor sharpening her voice. "I love God and Jesus Christ truly, but those red-robed cardinals and foul priests are my sworn enemies! My mother died due to a cardinal's selfishness, and my father, who would turn the other cheek to his cruelest enemy, was struck down with Cardinal D'Ailly's blessing. So I have sworn to fight for the righteous gospel taught by Jan Hus and Jerome of Prague and all those who carry the holy Word of God to the people. And I have vowed to take vengeance upon those who have hurt the people I love."

Feeling suddenly weary in the face of her fierce anger, John shook his head. "I can find no reason to spoil the peace of a convent or another lord's house with this ferocious temper," he muttered, turning his gaze to Novak. "Can you, Sir Knight?"

"No, my lord," the knight answered, sighing in what looked like relief.

John paused, taking a frank and assessing look at the girl before him. She had proved her bravery and courage, she had demonstrated her wit and skill with languages, and she was as educated as any nobleman's daughter. In truth, she might be an asset in the cause he had undertaken with Jan Hus. In the days to come they would need a scholar, a scribe, and perhaps even a woman who could slip unnoticed into council rooms and churches, past guards and priests. And, truth be told, she was a pleasure to look upon, even in men's clothing, and her reading a delight to the ears—

He learned forward, reining in his thoughts. He couldn't afford to be distracted by inappropriate romantic notions. The girl was half his age, and he had neither the time nor the inclination to court a woman pretending to be a man. But what could he do with her? She would not go quietly into one of his villages—he had the feeling she would not go quietly anywhere. Allowing her to continue in this masquerade was unthinkable, but surely she would not persist in this role forever. And while she served, she might be useful to Hus's cause.

"Then thus shall it be," he said, regarding her with a speculative gaze. "You shall spend the night in prayer, as any squire would, and if on the morrow you feel that God would have you join us in knighthood, you shall take a vow of fealty. But you shall not swear to serve me for life. You shall instead swear to serve me as long as I serve Jan Hus, the preacher of the gospel you cherish. And when I wish to discharge you from your vow, you must relinquish it."

Her face fell in disappointment. "I have taken a vow of my own and cannot deny it. If you discharge me before my own vow is fulfilled, I shall have to continue in this knightly path."

"But not as a knight of Chlum." John rested his chin upon his fingertips. "You can accept my conditions, or you can return to Prague." His conscience smote him as he spoke, for he would never willingly cast a penniless young woman into the streets. Maybe she would not know he was bluffing.

Her delicate face shone with courage and determination as she lifted her head. "As you wish, my lord," she said, bowing. "I will swear whatever you command."

Sinking back in his chair, John motioned for Novak to take her away and prepare her for the night-long vigil. And as he watched them go, he congratulated himself on finding an answer to a difficult quandary. He was, he thought, either one of the most clever men in Bohemia . . . or the most foolish.

Anika now found herself on the brink of joining an elect company of valiant men who vowed to follow the ideals of chivalry: to be brave and loyal, to be faithful to the king, to defend the Christian faith, and to protect widows and orphans, the old and the weak. For over four hundred years knights throughout the European kingdoms had pledged their lives to their masters and sealed the agreement by the giving and receiving of a kiss, a visible sign of peace and loyalty.

In return for a lifetime of service, a knight was trained, fed, lodged, and provided with weapons.

As her mentor, Novak was responsible for seeing Anika through her induction. After escorting her from the lord's chamber, he led her to a small room dominated by Lord John's wooden bathtub. Awkwardly, he cleared his throat. "You must cleanse your body as well as your soul this night," he said, pulling his eyes away in a rictus of embarrassment. He thrust a bundled garment toward her. "And there is this, for after. Remove your armor, cleanse yourself, dress in this, and go up to the chapel. Lord John and Vasek will meet you there."

Anika took the garment from him and placed it on a chair, then slowly closed the wooden door behind Novak. If she were male, this room would undoubtedly be filled with jesting squires and knights eager to "baptize" her into a new life, but Novak had forestalled that possibility by bringing her straight from the lord's chamber into this lavatory. She would be knighted on the morrow, but her comrades in the garrison would know nothing of it until sunrise.

After shedding her armor, hauberk, and gypon, the shirt worn under all garments, she turned a spigot that brought cold water from the cisterns on the roof, then climbed into the barrel-like tub. She gasped at the first shock of coolness, and then laughed, a tender little sound that seemed strangely out of place in this private and ceremonial act. But why shouldn't she rejoice? She had fooled them far longer than she had thought possible. And Lord John obviously admired something in her character, else he would have demanded that she leave when he first learned of her deception.

She scrubbed her skin until it was pink and tender, then pulled the plug and watched the water swirl out through a pipe that led to the moat. The memory of Novak's words brought a wry smile to her face: *If you take a man and woman and tell them to wash as well as they can, which water bucket will be fouler? The man's. For if you wash clay, you make mud, and if you wash a bone, you make no such thing.*

The water swirling away between her toes seemed clean enough, but Anika knew it was invisibly polluted with her old life. From sunset on the morrow she would no longer be Anika of Prague, but Sir Kafka, knight of Chlum, sworn to serve the gospel and avenge those who had died at the hands of corrupt priests, chief among them Cardinal D'Ailly.

After climbing out of the tub, she picked up the bundle Novak had thrust toward her. It contained two garments: a new white robe, simple and elegant, and another long-sleeved gypon which felt wonderful against Anika's clean skin. Over the gypon she draped the sleeveless robe, which fell in elegant pleats to her ankles.

One small parcel remained inside the bundle, and Anika's eyes filled with tears when she opened it. Inside lay fresh cotton strips and straw. Novak, despite his protestations, did believe in her, and he had proved it by providing for her womanly needs. The tender gesture touched her, and she smiled.

She pulled on her soft leather boots, then finger-combed her wet hair, realizing with dismay that it had grown over the tops of her ears. She would have to ask one of the kitchen women to cut it again, but she would no longer worry about the white streak near her temple. It no longer held any power as an identifying mark, for her old life had been completely washed away.

After piling her filthy old garments in a pile for the washerwomen, she paused by the doorway and took a deep breath. The iron hinges on the heavy door screeched in protest as she pulled it open, then she climbed the winding stone staircase that led to the chapel and murmured a prayer: "Holy God, Almighty Father, help me keep the vows I am about to make."

Just as Novak had said, Lord John and the chaplain, Vasek, were waiting when she entered. Lord John refused to look at her, but simply gave the chaplain a curt order: "Begin."

Anika advanced to the altar and sank to her knees at the simple iron railing. "Do you, Squire Kafka, wish to vow your life in the service of God and this family?" the chaplain asked, his voice cracking with age and disuse.

"I do."

She thought she heard a soft, strangled sound coming from Lord

John, but she ignored it, watching instead the graceful movements of the chaplain's hand as he traced the sign of the cross before her wide eyes. "Then spend the night in prayer, cleansing your soul as you have cleansed your body. And may the Lord reveal his will to you and lead you in the way of everlasting life. Amen."

"*Sepera in Deo, quoniam adhuc confitebor illi: salutare vultus mei, et Deus meus . . .*" As the chaplain droned on, Anika closed her eyes and mentally translated the Latin text: "Trust in God, for I shall yet praise him, my Savior, and my God."

And as she lifted her thoughts toward heaven above, she tried not to think about the handsome man standing behind her, the one to whom she was vowing her life . . . and to whom she was striving not to lose her heart.

Twenty-One

John clasped his hands and bowed his head, trying to pretend that this squire was like all the others. How many squires had he taken into his service? Thirty? Forty? He loved them all, as a father loves a son or one brother loves another, but he was finding it difficult to love this one . . . like the others.

He found himself studying her soft profile. In some ways she was very womanly, yet there was an attitude of determination about her that fascinated him. The very air around her seemed electric as she joined the chaplain in prayer, and John felt an unwelcome surge of excitement as he contemplated those green eyes, that fair skin.

What had initially been an interesting experiment had become a reality beyond his control. Other noblemen of his acquaintance would surely have ordered the girl away or imprisoned her for her impertinence, but he could not bring himself to hurt her. What made a girl abandon everything a woman ought to be in order to strive for an impossible goal? What thoughts filled that impish and unorthodox brain? And why did he feel compelled to explore it further?

Part of her attraction lay in her sheer unconventionality, he knew. And in the most honest part of his soul he had to admit that even under a layer of dirt and a mail hauberk, Kafka was beautiful. The features which made a rather pretty boy combined to create a stunningly beautiful woman, and when she had first entered the chapel, flushed, damp, and rosy, he had to avert his eyes entirely lest he find himself staring at her.

Chaplain Vasek, he thought, feeling a wry smile lift the corner of his mouth, would find that a little *too* interesting.

John lowered his eyes and cleared his throat. 'Twas only her vitality that attracted him, the very uniqueness of her situation. He knew few men who made vows as fervently and followed their dreams as doggedly as she did. She was quite singular, this young woman, but she could prove useful in the days ahead.

He leaned back, suppressing a sigh. She could be useful . . . or she could be a torment. Only God above knew which.

———

She was supposed to spend the night in prayer, but an hour after the chaplain and Lord John departed, Anika felt her thoughts wandering as her eyes lifted to the night sky above. The sun had set while she bathed, and outside the chapel window the stars blazed like gems in a sky as black as the grave.

Could her father see her now? Could Petrov? And would they approve her actions? Petrov, she thought, would have been proud of the way she tripped Manville's horse. She knew just where to apply the point of her lance, and though she was far weaker than the seasoned knight, a warrior was only as strong and swift as his war-horse. *When you are at a disadvantage, forget your weakness and find your strengths.* Petrov's insistent voice rang in her mind, and her blood soared with unbidden memories—Petrov teaching her how to parry, how to feint, how to look right and move left, how to feign an injury so the enemy grew bold and overconfident.

In a surge of recollection, another beloved voice touched her inner ear: *Men will carry swords until they learn to carry the cross.* With memory's kind and loving eyes she saw her father's face framed in the chapel window, his humorous, kindly mouth, the age lines about his lips and eyes, muting his strength with gentleness.

Would he have approved her plan of vengeance? Somehow she didn't think so. Ernan O'Connor had been a righteous man, unable even to nurse a grudge.

"Father God, help my father understand," she prayed, her eyes flitting over the stars in the night sky. "In the war between right and wrong, we cannot afford to be neutral. We must fight; we must defend ourselves and our right to the truth. Please, Almighty God, let him understand."

On and on she prayed, recalling those she had loved and lost, until the stars began to fade behind a blue velvet sky.

————

The sky was pure blue from north to south, with no more than a little violet duskiness lingering in the west when John stepped onto the portico of the castle. The knights, whom Novak had summoned, stood in a circle as they had the day before, but all signs of curiosity had vanished from their faces. As far as they knew, another squire had been tested and proved himself worthy to join the knights of Chlum Castle. Though the squire's curtailed test had been unusual, those with inquiring minds had been satisfied with the simple answer that Kafka's ingenious approach to unseating Manville was proof enough of his worthiness.

Now the knights stood arranged by rank in a formal circle, ready to witness the dubbing of yet another squire, a link in the chain of an endless succession of knights who had ridden into Chlum Castle as boys and had grown to manhood within its walls. Except this one, John thought, staring fixedly at the slender sword in his hands, had never been a boy and would never make a man.

In a moment she would descend those chapel stairs, kneel at his feet, and swear allegiance to him, his wife (if he ever took one), and his cause. He would promptly assign her to Master Hus, in part because it would remove her from his continual thoughts, and in part because if the preacher had known her in Prague, he might recognize her and persuade her to give up this ridiculous quest. If Hus discovered her identity, John was certain the preacher would waste no time finding her a suitable position with a godly family in Prague. John would have asked for the preacher's help yesterday, but Hus had locked himself in a solitary tower room to spend the day in fasting and prayer.

At a silent signal, the knights before him laid down their swords, uncovered their heads, and knelt in the sand. John knew without being told that she had appeared behind him. The trumpeters at his side lifted their horns and blew a long, resounding note. Then the chaplain raised his hands and opened the ceremony with a brief prayer in the Bohemian tongue.

John heard the soft swish of her garments as the smooth cap of her hair appeared in the corner of his eye. He looked to his right hand where Novak stood and saw the older knight staring, a gleam of incredulity in his eyes.

John looked down when she knelt at his feet. Upon the red carpet, with her white robe gleaming like snow in the sunshine, she pressed her small hands together in an attitude of prayer and lifted her eyes to his.

———

She raised her eyes to find Lord John watching her. Did he resent her, this man who would be her master for days to come? She had exchanged father and guardian and mentor for his protection, and she would like to believe that he at least thought fondly of her.

His dark brown eyes seemed to soften. "Do you wish, without reservation," he asked, gentleness in his voice, "to become my servant?"

"I wish it." Her voice was shakier than she would have liked.

He bent forward then and pressed her hands between his own, then lowered his head until it hovered just above hers. "I seal your vow this day," he said, his own voice simmering with emotion, "with a kiss."

She closed her eyes as his warm lips lowered to meet hers. Her first kiss. Her heart slammed into her ribs as an unexpected tremor shook her. She felt a rush of pink stain her cheek—would he see it?

Leaving her breathless and shaken, Lord John straightened and motioned to Novak, who stepped forward with Kafka's sword.

"Swear," Novak demanded.

Anika struggled to remember the words of the oath she had committed to memory: "I promise by my faith that from this time forward I will be faithful to Lord John of Chlum and will maintain toward him my homage entirely against any man, in good faith and without—" her gaze flew upward, meeting Lord John's, "without any deception."

He knew who and what she was. And still he accepted her.

Taking the sword from Novak, Lord John handed it to the chaplain, who murmured a blessing in Latin, then returned it to the master.

Lord John held the blade aloft for all to see, then lightly touched Anika on the right shoulder, then the left.

The bond was forged.

The chaplain stepped forward, a silken blue surcoat spread across his upturned hands. Anika fastened her eyes on the gold cross emblazoned in the center of the garment and felt her heart soar.

John took the surcoat, held it up for all to see, then dropped it over Anika's head. As the silky fabric fell around her, she lifted her gaze again to her master's.

"Go now, fair knight," he called, his voice ringing with command. "Be brave and upright, that God may love you."

As her heart pounded in an erratic and joyous rhythm, Anika stood, bowed to Lord John and Novak, then flew off the carpeted platform toward the stallion waiting just outside the knights' circle. As the others cheered, she mounted the war-horse, caught the lance Lev tossed her, and made a mock run toward a dummy someone had strung up on a pole.

It was all in show, good fun for men of war, a chance to show off all she had learned. As she lowered her head and spurred her horse, she knew many of the others were thinking that she might never use these skills again. After all, the knights of Chlum Castle had enjoyed peace for over twenty years.

But they were ignorant; they gave no more thought to the current state of affairs in Bohemia than to what they would eat for dinner. They had not listened to the supper conversations of Lord John and Jan Hus; they had not read the papal bulls and Hus's appeals.

They did not know, as she did for a certainty, that war loomed beyond the horizon.

Jan Hus

Twenty-Two

"And seeing the multitudes," Anika whispered under her breath, "he went up into a mountain. And when he was set, his disciples came unto him. And he opened his mouth, and taught them saying, 'Blessed are the poor in spirit.'"

"What are you mumbling about?" Lev asked, looking up at her with frank admiration. Ever since she had passed her test and earned the blue and gold surcoat of a knight of Chlum, he and the other squires had treated her with a reverential deference.

"Look at Master Hus," Anika said, jerking her chin toward the place where the preacher stood. "Denied a church, he will make a temple of the fields and flowers themselves. And throngs gather to hear him, just as they surrounded our Lord during his ministry."

"They are curious, that's all," Lev dared to contradict her. "They want to see the great preacher of Prague for themselves, the teacher who dares to defy an order of excommunication."

"It's more than that," Anika answered softly. "Look at their faces, observe their eyes, see the deep affection they hold for him. He cares enough to come and call them from their homes, fields, and workshops, and they are listening and learning. No matter what their reasons are for coming, they will not forget the truths they have heard here today."

Lev did not reply but ambled off to find less lofty conversation. Anika crossed her arms and let her eyes rove over the crowd, watching for trouble. For weeks she and the other knights had been accompanying Hus on these excursions into Husinec, Hus's birthplace, and other small villages of southern Bohemia.

When he was not preaching, Jan Hus closeted himself in a small chamber of Chlum Castle and called for Peter Mladenovic, Lord John's private secretary. With Peter's help Hus wrote long letters to both his friends and his opponents, patiently explaining his views, extolling the virtue of the Scriptures, and encouraging those who sought the truth.

Lord John and other sympathetic nobles urged the indefatigable preacher to rest, but Hus seemed not to know the meaning of the word. When the wet spring weather prevented him from venturing out to preach, he applied the pen to his thoughts, scribbling in a hasty shorthand on a wax tablet, which Lord John's secretary transcribed onto parchment.

Hus's constant employment of Lord John's secretary brought an unexpected opportunity into Anika's life. With Peter Mladenovic unavailable, Lord John found himself in need of a secretary, so Kafka was summoned from the garrison to handle her master's correspondence and recordkeeping. Lord John also brought her copies of Hus's latest letters, asking her to translate them into French or Latin, depending upon the parchment's intended audience.

Anika felt a silken cocoon of euphoria wrap around her when she picked up a quill again. She loved to write and was thrilled to help further the cause of reformation. As she penned the preacher's words, she saw herself as a tiny spark that would help ignite a much-needed revolution.

Any and all customs, Hus wrote, *which have been introduced contrary to Christ's law are naught but man's law and should therefore be put down. Christ has presented the light of his truth to the apostles, but for nearly one thousand years men have systematically clouded that light with legalistic rules, unscriptural doctrines, and false teachings.*

At the lord's dinner table—where Sir Kafka was now invited to sit—Anika heard from visitors that a literal war of words was being waged in Prague by the two opposing parties. Books and pamphlets flooded the streets and the university, and citizens were quick to take sides. The reformers sympathetic to Hus were known as "Wyclifites," because Hus's teachings were similar to Wyclif's, while the opponents of reform were unflatteringly dubbed "Mohammedans," because they supported their man-made doctrines with violent actions.

"Support of our cause is on the rise, and I believe we shall prevail," Lord John recently told his dinner guests. "A royal decree from King Wenceslas has just instituted a new method for making appointments to the Council of Prague. For the first time the council shall consist of Bohemians, not foreigners, and those who attempted to destroy Bethlehem Chapel will be silenced. Our people will finally be encouraged to hear the gospel in their own tongue, without the trappings of Romanism."

Yes, Anika reflected, the future looked bright for their cause. Favoring Hus, King Wenceslas listened to complaints from the Roman clergy with a bemused smile. The majority of Bohemia's barons now sided with Hus, and in recent days even the common people had come to treasure the preacher from Prague as a national prophet.

Now, as she watched, half a dozen yellow butterflies circled the preacher as if he were a gift from heaven, while behind him a brilliant sunset blazoned the western sky. The crowd would soon be begging him to stay through the night, but Lord John had expressly forbidden any overnight journeys. Hus took his life in his hands every time he ventured from the safety of Chlum Castle, and Lord John was not willing to risk either his knights or the preacher in order that a few more words might be shared.

Insects whirred from the tall grasses around Anika, and she looked up, startled by Hus's silence. The preacher had stopped speaking and bowed his head, lifting his hands to bestow peace upon the dozens of people who clustered around him. From the corner of her eye, Anika saw Novak give the signal to move forward. They would politely escort Hus to the master's carriage and set him back on the road to Chlum, and all would be in order.

Anika exhaled a long sigh of contentment as she moved away

from her post. Bohemia loved her son, Jan Hus. And Hus loved Bohemia enough to win her people to Christ.

———

The next afternoon, as the procession from Chlum made its way to the castle of Lord Venceslas of Duba, Anika deliberately let her horse slow until she rode abreast of the preacher's carriage. Hus sat within, his eyes glued to a copy of the Scriptures in his lap, his finger running quickly over the pages of script.

Anika pulled slightly left on the reins, willing the horse to move closer. Was Hus reading one of her own copies? She thought she recognized the writing.

The preacher must have sensed her presence. "Is that you, Sir Kafka?" he asked, not lifting his eyes from the page.

Anika felt an unwelcome blush creep onto her cheeks. She was not yet accustomed to hearing the other knights address her as "sir," and the name sounded particularly odd coming from her father's friend.

"Yea," she murmured, keeping her voice low.

Hus turned just enough for her to see the suggestion of a smile on his newly tanned face. "Do you know what I am reading?"

"The Scriptures, sir.'

"Not just any Scriptures, my friend. These were copied by a most unusual girl I knew in Prague. Her name was Anika." He lifted his face then, his dark eyes piercing the distance between them. "I am surprised you have never heard of her. She was a most talented young woman, as skilled in languages as you are. And, like you, she was quick with a pen."

Amid the creak of saddles and the rhythmic plodding of horses' hooves, his velvet voice wrapped around Anika's conscience, causing her to look away.

"If you'll excuse me for noticing," the preacher went on, a coaxing note in his voice now, "your eyes and hair are very much like hers. But she was an innocent, full of hope and light, while it is easy to see that you, Sir Kafka, have seen things to turn a man's soul dark." He paused, and when she turned to look at him again, his brows lifted. "What, little bird, would cause your soul to grow dark? Fear? Sorrow?"

Tears welled up in her eyes. Turning her gaze from Hus's compassionate face, she stared mindlessly over her horse's head. *Little bird!* Of course he knew. Though she had tried her best to avoid him, Jan Hus was an astute man. When had he realized?

When she was certain she could speak without her voice breaking, she looked across at the preacher again. "How did you know?"

He gave her a boyishly affectionate smile. "I am not as wise as some men, nor as observant as others. I must confess that I did not recognize your face, voice, or form—but your writing, Anika, is like none other. The first day I saw a copy of my letter to Lord Venceslas of Duba, I recognized your handwriting and style. You can imagine how surprised I was to discover that a knight in Lord John's castle was as fine a copyist as any in Prague."

His smile suddenly vanished. "The night you read the letter telling us of Petrov's death, I knew for certain. Your love for the old man shone on your face, and I realized I had found you. Sir Petrov said you had gone to an estate in the country, and there you were. Not as a chambermaid, but as a defender of the truth."

She stammered in surprise. "But you said nothing."

Through the carriage window, he tipped his face to the warmth of the sun. "I knew you were in danger from Laco—a danger that still exists, I believe. And since God and Petrov had approved your plan, how could I object? While it is not a course of action I would recommend," he said, surveying her with kindness in his eyes, "it seems to be one which agrees with you. Lord John is a godly and noble master—"

"No one could be better," she interrupted, feeling a dire need to explain herself. "And I have been useful to him. I worked hard, Master Hus, to prove myself."

"I am certain you did." His arched brows flickered a little. "Was your work well done and pleasing to our Savior? You have not deceived your master, have you?"

Her blood ran thick with guilt. "At first, Master Hus, I confess I did. Not in words, but in . . . actions. But now he knows who I am, as does Sir Novak. And Petrov did not lie when he brought me here. We strove to tell the truth always, to be honest and pure."

"I'm sure you did." He looked down at the road, the breeze ruffling the hair around his tonsure, then looked up and released a short laugh touched with embarrassment. "It is strange, isn't it, how God works? I never dreamed I would be an itinerant preacher, and you doubtless never dreamed that you would ride in armor with a sword at your side. But here we are, and who can say that God has not worked in our lives?"

She smiled back at him, more than a little relieved at his attitude. She had never thought it possible, but Jan Hus understood her.

"Are you happy?" he asked, his voice fading away to a hushed stillness.

"Yea, Master Hus, I am." She lifted her chin to feel the sun on her own face. Why shouldn't she be happy? She lived in one of the most noble estates in the country and served a lord as godly as he was handsome, with eyes as fresh and clear as the morning skies.

Hus nodded, one hand absently pulling on his pointed beard. "Good. But remember, my child, happiness is not our goal in life. We are to find our happiness in following the will of God. And while it is possible that God wills for you to be here and be a knight, I do not think he intends for you to deny the womanly qualities with which he has blessed you."

Anika shrugged to hide her confusion. "I have sought God's will, and this is where he led me. And I have sworn to serve Lord John as he seeks to serve you and the gospel."

"Even so, Sir Knight," Hus answered, a dark and troubled tone to his voice, "I am sure there will come a time when you will want to lay down your sword. When that time comes, do not resist the impulse. God speaks in a quiet voice, too. And his will lies in surrender."

His eyes suddenly filled with remoteness. "I never told you this story, Anika, but it bears repeating now. Do you remember when I was summoned to Rome?"

"Of course," she answered, shifting in the saddle. "You were right not to go."

The preacher shrugged. "I had my reasons, and they were good ones. But, deep inside, I refused to go to Rome because I was afraid. Pope John intended to kill me, and I did not want to die." His words, murmurous and uninflected, ran together in a soothing rhythm. "I forgot even the things I had learned as a student. Once, when I was reading the story of St. Lawrence, someone asked if I would have the courage to be roasted alive in an iron chair as Lawrence was. I didn't know, so I placed my hand on the fire in the coal pan, firmly holding it there until one of my companions drew it away."

Anika listened in horrified amazement, but Hus's eyes had focused on some distant point of the horizon as his thoughts journeyed back through time. "I only wished to test whether I should have sufficient courage to bear but a small part of the pain St. Lawrence endured," he whispered, his hand clenching and unclenching in his lap. For the first time, Anika noticed that a scar marked his right palm. "That courage was what I lacked when I was summoned to Rome. I should have been like Paul; I should have gone and joyfully counted the cost."

"You were right not to go," Anika insisted again. "Think of the hundreds of people who are receiving the gospel now. None of them would have heard if you were not here to preach to them."

"God could use these stones, if he willed it so," Hus answered, gesturing to the rocks beside the road. "The truth, my dear Anika, is that I was unwilling. God has convicted me, and now I am ready. Whatever summons I receive, I will obey. For God's will lies in surrender."

Hus's eyes had drifted toward the horizon again, and Anika had the feeling he was no longer speaking to her at all, yet his words had shaken her more than she cared to admit.

Puzzled by his abrupt change in mood, she nudged her horse, trotting forward in the procession.

———

In an effort to help Hus and bring peace to Bohemia, in the spring of 1413 King Wenceslas called together a synod between the two contending religious parties. The opponents of reform, who believed they finally had the troublesome Hus on the run, stood firmly against any sort of compromise. Steadfastly on the opposite end of the debate, the proponents of Hus's ideas demanded that Hus be allowed to appear before the synod to speak in his own defense—a demand which was adamantly refused by the other side.

After making no progress toward peace, the synod adjourned.

Anika was surprised that Master Hus seemed undaunted by the synod's failure. The preacher went about his work as if nothing had happened, often humming as he wrote and singing hymns as they rode to various villages where he would preach. Finally overcome by curiosity, Anika slipped into his private study and asked the reason for his cheerful countenance when defeat continually frustrated the reformers.

"This is not defeat!" he answered, his mouth opening in pretend horror. He dropped his pen upon the desk and lifted his hands in dismay. "My dear Kafka, how can you look at us and see *defeat*? Examine the men who come here from Prague—they carry copies of the Scriptures to Lord John's dinner table; they are examining God's Word for the first time in their lives. Men who once blindly accepted whatever the priests told them now question things they have heard all their lives."

"Is it wise to question so much?" Anika asked, frowning. "After all, God is God. Who are we to question him?"

"We are not questioning God, my dear knight," Hus answered, loosely draping his arm across her shoulders. "We are searching for truth, asking questions, waiting for answers. If my religion is true, it will stand up to all my questioning; there is no need to fear. We should question our beliefs continually—not God himself, not Christ our Lord, but what *other men* tell us about God and Christ.

Otherwise we are little more than the frozen statues you see in so many churches." He released her shoulders and picked up his pen again, then smiled in the calm strength of knowledge. "I am delighted to hear that men are questioning and seeking answers in the Scriptures. At last the sleepers are shaking off their slumber."

————

As spring passed into summer, Hus's opponents abandoned their plans to stop his work in Bohemia. The king was Hus's friend, and Hus served as Queen Sophia's Father Confessor. The university brimmed with scholars who found merit in Hus's scholarship and nothing but virtue in his character. While the nobles supported him, the common people revered the preacher who left his elegant stone church to share the truth of faith and salvation in their fields.

By the time autumn's chill winds blew over the mountains, Hus felt safe enough to return to Prague. He decided to celebrate his homecoming on the Lord's Day and wanted nothing more than to enter the walled city and proceed directly to Bethlehem Chapel to address his congregation.

Anika felt her heart leap when Lord John and Novak chose her to travel with the contingent that would escort Hus back to Prague. She had not been inside the city of her childhood since Petrov's death. Though she had said farewell to her old life, something deep within her yearned to see the spot where her father's bookshop had once stood.

They set out on a warm October day splashed with brilliant sunlight and canopied by a clear blue sky. Flaming colors lit the trees on distant mountains, and the horses moved at a brisk pace, as if they sensed that time was short and winter was coming. The miles flew by, and Anika was surprised at how quickly they arrived at the city gates.

Had a lifetime passed since she left this place? She had left Prague a frightened, insecure girl but was returning now a fully sworn knight. Though she could not reveal herself to anyone who might remember her, she felt as if the city itself somehow welcomed her and drew her to its breast.

Hiding behind the safety of her armor and concealing helmet, she joined ranks with her companions and rode in a close formation around Hus's carriage until the vehicle stopped at the threshold of Bethlehem Chapel. A riotous crowd awaited the long-lost preacher, and so many hands reached out to touch and welcome him that Anika worried about his safety. But Hus displayed no fear, plunging boldly into the mass of humanity which carried him along to the pulpit.

Anika hesitated at the edge of the throng. The other knights of Chlum had positioned themselves at the entrances and windows of the crowded building, but something called Anika away from the familiar church. There would be no time after the worship service to obey her heart's bidding, so she quietly turned and walked down a side street, away from the clamor of the gathering.

A thick gray veil hung over the city, an obscuring autumnal mist of chimney smoke compressed by low-hanging clouds. An almost unnatural silence prevailed in the streets, and Anika wondered if the entire city had turned out to line the walls of Bethlehem Chapel. This boulevard, which she had walked so often with Petrov and her father, usually rang with the laughter of children and the scolding of their mothers. Now there was no movement in the street, not even the whisper of a sound.

Like gauzy scarves from a lady's wardrobe, curls of smoke crossed the rooflines of houses that loomed against the sky. She had never thought Prague depressing, but now, accustomed as she was to the open vistas surrounding Lord John's estate, the narrow cobblestone roads seemed cluttered with timber-and-daub houses and tarp-covered carts. The street where her father and she lived seemed to be only a succession of darkened doorways and shuttered shops.

She stopped before a new structure that had been built upon blackened foundation stones. The fresh wood gleamed bright and new, a startling yellow against the dingy gray of the other weathered buildings. She lifted her visor to stare unimpeded at the bit of earth she had once called home.

There was nothing left. Not a single monument or sign or indication that her father and she had lived in this place, slept over these stones, dreamed beneath this section of sky.

She turned slowly, almost afraid to look over at the small structure that had been Petrov's house. To her surprise, she found that it had not changed. The door hung partway open, and the shutters wore a patina of dirt, but at least something remained of her previous life.

As if moving in a dream, Anika walked toward the tiny house. There was no light or movement within, but a rectangular sign advertising a tobacconist hung over the door. The memory of a similar sign ruffled through her mind like wind on water, and she walked forward and turned the sign over. On the other side a proud hand had written: *Ernan O'Connor, Copyist.* The paint had weathered and the letters faded, but at least this sign had survived the fire, probably knocked loose when the fiends set her father's bookshop ablaze and destroyed a lifetime of work. A pain squeezed her heart as she thought of her father hunched over his table, a pen in one hand, a straight edge in the other. He had taught her so much about books, and books had taught her about the world.

"I thought you might be here."

More surprised than frightened, she looked up to see Lord John standing behind her. She dropped her lashes quickly to hide the hurt in her eyes, then turned back to the sign, returning it to its new position. "This was my father's sign," she whispered through suppressed tears. " 'Tis all that remains of him in this place. I had hoped there might be something more."

"Do not expect to find your father here," Lord John answered, coming a step closer. "He lives on in your life and your future, Kafka." His voice, without rising at all, took on a subtle urgency. "Leave these things behind, and forget the past. You are needed now at Chlum Castle." Amusement flickered in the dark eyes that met hers. "I could no longer imagine life without you among us."

She pressed her fingers to her lips, searching anxiously for the meaning behind his statement. He had spoken so tenderly she might have believed his words to be a proclamation of love—or at least concern. But he was her lord, and she his sworn servant. Surely that was all he intended to imply. And he was here, not because he was concerned for her, but because one of his knights had disappeared from an assigned post.

His next words confirmed her thoughts. "Why did you leave, Kafka? Novak came to me because you could not be found, and we feared mischief from one of our enemies."

"You should not trouble yourself on my account," she said, forcing herself to look at him again. "You have made certain that I can handle myself. And the knights of Chlum are so esteemed no one would dare attack one who wears your blue and gold."

"All the same," he said, extending a hand, "I wish you would join us again. I would be more at peace if you were with us."

The expression in his eyes brought the color rushing into her cheeks. She forced herself to look away and ignore the hand stretched out for her comfort. "Of course, my lord. My work here is done," she said, moving stiffly past him to the street.

As Lord John checked his long stride to match her own on the walk back, Anika tried not to think of his closeness or the expression in his eyes when he had announced that he'd come looking for her. Why had he come? If Novak had reported her missing, Novak should have sought her.

She tucked the question away, unwilling to waste her time considering impossibilities.

Three months later, as the bitter January winds pierced the tapestry-lined walls, Anika entered the castle and climbed the stairs to her master's chamber, obeying a summons. Lord John's two mastiffs, Bela and Bilko, looked up as she approached but did not growl.

From inside the chamber, Lord John glanced up from his desk. "Sir Kafka," he called loudly, aware that others in the hallway might hear, "come in." He gave her a wry smile and in a lower voice added, "They did not growl at you, but they growl at every man who approaches. How do you explain it?"

Stepping forward, Anika paused to scratch each dog's ears. "I am certain you alone know the answer to that, my lord. Perhaps they know I love animals. Or it may be they know that I am no threat to you."

"'Tis more likely," John murmured, turning his attention back to the parchment on his desk, "they know you are no man. But no matter. I have brought you here to describe our work in the months to come. Of all my knights, you are the best suited to help us accomplish our aims."

Anika stood, astonished at the sense of fulfillment she felt at his words. *Of all my knights . . .* He had not only accepted her; he had come to value her.

"While Master Hus travels, preaches, and writes his letters," Lord John explained, "negotiations are being conducted for the meeting of a general church council to discuss the reforms we sorely need. Among those calling for the council is King Sigismund of Hungary, who has now been elected to imperial power. This Sigismund is astute enough to realize that being emperor of a divided kingdom is tantamount to not being emperor at all. He wants to rule Rome, but he does not want his life complicated with three popes and a confused people."

"The people of Bohemia," Anika inserted when Lord John paused to gather his thoughts, "care little for this man who calls himself emperor."

"They should." Lord John stroked his chin. "As King Wenceslas's brother, Sigismund is also heir to the throne of Bohemia. Wenceslas has no son, and upon his death Sigismund will be our king."

Anika waved the information away. "Who cares about kings and emperors? They are a secondary evil. We must have reform because the Church is not to be endured in its present state. The vices of the priests are a rank odor before heaven. They commit murder, they steal, in broad daylight they perpetrate acts which cannot be spoken without shame."

"*Some* of them," Lord John corrected. "But you are right, the time has come to halt their evil. The best minds in the world are calling for a meeting, and Master Hus has heard rumors that they will agree that a council of the entire church is superior to any single member of it, even the Roman pope himself."

Anika caught her breath as she realized the significance of his statement. "A council can overrule the pope?" She regarded her master with somber curiosity. "Truly?"

The suggestion intrigued her. This was what the church needed, and surely this was what Master Hus wanted. If that vicious Pope John were deposed, the entire Roman hierarchy could be reformed. Perhaps then truth could enter the ranks, and light could throw back the shadow of boundless iniquity that had shrouded the church for so long. The other antipopes were not nearly as powerful as John, and in time their influence would fade away.

"Your face!" Lord John murmured, breaking off her train of thought. "How like a mirror it is. I can see into your very soul, my friend, and the earnestness of your convictions puts me to shame."

"Tell me more," she breathed, kneeling on a cushion beside his chair. "What would you have me do? I stand ready and willing to serve, even if you would have me crawl to Rome on my hands and knees to beg this Sigismund to convene a council."

"My request is nothing so difficult," he answered, a trace of laughter in his voice. "But it is not without possible danger." His smile diminished slightly. "Pope John, of course, is not eager for this council of cardinals to convene."

"Cardinals!" The word flew from Anika's tongue like a curse as the rotund face of Cardinal D'Ailly rose to her mind. What would a gathering of vulture-like cardinals accomplish except to peck out the eyes of Truth?

Frowning at her interruption, Lord John continued: "I am certain that this pope has met every proponent of the council with bribes or threats, whichever will work to his favor. But the emperor has already set the time and place—Constance, in October of this coming year. And Sigismund, who now looks at Bohemia like a prospective bride, will not take a heresy-stained kingdom into his bosom. He has commanded that Jan Hus shall appear before the council, that Hus may prove false the rumor that Bohemians are sons of heretics."

Anika silently considered this information. Master Hus would consider it his duty to appear before the council, but if it were composed only of cardinals, the calcified backbone of the church, what hope had they of true reform? The cardinals were not popes, true, but living one heartbeat away from infallibility and nearly unlimited power tended to create a mass of power-hungry and ruthless men. Perhaps there were some high-ranking clerics who honestly sought the heart of God, but Anika could not forget that Pope John had once been a cardinal.

"A delegation from Sigismund will arrive here on the morrow," John answered, lowering his voice. "They will undoubtedly speak Latin, which many of my knights do not understand. I want you to remain at my side, listening with your sharp ears, and using that delightful sense of intuition you possess to note impressions I would miss. And if Master Hus elects to undertake the journey to Constance, I want you to go with us."

She stared at him, amazed that he would find it necessary to ask. She was his to command; as his knight she was sworn to obey his slightest wish. "Of course, my lord."

"Know this," he said, his tender voice almost a murmur. "There may be an occasion when I will ask you to remove your armor and venture out on our behalf in women's dress. It has occurred to me, and to Novak, that it might be advantageous to have a spy in Constance. It may well be that a woman may go where an armored knight cannot."

His suggestion both excited and aggravated her. She was thrilled to think she could provide a special service for her master, but something in his manner irritated her. Did he seek to spare her from what could be a dangerous undertaking? During her year at Chlum she had asked for neither mercy nor special treatment, and she did not want to receive either now.

But, on the other hand, if she could serve him in some way the others could not—her heart fluttered at the thought—she could not refuse him.

She inclined her head stiffly. "I will do whatever you think necessary, as long as it will help Master Hus's cause," she answered, her voice harsher than she had intended.

"You are angry." He folded his hands and regarded her with inquisitive eyes. "Why, pray tell? Why should it bother you to become what you are meant to be? You know that one day you must resume your woman's garments. I cannot deny that your disguise has worked thus far, but it will not always shield you, my Kafka. When the younger squires begin to grow beards and speak with the voices of men, do you not think they will wonder why you remain unbearded and speak in a woman's voice? I know Master Hus believes God has brought you to this place, but even he does not think you can continue many more months like this."

"I can!" she cried, gulping back her frustration and a horde of unspoken emotions. "At least until Master Hus is vindicated. I swore to serve you as long as you serve Master Hus, and you are still active in that service."

He leaned back in his chair, probably as exasperated with her as she was with him, and Anika bit her lip. She had also agreed that she would relinquish her vow whenever he asked her to, but she couldn't bear the thought of leaving him.

If Lord John asked her to leave, she'd beg for more time. Maybe he would agree to give her separate quarters in the stable, where she'd be removed from the other knights. But she couldn't leave Chlum Castle, at least not yet. Not while her vow remained unsatisfied . . . and Lord John remained unmarried.

If he married again, she would have to go. She wouldn't be able to abide the sight of another woman by his side at dinner. A wife would read to him after supper. She would answer his correspondence and listen to him discuss the affairs of king and country . . . all the things Anika had been doing for over a year.

"I can remain as I am for some time to come," she repeated, forcing herself to concentrate on the matters at hand. "I am quiet. The other knights don't notice me because I spend so much time copying for you in the castle. And you may place your full trust in me."

She turned on her heel and walked from the chamber, nearly bumping into Vasek in her haste to retreat.

Vasek pulled back, away from the startled young knight, then stood silently in the hall as Kafka moved gracefully away. He absently took a bite from the loaf of bread he carried in his hand, then chewed thoughtfully as he considered what he'd heard through the door. He hadn't heard the entire conversation, for Lord John had been facing the other direction, but Kafka's higher-pitched voice had carried easily. He'd heard something about a council, about cardinals, and something that led him to believe Kafka wasn't perfectly happy with the situation at Chlum Castle.

He took another bite of the bread—all he was allowed to eat during his self-imposed bread and water fast. Perhaps this Kafka held the same reservations that troubled Vasek. Lord John had always been a God-fearing and devout man, much like his father, but lately this Hus had addled the master's thinking. If Lord John was not careful, Hus would cause an irreparable breach in the church, and what would happen then to the thousands of men like Vasek who served the church while serving its nobles?

Hus had no idea how dangerous his ideas were. And like a maiden infatuated with a handsome knight, Lord John was content to blindly follow Hus.

He pursed his lips, thinking. If he could go to Prague, maybe he could talk to some of the priests in that city and see which way the political winds were blowing. Was Hus as popular with the people as Lord John believed? Or was his master committing political *and* spiritual suicide?

Vasek lowered the hard bread as his gut suddenly cramped. He'd been fasting with bread and water for a week, hoping that God would speak, but the only revelation he'd received thus far was the knowledge that naught but bread and water had a tendency to constipate the bowels.

Shaking his head, Vasek pressed his hand to his distended belly and hastened away to find a chamber pot.

Twenty-Three

The kitchen swarmed with activity the next day as the promised delegation descended upon Chlum Castle. Along with the representatives from Sigismund, several prominent members of the university arrived, primarily to entreat Hus to remain at home in Bohemia. Other lords from neighboring estates rode in, escorted by their knights, and valiantly offered to defend Hus in their castles.

At dinner, one of Sigismund's envoys actually stood and said to Hus, "Master, I speak now from my heart. If you go to Constance, be sure that you will be condemned. Listen to these men, and do not go."

"There is the promise of a safe conduct," another of Sigismund's representatives offered, standing to his feet. He bowed slightly to Lord John, then turned beady eyes upon the preacher. "The emperor will grant you a safe conduct which will guarantee an unmolested journey to Constance and a safe return to Bohemia. The emperor also promises that you will be allowed to speak before the council."

Lord John's chaplain, Vasek, leaned over his trencher and practically hissed at Hus. "It is what you want, isn't it?"

From where she sat at Lord John's right hand, Anika saw that Master Hus's face was resolute. He would go. He was eager to purge himself and the kingdom of Bohemia of the infamous charge of heresy. Her mouth curved with tenderness as she studied him. He would go, for she had never known Hus to refuse an invitation to preach.

"This is what I will do." Hus stood to his feet and nodded

respectfully toward the visiting nobles and imperial representatives. "I will post notices throughout the whole of Prague, offering to render an account of my faith and hope. I will obtain from Nicholas, the inquisitor of heresy for the city of Prague, a statement declaring me to be a true and Catholic man. Perhaps we can obtain a similar testimony from the archbishop."

Several of the nobles nodded enthusiastically.

"Then I shall go," Hus said, glancing down for a moment at Lord John. Anika saw a flicker of worry in her master's eyes but none at all in the preacher's. "With faith in God," Hus said, looking again at the crowd in the hall, "and buoyed by the testimony of my faithful brethren, we will go forward to meet the road ahead. It may be that we will be a candle in the darkness, shining the light of the Holy Scriptures into a void which has existed far too long."

Several of the nobles lifted their voices in supportive cheers, but Anika saw that others received Hus's proclamation with smug expressions.

"God knows I have taught nothing in secret, but in public," Hus went on. The smile he gave the crowd conveyed no reproach; rather it was almost apologetic. "My ministry was attended by masters, bachelors, priests, barons, knights, and many others. I thus desire to be heard, examined, and to preach not in secret but at a public hearing, and to reply with the aid of the Spirit of God to all who should wish to argue against me. I will not, I hope, be afraid to confess the Lord Christ."

His voice fell, and his face showed a delicate dimension of sensitivity. "And, if need be, to suffer death for his most true law. For he, the King of kings and the Lord of lords, the true God, being poor, mild, and humble, suffered for us, leaving us an example that we should follow in his footsteps. He who committed no sin, on whose lips no guile was found, who humbled himself, having by his death destroyed our death, has placed us under an obligation to suffer humbly and not in vain. For he said: 'Blessed are those who suffer persecution for justice's sake, for theirs is the kingdom of heaven.'"

A murmur of voices, a palpable unease, washed through the

room. Anika looked up quickly. Did Hus truly expect to suffer if he obeyed the emperor's summons?

"After turning this over in my mind, I, Christ's servant in hope, although unprofitable, have desired to induce both the clergy and the people toward his imitation," Master Hus continued. A spark of some indefinable emotion lit his eyes. "On that account I became hated, not indeed by all the people, but by those who oppose the Lord by their behavior. Having been very often cited by them to the archiepiscopal court, I have always proved myself innocent. Thus I commit myself into the hands of the most just Judge, for whose glory, I trust, the emperor will obtain for me a safe and public hearing under the protection of the Lord Jesus Christ."

Hus abruptly sat down, and Anika felt the wings of shadowy foreboding brush the back of her neck. Her father, were he alive, would surely tell Hus not to go to Constance. Even Petrov would warn the preacher that it would be foolishly naive to entrust himself to the goodwill of his examiners.

"Excuse me, Lord John?" From his place at Hus's left hand, Vasek leaned forward to catch his master's attention. "If I might, my lord, I would like to ride with the emperor's delegation when they return to Prague. It is not often that I have the opportunity to converse with scholars from the university."

"By all means, go," Lord John answered absently, his attention centered on Hus, who had closed his eyes as if in prayer.

From her place, Anika shivered as the sense of foreboding increased.

The knights of Chlum spent the summer months preparing for the journey to Constance. Hus remained at Chlum Castle to concentrate on the all-important confrontation ahead, while Jerome resumed Hus's place as preacher at Bethlehem Chapel. Now that Hus had commandeered Lord John's secretary again, Anika's days were once more filled with writing. In addition to the letters and records she transcribed for Lord John, she spent hours transcribing endless copies of Master Hus's proclamations to the people of Prague. Every citizen, from the lowliest farmer to the king and queen, would know of Hus's testimony, his doctrines, and his faith in Jesus Christ alone.

As a lowly preacher-priest, Hus had no income to speak of and thus depended upon friends and supporters to provision his journey. One afternoon at dinner Lord John entered the great hall with a bag of gold in one hand and a note in the other. Holding the gold aloft, he proudly announced that the esteemed lady in Prague had sent more than enough to provision the knights of Chlum for the trek to Constance. As the men erupted into cheers, Anika looked up at Lord John. Who was this esteemed and generous lady? Lady Zelenka? Lady Ludmila?

She waited until Lord John left the hall, then she approached Novak. "Who is this woman who sends such rich gifts?" she asked, trying to keep her voice light. "Is Lady Zelenka now trying to buy our lord's favor?"

Novak stepped back with a look of surprise as he broke into laughter. "Zelenka? I cry you mercy. How could you think Lady Zelenka would send money and request that her name be kept secret? If she sent a gift, she would emblazon her name upon it in gilded letters. No, our patroness is a married woman, and her concern is only for the gospel and Master Hus." Novak paused, arching his busy brows into triangles. "You wouldn't happen to be jealous of our lady friend, would you now?" he whispered. "Because I'd hate to have to explain *that* to the other fellows—"

"Of course not," Anika snapped, seething with sudden anger and humiliation. "I was curious, that's all. Nothing more. Nothing less. Forget it, Novak; put it out of your mind."

She hurried out of the castle and walked through the bright sunlight in the courtyard. A cool breeze from the mountains had swept away the heat of the summer day, and the western sky was awash with crimson and gold.

Anika clenched her fists as she walked toward the paddock where Svec and Lev sat on the fence watching the grooms break a new horse. What were these feelings that rose in her chest every time she looked at Lord John? These emotions—joy, warmth, and anxiety—

weren't exactly what the author of *The Art of Courtly Love* described. Love was supposed to be more refined, more predictable, and far more coy. This wasn't love she felt, it was . . . gratitude. Admiration. Perhaps a bit of infatuation. But nothing could come of these feelings. Lord John was a nobleman and she a humble merchant's daughter. Lady Zelenka, who continued to write long, gossipy letters to the master, would make him a better wife. Anika had received the distinct impression that the blond beauty was also waiting for Hus's case to be resolved. Then John would be less distracted and more ready to woo a bride.

With a grunted greeting, she climbed to a seat on the railing between the two boys. Svec gave her a smile, but Lev barely turned his head her way. He seemed intent upon watching the grooms with the horse, but from the expression in his eyes Anika knew his thoughts were far away.

"Is aught amiss, Lev?" she asked, leaning forward with her elbows on her knees. Like Lev, she kept her eyes turned toward the majestic stallion. "Maybe I can help."

"Sir Kafka." He spoke hesitantly, as if he were about to utter words he knew he would regret. "What do you know about girls?"

Anika nearly lost her balance on the fence. What did he mean? Had he discovered her secret? Perhaps Lord John was right—the squires were beginning to suspect.

"I know about girls," she answered softly, not willing to lie. "What would you like to know?"

Without warning, Lev's eyes slowly filled with tears. "There's a girl in the village; her name is Jana. I talk to her whenever we ride there to check on the harvest. And I think—I think I may be in love with her, but Lord John says I cannot marry until he gives me permission."

He looked at her then, and Anika saw wounded dignity in every line of his face. "How do I wait, Kafka? I see her, I want to be with her, I want to be at her side always, to make her happy—"

"How old are you, Lev?" she asked, sighing.

"Fourteen."

A smile tugged at Anika's lips. "Fourteen is a young age to find the love of one's heart. Why don't you listen to your father? He knows what is best for you. And while you are waiting, in my bag I have a book that will teach you what love is and how it is best pursued. You are a nobleman's son, and there are certain conventions which must be followed."

Lev nodded in what looked like relief, then turned his gaze outward again. "What about you, Kafka? You are older—have you loved someone?"

Anika felt a shudder of embarrassment and was grateful the boys had turned their eyes elsewhere. "I loved my father," she said, searching for words with which she could tell the truth and yet not reveal her heart. "I loved my mother, and I loved Sir Petrov. In a chaste and respectful way I love Master Hus."

"And so you must love Lord John, too," Svec observed, his young face brightening at the suggestion.

Anika felt her flesh color. "All the knights of Chlum love your father, for they are sworn to serve him," she answered quickly, determined to change the subject. "And why are you so formal? He is your father; you should refer to him as such. My father was as dear to me as my own life, and I never would have called him 'Ernan O'Connor.'"

"Lord John wants us to be like everyone else," Lev answered, rhythmically swinging his leg from the fence. "He doesn't want us to have special attention or special favors."

"You ought to at least have his special love," Anika answered, disappointment and frustration bringing a hard frown to her face. Why did her master keep people at arm's length? She could understand the social gap that kept him distanced from his knights and servants, but these two precious boys were his *sons.* They had no mother, and as long as Lord John continued to remain aloof, they did not have a father, either.

"I'll get that book for you later," she promised Lev as she slipped from the fence. "As soon as I've returned from speaking with your father."

She found Lord John in the kennel, his arms crossed and an expression of extreme satisfaction on his face as he looked at a bloodhound nursing her new litter in a sturdy crate. The mastiffs, Bilko and Bela, crouched by his side as usual, their alert faces tilted toward the mewling puppies as if they couldn't quite understand the reason for these new additions.

Anika cast the puppies a perfunctory glance, then braced herself for the confrontation. Lord John would not want to hear this from her, from anyone, but someone had to tell him he was hurting his sons. Apparently none of the other men cared enough, or maybe they didn't feel a responsibility toward Lev and Svec. But Anika understood how the boys felt; she sensed the hurt behind Lev's dark eyes and Svec's quiet whimpers in the dark. These boys were *lonely*, and they needed their father's affection.

"My lord."

He looked up, his eyes glowing with enjoyment. "Look at them, Kafka. Finer hounds are not to be found in Bohemia. These pups will be like their father, able to finish any stag the greyhounds chase."

She would not let herself be distracted. "My lord, I would speak to you of another father—my own. Because my mother died when I was young, he was closer to me than any other kin. He taught me, he fed me, he listened to me."

He offered her a distracted smile. "You have mentioned him several times."

"Yes, my lord. And now it seems to me that you ought to do the same for your sons." She took a deep breath and plunged carelessly on. "I used to think you were wise to put your sons with the men, but I have spent many hours with Lev and Svec, my lord, and they are unhappy. They love you as their master, but I fear they do not know you as their father—"

He whirled to stare at her, quick anger rising in his eyes. "Why do you speak of my children? They are nothing to you."

She felt suddenly weak and vulnerable in the face of his anger, but she could not back down. "In truth, my lord, they mean much to me. Lev has been a friend since my squire days, and Svec is still but a child, and he needs a father."

"They have a father." His dark eyes blazed amber fire. "They have me. They have more than the other squires. Most of the men in my garrison were raised to knighthood from their youths, and none of them were spoiled by a father's hand. If my sons are to be strong, if they are to be heirs of this estate, they must not be pampered and coddled."

"Pampered and coddled?" Anger singed her control. "Is that what you think I was? Pampered? Spoiled? Loving a child is no more pampering him than—" Sputtering for words, her mind went blank. "There!" she said finally, grasping for something he could understand. She pointed toward the newborn puppies. "Would you take these infants and toss them out into the courtyard with a pack of curs? Of course not! They need their mama! Likewise, your sons need you! There comes a time when you should not act the lord, but the father!"

He stood there, tall and angry, his eyes black and dazzling with fury. "Who are *you*," he said finally, an undertone of cold contempt in his voice, "to tell me what I should be? Look at you. You are neither woman, nor daughter, nor wife. What gives you the right to reproach me?"

She took a half-step back as his words pierced her heart. Who was she, indeed? She had felt certain that this confrontation was right, that he respected her enough to heed her advice. They had spent so many hours working together—he knew her secrets, and she thought he understood the deepest motivations of her heart. Her head swam as she reversed the situation and considered his point of view. He would think she had glibly gone to him to point out the speck in his eye, forgetting that she bore a beam in her own.

"You know who I am," she whispered, stunned by the sudden declaration of war between them. "You, more than anyone. But I'm beginning to think I don't know you at all!"

She turned to run away, but his right hand caught her elbow. He pulled her roughly toward him, his hand now locking against her spine, drawing her into his arms. "You know me," he whispered into her hair, a possessive desperation in his voice. "But you should not."

Spellbound with new and compelling sensations, Anika could not answer. A trembling thrill raced through her as he lifted his palm to her cheek, and she wondered if he could feel in it the pounding of her pulse. The touch of his hand was suddenly almost unbearable in its tenderness, but none of this made sense, none of this should be happening.

As if he had read her thoughts in her eyes, he abruptly released her. Backing away, he stared at the ground for a moment, then whistled for the mastiffs and strode out of the kennel.

What had he been thinking?

John walked past Demetr with an uplifted hand, not willing to take time to hear the steward's list of complaints. Anika had come to him out of concern, and he had attacked her feelings and her respect for him, and then he had reached out to touch her—

Foolishness. Complete and utter foolishness. He had already broken one woman's heart; he would not toy with another's.

"Lord John—" Demetr padded after him, waving a parchment.

John turned abruptly and thrust his hand into his belt. "Later, Demetr. I need some time alone. Grant me a few moments privacy, at least. If you have questions, take them to Sir Novak or Peter or—"

"Sir Kafka, my lord?"

John glanced up in suspicion, but Demetr's face was seamless and bland. The question was most likely an innocent one, since Kafka had been helping with so many of the estate's records. "Yes. Take your questions elsewhere. But pray leave me alone."

Demetr nodded and hurried away. John let himself into his empty bedchamber, then sank into a chair. Bela and Bilko collapsed gratefully at his side, probably as confused as he about the events of the morning.

Lowering his head onto his hand, John grasped at the strings of reality and held them tightly. He was the lord of a vast manor; he had responsibilities to his villagers, to his king, to his friend Jan Hus, to God Almighty. He fulfilled his responsibility to his sons by taking care of the estate which would one day be Lev's and by training Svec for knighthood. Surely that ought to be enough.

His mind burned with the memory of Kafka's accusing eyes. No. It wasn't enough. He worked his hand through his hair, resisting the truth. Kafka's words, spoken in honest concern, had laid bare the mere tip of a long seam of guilt that snaked its way back through the years.

He never should have married Frantiska, his sons' mother, but the marriage doubled the size of Chlum estate. His widowed mother, eager to secure a place for her son, had arranged everything from the size of the dowry to the blushing bride's wedding gown. And in those early days, John had appreciated Frantiska's gentle and overwhelming beauty. She was an exquisite moonbeam too delicate for daylight and too ethereal for the vagaries of political life. Born with a desolate, shallow soul, she often wilted like a flower in the cold winds of a disagreement. She had no values or dedications beyond her own walls, and as the years passed she remained pathetically girlish in behavior.

Yet John believed Frantiska was all a wife should be. And his feelings for her—which varied from the pride one feels for a lovely possession to indifference—were all he knew of love. As time passed and the boys were born, Frantiska remained majestic and beautifully aloof, yet somehow seemed shadowed, even with an aura of sunlight around her. She withdrew into herself, shunning John's company and her sons' affections. And one morning while the boys studied with Vasek and John hunted with his knights, she hanged herself from a beam in the stable.

Later Vasek assured John that the girl's temperament was flawed. John should not blame himself for Frantiska's tragic end, the chaplain said, for 'twas obvious that the humors of cold and dryness made hers a negative, obsessive, depressive, and brooding temperament. The theory was proved by the fact that she chose to end her life in autumn, in the period between noon and six P.M., the time when the melancholic temperament was strongest and life waned out of the earth.

Despite Vasek's logical explanations, guilt still plagued John. In honest moments alone John admitted that he had given her less time and attention than he routinely gave his dogs. He had intended to cherish and respect her, and to every public eye he had seemed a model husband, but his heart could never rise to the level of his own expectation. He had cared for her, protected her, fathered two sons with her. But he had never loved her.

And Kafka had just told him that he did not know how to love his sons.

He shuddered inwardly at the thought that he might compound his error, but he had set his course and could not turn back. The boys were safe in the garrison, for over forty pairs of eyes watched over them. They knew their station, they knew he was near, they knew he would listen to their concerns as readily as he listened to any man in the garrison with a complaint.

But love was not for him. God had filled his life with other responsibilities.

Twenty-Four

Throughout the next several weeks, Anika felt a wretchedness of mind she'd never known before. Lord John sensed it, she was certain, for he did not send for her unless there were others present in the room—as if he could not trust her not to rail at him again.

She watched him with sorrow in her eyes, wishing she could tell him that her anger had faded to concern and compassion. Obviously some secret pain kept him from enjoying his sons' company—did he miss his wife so much that the mere sight of the boys distressed him? The woman had been dead for nearly five years, but Anika knew her father had mourned his wife at least that long.

Why? She quizzed him silently, watching her master stare out the window as she copied a letter about Hus's upcoming journey. *Why can't you leave the past behind and see that two loving sons need you very much?*

But his eyes, when he turned to her, were indecipherable. And so she turned back to her parchments, seeking in work the mindless activity that helped her escape—at least temporarily—the deep despair of her loneliness.

By October 11, 1414, the designated day of departure, Anika noted that the Constance-bound procession had grown to include not only Lord John, Peter Mladenovic, Vasek, and a full company of knights from Chlum, but also Lord Venceslas of Duba; Jerome, Hus's assistant and chief disciple; and John Reinstein, a sympathetic parish priest from Prague.

The crisp morning air, bathed in orange sunlight, carried faint hints of coming winter days as the company set out from Chlum. By the time the sun climbed overhead, the procession had entered Prague's city gates. As they moved paradelike through the city, Anika watched in amazement as the houses, shops, and university emptied. A huge throng followed Hus's carriage to the western city gate, where weeping men and women waved their kerchiefs and promised to pray for him.

Upon her horse behind Hus's carriage, Anika heard the shouts of blessing and approval and felt her heart pound beneath her disguising armor. She was glad to leave Chlum, for there she spent too much time in close proximity to a man for whom her feelings grew more confused each day. Her armor, sword, and shield now reminded her why she had set out to become a knight. She had vowed to defend the truth and gain vengeance against those who had destroyed her loved ones. She should rejoice that they had left Chlum Castle, for God had finally placed her feet upon the path she had sought so long.

She now saw with abrupt clarity that the time had come to put thoughts of Lord John, his children, and his sorrows behind her. From this day until her parents were avenged, she would concentrate on the task she had yet to complete.

"Lord John, halt!"

John pulled back on his reins, recognizing the advancing rider's blue and gold standard as his own. This would be Sir Manville or Gregor, both of whom had been scouting the countryside ahead for a possible ambush.

The knight came closer and slowed his horse, then lifted his visor. Through the opening, John recognized Manville's ruddy face. "Ho, Sir Manville, and how is the way ahead?"

"Clear as a mountain stream, my lord," Manville answered, shooting John a lopsided grin. "There's an inn about an hour's ride from this place, and there I met other scouts on patrol."

"Oh?" John folded his hands across the pommel of his saddle.

"And as you lifted a tankard to my health, did you hear any interesting gossip?"

Manville grinned. "Aye, Lord John. It seems that Lord Laco of Lidice and his knights are venturing out to Constance, too. They are ahead of us, though, by two days, so we should not encounter them on the road."

"Laco, eh?" John asked, trying to appear nonchalant. An oddly primitive warning had sounded in his brain at the mention of that nobleman's name, but he had to sheath his inner feelings. After all, Laco had done nothing wrong. He was known to be ambitious, conniving, and ruthless, but though he was a frequent associate of Cardinal D'Ailly and several other prelates, he had made no public condemnations of Master Hus.

But his son had threatened Anika.

John gripped his reins and glanced behind him. Anika rode next to Lev near the end of the procession. Surely she was safe, for no one looking at her in armor would suppose her to be a woman . . . but John could not ride in peace knowing she might be exposed. Only two months before, he had heard that Laco's men were still searching for the elusive red-haired maiden, even offering a reward for anyone who found her.

"Very good, Manville," he said, nodding his thanks to the knight. "And will you do me the service of riding behind Kafka and Lev? Those two young ones talk too much on the journey. I fear they might wander off in the woods and lose us."

If Manville thought the request odd, he gave no indication of it. "Aye, my lord," he said, inclining his head. As Manville turned his horse and moved toward the back of the line, John slapped his reins and urged his own mount forward.

The procession moved on into the countryside, and as the swollen sun hung low in the west, Anika spied their destination: the castle belonging to the Earl of Tesar, an old friend of Lord John's. The deforested pasture surrounding the castle gleamed like copper in the fading light, and the sun's bright beams gilded the castle's massive stone walls. On a pair of imposing twin towers flags emblazoned with the earl's family crest fluttered in the slight breeze. Anika thought of the knights who lived in those towers and shifted uneasily in the saddle, wondering if she would have any trouble in the night. She had never encountered difficulty in the garrison at Chlum with her comrades; each man instinctively left his fellows alone in the dark, affording each other a modicum of privacy. But tonight after supper she would have to find a place to sleep in the straw, for Tesar's knights surely would not give up their bunks to a band of competitive visitors.

The earl had obviously been alerted to their approach. The gates yawned in welcome and the knights of Tesar lined the drawbridge and the indented ramparts. Several men on horseback were now approaching, their pennants streaming in the wind. Anika thought she could smell the mouth-watering aroma of roasting beef, and her stomach clenched in anticipation of a hearty meal. They had not eaten since leaving Chlum, and she was as hungry as a nun on the last day of Lent.

With the others, she spurred her horse into an easy canter, and watched the castle rise up before her.

The knights of Chlum were greeted with much slapping on the back and roughhousing, and Anika quietly thanked God that her slight form forestalled the inevitable challenges the knights tossed at one another. No one wanted to challenge a scarecrow, Novak told her, so she'd be safe enough.

After supper there would be jousting and wrestling and fencing in the field, dangerous enough exercises in the light of day and hardly appropriate activities for torchlight. But the knights of Chlum were eager to expend pent-up energy, and the knights of Tesar were anxious to prove their valor. Manville and Novak, due to their size and reputations, were challenged immediately, and Anika stepped back into the shadows of the stable, unwilling to attract attention. The long day of riding in heavy armor had done nothing but weary her, and after supper she planned on staking out a quiet spot in the barn and losing herself in sleep.

The flare of torchlight from an upper balcony caught her eye, and she stepped forward, hoping the light meant that supper would soon be served. In the orange red glow Anika saw Lord John, Jan Hus, and the shadowy forms of a man and woman. The unknown man stepped forward. The Earl of Tesar—for surely this was he—had a wide-shouldered, square body and black hair that flowed from his face like a crest.

"Welcome, knights of Chlum!" he called, his confident voice ringing over the courtyard. "You grace us with your presence and your bravery, and our prayers will go with you on the morrow as you carry one of Bohemia's most precious sons to do God's bidding!"

Cheers rose in great waves from the assembled knights, bringing a blush to Master Hus's face. He stood silently, his hands clasped in front of him, his eyes focused on his host's face.

"I am the Earl of Tesar," the man continued, playing his role with great relish, "and this fair beauty you know, my lovely daughter Zelenka."

Anika blinked in dismay and surprise as the earl took the woman's hand and led her from the shadows into the torchlight. Lady Zelenka! Anika had not seen that lady in over a year, and some part of her hoped that the bloom had faded from the rose. But there Zelenka stood, still lovely, still eager to smile at Lord John.

Zelenka lifted her hand to the knights in a graceful salute, then allowed her eyes to roam over the crowd like an eagle searching for prey.

"I wish I could bring you all in to sup with me and your master," the earl was saying, but Anika could not look at him. Her eyes were fastened instead upon Zelenka, who stood with her bare shoulder brushing Lord John's arm, a few strands of her golden hair clinging to his cloak as if drawn by some magnetic force.

"Father." Zelenka's voice, though quiet, carried throughout the courtyard. At the sound of her silvery tones even the background sounds of activity ceased. Every man present leaned forward in anticipation of her next words. A smile nudged itself into a corner of the lady's mouth. "Father, I see an old friend, a knight I met at Chlum. Will you allow me to invite him in to dine with us?"

Surprised out of his graciousness, the earl turned and gaped at her. "One of the knights?" he stammered, obviously reluctant. "At our supper?"

"Yes." The girl threw the crowd a triumphant smile that set the knights to cheering. Anika felt her heart contract in pity for whatever unfortunate the girl had singled out. The other knights, with the sole exception of Novak, leaned forward, hoping for the summons from on high. Zelenka's pale arm lifted, the delicate finger pointed—in Anika's direction.

"The wee one," Zelenka called, her voice brimming with false sweetness. "The little knight there, in the hooded hauberk. I believe his name is Sir Kafka."

Anika's heart turned to stone within her chest, weighing down her legs so she could not move. She saw—no, felt—every head in the courtyard turn and strain to see her, and suddenly she wished the sand under her feet would part so the earth could swallow her whole.

"I don't suppose one wee knight will disturb our fellowship. Have the man come up." The earl raised his daughter's hand in an elegant gesture and turned to leave the balcony. Anika lifted her eyes in time to see Lord John look toward her with an inscrutable expression on his face, while Master Hus sent her a smile of bemused pity. *You have made your bed,* his smile seemed to say. *Now lie in it.*

And while the other knights slapped her on the back and made insincere jokes about how lucky Kafka was to have caught the lady's eye, Anika clenched her hand until her nails entered her palm. Lord John had told her that Zelenka had seen through Anika's disguise. The earl's daughter was fully aware that she had just invited another woman to her father's table.

What sort of torture was this? *It is nothing. It means nothing. Zelenka only means to toy with me; this has nothing to do with Lord John.* Desperate to prove to herself that she was immune to anything that might happen in her master's presence, Anika straightened her shoulders, brushed the dust from her surcoat, then strode toward the doorway that led to the earl's banquet hall.

Though she was starving, Anika could eat little, for her stomach churned with anxiety and frustration. She remained silent throughout the meal, content to be ignored so she could listen to her master's voice, but her attention to the conversation was distracted by Zelenka's actions and attitudes. The earl's comely daughter sat across from Anika but next to Lord John, and her face proved to be a study in contrasts. One moment she pouted, her rosebud lips pointed down in a gesture clearly designed to indicate her displeasure, but the next moment her hand was on John's arm and her blue eyes bright with admiration as she gazed up at him. Though many months had passed since she had visited Chlum, Zelenka looked more beautiful and irresistible than ever, and Anika found herself comparing her callous and ink-stained hands to Zelenka's dainty palms.

Why would John prefer the company of a girl whose face was streaked with dirt when he could have one who had painted her cheeks as prettily as a rose? Why would he cultivate friendship with a scrawny girl with chopped coppery hair when he could have lustrous golden braids streaming through his fingers? Zelenka displayed her smooth bosom and arms to her advantage, while Anika wore dusty layers: a linen shift, a mail hauberk, plates of iron, a shapeless surcoat.

Why would Lord John even think of Anika as a woman when he had Zelenka to fill his dreams? 'Twas a wonder he did not forget who and what Anika was, so well had she hidden whatever charms she might have had . . . once.

Swallowing the despair in her throat, she looked down at her trencher and uselessly moved her uneaten food with her spoon. Zelenka's laughter cut through the silence, a soothing sound like music on a quiet night. Anika lifted her head. Through tear-filled eyes she saw Zelenka smiling, her hand on John's shoulder, her eyes glowing with—love?

The earl stood and pushed back his chair, and instantly Master Hus and Lord John followed suit. Anika nearly sat still until she remembered that as a man she, too, must rise, so she sprang immediately to her feet.

"This knight of yours has said little tonight," the earl told his daughter, a faintly reproachful note in his voice. "I think he might have preferred to eat with his comrades in the yard below."

"No," Zelenka answered, her eyes crossing to meet Anika's. "We will have a private word now, my friends, as you go your way. Good night, Father, Master Hus." She looked up at Anika's master with dreamy eyes. "Good night, my lord."

Amid much shuffling and the exchanging of pleasantries, the men left the room. Anika bowed stiffly and tried to follow, but a stern command from Zelenka stopped her.

"I know your little game," the lady said, resting her elbows on the arms of her chair. She tented her dainty hands and stared at Anika over the tips of her manicured fingernails. "I know you are a woman. And if you think you can win Lord John's heart through this little pretense of yours—"

"My lady, I can assure you nothing lies further from my mind," Anika interrupted, keeping her voice low. "Lord John is my master, and I have sworn fealty to him. That is all I ever wanted to do."

"Oh?" A sudden icy contempt flashed in the other woman's eyes. "If all you ever wanted to do was become a knight, why do you remain at Chlum Castle? You have proved yourself; you are no longer a lowly squire. Are you so unnatural that you do not long for the love of a good man? Do you not wish to raise sons and daughters? To feel a man's arms around you in the night?"

Anika closed her eyes against the unexpected emotions that rose in her breast. "No," she whispered, her voice strangled by anger and jealousy. "I only wish to serve him—and to fulfill a vow I made. And that vow has nothing to do with Lord John."

"Then you are the most unnatural of women," Zelenka answered. She gazed at Anika with chilling intentness for a long moment, then pursed her lips in a suspicious expression. "And yet, something tells me you are not."

"How do you know anything about me?" Anika countered, irritated by Zelenka's mocking tone. "You do not know me at all. We have nothing in common."

"But we do," Zelenka answered, lightly bringing her fingertips to her lips. Her mouth pursed up in a tiny rosette, then unpuckered enough to continue. "We are women, and women understand each other. I can see from the look in your eyes that you love your master, even as you see that I am clearly out to claim the prize you cannot have."

Shock flew through Anika. She stood by the side of the table, blank, amazed, and very shaken, until her tongue loosened enough to reply. "I am surprised," she finally managed to say, "that you have waited so long for Lord John. Surely there are other unmarried lords with vast estates."

"None so vast as Chlum," Zelenka answered. She leaned back in her chair and contentedly sipped from her glass. "And there are no lords so handsome as Lord John. I will wait forever, if need be, or at least until this matter with the preacher is settled. Master Hus occupies Lord John's mind now, but soon that matter will be finished. And when it is, I shall be ready to return to Chlum . . . as its mistress."

A flurry of protestations rose to Anika's lips, but she bit them back with a discipline forged on Novak's relentless training field. "If you have no further need of me," she said, turning to face Zelenka in a deliberately casual movement, "I would like to join my comrades."

"Go." Zelenka leaned toward her, her eyes cold. "I hope I never see you again."

"If God is good to us, my lady," Anika answered, each word a splinter of ice, "you will not."

She could not love Lord John. It was impossible. As the procession of mounted knights, clerics, and nobles moved southwestward through the Bohemian Forest, Anika reminded herself that her master had courted daughters of nobles, many of whom would bring dowries that would further enrich his estate. Many of them, like Zelenka, were beautiful and witty, others sweet and holy. When he could have his choice from any of them, why would he even consider her? He thought her strange, and though he respected her work, he probably thought her more fit for perdition than matrimony. He only allowed her to remain at Chlum because she was skilled with a pen and languages; he had no patience for her dreams and no understanding of her motivation.

Why, then, did her heart ache every time he walked by? And how had Zelenka known this? Had Anika somehow revealed her emotions on her face?

She was secretly pleased when Lord John decided to ride today in the carriage with Jan Hus, Jerome, and Lord Venceslas of Duba. Their days were filled with plotting and strategies, Anika suspected, and Lord John would have no time for romance or longings for Zelenka. If she concentrated on her work, perhaps her attention would be distracted as well.

Anika sighed. Passing a single hour without thinking of Lord John seemed about as impossible as counting the stars in the night sky.

Twenty-Five

B aldasarre Cossa, more commonly known as Pope John XXIII, leaned forward in his gilded carriage, annoyed that a herdsman with an unstable flock of sheep had blocked the road. "Driver," he called, rapping on the roof of his conveyance with his walking stick, "run them over, do you hear? The man obviously has no idea who rides in this carriage. Run over the filthy beasts, and let the man count himself blessed that God's representative has noticed him today."

The crack of the whip rang out, the carriage jolted forward, and Baldasarre cursed softly under his breath as he was thrown off balance. What a lot of foolishness this council was. He hadn't wanted to leave Rome. He had only agreed to this council because not agreeing would most certainly lead to his condemnation from afar. And though he didn't know how they would evict him from his Roman palace, he feared that someone might try to do it by subtle means. After all, he had assumed the pope's crown after feeding his weakling predecessor, Alexander V, a healthy dose of poison.

Uncertainty gnawed at his confidence. One could never be too sure which way the winds of fate might blow. In his lifetime, Baldasarre had been many things—soldier, scholar, pirate—and through all his journeys he had come to see that only one thing mattered: power. With power came money, renown, and women, all the pleasures that lightened a man's soul, but without power a man was little more than the dust of the earth, as useless and worthless as peasants who worked the soil outside a nobleman's estate.

And so he had cultivated power. Among the retinue of cardinals and bishops that followed him now in ornate carriages he had few friends; Baldasarre preferred to anchor his future to strongholds *outside* the church. He had paused in Tyrol to confirm his alliance with Duke Frederick of Austria, a genteel nobleman with no money and a great love for creative melodrama.

"Your Holiness!" A brightly uniformed servant rode up on horseback, bringing a choking cloud of dust into the carriage. Baldasarre bit back an oath and stared at the man.

"Constance is just ahead, Your Holiness. I thought you might like to know."

There went that instinct again, seizing him by the guts and yanking for his attention. Fear blew down the back of Baldasarre's neck, but he shook it off and hunched forward, gesturing for the servant to fling open the door of the carriage.

"Let me out!" he screamed, not waiting for the red carpets which were usually spread before he would descend. The princely procession had halted atop a hill, and below, in the valley, Baldasarre could see the city of Constance glittering like a jewel by the shore of the lake.

Despite his earlier apprehensions, his confidence spiraled upward. "'Tis a pit for catching foxes," he proclaimed, holding up both hands in delight. As his bewildered bishops scrambled out to see what had caught the holy father's attention, Baldasarre gathered his robes and climbed back into his regal chariot.

"Drive on!" he bellowed.

The route to Constance had taken Hus and his party through Barnau, the imperial free city of Nuremberg, and numerous other small towns. Everywhere they journeyed, even in the German territories, Anika was amazed and pleased at how well Jan Hus was received. Any and all suspicions the people might have harbored after hearing lies about the preacher from Prague vanished as the man himself won supporters with his earnestness and humility. By the time he left, the common people and humbler clergy felt that he fought for them.

At Nuremberg, their hearty welcome forced a delay of several hours, for the people were eager to see Hus and hold a public disputation. Priests, a doctor of theology, and several magistrates were assembled in the city hall, waiting for Hus. After a few hours of debate, public opinion had swung firmly to the reformer's side.

That night Anika helped Hus pen a letter to friends in Prague. "I have not," he dictated, "met a single enemy as yet."

Reports of Hus and his speaking skills spread like wildfire through the country, and soon they had to stop and let the preacher speak at every village the procession passed through. In each place the priests and religious scholars engaged the Bohemians in theological discussion. In Biberach, Anika had to smother a broad smile when Lord John took so prominent and enthusiastic a part in the debate that the citizens believed him to be a doctor of theology. From that day forward, Hus jokingly referred to Lord John as "the doctor of Biberach."

"Do not forget your own name, O goose," Lord John replied, enjoying the gentle sparring.

On November third, not quite a month after leaving Prague, the Bohemians arrived at Constance. The picturesque beauty of the town stunned Anika. Situated on the south bank of the Rhine, the imperial free city normally boasted a population of fifty thousand. But now that the world's attention had focused on the city, the population had doubled. The streets blazed with gorgeous color—red-robed cardinals moving among blue surcoats and bright gowns of women. Horses with waving plumes pranced in the streets, ridden by knights in polished armor trailing gleaming standards. The pope and the emperor would both join the convention, Anika reminded herself, and with each would come a numerous and dazzling array of officers and attendants.

In addition to all the invited participants, a throng of merchants, artisans, retainers and curious visitors jammed Constance, drawn by curiosity, the possibility of making money, and the probability of pleasure. Anika heard Lord John remark that this was the largest congress the world had ever seen.

Because the inns were full, booths and wooden buildings were hastily erected for the accommodation of visitors, while thousands more camped in the surrounding countryside. Lord John arranged a hasty encampment for his men, though he fully intended to remain at Jan Hus's side for as long as possible.

Through an arrangement with the council, Hus himself was lodged in the house of a righteous widow named Fida. Her modest dwelling was not far from the episcopal palace where the pope and his entourage were headquartered.

After seeing Hus safely to his room in Fida's house, Lord John turned to Anika and Novak, who alone had followed him into town. "With all respect to you, Mistress Fida," John said, bowing deeply while the elderly woman twittered in pleased surprise, "my knights and I must report Master Hus's presence here in the city. We will return, but if anyone gives you cause for concern regarding Master Hus's safety, please do not hesitate to send me word."

The woman nodded, a clump of white hair clustered in short curls around her heart-shaped face. "I will take good care of Master Hus." She spoke in a tone filled with awe and respect. "You need not fear for his safety while he is here. The archbishop of the city has assigned a guard to my house at night; 'tis one of the safest in Constance."

"Thank you, gentle lady." With a gallant gesture, Lord John bent to kiss the woman's plump hand, and Anika smiled at the blush of delight that rose to the woman's cheeks.

The episcopal palace, home to the archbishop of Constance and now to Pope John XXIII, dwarfed Chlum Castle in size and majesty. Anika could not tell if the treasures inside the plastered and painted hallways had been brought in for the pope or resided with the archbishop, but either way she thought it unseemly for churchmen to indulge in such an ostentatious show of wealth. The church elders had gathered in Constance, after all, to discuss reform so that the common people might benefit from the church, and such a show of affluence only accented the great gulf which existed between the clergy and those they supposedly served.

They were kept waiting for the space of half an hour, then a pair of servants in bright red and gold livery opened a pair of gilded doors and admitted them into the presence of Christ's representative on earth.

Standing beside Novak, a few paces behind Lord John, Anika stared at the robed figure seated on a gilded chair. Her first thought was that John XXIII was no servant of Christ—or anyone else. Aloof on his golden throne, he had an air of authority and the appearance of one who demanded instant obedience. Massive shoulders filled the spotless white robe he wore, and from the flowing sleeves two impatient hands tapped against the armrest of his chair. Thick, tawny-gold hair fell from the tonsure on his pate, and his square, florid face was shaped into lines and pouches of sagging flesh that suggested dissipation rather than age. He did not look capable of any pleasant emotion.

His square jaw tensed visibly as the trio approached.

"You are Lord John of Chlum, are you not?" the pope barked, not waiting for a formal introduction.

"Yes, Your Eminence."

Anika watched with muted pride as her master bowed formally to the man who had no right to wear the crown of Christ. The correct form of address when speaking to the pope was "Your Holiness," but her master had used the address reserved for cardinals. While others might think his greeting a mere lapse in memory or a fault in manners, Anika knew Lord John was making a point—a very sharp one.

The pope's dark eyes flashed imperiously. "You have brought Jan Hus?"

"Yes." Lord John nodded abruptly. "He is safely ensconced in the widow Fida's house."

"*Bene.*" The pope seemed to measure the three of them in a cool, appraising look. "It is my duty to reassure you that your friend is in good hands. No one will be allowed to molest him, and I myself will preserve his safety. His sentence of excommunication is suspended while he remains here, so the city will not be subject to interdict on his account."

"How kind . . . and convenient of you."

Anika was alarmed at a certain reckless note in her master's voice.

Before Lord John could turn to leave, the pope lifted his jeweled hand. "All I require," he said, eyeing them with a prim and forbidding expression, "is that you ask Master Hus to remain in the widow's house. To avoid scandal, let him not attend public worship. He may receive guests as often as he likes, and the widow Fida shall, at my provision, supply all his needs."

"What about mass?" Lord John asked, shifting his weight and folding his arms. "My friend is a pious man and would like to partake in Holy Communion."

"He is a priest, isn't he?" Sudden anger lit the pope's eyes. "Let him say his own mass in the privacy of his room. It shall be enough."

Anika bit her lip, half-afraid her master would return the pope's contemptuous words with a few of his own, but after a half-second, her master inclined his head in a small gesture of thanks. "You are right, it is enough," he answered, his voice pleasant. "Jan Hus has never needed any man's help to reach the heart of God."

As her own heart brimmed with pride, Anika stepped aside to let her master pass. Then she and Novak followed him from the pope's pretentious chamber.

Cardinal D'Ailly ducked behind a statue as Lord John and his knights exited the chamber. He felt a sudden darkness behind his eyes and a chilly dew on his skin. John of Chlum's presence could mean only one thing—Jan Hus had arrived in Constance. The schismatic who would destroy a thousand years' work of refining religion would soon stand before them to have his heresy exposed.

D'Ailly took a deep breath to calm the erratic pounding of his heart. The fox was near the trap; he ought to be relieved, but doubts and apprehensions still clouded his brain. Hus had the luck of the devil; he had escaped their carefully laid snares before. And each time he had stolen souls from the church. Hundreds of men and women who had faithfully trusted in Holy Mother Church were now following the dangerous winds of dissension, riding first one current of heresy, then another. Hus claimed to interpret the Holy Scriptures and give them to the people, but common people could not understand the things of God. Only men who had studied the Hebrew and Greek could be trusted. Only men who had studied the laws of the church should be allowed to teach and preach.

Hus had become dangerous, and so had his friend, this John of Chlum. Fortunately, however, D'Ailly had one friend in Chlum's camp—the chaplain. Though D'Ailly could not remember the little man's name, he was certain the priest would soon appear.

Unlucky coins and impoverished relatives always turned up.

———

Swiveling his head to keep his master in view, Vasek waited until Lord John and the two knights disappeared. Then he skulked out of his hiding place and tugged on Cardinal D'Ailly's sleeve. The cardinal ought to remember him, for they had met more than once in Prague.

"Cardinal D'Ailly, a word," Vasek whispered, glancing left and right to be certain his master would not reappear. "I must see His Holiness." He indicated the door with a jerk of his head. "My master has just left the pope, and I have news which may be helpful. I promise you, His Holiness will be pleased to hear from me."

The cardinal stiffened and turned up his nose at Vasek as if he had caught a whiff of some vile smell. "What did you say your name was?" he asked, distrust chilling his hooded eyes.

"Vasek," the chaplain replied, wiping his hands on his tunic. "Surely you remember me. I serve Lord John at Chlum Castle and have traveled for the past month with the one called Jan Hus."

At the mention of Lord John's name, the cardinal gave Vasek a fixed and meaningless smile. "What news have you to offer His Holiness?"

Vasek gave the man a tentative smile. "I know what the Bohemian preacher plans to say. I have heard him rehearsing his arguments. I know he hopes for a public hearing so he may further spread these heresies."

"Wait here." D'Ailly turned soundlessly and slipped through the double doors, then reappeared before Vasek had finished reciting the *Our Father.*

"His Holiness will see you," the cardinal remarked, his eyes as hard as dried peas and his mouth drawn into a knot. "Make certain that your news is trustworthy, or you may regret having approached us today."

———

As freely as a cascading waterfall, Vasek let all he knew of Jan Hus flow from his tongue. The pope listened silently, his heavy cheeks falling in worried folds over the stole around his neck. Three other cardinals hovered nearby, their beaked and surly features turned toward Vasek like hungry birds of prey.

When Vasek had emptied himself of all the information he thought useful, he lifted hopeful eyes toward the pope. Silence settled upon the group, an absence of sound that had almost a physical density. Vasek found himself struggling to breathe the strangely thickened air.

Then Cardinal D'Ailly spoke. "Why have you come to us?" he asked, his eyes cold and polished as obsidian beads. "You are a servant of Chlum. How do we know this is not a trap?"

"It is not; by my honor, it is not," Vasek explained, thrusting his hands forward in an open gesture. "I am disturbed, Your Eminence, Your Holiness, by what I see happening in my beloved country. The old ways are under attack. The priests are overthrown and tossed out of their churches. I have seen bishops' houses ransacked and their treasures taken out and given to the poor. The nobles who once sided with the Holy Mother Church in all things now follow Master Hus.

I love my master, but I believe Hus has infected his soul with heresy. I only want to restore greatness and truth to the house of Chlum before its nobility and strength disappear."

"I think," the pope said, a thin smile on his lips, "a more apt question might be what you expect of us. What do you require of us, Vasek of Chlum? If we accept your help in this matter, what do you expect in return?"

Vasek paused as the question hammered at him. He had come for noble purposes only. He certainly had not intended to achieve material gain, but if the pope was offering something, he might be a fool to refuse. If he appeared greedy, however, His Holiness might show Vasek the door and expose his disloyalty to Lord John.

He lowered his eyes in what he hoped was a humble expression. "Your Holiness, I am a servant of Christ's Holy Church. As God is my witness, I came here with no thought of personal profit."

"But if you do us a service, you deserve recompense." The pope's voice was like velvet lined with steel. "Do not be foolish, Vasek. Do not even the Scriptures say that a servant is worthy of his hire? Even so, if you aid us, God will reward you. We are pleased to be his hands and his mind in this matter."

Vasek looked up, hope lightening his heart. "I am only a servant of Christ's Holy Church," he repeated, "but since I will be unwelcome at Chlum Castle if Master Hus is discredited through my efforts, I had thought that I might like to take charge of one of the churches in Prague. There is a nice church on the south side of the city whose priest died last summer—"

"A mere priest?" A smile crawled to D'Ailly's lips and curved itself like a snake. "You are a humble man, Vasek. Why not wish to become a bishop? Archbishop of the city? Such things could be accomplished, you know. And perhaps God shall work in this way. Everything will depend upon the service you render to Christ's Holy Church."

"What more can I do?" Vasek cried, groping through a haze of feelings and desires. He hadn't expected this. He had thought he would tell what he knew and be done with everything.

"We need to arrest him," another cardinal said, interrupting Vasek's thoughts. "And we cannot do it without cause since the Holy Father has given his word that Hus will not be molested. We need a cause, Vasek. We need you to entice Master Hus to do something for which he can be arrested and taken into our custody."

Vasek lowered his gaze in confusion. "He is a godly man. He has no faults, no vices for which you could arrest him."

"Find something," D'Ailly urged, stepping closer. "Use your imagination. Has he a fondness for women? For gold? Perhaps among his papers you could find a copy of that heretic Wyclif's writings. That would be grounds for arrest. All you must do is report to us, and we will take care of the matter. No one else need ever know of your part in it."

Vasek stepped back, momentarily rebuffed as a war of emotions raged within him. Why, they spoke as if he were about to commit some sort of shameful act! Why should he be ashamed of helping them expose a traitor and schismatic?

Pope John held out a soothing hand. "My son," he said, his voice losing its steely edge, "we will support you in whatever you do. We know your heart is loyal to the Church, and we are confident that God will give you opportunity and wisdom." He folded his hands and gave Vasek a disarming smile. "Go in peace, my son."

Vasek felt his heart fall. Was he to be dismissed so soon?

"If you think of anything which might aid us," D'Ailly added, with no expression on his face, "come again. You will be admitted."

Vasek gathered the rags of his dignity and bowed to the Holy Father. As he turned to leave, he congratulated himself on keeping his honor and his wits firmly about him.

———

Two days after the Bohemians' arrival in Constance, Lord Venceslas of Duba brought the safe conduct from Sigismund. Hus, Lord John, Novak, and Anika gathered around to read it:

Sigismund, by the grace of God, King of the Romans, etc.:—To all princes, ecclesiastical and lay, and all our other subjects, greeting. Of our full affection, we recommend to all in general, and to each individually, the honorable man, Master John Hus, bachelor in theology and master of arts, the bearer of these presents, going from Bohemia to the Council of Constance, whom we have taken under our protection and safeguard, and under that of the empire, requesting, when he arrives among you, that you will receive him kindly and treat him favorably, furnishing him whatever shall be necessary to promote and secure his journey, whether by water or by land, without taking anything from him or his, at his entrance or departure, on any claim whatever; but let him freely and securely pass, sojourn, stop, and return; providing him, if necessary, with good passports, to the honor and respect of the imperial majesty. Given at Spires, October 18, 1414.

"Well." Hus thrust his hands into the pockets of his cassock, well pleased with the document. "I suppose we should be glad we did not need the safe conduct on our journey. But it will suffice to get us home, no matter what the council's decision." He looked at Anika and Novak and smiled in earnest. "I know you were looking forward to using your swords in my defense, so I am sorry to disappoint you."

"Do not tease us, sir," Anika whispered, unable to return his smile. "Have these men not lied to you before?"

"Sigismund does not want to alienate Bohemia and her people," Hus replied, turning now to the nobles seated at his table. "Surely you, my lords, understand that this parchment is an honest promise."

Venceslas of Duba nodded, eager to agree, but Anika saw a shadow of doubt upon her beloved master's face. "We will wait and see," Lord John said, his eyes moving to Anika's as if he, too, shared her misgivings. "Time, my friend, will tell the tale."

Twenty-Six

A lone in his regal bedchamber, Baldasarre Cossa wrestled with the sheets on his elevated bed and struggled to sleep. Too many thoughts crowded his brain, too many fears and doubts, too many misgivings. The misdeeds and sins of his past rose up in the dark like vengeful ghosts waiting to accuse him, and no matter how he turned and squirmed, they would not go away.

He didn't fear them—his conscience had been too thoroughly seared by time and hate. What he feared was loss—the loss of his power, his position, his abundance. He had already lost much of his wealth, for on his way to Constance he had doled out heaping bags of gold and priceless treasures to countless nobles, cardinals, and bishops. He had bestowed bribes as freely as a dog shares fleas, and he fretted that his endless wealth had been diminished . . . all because of Jan Hus.

There were others, of course, who knew of Baldasarre's indiscretions, but no one else had pointed them out as openly as the preacher from Bohemia. And none but this preacher had the purity to withstand the moral pressure Baldasarre tried to apply in return. A humble man without unconfessed sin had cast the first stone, and to Baldasarre's endless surprise, the world had paid attention.

Something would have to be done. Frustrated officials from Bohemia had plagued Baldasarre for months, frustrated by their inability to rid their own kingdom of this revolutionary. The pope alone, they cried, had the power and authority to send a man to hell, but even excommunication had not silenced Hus's battering tongue.

Perhaps this council, already decreed to be of higher authority than the pope, could rid Christendom of this troublemaker . . . as long as the beast did not turn on its own head.

Baldasarre shifted on his bed and pulled the sheets to his chin, breathing heavily. The sworn enemies of Hus had already begun to arrive in Constance. Foremost among them was John the Iron, Bishop of Litomysl. A notorious simonist, he had made a vast fortune selling indulgences and heavenly pardons until Hus's ravings caused the people to reconsider the validity of man-made forgiveness.

Michael de Causis, Stephen Palec, Lord Laco of Lidice, and a dozen other Hus-haters had also visited the episcopal palace, pledging their allegiance and efforts to aid the pope and the council, to do whatever must be done to destroy Hus. With funds donated from clergymen throughout the region of Bohemia, they had engaged a network of informers and spies.

The anti-Hus crusade had already begun. Within two days after Hus's arrival in Constance, his enemies placarded him on church doors as the vilest heretic. The publication, Baldasarre had heard, reported that Hus was a dangerous mind reader who could divine the thoughts of those who attended his services, thus explaining why so many leaped up to proclaim their sins at the conclusion of his preaching.

With the bitter fidelity of fanatics, the enemies of Hus buzzed through the chambers of cardinals, archbishops, and prelates, demanding that something decisive be done. But what could Baldasarre do? He, like Hus, might find himself under investigation in the Council hearings, and though he had more money with which to defend himself, he sorely felt the lack of the Bohemian preacher's strongest asset: a clear conscience.

Vasek glumly followed in the footsteps of his lord and the train of knights, wishing again that they had been allowed to bring their horses into town. Due to the press of the crowd and the heightened agitation since Jan Hus's arrival, the city magistrates had requested that all horses be tied outside the city walls to keep the streets fit for walking. Though he had never been as keen a rider as the horse-happy knights, Vasek keenly felt the lack of a carriage. For twenty-five days they had marched into town, escorting their master as he attended to Hus's needs, then marched back out to the camp where they were stationed. It was exhausting, cold, thankless work, and there was no end in sight. Though Hus had been promised a public hearing, no one had approached him about when his hearing might be held.

As they passed the Schnetz gate of the city, Vasek hung back, leaning against the city wall. He placed his hands on his knees and fought to steady his breathing. He was unaccustomed to such strenuous walks over the sloping streets; his activity at Chlum Castle consisted mainly in climbing the stairs to his chapel once or twice a day.

In the distance, he heard the widow Fida's enthusiastic greeting and Lord John's baritone reply. John would spend an hour or two inside with Hus, taking that young knight Kafka with him. Vasek had no idea what they did inside the preacher's room, but Kafka's presence gave him reason to suspect that some sort of dictation was taking place. The boy did have a skilled and fine hand.

Vasek straightened suddenly, startled by the sight of a hay cart on the road. A vehicle! The cart was pulled by a donkey, not a horse, so why hadn't he thought to ask Lord John if he might have a donkey for this ridiculous journey? If donkeys were allowed while horses were forbidden, he could find a donkey and spare himself this strenuous daily walk.

As Vasek coveted the donkey, the hay cart paused outside the widow's house. The knights of Chlum, who were loitering outside, sprang to their feet and surrounded the cart, eyeing it with suspicion. While the driver knocked on the widow's door, several of the knights surrounded the cart and thrust their swords into the straw, doubtless checking to be certain that no murderers were hidden therein.

A man could easily hide in the hay. 'Twould be foolish to attempt such a thing in broad daylight with so many eyes about, but if the cart were left here overnight . . .

Suddenly his mind blew open. Turning toward the episcopal palace, Vasek hunched forward and disappeared quickly into the milling crowd.

"A hay cart?" Baldasarre's nostrils flared with fury as he stared at the stupid little chaplain from Chlum. "What do you mean, our answer is the hay cart?"

"If it please Your Holiness," the man said, bowing again, "as I watched our knights prick the hay with their swords, I realized they were checking for anyone who might do Master Hus harm. They thought a man could have been hidden in the straw, and since there are not many vehicles in the streets—"

"A hay cart!" D'Ailly breathed the word almost reverently. Baldasarre glared at the cardinal, irritated that he had again missed the point.

"Don't you see, Your Holiness?" A shadowy ironic sneer hovered about D'Ailly's heavy mouth.

"We didn't send a hay cart," Baldasarre whispered, irritated at the thrilling current moving through the room. "Unless John the Iron or that Laco of Lidice sent someone—"

"No, no." D'Ailly gave the chaplain a smile of pure admiration, increasing Baldasarre's annoyance even more. "The cart is harmless. But how do we *know* it was not intended for Hus's escape? There it was, on a street with no other vehicles, surrounded by knights of Chlum while the master and the preacher conspired inside the house. Do you not see it?"

Baldasarre listened, then laughed. Of course! They didn't have to do anything but convince the council that Hus had *planned* an escape. He had called his friend John of Chlum to stand guard, and then a hay cart had mysteriously shown up on the doorstep of the widow's house, ready to spirit the heretic away.

"Quickly," he said, motioning to a servant who stood nearby. "Send two bishops as my representatives, the burgomaster of the city, and a respected knight to cite Hus with attempted escape. When you have taken him into custody, bring him here."

As the servant scurried off, Baldasarre turned his eyes again to the little chaplain. The man might be a country bumpkin, but he was not stupid.

"Chaplain Vasek," he said, noting the look of dazed happiness that filled the man's eyes. "How would you like to spend the rest of your days serving God with me? There is only one more thing you must do . . ."

Vasek approached the widow's house with a light step and an even lighter heart. His task was so simple, so completely innocent that he would be able to sleep for the rest of his life with nothing heavier than air on his conscience.

He joined the knights outside the widow's house and waved to get Novak's attention. "Have you heard, Novak?" he called, the joy in his heart spilling naturally into his voice. "The brewmaster down the street is offering free ale to all knights in livery today. All a thirsty man has to do is ask, and he can drink all he likes."

"In sooth?" Novak's wide smile broke through his beard.

"Truly." Vasek paused to scratch his nose. "Why don't you take the fellows down there for a spell? I'll stand by the house and inform the master when he comes out."

Novak hesitated only for a moment. For twenty-five days they had met with no trouble or resistance, and surely it seemed ludicrous to have thirty armed knights loitering outside a harmless widow's house.

"We're off then," Novak called, flashing Vasek a gap-toothed grin. "I'll lift a glass in your name, chaplain."

"Do that," Vasek called, sinking to the widow's porch step. He waited, watching passersby on the street, until he was certain the last of the Chlum knights had wandered well away. Then, whistling, Vasek stood and retraced his steps, returning to the episcopal palace and a more appreciative master.

"Cleanse my heart and my lips," Jan Hus prayed, offering mass to Anika and Lord John in the sanctuary of his room. "O Almighty

God, who cleansed the lips of the prophet Isaiah with a burning coal, in your gracious mercy deign so to purify me that I may worthily proclaim your holy gospel. Through Christ our Lord, amen."

"Lord," Anika and Lord John replied together, "grant us your blessing."

"The Lord be in your heart and on your lips that you may worthily and fittingly proclaim his holy gospel," Hus finished. "In the name of the Father, and of the Son, and of the Holy Spirit—"

A rapid tapping at the door interrupted him. Anika turned toward the doorway, startled by the sound, but Hus continued. "Amen," he said, his bowed head lingering over his folded hands.

Respecting the preacher's silence, Lord John rose from his knees and opened the door. The widow Fida stood there, her eyes bright with worry. "I'm sorry, my lord, but there are men at the door. A knight, with his sword drawn, and the burgomaster of the city, with two bishops. They say they have come to see Master Hus."

Lord John turned to Hus with a blank expression, but Anika could see the arteries throbbing in his neck. When the preacher lifted his head from prayer, a weight of sadness rested upon his thin face.

"I'm afraid the trouble begins now," Lord John said.

Hus managed a smile. "We have a safe conduct, John. I don't know what this is about, but I am sure it is nothing of import."

He had scarcely finished speaking when a knight shouldered the poor widow aside. Lord John's face darkened in anger, and for a moment Anika nearly forgot what she was. She leaped from her knees, ready to retreat to a corner, but as her hand went to her throat she felt the coldness of woven mail beneath her fingers.

She was a knight. She wore a sword, and she had sworn to use it in defense of righteousness and truth. And if ever two men were righteous and true, Lord John and Jan Hus were.

She placed her hand on the hilt of her sword, but before she could draw it out, the strange knight and the city's burgomaster pushed their way into the room. Behind them, clad in stately black robes, came two bishops, neither one of whom she recognized.

Hus was the first to recover his tongue. "Grace and peace to you," he said, not moving from the place where he had just concluded mass. "How may I be of service?"

"We mean you no harm," one of the bishops said, offering a tentative smile of goodwill. "We seek only to avoid a public scene. The cardinals wish to discuss an important matter with you."

"Jan—don't listen to them," Lord John said, staring at the knight's drawn sword in a horrified expression of disapproval. "Do they send a sword if they mean you no harm?"

"Perhaps the sword is for my protection," Hus answered calmly, lifting his chin slightly as he stared into the eyes of his fellow priests. "If I cannot trust a brother in Christ, then the entire world is untrustworthy. I am willing to obey this summons." He looked pointedly now at the red-faced knight. "Put your sword away, Sir Knight, lest you hurt someone. My friend Sir Kafka is no less skilled with a sword than you, but I would hate to see such a young knight put to the test so soon."

Anika stiffened, momentarily abashed. Even in the face of his own arrest, Master Hus was thinking of her. In his words she heard a warning that she should not fight for his sake.

Hus looked at her then, his eyes sparkling as though he was playing a game. How could he be so naive? He ought to know by now that his fellow churchmen could not be trusted. Jan Hus was a lovable fool; for all his wisdom, he had neglected to obtain a healthy portion of common sense.

"If you insist upon going, I am going with you," Lord John answered grimly. He looked up at Anika. "You, Sir Kafka, will remain here until you are at liberty to leave. Then you will return to our camp and tell them all that has happened."

She heard his unspoken message as well: *Find out what happened to our men outside, and send them to help.*

Without resistance, Jan Hus followed the two bishops from the small room, the knight dogging his footsteps, Anika and Lord John trailing behind. In the hallway, the beneficent widow fell to her knees and clasped Hus's hand, weeping wordlessly.

See, Anika told Hus with her eyes. *Even this simple woman knows*

*the truth. These men cannot be trusted, and you are but a noble fool if
you place faith in them.*

Hus murmured a blessing over the woman's white head, then
proceeded from the hall. As the party moved down the steps of Fida's
house, Anika overheard one of the bishops say, "Now you will no
longer officiate or say mass."

Outside, the street boiled with soldiers—not the knights of
Chlum, but the red-surcoated guards of the episcopal palace. Hus
was immediately mounted upon a poor, swaybacked horse and
placed between two guards. Lord John planted himself firmly beside
Jan Hus, determined to follow on foot.

Before the arresting party moved away, Lord John caught Anika's
gaze and mouthed a silent command: *Do what you must. Do what you
can.*

Inside the house, the widow sat down, radiating bleakness.

"Widow Fida," Anika whispered, moving swiftly toward her, "do
you know a boy who will serve as a messenger?"

"I have a nephew," the woman answered, her red-rimmed eyes
lifting to meet Anika's. "He is young and able."

"Good." Anika reached out and hauled her from the chair. "I'm
going to go into the preacher's room and write a letter. You are going
to fetch your nephew."

Anika was pleasantly surprised when the woman did not hesitate
but moved through the doorway as quickly and quietly as a ferret.
Why shouldn't the woman obey? She was, after all, taking orders
from a knight.

Anika moved to Hus's room and scrawled a hasty explanation of
the day's event upon a parchment, then rolled it up and sealed it with
wax. There was no need for a signature. Novak would recognize the
handwriting and would waste no time marshaling Lord John's forces.

Anika had scarcely finished sealing the parchment when the
widow returned, her face flushed and a line of perspiration above her
brow. "He's coming," she panted, lifting her skirts as she pulled herself up the stairs. "He'll be here in a moment."

Anika nodded, then placed the letter on a table in Fida's hall. "Ask him to take the letter straightway to the knights of Chlum," she said. "He'll find them encamped outside the northern wall of the city. Tell him to ask for Novak, captain of the Lord's guard, and to put this letter directly into Novak's hand."

The widow nodded, her eager eyes fastened to the parchment.

Anika straightened and took a breath. "After you send your nephew, Widow Fida, you must help me. And you can tell no one what we are about to do, not even the closest soul to you on earth. It is for the good of the preacher, do you understand?"

Speechless with surprise, Fida nodded again.

"We will need a dress, a fine lady's gown, and a veil," Anika said, mentally clicking off the items she had thought she might never put on again. "Undergarments, if you have them. And a hooded cloak, if you can spare one."

"For whom, Sir Knight?" the widow squeaked, her eyes large and liquid.

Anika felt a wry smile cross her face. "For me."

Twenty-Seven

Fortunately for Anika, the Widow Fida was a charitable and frugal soul whose wardrobe chests bulged with garments she had worn in earlier, slimmer days. Anika found an elegant gold gown with long, trailing sleeves and an upturned collar with a cloak to match. While the widow stared in wordless amazement, her hand at her throat, Anika unbuckled her armor and shed her hauberk and shirt, standing before the widow in a thin chemise, pale and obviously female.

The poor widow clapped her hand over her mouth, barely able to control her gasp of surprise, but a pounding at the door interrupted the proceedings.

"That might be your nephew," Anika pointed out, lifting the gown and robe into her arms. "See to him and give him the note, while I dress in this."

Flustered and embarrassed, the widow left the room, leaving Anika to fumble once again with collars, fur trims, and high waistlines. Perhaps, she mused as she prodded the collar to stand up around her tanned neck, if this were not so serious an occasion she might have enjoyed putting on a woman's kirtle again. But she had no time for dwelling on those things now.

The widow returned, her lips pressed together, her eyes like two bright torches.

"Your nephew?" Anika asked, bending down to fumble through the trunk for a suitable pair of slippers.

"Yes." The widow clasped her hands at her waist. "Sir Knight—but you're not a knight, are you? Can you tell me what is going on? Can it be true that Jan Hus is a heretic? Surely he would not have condoned your unnatural masquerade—"

"Jan Hus has nothing to do with this," Anika answered, standing. She pulled a pair of flat leather slippers from the trunk and placed them on her feet. They were too long; her heels would be blistered by the time she returned, but it couldn't be helped. "I was orphaned, and an evil nobleman sought to take advantage of me. As a woman, I had no means of escape. As a knight, I earned my freedom. Jan Hus is my friend. He neither condemns nor supports my knighthood. But I will do all I can to support him."

Anika turned and lifted her arms, inviting Fida's inspection. The widow sank onto a bench against the wall and crossed her arms, staring at Anika as if she had suddenly sprouted horns. "You make a very pretty woman," she said, her round face melting into a tentative smile. "But you will have to do something about your hair. No woman goes about with her hair shorn like that."

"Have you a veil?"

"I have a hat." She rose from her bench and pulled a rolled hat from a box under her bed, then reverently offered it to Anika. "The black veil on the back will cover any wisps that peek out," she said, helping Anika push her stubborn locks under the brim. When the veil was adjusted, the widow stepped back and pinned Anika with a long, silent scrutiny.

"Well?" Anika asked, impatient to be on her way.

The widow nodded. "You are a very pretty woman, my dear. I don't know what you intend to do, but you are very well dressed for whatever part you must play."

"I intend to go to the hearing," Anika said, pulling the long black cloak around her shoulders. She tied the strings at her neck, then carefully pulled the wide hood up over the cumbersome hat.

She paused at the doorway. "Hide my armor; I will come for it later. And if any ask you what lady left your house after noon today, tell them Lady Anika of Prague paid you a visit."

Anika found her way much easier than she had imagined. In such an august gathering of men—bishops, scholars, priests, cardinals, prelates—a woman, especially a pretty one, elicited such surprise that no one thought to detain or question her. She marched boldly up the wide steps of the episcopal palace, then calmly asked a guard where the hearing for Jan Hus was taking place. The guard, probably as stunned by her effrontery as by her presence, merely pointed down a long corridor.

Anika blended as well as she could into the sea of dark robes until she spied a pair of open doors. A long table had been set up inside, and she could see Lord John and Jan Hus standing before the table.

Her heart pounding, she eased into the room and took a low seat against the wall, willing herself to be as inconspicuous as possible. But a cold knot formed in her stomach when she recognized the voice and face of the man presently addressing her master and her friend.

"Many complaints against you have been forwarded to us from Bohemia," Cardinal D'Ailly was saying, his eyes burning into Hus.

"I have come freely to the council and freely to this room," Master Hus answered, standing straight and tall. "And if I am convicted of error, I will gladly accept instruction."

"It is well spoken," another cardinal answered.

Anika watched with acute and loving anxiety. Deliberately or not, the cardinal had misunderstood Hus's words. Master Hus wished to be convinced by reason and the Scriptures, but the council would want him to bow blindly to their authority.

"What they call instruction I would not wish on my worst enemy," Anika murmured, clenching her hands as a pair of guards took hold of Hus and Lord John and led them out through a far door. Jagged and painful thoughts moved restlessly through her brain as she rose from her seat, trying to follow them with her eyes.

In spite of the emperor's pledge and the pope's promise, Hus was a prisoner. Anika's base suspicions had proved true, while Hus's optimistic hopes had proved false.

A long, brittle silence filled the room as the two prisoners exited, then the cardinals at the table leaned back, crossed their arms, and cast sly grins at each other.

"Ha!" D'Ailly cried, rising to his feet. He clapped his hands in simple delight, mindless of the observers in the room. "Now we have him, and he will not escape us till he has paid the uttermost farthing."

While Anika coiled into the shadows and watched in horror, the overconfident cardinals rose to their feet and began to dance about the room in mindless merriment. One priest, John Reinstein, stood and shouted his objections, but the din of celebration overwhelmed his voice.

Late in the afternoon, the council sent word that Lord John of Chlum, having done no wrong, might depart to his camp. Still in her woman's dress, Anika spied a pair of guards escorting her master to the street. She rushed forward, mindful that she was playing a role before a crowd rife with spies and informers.

"Lord John!" she cried, hurrying to his side.

Startled by the sound of her voice, he glanced up. Anika lightly placed her hands upon his arms and stood on tiptoe to give him a kiss, an affectionate salute that would not be misinterpreted.

"Kafka?" he whispered when her lips brushed his cheek.

"Lady Anika of Prague," she answered, pulling away so he could read the message in her eyes. "I have crept today where no knight of Chlum could go, my lord, and I have much to tell you. But stay with me now, and let me act the part of a nobleman's daughter."

He nodded in a barely perceptible movement, then took her hand and gallantly linked it through his arm. "Walk with me to the widow's house," she whispered, modestly lowering her eyes before the prying gaze of a guard who had watched her greet her master. "And I shall unfold the tale to you there."

While the cardinals celebrated downstairs, Baldasarre poured wine and drank a toast to his new comrade, Vasek. "The fox is caught," he said, pausing to sip the red wine. He smacked his lips appreciatively, then gestured to the country chaplain. "Try it, my friend. The vintage is a good one. Even the priests serving mass don't taste anything this fine."

A commotion out in the hall broke his concentration, and Baldasarre heard a loud and angry voice rise above the babble of his guards. Vasek, the foolish chaplain, went pale in one instant and scurried toward the water closet in the next.

The doors to the chamber suddenly burst open. Startled, Baldasarre spilled wine onto his cassock, then looked up to scowl at the fool who dared disturb his privacy. He recognized the man before him: the Bohemian noble, Lord John of Chlum. Tonight the nobleman was red faced with anger, his hair tousled by the wind, his eyes smoldering with fire.

"Who let him in?" Baldasarre demanded of his servants, jabbing a finger toward John of Chlum.

The nobleman ignored the gesture. "What of your promise to Jan Hus?" he said, bitterness edging his voice. "He has today been arrested."

Baldasarre lifted a shoulder in a shrug. "I am powerless in the matter."

"You are the pope! Whether rightly or not, you wield power enough to have this man released!"

"I am helpless," Baldasarre continued, idly stirring his wine with his finger. "My brethren the cardinals, as you know, have more authority than I. They are quite beyond my control."

Through narrowed eyes, Baldasarre watched the man carefully. John of Chlum was in an Old Testament mood now, unwilling to turn the other cheek, unable to play the games of power and position.

"You—" John of Chlum lifted an accusing finger toward Baldasarre, "you will pay for this. In this life or the next, you will pay for this treachery."

"You forget," Baldasarre countered gamely, "that as the pope I hold the keys to heaven and hell. I decide who pays—in this life *and* the next."

Their eyes locked in open warfare for a moment, anger hanging in the air between them like an invisible dagger. Then John of Chlum whirled and stalked away, probably to vent his anger in the apartments of a succession of cardinals.

But it wouldn't matter, Baldasarre thought, dipping his finger into the wine again. He ran his wet finger across his lips, then smiled at the cowardly chaplain who peered from behind the door to the water closet.

"Come out," he told the little man. "You have done nothing worthy of shame."

"I only wish I could agree with you," Vasek croaked, his face red and blotchy with humiliation as he crossed the room to resume his seat.

Baldasarre shot him a twisted smile. "Have no fear. As long as you please me, you'll enter heaven. Eventually."

"My poor lord John." The chaplain's eyes bore a tinge of sadness and regret. "He is so caught up in this matter with Master Hus. I fear he has been deceived, and yet I know him for an honest and godly man—"

"That is why you must return to his camp," Baldasarre answered, setting his cup on the table at his side. "You will be of more use to God there than here. Go back to Lord John of Chlum, act as my eyes and ears. And if your master and his comrades plan anything that would injure our cause, report immediately to me."

Vasek the chaplain looked up, his eyes like black holes in his pale, unhappy face. But he nodded in agreement, and Baldasarre leaned back, content with the knowledge he had enlisted another spy.

The next morning, Anika rose from her place in the straw at the knights' camp and took a quick inventory of her women's garments. After returning to the widow's house, the woman had helped Anika dress again in her armor but had insisted that she keep the gown, cloak, and hat. "You do not know when you will need these things again," Fida had whispered, a strong note of approval in her voice. "I don't know how you did it, child, but I applaud the service you have done Master Hus. I am pleased to know you."

The garments were now wrapped in an oilcloth and hidden at the bottom of a trunk filled with kitchen supplies. Anika thought she would be able to find them again if needed, and if someone else stumbled upon them she would not necessarily be exposed. Anyone in the camp could have placed them there.

One of the knights had slain a buck in the nearby forest, so after a brief breakfast of roasted venison, Anika looked up to see an armored knight in blue galloping down the pathway leading to their camp. "Master John!" the knight called, his voice muffled through his visor.

Lev caught the man's foaming mount. Then the knight dismounted and removed his helmet. Anika recognized Manville, who had been sent into town to keep watch over Hus.

"They removed him in the night!" Manville shouted, hurrying toward the canopy under which the master had breakfasted with Anika and Novak. "They took him from the episcopal palace to the house of the precentor of the cathedral. Hus is closely guarded."

Lord John took in Manville's harried appearance in one swift glance. "Did you see them move him?"

The knight nodded. "Aye, my lord. I have been so long in returning only because I was not able to find a mount until I reached a stable on the outskirts of the city. All I had to do was speak the name of Master Hus, though, and the smithy there gave me his own mare and wished me Godspeed."

"When you return the horse, give the man my thanks," Lord John answered. Without thinking, he lowered his gaze until it met Anika's, and she thrilled to think that he considered her a comrade. "What do we do now?" he murmured, almost speaking to himself.

"I cannot believe they will keep him at the precentor's house for long," Anika answered, her mind racing. "If he was a threat in the widow Fida's house, the threat will not be removed as long as he remains in Constance. There are too many here who love Jan Hus, and those who fear him will not rest if he sleeps behind the city walls." She took a deep breath and moved her gaze into his, seeing nothing else. "They mean to kill him, my lord," she said simply, tearing the words from her soul. "They are evil men, servants of Lucifer himself."

"Anika!" He spoke her female name without thinking, and she blinked in surprise. Manville would think he had made a mistake, but she felt her heart turn over at the realization that he not only saw her as a comrade, but as a woman.

Abruptly he pushed his chair back from the table and stood. "I will not give up while breath remains in my body."

Anika

Twenty-Eight

———◦◦◦———

The Bohemians passed the winter of 1414–15 in the darkest possible circumstances. Lord John and the knights of Chlum remained encamped outside Constance, not willing to return to Bohemia while Hus remained in prison. While they waited, the knights grew bored and restless, and many fell ill with diseases brought on by the cold, harsh weather.

Anika knew the nobles worried about matters back home. Both Lord John and Lord Venceslas had left their estates in their stewards' capable hands, but some things even a steward could not handle. With a pang of sorrow Anika recalled that Lord John had left his youngest son behind. Svec would be several months older by the time they returned, precious time that could never be recaptured in the child's life.

But Jan Hus fared far worse than his fellow Bohemians. After one week in the precentor's house, where he was closely guarded and allowed no visitors apart from council representatives, guards moved Hus to a Dominican monastery situated on a small island in the center of Lake Constance. When Anika first learned that Hus had been transferred to the graceful building near the water, she wept in relief, but her relief turned to despair when she learned Hus had been cast into the dungeon of a round tower only a few feet from the monastery sewer and the water's edge. In this dank and dismal place he remained for over two and a half months. Not until a noxious fever seized him did news of his pitiable condition reach those who prayed for and worried about him.

"The pope," Lord John told his Bohemian allies one afternoon when he had returned from another fruitless round of meetings with the pope's emissaries, "does not want Master Hus to die a natural death. They tell me Master Hus was at death's door, but the pope sent his own physician to restore our friend to health. On the doctor's orders, Hus has been removed to a more healthful cell and treated with greater humanity."

While the physicians worked over Jan Hus's body, prelates scoured his soul. After the doctors left Hus's cell each morning, witnesses from the council entered the small chamber and worried the preacher with complex questions. Once when Hus lay at his weakest, his mind wearied by fever and unrest, they brought fifteen witnesses who peppered him with sly questions, hoping to catch him in some mistake or heresy.

The attack against Hus advanced on a third front, as well. The council appointed three prelates to investigate and report on Hus's public statements. Michael de Causis and Stephen Palec drew up a series of accusations based on Hus's treatise on the church, *De Ecclesia*. Hus's beliefs, as set forth in this document, were a declaration of independence for the individual believer in Christ, for he effectively reduced the cumbersome system of priestly rule to rubbish. Hus stressed that faith, not connection with the Roman Catholic body, was the true basis of membership in the spiritual Church of Christ. And he steadfastly maintained that human distinctions of clerical rank paled to insignificance when considered in the light of Christ's admonition that "whosoever will be chief among you, let him be your servant." The concepts of *De Ecclesia* frightened the cardinals, and with the aid of Palec and Michael de Causis, the commissioners twisted some of Hus's statements and fabricated others to make the document appear heretical.

And yet, through all his trials, Jan Hus did not slip or falter. He did ask for help, begging that he might be allowed to employ an advocate for his defense, only to hear that a man accused of heresy had no right to expect the protection of the law.

In the end, the council members had only lies and misrepresentations with which to accuse him. Peter Mladenovic, Lord John's secretary, kept a careful account of the proceedings as news trickled out and wrote that the final formal accusations against Hus, forty-four articles drawn from *De Ecclesia,* were totally misleading. "These have been falsely and unfairly extracted from the book by Palec," he wrote in his journal, "who has mutilated some sentences at the beginning, others in the middle, others at the end, and who has also invented things that are not contained in the book at all."

For months, Anika and the other knights helped Lord John and Lord Venceslas of Duba attempt to free the Bohemian preacher. The nobles wrote countless letters to the emperor and badgered cardinals in their offices, trying to rouse all of Constance in Hus's defense. Their efforts were fruitless, but when Emperor Sigismund finally arrived in the city at the end of December, a ray of hope dawned. Anika knew Lord John placed great faith in the emperor—after all, Sigismund had provided Hus's safe conduct, and was King Wenceslas's brother. He should prove to be an ally.

For a day or two, Lord John's hopes were fulfilled. After his arrival, Sigismund sent a message commanding the cardinals to release Hus according to the terms of the safe conduct. But his demand was refused. "Faith need not be kept with a heretic," the cardinals replied, "since he has none."

Though sick, weak, hungry, cold, and often burning with fever, Hus was not forgotten or abandoned. In spite of the vigilant spies who surrounded him, Bohemian visitors managed to smuggle letters in and out of his prison. One of Hus's jailers, a man called Robert, proved particularly helpful, and Hus often referred to him in his letters as "that good man" and "the faithful friend." Despite the preacher's physical weakness, he wrote almost daily from his prison cell. When his letters reached friends encamped outside Constance, they were copied, translated, and spirited away to those who prayed for him in Bohemia.

In one letter addressed to Lord John, Hus asked for a Bible. Anika could almost see him as he wrote, his hands trembling upon the parchment, his eyes still blazing with faith and a hint of mischief:

Acquire for me a Bible and send it by this good man. If your scribe, Peter, has any ink, let him give me some, as well as several pens and a small inkwell. I know nothing about my Polish servant or about Master Cardinal, I only hear that your lordship is here and is with the lord king Sigismund. Accordingly, I beseech you to pray his royal majesty, both for my sake and for the cause of the Almighty God, who has so magnificently endowed him with his gifts, as well as for the sake of manifesting justice and truth to the honor of God and the welfare of the Church, to liberate me from captivity, that I may prepare myself for and come to a public hearing. You should know that I have been very ill, but am already convalescing.

Written with my own hand, which your scribe Peter knows well. Given in prison.

———

Sitting in the tiny closet that served as a lavatory in his vast apartments, Baldasarre Cossa blew out his cheeks and tried to ignore the rumbling in his stomach. He felt the grip again in his gut, the scratch of fear that had arisen to plague him ever since Sigismund's arrival in Constance. For two months he had been the highest power within a week's ride, the ruler of his immediate universe, but now he sensed a subtle shift in power, almost as though the stars overhead had turned on their axes to shine the light of authority upon someone else's head.

His nervous fingers found a bit of hardened skin along his cuticle, and he brought his finger to his lips, gnawing away the offending flesh. He had hoped to distract the council from the issue of papal power with the controversy surrounding Jan Hus, but while the preacher underwent examination, those who intended to heal the great schism worked, too. Three popes were too many, they said. Of course! So why didn't the other two surrender to *him*? He was the one in Constance, cooperating with the council. The others, that cowardly Benedict and troublesome Gregory, hadn't even bothered to appear.

Baldasarre bit hard on his finger, ripping away a shred of skin, then cursed softly as the bite exposed the tender flesh. He should be more careful. Every man in the council room tomorrow would have to kiss his ring, and the shrewdest of them, in an unguarded moment, might notice his bitten fingernails and wonder if he had cause to be nervous. And if they wondered about him—as many of them already did, he knew—they'd soon be calling for his head. He might be imprisoned, even burned at the stake, for what the council would perceive as excesses and abuses of power.

He had whited too many sepulchers to be easily deceived. Of all the men in Constance, he had the most reason to be wary because he had the most to lose. His spies had been busily ferreting out all sorts of information, including a report that the council was about to propose that Pope John follow the example of Christ, who willingly laid aside the glories of heaven to serve a fallen world.

They were such fools! He'd lay down his crown when those cursed cardinals gave up their palaces, their rings, their wealth. They would never relent, and neither would he, which might make for a violent end unless . . .

His mind drifted back to an Austrian castle he had visited on his way to Constance. Beside a roaring fire he promised Duke Frederick a fortune in exchange for a promise of help, should the need arise. Frederick had conveniently followed Baldasarre to Constance and now waited for the time when he might prove useful.

Grunting, Baldasarre pulled himself up from the chamber pot, peering through a crack between the door and the doorframe to make certain no one lingered in the room outside. Without a doubt, the time had come to send word to Frederick. This impasse would not last long.

Four days later, the knights of Chlum received an invitation to a spring tournament hosted by Duke Frederick of Austria, a nobleman who sought to provide comfort and entertainment for the hundreds of men who had to remain in Constance while the council conducted business. The council would adjourn for the special tournament, the messenger told them, so the cardinals and even His Holiness might witness the skillful knights' exploits.

"Should we enter?" Manville asked, turning to Novak. " 'Twould give the men something to do besides hunting. Nervous energy does a man no good, and a tournament might take the edge off their raw nerves."

"The knights of Lidice have already entered," Lev added hopefully. "Lord Laco has sent a contingent of men to prepare for the jousting. His captain rode by here earlier and asked if we would participate."

"We do not play games when one of our own is imprisoned," Novak snapped, his eyes darting toward Anika at the mention of Laco's name. "Let the knights of Austria and Lidice make sport. We are here for one reason only: to protect Jan Hus. And until he is free, we have no time for games."

Anika pressed her lips together and smiled at Lev, signaling that she understood his intentions were innocent. Something in her would have liked to see if she could challenge one of the other knights, but the stronger voice of reason was content to let the challenge pass. She hated to admit it, but since she had worn Fida's kirtle and seen Lord John's eyes light in appreciation, her suit of armor had begun to lose its appeal.

Five days after the tournament, Manville rode breathless into camp again. "Lord John!" he called, his voice hoarse. "Sir! The pope has escaped!"

"What?" Lord John stepped out of his tent and gave the knight a sidelong glance of utter disbelief.

"It's true," Manville answered, swinging his tree-trunk leg over the rear of his horse as he dismounted. "He has not been seen since the tournament. One of Frederick's servants reports that the pontiff disguised himself as a groom and escaped in the crowd."

"He knew the council would destroy him," Anika said, looking toward her master. "Lord John, if the cardinals would not spare one of their own, what do you think they will do to Master Hus? He has no opportunity for escape. While the pope dined on duck and beef in a palatial chamber, Master Hus has been chained in a dungeon—"

She stopped, silenced by the guilty look on Lord John's face.

Vasek, who had been standing nearby, came forward and held up his hand as a strange livid hue overspread his face. "Is the pope's retinue gone, too? His guards, his servants, everyone?"

Manville nodded. "Yes. They are probably gathered around an Austrian banquet table by now. It is widely assumed that Duke Frederick helped that rascal escape."

Lord John's brow creased with worry. "If the pope and his people are gone—who is tending Master Hus?"

They found him in chains, faint and prostrate, but alive. Anika, Novak, and Lord John had ridden immediately for the monastery after hearing Manville's news, and there they found a lone monk at the preacher's cell door. Hus had received neither food nor drink since the pope's departure and had survived by using his tongue to gather moisture from the damp walls and floor.

Lord John would have removed Hus from the place by force, but the monk threw himself at the nobleman's feet, declaring he would be imprisoned if the cardinals discovered that their prisoner had escaped. John finally relented but demanded that Anika and Novak be allowed to remain with the prisoner until he returned with news from the emperor.

"With the pope gone, Sigismund is now the master of the city," he told Anika, giving her a tentative smile as he prepared to go. "And since the emperor was willing to release Master Hus only a few weeks ago, we can certainly hope he intends to keep his word. I will return shortly with good news for all."

But Baldasarre Cossa was not the only authority to sense a shift in power. When Sigismund learned of Hus's situation, he refused to hand the preacher over to Lord John, but instead sent word to the council. In consultation with Cardinal D'Ailly and other leaders, Sigismund decided that Hus should be committed to the custody of the Bishop of Constance. As the moon hid her face in the clouds on the evening of Palm Sunday, March 24, guards transferred the preacher from the monastery dungeon to Gottlieben, a castle on the Rhine.

Situated four miles outside the city, Castle Gottlieben was a majestic, sturdy structure with two quadrangular towers, each nearly two hundred feet high. A small wooden cage of two compartments had been built just beneath the roof of one tower, and into one of these Jan Hus was thrust. His jailers pinioned one arm to the wall, then chained his feet to a block.

While Lord John and the other Bohemians continued their daily efforts to have the preacher released, Hus waited in solitary confinement, suffering from hunger, cold, and painful attacks of neuralgia and hemorrhage. The damp spring winds swept almost continually through a small ventilation window. His brutal keepers did nothing to assuage his misery, hoping his spirits would be brought low enough to confess to almost anything when he was finally brought before the council.

Once he had been comforted by visits from his friends, but now only the commissioners assigned to torment him were allowed to enter his dismal cell. And while Hus endured their ridiculous questions and denied their false charges, he consoled himself with something Lord John had once told him: "There are many things worse than defeat, my friend, and compromise with evil is one of them."

Twenty-Nine

"You needn't push me, young man," Baldasarre snapped, turning to the chubby-faced guard who held his right arm. "Though it may give you pleasure to push one of your superiors up these stairs—"

"Don't mind him," the other guard replied, sharing a smile with the clumsy youth. "He still thinks he's the blessed pope."

"I may no longer wear the Crown of Christ," Baldasarre answered, his voice brimming with distaste, "yet still I am your superior. I am, and I will always be. So mind your words and your actions lest they come back to haunt you."

The guards eased their grip on him then, though their smirking faces lost none of their insolence. Baldasarre lifted his robe and climbed steadily up the winding staircase, holding his chin as high as his fractured pride would allow.

Duke Frederick had proved to be a fickle friend. Though he had been true enough to help Baldasarre escape from Constance, Frederick's eagerness to ingratiate himself with Sigismund had been Baldasarre's undoing. The price of Frederick's friendship with the emperor was one ex-pope, bound and delivered. Two mornings ago Baldasarre had awakened in his plush bed at the Duke's castle to find himself surrounded by half a dozen imperial guards.

In a hastily arranged trial by the council, the former Pope John was convicted of fifty-four charges and declared to be "the mirror of infamy, an idolater of the flesh, and according to all who knew him a devil incarnate." The audacious council—several of whom owed their cardinals' robes to *him*—sentenced Baldasarre to imprisonment. In a fit of spiteful glee, Sigismund commanded that Baldasarre be brought to the Castle Gottlieben, only four miles from the brouhaha he had escaped at Constance.

Baldasarre stopped and inhaled deeply when he and his guards reached the landing at the top of the tower. By a stream of light through a small window, Baldasarre could see a wooden cage with two compartments, one of which was occupied by a stooped, shadowed shape. The stench of rotting food, human waste, and infected air filled the atmosphere like a palpable fog, clogging his nostrils. He could not survive in this place, and he would not bear it.

"Am I to be thrust in here like an animal?" He threw back his head and thumped his manacled hands against his chest. "I am no beast, not like this criminal. Tell your royal master that I protest. I have done nothing to warrant this kind of barbaric treatment."

His reaction seemed only to amuse the guards. A small rustling sound shattered the stillness in the cage; the shadowed man stirred. Did he dare to laugh, too?

"In you go," the older guard said, unlocking the wooden door on the first cell. Baldasarre resisted, but felt the insistent prick of a sword through his robe. Slowly and reluctantly, he moved into the cramped space.

"Hear me!" he cried, even as the guard slammed and locked the door. Lifting his chained hands to the bars, Baldasarre fixed the younger guard in the stare that used to make subordinates cringe. "I am not an animal, that you can lock me in a cage! I am a man of God! I hold the power of life and death in my hands! Almighty God himself will punish you for this injustice!"

Laughing, the two guards disappeared down the stairs, their light steps tripping over the stones like rhythmic applause.

Baldasarre leaned his back against the wall and slowly sank downward, dimly aware that he was ruining what had been a very costly robe. Sigismund, the jealous fool, was doing this to teach him a lesson. The emperor was flaunting his power, but he had forgotten that Baldasarre always won in the end. Sigismund would free him as soon as he needed a favor. Or maybe the new pope, whomever the council elected, would need advice. In either case, Baldasarre would be freed. He might never again be pope, but he would return to the glorious life of a cardinal. He could accept no less.

He glanced up, some sixth sense having brought him back to reality. As nightfall approached, the light was fading fast, color bleeding out of the air. The dark figure in the other chamber, even more shadowed and indistinct than a moment before, sat hunched in the corner, one limp arm hanging from the wall, the other resting on a bent knee. The bearded stranger sorely needed a haircut. The fingers of his hands seemed devilishly long and gaunt, but bright eyes burned from the center of that skeletal face.

The head moved in a barely discernible nod as the apparition spoke: "Grace and peace to you, Baldasarre Cossa." The words hung in the miasma between them.

Baldasarre winced slightly, as if his flesh had been nipped. What sort of criminal was this, and how could he know Baldasarre's name? "Who are you?" A sudden whisper of terror ran through him. "How do you know me?"

"I am Jan Hus," the man replied, his voice soft and eminently reasonable. "The man you persecuted."

Baldasarre waited, knowing the man would gloat, curse, or rail against him . . . but darkness fell, and the Bohemian preacher spoke only once more: "May the Lord bless you and bring you peace."

Half-blind with unreasoning terror, Baldasarre leapt to his feet and pounded on the door, screaming that he would go mad unless his captors released him.

Vasek stood as tense and quivering as a bowstring, but managed to bow before the assembled council. A letter from Lord John lay on the table before the prelate in charge. "Your master begs us to release Hus from custody that he might recover his health for a public examination," the cardinal read, summarizing the letter for those assembled. "And he offers to provide sureties to guarantee Hus will not attempt to leave Constance before his case is judged."

"That is correct, Your Eminence," Vasek said, inclining his head. He took a deep breath to quell the leaping pulse beneath his ribs. "There are several noble lords in league with Lord John of Chlum, and they have all promised to lend their men and their resources to abet my master."

"The request is absolutely refused." The prelate laid the paper on the table and folded his hands over it. "We will not release Jan Hus under any circumstances, and we are not inclined to grant him a public hearing. The key to containing apostasy is to prevent its spread; how then can we willingly allow the public to receive seeds of heresy from this apostate's lips?"

"I agree with you that heresy should not be spread," Vasek said, opening his hands to the council. "But I am employed to convey my master's wishes. And—are we certain that Master Hus is a heretic? The council has not yet decided."

"The council will decide soon enough." Cardinal D'Ailly leaned forward, his eyes dark and powerful. "But where do your sympathies lie? There are some, Chaplain Vasek, who fear you were close to that deposed pope."

"I have always supported the Holy Mother Church." Vasek had been forcing a smile, but now he felt it fade as he looked into D'Ailly's hypocritical eyes. Hadn't *he* been in league with Pope John? But that no longer mattered. The tide had turned, and D'Ailly now rode at the pinnacle of power. "I have always stood against heresy," Vasek continued, his blood pounding thickly in his ears. "Even when Master Hus visited Lord John at Castle Chlum, I was faithful to point out the fallacies of his teaching."

"Then why do you still serve this Bohemian lord?" Another cardinal shot the question from across the chamber.

"I had thought," Vasek dropped his gaze before a dozen pairs of steady eyes, "that I might prove useful to the Church in my present position."

Vasek paused, weighing the impact of his words. When the pontiff fled only to be arrested and convicted, Vasek had lived for days in a state of terror, afraid he would be charged with some crime as well. But apparently only D'Ailly and a few other cardinals knew of Vasek's papal connections, and they were not eager to advertise their own visits to that miscreant.

By God's merciful grace Vasek had escaped his lord's notice the night Lord John stormed into the pope's chamber. He had been spared not once, but twice. Perhaps it was a sign. Perhaps there might still be a place of power and influence for him, even with the former pontiff in chains. If he could only manage to balance himself between his ecclesiastical superiors and his master.

"My brother the chaplain is a noble priest," D'Ailly said, his gaze darting toward his fellow cardinals. "A weapon against Lucifer stands before you, so why do we not use him?" When he turned back to Vasek, his faint smile held a touch of sadness. "Go back to your master, Chaplain Vasek, and continue to serve him with the best of your ability. But know that we are opposed to a public hearing for Hus just as we are opposed to Hus's release. His heresy is like the plague: It moves swiftly and fatally, and we would not infect Constance with it." His dark eyes narrowed. "Do you understand?"

For no reason he could name, D'Ailly's voice raised the hairs on the back of the chaplain's neck. Slowly he nodded. "I understand completely, Your Eminence."

The days fell like autumn leaves from an oak tree, one after the other, indistinguishable. While the Bohemian nobles continued their efforts to obtain a hearing or release for Jan Hus, their knights chafed in uselessness. Spring greened into summer; the days ticked by with tedious monotony, but Anika knew the impasse would not last forever. Her father had always predicted that war would come, but now it appeared that the conflict would extend far beyond Bohemia's borders. Both the forces of freedom and the warriors of Holy Mother Church were readying for battle, and the resulting clash would be heard round the world.

One morning in late May, Anika sat at Lord John's table with

Novak, Vasek, and Peter Mladenovic. A letter from Sigismund had just arrived, promising that the emperor would do his utmost to guarantee that Hus would receive his promised public hearing.

"This is a victory," Lord John said, waving the parchment. "They thought they could let him languish away in prison, but Hus will be heard. For this he has prayed; for this we have all worked. May God grant that the day will speedily arrive."

"Why would they fear a public hearing?" Anika asked, idly trying to capture a slippery piece of beef on her trencher. "Though the people of Bohemia would rise up to defend him, the people here don't know him."

"They fear his voice," Vasek inserted.

"They fear his *wisdom*," Lord John amended. "They realize the power of his eloquence, and they fear its effect. In the past few days many of them have felt the blows of Hus's logic, and they cannot argue with his intellect. He stands for truth, and it is time truth is heard."

"But is this action really wise, my lord?" Vasek asked, his gray eyes as flat and unreadable as stone. "Surely it will not benefit your cause if the populace is roused to revolt."

"Why wouldn't a little revolt be useful?" Novak looked directly at the timid chaplain. "We are knights, sworn to fight for truth. Why shouldn't we try to raise forces who will fight with us? If Master Hus convinces the people of Constance that he speaks truly, we ought to be able to raise an army from the folk here. We could then rescue him from Gottlieben and escort him back to Bohemia."

"He wouldn't go." Lord John emphatically stabbed the air with his knife. "He will not leave Constance until his trial is done, I promise you. He believes God has brought him here for the purpose of publicly setting forth his views and having them judged as right or wrong. It would be easier for him to die than to resign this task. He will persist until the end, whatever end that may be."

His bold statement took Anika's breath away. "Does he want to die?" she asked, remembering the somber look in Hus's eyes when he told her that God's will could be found in surrender. Surely he didn't want to surrender his life!

"Why should he die?" Novak spoke up. "I thought the council's purpose was to reform the church. Master Hus is a reformer. Why can't they work together?"

"They hate him," Anika answered, meeting her mentor's open gaze. "They want reform only so long as it enables them to keep their petty powers. Master Hus wants the church to return to the ideals set forth in the Scripture. He values the Word of God over the traditions of men and the liberty of conscience over the tyranny of authority." She leaned toward Lord John, resisting the impulse to place her hand over his. "My lord, we could take him out of Gottlieben. There is no need for him to die. He can speak from Bohemia, and the world will hear his message through copies of his sermons! He can live in peace, even if he must minister as an itinerant evangelist."

"He would love that life," Lord John answered, his eyes gentle and contemplative. For a moment Anika saw an almost hopeful glint in his eyes. Then he shook his head. "No. Jan Hus has come to his moment of accounting, and he would rather die than deny what he is," he said firmly, his eyes boring into her soul. "We should all be as true to ourselves and God. Do you agree, *Sir Kafka?*"

Anika sat back, stung. None of the others understood the subtle emphasis of his words, but his meaning was clear enough to her. Once again he was chiding her because she had chosen to live as a knight. But she *was* being true to herself! Why couldn't he understand that she would rather die than deny her vow? He understood Jan Hus readily enough, but he would not grant her the liberty to reach her goals.

"Excuse me, my lord," she replied, stiffly rising from the table. "I think Lev and I could use some practice with the sword. I'm afraid we may sit here too long and forget how to fight."

———

The morning of June 5 dawned hot and clear. Restless and irritable in the unseasonable heat, Vasek paced outside the Merchants'

Exchange, the rectangular stone building which served as the council's official meeting place. A few nights before, Hus had been transferred from Gottlieben to a Franciscan monastery in Constance. His jailers were allowing him to write again, and letters to and from the Lords Duba and Chlum had flown back and forth with increasing regularity as Hus prepared for his long-awaited public hearing.

Yet another gilded carriage pulled up outside the council's meeting place, and Vasek bowed automatically to the cardinal who stepped out. The council members had begun to arrive even before the sun crested the horizon.

The plan to meet early in the morning had been Vasek's idea, born of necessity and prudence. "If you tell the preacher June 5, but do not tell him what hour, he cannot say you were negligent if you meet early," Vasek had suggested. "I know Master Hus. He will rise early on that day. He will spend hours in prayer, he will study his notes, he will read the Scriptures, and then he will make ready to come. If you call upon him to speak and he is not in attendance, you can progress with your work."

The cardinals proclaimed Vasek's idea a stroke of genius. Though he had been hailed as a hero and promised a bishopric for his help, the council's promises did nothing to lift Vasek's heavy heart. Guilt avalanched him now, pressing him down with its weight.

He had been disloyal to Lord John.

He had been disloyal to Jan Hus, who still called him friend.

But most unpardonable of all, by arranging this hasty hearing so that Hus would be condemned before he even arrived at the meeting place, Vasek felt he had somehow been disloyal to his calling. This was a liar's trick. Only people like Baldasarre Cossa resorted to such low tactics.

Another carriage arrived, churning up the gravel in the street. Vasek watched a cloud of dust rise, then lazily drift toward the ascending sun.

Following his heart, he lowered his head and lengthened his stride, praying he would not be too late.

"They have already prepared the document," Vasek panted, trying to find the courage to look Lord John in the eye. "They planned to satisfy Sigismund by holding a public hearing, but in Hus's absence. The document will be read to all assembled in the hall, and condemnation passed. If Hus is not present before they pass condemnation, the cardinals can truthfully say they held a public hearing, but the accused did not appear to speak."

"Snakes!" Lord John muttered, tossing his shirt over his head. "Lower than snakes, that passel of vermin! Whoever could have put this idea into their heads? 'Tis an invention of the very devil himself."

An image rose in Vasek's mind: Adam and Eve in the Garden. Eve had tasted the forbidden fruit in order to be like a god; Vasek had done it in order to be a bishop. Surely their hearts were much alike.

"My horse!" John called to a servant. "And my knights! Have all who are dressed mount up and ride with me at once. We go to inform Sigismund that those crafty cardinals seek to circumvent his intention. We ride at once!"

"Hurry, my lord," Vasek murmured as Lord John blazed past him. "I wish you Godspeed."

"We were successful," Lord John reported later that night as Anika and the other knights gathered round the campfire to hear his news. "The emperor halted the hearing until Master Hus could be brought from his cell."

"We tried to join you," Novak growled, jabbing his dagger into the soil. "But they said no armed men could enter the assembly hall. They must fear our swords."

"I think," Lord John answered, his eyes meeting Anika's, "they feared your brave hearts more. Having you there would have greatly encouraged Master Hus. You might have given him the courage to silence his opposition."

"Is all lost?" Anika asked quietly, a heavy feeling in her stomach. "Is Master Hus condemned?"

Lord John shook his head and smiled. "No. He will have his public hearing, though I doubt it will be all he hoped for. They allowed him to address only the council and a few observers, when he had hoped to give an extended address to a great congress. After his arrival, one of the cardinals read articles of accusation from *De Ecclesia*. Hus declared that if there was anything evil or erroneous in his writings he was prepared to amend it, but then his accusers brought statements of false witnesses to accuse him."

"They dared to lie before God?" Manville's face flushed with honest fury.

Lord John nodded grimly, his countenance like gold in the flickering firelight. "Hus attempted to reply to the falsehoods, but their loud cries interrupted him. He was obliged to turn first toward one cardinal and then toward another to answer those who argued against him. He tried to explain how he had been misquoted and misrepresented, but they screamed at him and demanded that he reply only 'yes' or 'no.' Finally, when he followed the example of our Lord and fell silent, they exclaimed, 'Behold, you are silent; you have admitted your errors!' "

Lord John picked up a stick and silently stirred the fire, sending a volcano of sparks into the night sky. "They worked themselves into a rage like wild boars. If they had been animals—and I am not certain they were not—the bristles on their backs would have stood on end. They lifted their hands to their brows and gnashed their teeth, yet amid all the confusion our friend the goose was not dismayed. When the pack of accusers finally grew silent, he remarked, 'I supposed there would be more fairness, kindness, and order in the council.' "

Anika felt her heart melt when Lord John looked at her again, his eyes seeking comfort. "I took satisfaction in seeing that at least some council members were shamed by his remark. To save whatever remaining honor the council had, they requested that the meeting be adjourned until the day after the morrow."

Lord John looked around at his men, appreciation and affection gleaming in the depths of his dark eyes. "To each of you who have remained beside me and our friend Master Hus, I owe thanks," he said, his voice husky and deep. "I know you have sacrificed wealth to remain here, and some would say you have sacrificed even your honor. I cannot but believe that our travail here is drawing to a close. Master Hus's trial will be concluded soon, and we shall be going home in victory. And now," he said, smiling again as he rose to his feet, "I suggest that you all retire to your beds and get some sleep."

Anika waited until the circle of knights broke up, then hurried forward in the darkness, following her master. She found him outside his tent, standing alone in a stream of moonlight that poured through a gap in the branches of an oak. "My lord," she called softly, daring to use her woman's voice as she drew nearer, "will they really release Master Hus? You sounded so optimistic—"

He turned to her then, and in the darkness she could not see his face. "What do you think, Kafka? Would you be happy if Master Hus were released?"

"Of course," she answered, surprised and hurt by the question.

"But you do not think he will be."

Anika cast about for words, lifting her open hands in the darkness. "From what I know of these prelates, my lord, I do not believe them capable of such a noble act. They are evil. Do I want to see Master Hus restored? Yes. But do I believe these men capable of such righteousness? No. War is the devil's madness, and yet these men are pushing it toward us. They will drive us to revolution—"

Lord John turned slightly, moving into the light. "This mystery will never cease—the priest promotes war, the warrior, peace."

"What, my lord?"

"A poem I learned in childhood." He paused for a moment, then extended his hand to her. "Please—come into the light where I can see you."

Hesitantly, Anika gave him her hand. He pulled her toward him until they stood facing each other in the dazzling light of the moon. "Anika of Prague," he said, taking both her hands in his own, "What a thorn you are in my side! Your heart is as resolute as thunder, your mind as quick and nimble as a panther. You are courageous and beautiful, and yet you have set your heart on an obstinate path."

"Not so, my lord," Anika protested, feeling the chasm between them like an open wound. "I have set my heart to serve you."

An inexplicable look of withdrawal came over his face. "If you would serve me, Kafka, knight of Chlum, forswear this foolish quest of vengeance. Put aside your armor and sword and become Anika again. Be content with your womanhood and with whatever the morrow brings."

"Be content?" She wanted to behave like one of the men and spit with scorn. He had never suffered as she had—his parents had died natural deaths on their beds, their arms folded peacefully across their chests. He was a man, able to undertake and accomplish almost anything he set his heart and mind to do. He had never been forced to hide to preserve his virtue and his life.

"I am content to serve you, my lord," she answered, her voice a great deal shakier than she would have liked. She pulled her hand from his grasp. "As a *knight*. 'Tis what I have sworn, and 'tis what I will perform. As long as you serve Jan Hus, I am sworn to serve you."

"Anika—" His outstretched hand reached for her still. "Jan Hus's fate will soon be decided. What will you do then? Surely you can forget this foolishness of fighting and seek a more womanly life."

"No, my lord," she whispered, backing away. "I have a vow to fulfill before I can think of setting aside my sword." She lifted her chin to conceal her inner turmoil. "And it is not seemly for us to be together like this. What would your men say if one of them saw us?"

For a brief moment his face seemed to open so that she could look inside and watch her words slowly take hold. She saw bewilderment there, a quick flicker of temper, then resignation.

His hand fell to his side. "Good night, then," he said, turning into his tent.

"Thirty-seven." Alone in the woods, Vasek swung the instrument of external penance over his bare shoulder. The device, a small metal ring with five chains suspended from it, was intended to take his mind off worldly things so he could focus solely upon God. But ever since the pope fled into hiding, Vasek had been able to focus only upon his guilt. A man would not run unless he had something to hide. Vasek had visited the pope in the certain faith that His Holiness was the representative of Christ on earth, but Jesus Christ would never have fled into the night like a common criminal.

"Thirty-eight." The tiny hooks, one suspended from the end of each chain, bit into his back and scraped across the taut skin as he yanked the chains forward again. Private self-flagellation seemed the only way to correct his grave mistake. God had been merciful in one respect—as far as Vasek knew, neither Lord John nor Jan Hus realized that Vasek had been instrumental in having Hus arrested. Not even that nosy little Sir Kafka had picked up any clues.

"Thirty-nine." He winced as the little metal teeth opened a new patch of skin, then gritted his teeth. A headache asserted itself above his right eye, the pain digging into his brain. His stomach roiled in a sea of nausea—good, good, it was all good. Let God punish him out here in the woods, where he could bleed and vomit and suffer and moan his prayers of contrition.

In a few hours, or even on the morrow, he'd rise, bathe in the stream, and pull his tunic over his broken and bruised skin. And he would serve his lord and master with a will, trusting God and Lord John to do as they would.

He had taken matters into his own hands, and he was grievously sorry for it.

Bracing himself for one final blow, Vasek took a deep breath and readied the chains for another swing. "Forty."

Thirty

Later that night, a guard woke John from a deep sleep and pressed a letter into his hand. John fumbled for the lamp, then saw that the handwriting was Hus's. He smiled to himself as his eyes skimmed the first line—a tongue-in-cheek reminder of the time when John had debated theology in the town of Biberach.

To my good friend, the esteemed Doctor of Biberach:

How I miss the days when we were about the work of spreading the gospel! You, the doctor, and me, the goose! Together I believe we have made a difference.

The Almighty God today gave me a courageous and stout heart. Two articles of condemnation are already deleted. I hope, moreover, that by the grace of God more will be deleted. Almost all of them shouted at me as the Jews did at Jesus. So far they have not come to the principal point—namely, that I should confess that all the articles charged against me are contained in my treatises.

Greet our faithful nobles and friends of the truth, and pray God for me, for there is need of it. If only I could be granted a hearing that I might reply to the arguments of those who wish to impugn the articles stated in the treatises! I imagine that many who shout would turn dumb! But be it according to the will of heaven!

A freakish eclipse of the sun ushered in the morning of June 7, the day Hus's trial resumed. The more superstitious of Lord John's men cited the darkened sky as an evil omen, but Vasek murmured a hasty blessing over the group and told them that the unnatural darkness was only a trick of the devil.

Ignoring the others' uneasy murmurs, Anika pulled her bundle of women's clothing from its hiding place and slipped into a forest thicket. Though she had privately resolved that nothing good could come of Lord John again seeing her as a woman, the lure of Master Hus's trial proved stronger than her resolution. Since no men of arms could enter the assembly, perhaps a woman could.

The other knights had already ridden away through the gloom by the time she emerged from the woods, but she quickly mounted a horse and followed, praying no one would notice that under her billowing cloak the lady rode astride, her kirtle pulled up around her knees. When she reached the city gates, she tethered the horse at a hitching rail outside and blended into the crowd, carefully avoiding any knights in blue and gold surcoats.

An unruly mob waited outside the assembly hall, but in the midst of the gathering she spied Lord John's handsome profile. She threaded her way through the crowd until she reached his side, then smoothly slid her arm under his.

"Well met, my lord," she said, tilting her head. "I hope you will vouch for me so I may enter."

His eyes grazed her with a look of mingled amusement and admiration. "Lady Anika of Prague, is it?" he murmured, leading her forward as the doors opened and the crowd surged toward the building. "I thought you might appear today."

"Yes, my lord," she answered, tearing her eyes away from his face. By heaven above, she had not thought this action through. In the light of his words the other night, he might think she had donned this dress just to please him.

"I wanted to see my friend Master Hus," she said, lowering her voice as she offered an explanation. "This disguise seemed to be the best approach."

"Disguise? Since when does a woman wear a kirtle to disguise herself?"

She frowned at the laughter in his voice. "You know my meaning. And if you will vouch for me and let me enter on your arm and sit at your side, we shall soon be done with this. I will return this kirtle to the widow Fida as soon as our venture here is finished."

"Whatever you wish, Lady Anika," he said, his smile now utterly without humor.

By the trial's appointed hour, the sun had not come forth from behind whatever dark cloud God sent to hide it, and lamps had to be lit in the assembly hall when the hearing resumed. Anika felt her stomach churn with loathing when Cardinal D'Ailly, the self-professed "hammer of heretics," took the center chair to preside over the proceedings. He stood and lifted his hand, ready to bestow an invocation upon the gathering, but halted in midgesture, staring toward the doors at the rear of the room. Anika swiveled her head in time to see the emperor Sigismund himself stride forward. As an astonished silence fell over the group, he took a seat near the front of the room, apparently eager to observe and approve the trial.

Recovering quickly, Cardinal D'Ailly began the proceedings. After an opening prayer, an accuser again read the articles against Master Hus. Anika listened in rapt concentration as Cardinal D'Ailly began to smite the preacher with pitiless, hardhearted logic. But Hus, ever the scholar, defeated each point of contention with a scriptural quote and example.

Then, to Anika's horror, a prelate summoned a panel of witnesses. Through their testimony D'Ailly attempted to show that Hus depended entirely upon Wyclif's writings, for the views of that Englishman had already been condemned as heretical. Hus attempted to explain that he did not blindly approve all of Wyclif's teachings, but each time Hus opened his mouth, the cardinals interrupted with loud cries.

Prelates read eight additional articles of accusation. At the mention of Hus's appeal to his Savior, Jesus Christ, the assembly broke into loud jeers and mocking taunts. Anika stared at the cardinals' proud, stubborn faces, and in a breathless moment of insight, she understood why they hated Hus.

The council was *jealous*. Jealous of Master Hus's allegiance to Jesus Christ, and possessive of its own supremacy. Hus supported only one authority, that of Jesus Christ as revealed through Holy Scripture, and the council earnestly desired that preeminent position. These cardinals had pulled a pope from his ecclesiastical throne, but they would not allow themselves to be usurped. "Not by Jan Hus, not by the Scriptures, not by the blessed Lord himself," Anika murmured to herself.

As the day ended, Cardinal D'Ailly advised Hus to submit to the council. "If you do this," he said, an oily tone creeping into his voice, "you will best consult your safety and your standing."

The entire room jerked in startled amazement when the emperor's hand slammed down upon the arm of his chair. "There you have the answer," Sigismund cried, leaning forward to stare at the exhausted Hus, who had stood throughout the entire day of examination. "If you will but admit the council's supremacy in all matters of faith, your situation will be eased. Recant, Master Hus. I will grant no protection to any heretic who is obstinately determined to hold fast to his heresy, so I counsel you to fling yourself on the council's grace—the quicker the better, lest you fall into a worse plight."

"This I cannot do."

Anika jerked her head toward Hus, not certain she had heard him correctly. A wise man would have obfuscated the issue, suggested some sort of compromise, or murmured something about needing time to reflect. Surely Hus had spoken without thinking.

"I am willing to amend my teaching if it can be shown to be false according to the Scriptures," Hus said, the point of his beard grazing his robe as he lowered his head. "But if no man can prove the error of my ministry, then I cannot resign the truths I understand."

"Please, Jan!" John Reinstein, the priest who had journeyed with them from Prague, stood from his place in the assembly. "Please, for the sake of our Lord and his church, do not allow this issue to divide us!"

Hus smiled at the priest's concern, but his countenance reflected a distracted, inward look, as though he listened to something far off that only he could hear. "I cannot," he repeated, his voice like steel, "resign the truths I understand."

Rigidly holding her tears in check, Anika sat as still as a statue while the guards led Hus away.

———————

John was not surprised when Anika found him again the next morning. Her delicate features were composed, but her face was pale and her eyes wide, as though she had passed a sleepless night.

John had not slept, either. Another midnight messenger had brought a letter from Master Hus, the text of which lay as fresh in John's mind as if he had just read it:

> *To the good Lord John of Chlum and my friends in Constance:*
> *Would that I knew how the bearded Jerome, who refused to obey the counsel of friends and return home, is faring!*
> *Since they have my book, I no longer need this paper. Save the copy of the first articles with the proofs. Should there be need of proving some of the articles, note it there. Among them will most likely be the article, "A virtuous man, whatever he does, does virtuously."*
> *I am now suffering with toothache. At the castle Gottlieben I suffered with vomiting of blood, headache, and the stone. These are the punishments due for sins as well as the signs of God's love toward me . . .*

"Well met, Lord John," Anika murmured, slipping her arm through his in a companionable manner. He knew she did it merely to convince any spy that they were equals and old acquaintances, but she did not know her touch stoked a steadily growing fire. He had been unable to think of any other lady since realizing that his squire was more woman than any of the females he knew. Her commitment and passion for truth inspired his heart in a way no other woman could, but he could never let her know the depth of her effect on him. She was determined to follow her own path, and he was duty bound to let her.

"Will it end today?" she asked, glancing up at him.

"I cannot imagine that the trial will continue much longer," he answered, averting his gaze from the silky expanse of her neck. What a weakling he was, allowing himself to be distracted by temptations of the flesh while his best friend endured a trial for his life.

The crowd surged into the room, and the players entered as they had the day before. An air of isolation clung to Hus's sword-thin figure when the guards brought him in. John felt his heart contract in pity for his friend.

Cardinal D'Ailly wasted no time before launching his attack. Thirty-nine articles of accusation, collected by Michael de Causis and Stephen Palec, were read out. Article by article, Hus's accusers tried to show that the reformer had written against priests, the selling of indulgences, the pope, official doctrine, and the organization and administration of the Church.

Lord John found one point particularly interesting. They charged Hus with saying that no outward sign and no work of man could grant a man membership in the Church of Christ, but only the electing grace of God. Hus freely admitted the charge and illustrated his point by saying that Judas Iscariot, who did not have this electing grace, was not part of the body of Christ even though he possessed every outward sign and demonstrated the same deeds as the other disciples.

"Bravo, Jan!" John muttered under his breath. "Good thinking!"

But the council simply ignored his logic. They moved on to other arguments, accusing Hus of celebrating mass while under the ban of excommunication and preaching against priests who committed scandal.

"And what of this?" D'Ailly shrilled, pointing to another document on the table before him. He held it aloft as if Hus could read it from across the room. "You have written that if the pope, a bishop, or a prelate is in the state of mortal sin, he is not a pope, bishop, or prelate."

Hus's eyes, sharp and assessing, never left D'Ailly's face. "True enough. He who lives in a continual state of sin cannot rightly be a king before God, as is shown by the book of Samuel, chapter fifteen, verse twenty-three. There God, through Samuel, said to Saul, 'As you have rejected my word, I reject you from being king.'"

John caught his breath. Hus's response, though bold, was not the most prudent thing a man on trial for his life could say to men he had accused of sinning. D'Ailly flushed crimson, then smiled with satisfaction and looked toward the emperor's chair. When he found Sigismund's chair empty, the smile vanished.

"The emperor has stepped out into the hall," Anika whispered, following John's gaze.

D'Ailly murmured something to his aides, and immediately two prelates left the chamber. The gathering waited in silent expectancy for three or four minutes, then the emperor returned, escorted by the two prelates. With one brow raised in inquiry, he resumed his seat.

"Your highness," D'Ailly said, smiling in false humility, "we thought you would find this part of the trial particularly interesting."

Hus, completely aware of all that went on around him, did not flinch from speaking his mind. "Yes," he went on, meeting D'Ailly's steely gaze with his own, "unworthy rulers should rule no longer. Look at this council's own example—if John XXIII was truly and deservedly pope, why was he deposed?"

Again, Hus scored a point in his defense, and again D'Ailly ignored him. John Reinstein took advantage of a lapse in the proceedings to stand and give an impassioned defense of Hus's work in Prague and at Bethlehem Chapel, but D'Ailly quickly dismissed that priest's opinions and declared Reinstein out of order. A prelate read more articles; D'Ailly disregarded more of Hus's explanations. Over and over a few brave and sympathetic cardinals urged Hus to recant his teachings, and over and over the Bohemian preacher refused to relent.

John shifted in his seat, a tremor of mingled fear and anticipation shooting through him when D'Ailly turned and spoke to the council members. As the cardinals huddled in discussion, John cut a glance toward Anika. The customary expression of good humor had vanished from the curve of her mouth, the depths of her eyes. Her delicate features had hardened in a stare of disapproval, and he felt a strange lurch of recognition in her expression. She had worn the same look when she told him she had sworn vengeance . . . upon Cardinal D'Ailly.

He pressed his hand to his chin and looked away. This day might hold tragedy for Anika as well as Jan Hus. The anger and bitterness in her young heart would only be fed by the fires of execution. If the council condemned Jan Hus, Anika might never learn to forgive.

Finally Cardinal D'Ailly announced the council's threefold decision: First, Hus should humbly declare that he had erred in all the articles cited against him; second, he should swear not to teach them in the future; and third, he should publicly recant these beliefs.

The cardinal, his lips curving in an expression that hardly deserved to be called a smile, then gave Jan Hus two options: He must humbly submit to the council, which, in consideration of Emperor Sigismund and his brother, King Wenceslas of Bohemia, would treat Hus with humanity and kindness. In punishment for the scandal he had caused, Hus would be imprisoned for life in a Swedish monastery, in a cell that was to be walled up, leaving only a small opening through which food and drink could be handed to the prisoner.

"Should you not wish to submit and instead choose to defend your views," D'Ailly finished, "a hearing will not be refused you, but you will thus act at your greatest peril."

"I do not wish to maintain any errors," Hus replied, his expression grim as he faced the council, "but I cannot say that I held erroneous opinions which I never did hold. I beg that I might be allowed to express my views regarding the accusations made against me."

His request was met with indignant sputtering and much whispering. A few of the more sympathetic council members called out that he should recant, and even the emperor leaned forward and urged Hus to disavow his heretical views, even if he had never held them.

"No, your Highness," Hus answered, bowing his head in respect. "This I cannot do."

Beside him, John heard Anika release a muffled sob.

The guards strode forward to claim their prisoner, and Jan Hus turned to walk through the crowd. Too shaken for words, John stood and reached out, grasping Hus's hand and holding it firmly until a guard reached forward and broke the fragile human contact.

John sank back into his seat, an inexplicable feeling of emptiness at the center of his soul. He was dimly aware that Anika's hand lay upon his arm, and he found comfort in her touch, knowing that she loved Hus as much as he did.

As Hus left the room, Sigismund stood to address the assembled prelates. "Hus should be burned alive," he announced, not mincing his words and apparently not realizing that Bohemian nobles remained in the chamber. "Even if he recants, he should not be allowed to return to Bohemia. He is dangerous; he and his kind must be destroyed. Wherever bishops find others holding similar views, they should punish the offenders so this heresy might be destroyed root and branch. This council should make an end of Hus's secret friends and followers, especially his disciple Jerome, who is now in your custody."

John let out a choked, desperate laugh as his mind reeled in shock and amazement. He and his friends had placed so much faith in this emperor, and yet Sigismund had just proclaimed that anyone who agreed with Hus should be punished—including, apparently, John of Chlum, Venceslas of Duba, even King Wenceslas and Queen Sophia, the noble lady and anonymous friend who had given so much of herself and her fortune to advance Hus's cause.

John lowered his head, suddenly overwhelmed by the torment of the past few weeks. Perhaps Anika was right. War might indeed loom in Bohemia's future. And right now, John had to admit, vengeance would certainly taste sweet.

Thirty-One

To Lord John of Chlum, dearly beloved friend in Christ!

Lord John, most gracious and most faithful supporter, may God be your reward! I beg you, do not leave until you see the end consummated. Surely you would rather see me led to the fire than to be so craftily stifled! I still cherish the hope that the Almighty God may snatch me from their hands on account of the merits of the saints. Greet all our friends in the kingdom, requesting them to pray God for me that if I am to remain in prison, I may humbly expect death without apprehension.

My hope in the Lord is ever firm.

I thank all the barons, knights, and squires of the kingdom of Bohemia, and particularly King Wenceslas and the queen, my gracious lady, that they have dealt affectionately with me, have treated me kindly, and have striven diligently for my liberation. I thank also King Sigismund for all the good he has shown me. I thank all the Czech and Polish lords who steadfastly and firmly strove for the truth and for my liberation; I desire salvation for all of them, now in grace and afterward in everlasting glory. May the God of all grace guide your life in the health of soul and body to Bohemia, that serving there the King Christ, you may attain the life of Glory!

Written in prison, in chains, the Friday before the Feast of St. John the Baptist.

Jan Hus

Jan Hus spent the last month of his life engaged in two activities: answering members of the council who urged him to recant, and writing letters to his friends and supporters. The sympathetic cardinals, fearing that Hus's martyrdom would worsen the already strained relations between the council and the kingdom of Bohemia, pestered the preacher every day.

By night Hus wrote of his trials. Robert, his faithful jailer, conveyed the messages to Lord John, who gave them to Peter and Anika so that copies might be made and carried to Hus's supporters. Anika worked more diligently than she ever had in her life, but often she would have to begin anew, for she found herself watering the parchments with her tears as she moved her pen over the smoothed page.

Her hand actually trembled as she copied one of Hus's last letters. *Having these things before your eyes,* Hus wrote, *do not allow yourselves to be terrified into giving up the reading of what I have written or into surrendering your books to be burned. Remember what our merciful Savior told us as a warning in Matthew 24, that prior to the Day of Judgment 'there will be so great a tribulation as has not been from the beginning of the world and never will be afterward.' Remembering that, dearly beloved, stand firm! The council will not come from Constance to Bohemia! I think that many of that council will die before they wrest your books from you.*

The books. Her hand trembled with the rueful acceptance of a terrible knowledge. If the council had its way, all that would remain of Jan Hus were his books and letters—documents she had helped produce, that she could *continue* producing for as long as she lived. Many of Hus's original works had been burned in the fire at the bookshop, but Lord John had copies in his chamber, and Lord Venceslas of Duba undoubtedly had others.

She lowered her pen, an idea slowly germinating within her. Jan Hus would never be defeated. They might take his life, they might destroy his body, but his soul and intellect lived on in the pages of his books! And books traveled as far as the wings of the morning, especially when released in a university city like Prague. She could earn a living copying and renting Hus's works, supporting herself and enlightening souls at the same time.

Her father and Petrov would have approved this plan. Maybe,

she thought, her lips twisting in a wry smile, even Lord John would approve, providing she gave up her knight's armor.

She gave herself a stern mental shake. She loved writing, and she believed in Hus's work, but she was not yet ready to give up her sword and surcoat. She had worked too hard to become a knight, and she would not surrender her silver sword as long as evil prelates like D'Ailly held control over Bohemia. She had sworn to take vengeance, and she would not be denied.

She shook her fanciful ideas from her head and picked up her pen again, then dipped it in the inkwell. She and Jan Hus had both been set on an irrevocable course. They had no choice but to follow the path to whatever lay ahead.

On July 5, the Friday after St. Procopius, John prepared to obey a command which had come to him from Sigismund the day before. He, Lord Venceslas of Duba, and four bishops were to visit Jan Hus and see if the preacher could be convinced to recant. This would be the emperor's final effort on Hus's behalf, John realized. That thought rose above all others, killing any hope of joy.

Shortly after John and the others arrived at the prison, a pair of guards brought a pitifully bedraggled Hus out to them. Hus's hands were shackled behind his back, his beard untrimmed and foul, his hair matted. But he walked between his jailers in an attitude of self-command and studied relaxation, and John felt his heart twist in a feeling akin to envy. Would he conduct himself nearly as well if he found himself on trial for his faith?

Jan stood before him, his deep brown eyes large and surrounded by dark shadows.

"Look, Master Hus," John began, goaded by frustration and a desire to preserve his dear friend's life, "we are laymen and know not how to advise you; therefore see if you feel yourself guilty in *anything* of that which is charged against you. Do not fear to be instructed therein and to recant. But," John struggled to maintain an even, conciliatory tone, "if indeed you do not feel guilty of those things charged against you, follow the dictates of your conscience. Under no circumstances do anything against your conscience or lie in the sight of God; but rather be steadfast until death in what you know to be the truth."

It was a fitting time and place for tears, and Hus hung his head and wept them. Slowly, humbly, he answered: "Lord John, be sure that if I knew that I had written or preached anything erroneous against the law and against the Holy Mother Church, I would desire humbly to recant it—God is my witness! I have ever desired to be shown better and more relevant Scripture than those I have written and taught. And if they were shown me, I am ready most willingly to recant."

One of the bishops sneered. "See how obstinate he is in his heresy?" The prelate gestured to the guard. "Take him back to his cell. This matter is finished."

The guards pulled on Hus's arm, turning him, but the preacher's gaze caught and held John's. "Remember you the Goose!" Hus said, looking at John with a smile hidden in his eyes. "Go with God, my friend."

As he turned to leave, John clenched his hands into hard fists, fighting back his own tears of anger and frustration. Now, at least, he understood some of the passion that filled Anika's heart. If he did not take care, he would soon be as vengeful as that little knight.

But the prayer inscribed in Hus's last letter sustained him. *O holy Christ,* Hus had written, *draw us after you. We are weak, and if you do not draw us, we cannot follow you. Give us a strong and willing spirit, and when the weakness of the flesh appears, let Your Grace go on before us, accompany, and follow us. For without you we can do nothing, least of all suffer a cruel death for your sake. Grant a willing spirit, a fearless heart, true faith, steadfast hope, perfect love, that for your sake we may, with patience and joy, surrender our lives. Amen.*

On Saturday morning, July 6, the archbishop of Riga led Master Jan Hus to the cathedral of the city of Constance. Inside the cathedral, a general session of the prelates had convened with Emperor Sigismund presiding. The archbishop accompanying Hus had to wait outside the building while mass was being celebrated within, for no incorrigible heretic could be present where the sacred body of the Lord was being consumed.

Anika, dressed in her armor, stood outside the cathedral with the other knights of Chlum. The brooding sorrow present within each of them seemed to spawn and spread until it mingled with a million sorrows of past and present. Watching Master Hus's tired face, Anika wondered if she would ever feel joy again.

At the conclusion of the high mass, the archbishop led Jan Hus into the cathedral. At once, the massive crowd surged forward behind him. This assembly was open to anyone who wanted to attend, for the Council wanted to demonstrate in public the fate which awaited heretics.

Lord John had said little to her all morning, yet Anika stayed close to his side. She did not want to suffer alone. A future without Jan Hus seemed dark and dim indeed. Of all the Bohemians, she, Lord John, and Peter Mladenovic had been closest to Master Hus, probably because they spent so much time listening to and transcribing his thoughts.

Anika crowded into a pew, then gasped when she saw Hus kneeling upon a small temporary platform in the center of the church. Next to him on the platform stood a table laden with a priest's vestments. Hus was praying silently, the marks of suffering clearly evident upon his ashen face. Anika had never seen his cheeks so sunken, his limbs so weak and trembling. But his eyes, when he lifted his head, flashed with an unbroken spirit.

The heretic's platform rose from a sea of gold and purple and red robes, finery worn by the prelates. Sigismund sat on a throne near the high altar, his courtiers clad in splendid armor and nodding plumes. The treacherous Cardinal D'Ailly was also present, garbed in an ornate cassock and wearing a jeweled miter. Before this spangled gathering Hus rose to his feet in silent poverty, his poor brown robe soiled and worn.

Eager to begin, the Bishop of Lodi offered a short and nonsensical sermon on the text "that the body of sin might be destroyed." A second bishop then read a report of the council's past proceedings, including the articles cited as heretical from Hus's writings. As another prelate read the articles, Hus tried to explain his views but was immediately commanded to remain silent.

Anika stared in a paralysis of astonishment when one of the bishops charged that Hus had claimed to be a fourth member of the Godhead. "Name the doctor who testified that against me!" Hus objected, stunned.

The bishop looked up and frowned. "There is no need that he be named now."

Hus shook his head. "Be it far from me, a miserable wretch, that I should want to name myself the fourth person of the Godhead, for that has never entered my heart. I unswervingly assert that the Father, the Son, and the Holy Spirit are one God, one essence, and a trinity of persons."

On and on the charges went, ranging from minute twistings of Hus's words to blatantly ridiculous claims. At the conclusion of the list, Hus looked directly at Emperor Sigismund and reminded everyone present how he had come to Constance: "I came to this council freely, having the safe conduct of the lord king here present, desiring to show my innocence and to give account of my faith."

The flush on the emperor's face receded, leaving two red spots on his pale cheeks.

Anika felt Lord John stiffen beside her, then heard his whisper, tense and clipped: "This emperor is a disgrace. If honor were banished from every other home, it ought to find a refuge in the heart of kings."

When all the articles had been read, an aged Italian prelate proclaimed the formal sentence of condemnation. Hus's writings, both in Latin and Bohemian, were to be committed to the flames. Hus himself was declared to be a true and manifest heretic, to be delivered over to the secular authorities for punishment.

At this point, Hus knelt and prayed with a stentorian voice that echoed through the vast cathedral: "Lord Jesus, I implore you, forgive mine enemies! You know that they have borne false witness against me. Forgive them for your boundless mercy's sake!"

At the sound of his prayer, Cardinal D'Ailly burst out in loud, sardonic laughter.

"Sir Kafka," Lord John whispered, leaning so that his arm nudged Anika's shoulder, "Perhaps you should leave now."

"No," she answered, staring at Master Hus's helpless form. "I will remain until it is over."

"It will not be easy to bear," her master answered, unspoken pain alive and glowing in his eyes. "I have never seen one of these trials, but I know there is great suffering to come."

"We will bear it together, then," Anika answered, sliding her hand to the hilt of her sword. The smooth coldness of the metal against her palm gave her little comfort. No matter what they did to her friend, when war came, she would make them pay—beginning with Cardinal D'Ailly, who was now smiling at Hus, his bulging cheeks reducing his eyes to sparkling black circles.

Upon the platform, the cardinals had begun the cruelest and most bizarre ritual Anika could have imagined. Hus was commanded to array himself in the priestly vestments upon the table, then a chalice and paten were placed in his hands. As Hus held the containers for the wine and bread used in Holy Communion, he was once again exhorted to recant. Facing the vast crowd, he lifted his eyes to heaven and said in a trembling voice, "Behold, these bishops demand that I shall recant and abjure. I fear to do this. For, if I complied, I would be false in the eyes of God and sin against my own conscience and divine truth."

He looked out at the crowd with determination in the jut of his bearded chin. "There is another reason why I cannot recant. I would thereby not only offend the many souls to whom I have proclaimed the gospel, but others also who are preaching it in all faithfulness."

The prelates called him down from the platform. Through a blur of tears Anika saw them wrest the cup from his hands, then the paten. With each of the other vestments they removed from him—

the stole, the chasuble, the alb—they pronounced a curse. And each time, Hus humbly and gladly embraced their defamations for the sake of the Lord Jesus Christ.

Anika blinked in astonished silence as the bishops then began to argue about how they should obliterate Hus's tonsure, the mark of the priest. Some wished to shave his head with a razor, others insisted that cutting it with scissors would be enough. In the midst of the bedlam, Hus turned to the emperor and called in a loud voice, "Look, these bishops cannot even agree in this vilification!"

Without hesitation, D'Ailly himself strode forward with scissors, disfiguring Hus's tonsure by cutting his hair to the scalp in four places—right, left, front, and back. When his tonsure had been thus distorted, another prelate gleefully lifted up a paper crown which had been painted with a picture of three horrible devils about to seize a soul and tear it with their claws. When he had placed the crown on Hus's head, he called out, "We commit your soul to the devil!"

At this Hus lifted both hands to heaven: "And I commit it to the most merciful Lord Jesus Christ." His voice wasn't much above a whisper, but the effect was as great as if he'd shouted. Of the paper crown, he said, "My Lord Jesus Christ, on account of me, a miserable wretch, bore a much heavier and harsher crown of thorns. Being innocent, he was deemed deserving of the most shameful death. Therefore I, a miserable wretch and sinner, will humbly bear this much lighter."

A mayhem of noise ripped the air and seemed to vibrate the very foundations of the cathedral. Many of the cardinals, furious at their inability to coerce this stalwart scholar, pounded their pews and vented their fury while Hus remained solid and unbending through the cacophony. Anika saw two or three cardinals, however, staring in silent pity and despair, their countenances marked by lines of heart-sickness and weariness. Not all the cardinals were evil, she realized with a pang of remorse. But far too many of this panel had been infected with Cardinal D'Ailly's malice and jealousy.

At the sight of Hus's lonely form, Anika's face twisted. Her eyes closed tight to trap the sudden rush of tears, but there were too many. They streamed from her lashes down her cheeks, dripping onto her clasped hands.

When she opened her eyes again, Hus had disappeared from the platform and Lord John was tugging at her elbow. "They have taken him out to the churchyard," he said, his voice—like her nerves—in tatters.

Without question, she rose and followed him.

Thirty-Two

A stream of spectators—Hus's supporters, enemies, and a few folk who were merely curious—followed the preacher. His executioners led him through the churchyard where at that moment a group of prelates were setting fire to a collection of Hus's books. Lord John felt his spine stiffen as the tongues of flame lapped at the parchments. How many hours, how much sacrifice had gone into those books! A scribe like Anika had labored to produce them, a saint like Hus had labored to *live* them. And now they would be paid for with a martyr's blood.

John turned and lifted his head, trying to see over the crowd to catch a glimpse of Hus. The gaudy heretic's cap was easy to spot, for it rose nearly eighteen inches over Hus's head, and John felt his heart leap when he found the face he had been seeking. Hus was watching the fire with an expression of pained tolerance, then suddenly his countenance brightened in a smile. Had Hus seen him? John wondered. Or had his grief been lessened by a comforting touch from the Holy Spirit? Perhaps he had remembered that though his books might be destroyed at Constance, many more remained in Prague and throughout the castles of Bohemia.

The procession did not linger long at the churchyard, but continued to a quiet meadow known as the Bròhl. John saw the executioner's stake and stopped abruptly, anger and fear knotting inside him. *Why, God, has it come to this?*

Talk wrapped around him like water around a rock, but John ignored it all as his eyes fastened on his friend. When Hus first neared the stake, the buzz of conversation from the crowd ceased as he knelt and began to pray. In a resonant voice, Hus recited the Thirty-first and Fifty-first Psalms with such great emotion that the people around him wept. John overheard one man whisper to his companion, "I did not know how he acted or what he said formerly, but now in truth I know that he prays and speaks with holy words."

As the executioner commanded Hus to rise, the preacher urged all who watched not to believe that he in any way held, preached, or taught the articles with which he had been charged by false witnesses.

John felt his face burn in humiliation when the guards then stripped Hus of all clothing but the horrid heretic's hat. As a choir of innocent sparrows sang in the trees bordering the meadow, the executioners tied Hus to the thick wooden stake with wet ropes, his hands behind his back. Then another man placed a blackened chain around Hus's neck.

In the midst of these dire ministrations, John saw another smile light Hus's face. "The Lord Jesus Christ, my Redeemer and Savior, was bound by a harder and heavier chain," he said, his dark eyes roving over the crowd. "And I, a miserable wretch, am not ashamed to bear being bound for His name by this one."

The executioners stacked two bundles of wood under Master Hus's shackled feet. Systematically, the guards emptied two cartloads of wood and hay, piling the bundles around Hus's body to the level of his chin.

Before the fire was kindled, Sigismund's imperial marshal, Hoppe of Poppenheim, approached to offer Hus one final chance to recant his preaching and teaching. But Hus, looking up to heaven, answered resolutely: "God is my witness." His voice rang over the gathering and echoed on the wind. "Those things that are falsely ascribed to me I have never taught or preached. The principal intention of my preaching and of all my other acts or writings was solely to turn men from sin. And in that truth of the Gospel I wrote, taught, and preached, I am willing gladly to die today."

Forgetting herself, Anika clasped Lord John's arm and hid her face in his cloak. She heard the crackling of the flames, smelled the acrid scent of burning hay and wood, and listened in stunned disbelief as Hus's song lifted above the roaring inferno: "Christ, son of the living God, have mercy upon us," he sang in Bohemian. "Christ, son of the living God, have mercy upon me."

Flinching at the sound of her beloved friend's voice, she lifted her eyes. The wood around Master Hus seemed to thirst for the flames that beset it. "Even so, my soul thirsts for you," she murmured, recalling a Scripture verse Hus had often quoted in his writings.

The flames leaped upon the straw with fiendish exuberance, but she could no longer see Master Hus. Around her several people murmured the "Our Father" as an incantation against evil. But Anika turned her back on the sight and rested her hand on Lord John's strong shoulder as she resisted the nauseating sinking of despair.

This battle was over. The cardinals had won again, and this time they would not be satisfied with mere murder. The executioners would pull the charred body down and add more wood, burning Hus's remains until not even a bone was recognizable. Then the ashes would be strewn into the lake. The Church did not want any remnant of Jan Hus to remain, nothing that could serve as a relic or a bit of inspiration to those who sought the truth.

The council, the clergy, the corrupt church had claimed another innocent soul—but they did not know about the books . . . or Anika's sword.

"Jan Hus," she murmured, wondering how one horizon could look so peaceful while the opposite skyline boiled with fury and shame, "*exustus non convictus.* Burned but not convicted." Her hand gripped the hilt of her sword. "Murdered, but not forgotten."

Thirty-Three

In the late summer of 1415, Lord John and his party returned home to find Bohemia in tumult. All classes, from the serfs to the nobility, had been profoundly moved by Jan Hus's death. Many who had been timid followers of his teachings stepped boldly forward to proclaim their belief in scriptural authority.

In Prague, home to the university and the kingdom's foremost scholars, mobs drove ungodly priests from the city, plundered their houses, and filled their places of leadership with clergymen who followed Hus's teachings. Even Archbishop Albik found himself besieged in his palace and was forced to flee the kingdom.

Just as the Roman sword of persecution scattered believers and fanned the flames of belief in the years following Christ's death, so Jan Hus's blood proved to be seed. Everywhere the tale of his death was told, men were compelled to question why church authorities could execute a priest who steadfastly adhered to the gospel of Christ.

Though the misery of Constance still haunted her, Anika was privately delighted by the religious fervor sweeping the kingdom. Her father had been right all along—and she, his fiery-haired daughter, would yet live to fight in the coming confrontation. The battle was as inevitable as birth and death, and Anika entered into her duties at Chlum with renewed vigor. She spent her mornings training with Lev and Svec, sharpening both her skills and theirs, and passed the afternoons copying Hus's letters and treatises. The council had taken his life, but the *spirit* of the man lived on in his words.

That spirit—for God and truth and righteousness—could not be allowed to die. Men like Cardinal D'Ailly had nearly vanquished it, but she had seen heartfelt sorrow on some of the other cardinals' faces. The Church had not become entirely evil. The spark of holy purity still lived in some men of God, and as soon as she was fully prepared and in reach of her goal, she would do her part to excise the malignant tumor that drained Christ's church of her lifeblood. With the killing of Cardinal D'Ailly, her vengeance would be well under way.

She passed her days contentedly, but with an ear toward Lord John's intentions. He had originally said she could serve him as long as he served Master Hus, and she knew he could rightfully dismiss her at any time. So she labored diligently on Hus's manuscripts, hoping Lord John would see that she was continuing to promote Hus's cause. If he asked her to leave, she sternly told herself, she could. She would simply go to another castle and establish herself there. But she would never find friends as true as the Chlum knights or a master as wonderful as Lord John.

On September 2, in a formal response to the council's action against Hus, more than four hundred fifty lords and knights, including those of Lord John's household, signed a document affirming Hus's innocence. This letter of protest was immediately dispatched to the still-convened Council of Constance.

Lord John remembered Sigismund's bold assertion that all followers of Hus should be sought out and punished, and he warned his fellow reformers that their actions might be fraught with grave danger. To unify and strengthen themselves against opposition, Lord John's allies formed the Hussite League. Binding themselves by a solemn covenant, they pledged to allow the free preaching of the gospel on their estates, to accept no orders from the Council of Constance, to obey only those commands of the pope and bishops which harmonized with the Holy Scriptures, to resist all unjust bans of excommunication, to arrange for the defense of the country, and to regard the University of Prague as their authority in doctrinal matters.

In reprisal, the Bohemian nobles in agreement with the Council of Constance formed the Catholic League. These nobles were not as numerous as the Hussites, but many of them were powerful. Pledging themselves to adhere to the council's decisions and continue support of the Roman church, this group, led by Lord Laco of Lidice, steadfastly continued to contribute gold, men, and assistance to the Roman Church.

But most Bohemians had borne enough. Scholars and theologians at the University of Prague set forth four articles designed to govern religion throughout Bohemia. Lord John's knights cheered when he announced the four articles at dinner:

> *The Word of God is to be preached, in a proper way, by the priests of the Lord, without let or hindrance, throughout the kingdom of Bohemia.*
>
> *The sacrament of the Holy Eucharist, of bread and wine, is to be administered according to the institution of the Savior, to all believers not disqualified to receive it by reason of mortal sin.*
>
> *The secular dominion exercised by the clergy over worldly goods and possessions is to be taken away from them, and the clergy are to be brought back to the evangelical rule and apostolic practice of Christ and his disciples.*
>
> *All mortal sins, especially such as are public, are to be punished by those to whom they pertain.*

Bohemia, the unorthodox kingdom whose heathen ancestors had embraced the gospel from unconventional missionaries, rejoiced in the reform her own people had instigated.

But as Lord John sat alone in his chamber and listened to the nighttime sounds of his celebrating knights, he wondered how long the victory would last.

Rome had never allowed her errant children to escape retribution. And by establishing the Hussite and the Catholic Leagues, the nobles of Bohemia had created their own great schism and sown the seeds for civil war.

———

Autumn days fell into winter weeks, which melted into spring showers that dried under the hot summer sun. Anika continued her work at Chlum, writing with an almost furious intensity, buoyed by the success of the Hussite League but shadowed by the certainty that this freedom could not last long. The Council of Constance would not convene forever, and when it dispersed, the evil Cardinal D'Ailly would doubtless return to Bohemia, spreading his malevolence and evil like the plague. Then she would have her opportunity for vengeance . . . but how many lives would he destroy before she could stop him?

D'Ailly had continued to wreak destruction in Constance. In the late spring of 1416, in an effort to further vent his displeasure against Jan Hus, D'Ailly convinced the council to condemn Jerome of Prague, Hus's chief disciple. On a balmy June day, Jerome was escorted to the same meadow where his mentor perished, and there he also met death in flame. In Bohemia, the Hussite League stormed in protest, and another flurry of letters flew off to Constance.

Each action in Constance gave impetus to the growing movement among the Bohemian people. Hussite evangelists sprang up like wildflowers, preaching in private homes and open fields, offering the cup and the bread to anyone who professed belief in the Savior.

While evangelical fervor blossomed among the populace, another kind of fervor burgeoned among the knights. Rumors filtering in from Constance suggested that the new pope, whenever he was elected, would be expected to inaugurate an immediate crusade against the Hussites.

"War is coming," Novak told his knights in the garrison one night. "All of Christendom may be summoned against us." His gray eyes took on a remote, reserved look, and Anika knew he did not look forward to the fight. His hair had completely grayed in the four years she had been at Chlum, and war was for younger knights. "The Swiss with their halberds, the English with their billhooks and longbows, the French with their sharp glaives—we shall have to face them all."

"What do the Scriptures say?" Anika countered, rising to her feet. She looked at the others gathered around the fireplace. "No weapon formed against you shall prosper. If the Lord is with us, who can stand against us?"

"The Lord was with Master Hus, but the fires consumed him," Lev pointed out, his voice dull and troubled.

Anika's heart sank with swift disappointment at Lev's words. She suspected that the younger lad had been profoundly affected by Master Hus's death, but the only signs of his distress were his muffled cries in the night. When she tried to draw him into conversation, he only rebuffed her, scorning whatever kind attentions she tried to give him. Anika yearned to tell Lord John about Lev's torment, but if the boy would not admit his problem to her, why would he open up to the father he saw only as a master?

"Why are we talking about the past?" Manville spoke up. "We should be sharpening our skills and preparing for the battles to come. With proper training, even our peasants might be shaped into an army. Of course they will never be as disciplined as a corps of knights, but even such meager weapons as lances, slings, iron-pointed flails and clubs can beat down an armor-clad knight—if the peasant is properly motivated."

Indeed, Anika thought, looking around at the men who had become her peers, *if you can train me to wield a sword and a shield, you can surely train a farmer.*

"Sir Kafka." Anika looked up. Demetr, the steward, stood at the edge of the knights' circle, his hands clasped before him. "Lord John wishes to see you in his chamber. At once, if you please."

Anika pressed her lips together, then stood to her feet. Her master had not sought her counsel in months, and they had exchanged less than two dozen private words since their return to Chlum. What could he want with her now?

As she stood to obey, she felt her stomach drop, replaced by a frightening hollowness. What if he had decided to dismiss her? Was he about to cast her away?

A bead of perspiration traced a cold path from her armpit to her rib, but she nodded at the steward and followed him into the castle.

Lord John was seated in his chair by the balcony, his untouched supper plate on a small table at his right hand, the two mastiffs at his feet. Bilko lifted his head in curiosity as Anika entered, then lowered it with a resounding sigh.

"Sir Kafka, my lord," Demetr announced. Then he bowed and backed out of the room.

Anika moved stiffly forward. "You wanted to see me, my lord?"

"Yes. Thank you for coming."

Her heart contracted in pity as she looked at him. The previous months seemed to have aged him, and in the torchlight his flesh seemed so rarefied through suffering that now only his soul showed.

"I have spent the last day and night in prayer," he said, one hand idly caressing Bela's broad head. "And I have heard the rumors that Novak shared with the knights tonight. These stories have persisted for months." With his feet on a low stool, he frowned into the darkness beyond his balcony. "Though it has caused me great distress, I wanted to tell you that I and my household will withdraw from the Hussite League."

Completely stunned, Anika uttered an indrawn gasp. "Withdraw?" she asked, her voice rising in surprise. Her mind reeled with confusion. "You would withdraw your support from our allies?"

"This has not been an easy decision for me," he went on, looking up at her from beneath craggy brows. "I have agonized over it even as Master Hus agonized over the decision whether to recant."

"But Master Hus did not recant," Anika protested, struggling to find words. She pulled her gaze away from his; she couldn't think under his steady scrutiny. "Master Hus held firm. But you—if you withdraw, you are forfeiting a promise! You are abandoning the cause!"

"Hus did not die for a cause!" Lord John's eyes darkened dangerously. "He died for the truth! They are talking now of war, Anika, *real* war where men die and others are forever maimed. Jan Hus did not resist arrest; he would not allow me to mount an armed defense for his sake. He was not a warrior; his sole purpose was to lead men to Christ."

"His sole purpose was to reform the corrupt church!" Anika blazed back. "And he gave his life, all he had, in that cause. And now that things have come to a difficult pass, you want to back out!"

"I am no coward!" His burning eyes held her still, radiating disapproval, and Anika felt it like a hot wind in her face. His anger frightened her, but she could not allow him to retreat.

"If you are not a coward, then why would you abandon your fellow nobles?" she asked, her voice cold and lashing. "They have risked their lives, their estates, their sacred honor—"

"He that preaches war is the devil's chaplain," he interrupted. "Have you never heard that, Anika? Those who encourage war are not speaking for Christ. The Savior never advocated war, and neither did Jan Hus. The psalmist wrote, 'Scatter the people that delight in war,' and I fear we shall be scattered if we persist in fighting."

"Would you rather we lie down and surrender to the Roman church?" Anika asked, horrified. "Are we to be mindless sheep led to the slaughter? Master Hus was a gentle man; 'twas not in his nature to fight. But you and I and the other knights were born and bred to battle—"

She heard the lie in her words and halted, tripping over her own tongue.

"You?" His eyes froze on her lips, and Anika felt heat stealing into her face. "Were you born to battle, gentle Anika? Or was this desire wrought by something other than God? Something a great deal less than God?"

She turned away so he could not read the emotions on her face. He was clever, too clever, but he was wrong. Maybe, in time, she and Novak could convince him to continue his support of the Hussite League. Lord John was one of the most powerful and influential nobles in the region; his withdrawal would undermine the struggle against the Catholic league.

"Between Christ and war there is unalterable opposition," he said, a fierce intensity in his lowered voice. "There cannot possibly be harmony. The day of war is nothing but a harvest for the devil, and I will not involve my knights in it. I will defend my people, I will defend Chlum. But I will not go forward to fight those who bear the name of Christ."

"I am sure, my lord," Anika answered, speaking in as reasonable a voice as she could manage, "that you will do what is right when the time comes. After all, no one has yet mentioned war. It may be that war will not come, though it appears the council will soon elect a new pope. And when they do, he will have the power to launch a crusade against us—"

"Which the knights of Chlum will not go forward to meet," Lord John finished. "I intend to tell the other knights in three days, Anika. I will expect them to defend this estate and the villages under my protection. They are free to defend themselves, their wives, and their children. But I will not send my knights to kill in God's name. And if Jan Hus were here now, he would approve my decision. God has approved it."

Anika stared at him in silence, trying to comprehend his unspoken message. If he was waiting to tell the other knights, he had a particular reason for telling her early.

"I have brought you here," he went on, staring now at his hands, "because I know your heart burns to take your vengeance. And so, if you must fight, I will release you from your vow of fealty." He looked up and offered her a smile. "It was given under false pretenses, as I recall."

She felt ice spreading through her veins. "You want me to leave?"

"No, I do not." Rising fluidly from his chair, Lord John walked to stand in front of her, then took both her hands as he had on a moonlit night many months before. "I want you to forswear your vows of vengeance and remain here. I am sure knighthood is not as appealing as it once seemed to you, so leave this armor and become my scribe, Anika. Let the past be buried. Help me further Hus's cause by propagating the gospel through the written word. Together we can change the future."

"The future?" He radiated a vitality that drew her like a magnet, but such an attraction would be perilous. He did not understand her past; he was asking too much—and yet not enough. He wanted her as a scribe, nothing else. Just another house servant, someone to do his bidding, to help him win the world. Even after she had worked at his side for nearly four years, he was not willing to let her into his heart.

"War *is* coming, Anika," he whispered, tightening his grip upon her hands. "And I will need your help in the days ahead. Novak and the knights will protect Chlum, Vasek will pray that God will give us wisdom, Demetr will oversee the estate, Peter will help with my correspondence. I need you, though, to aid me with the translations of Hus's work."

"The translations?" She closed her eyes, her heart aching. "Is that your only reason for wanting me to remain here?"

"Of course not." He smiled, but a wall of reserve came up behind his eyes. "You knew Hus as well as I, and despite your youth, you have strength and knowledge. You are well read. And you have been a blessing to my sons. You were right; I should have shown them more affection, but you have been nearby to see that they lacked for nothing."

Dropping one of her hands, he placed his fingers under her chin in an affectionate gesture of gratitude, and the touch of his flesh sent a warming flush through her. She pulled away, not willing to be drawn into his spell. If she was not careful, she'd surrender to the temptation of his offer just to be near him, just to hear his voice and sit in the chamber where he worked every day.

"You will inform the other knights in three days?" she whispered, her voice strangled. She forced herself to look away. "I have until then to make my decision?"

"Yes." His tone was now cold and exact.

"Then I will give you my answer in three days," she whispered, backing out of the room.

A flash of loneliness stabbed John as Anika left his chamber. He should have known how she would react; for years his energies had been wasted against her granite stand. He could tell her that God himself had sent an archangel to deliver the message that Sir Kafka should vanish so Anika could step forth from that disguising armor, and still she would not believe.

Bela looked up at him, her brown eyes mirroring the sadness in John's own soul. "I tried, girl," he whispered, reaching out to caress the dog's head. "But she is set in her ways. I don't think we can convince her to stay with us."

Responding to his voice, Bela stood and came toward him, lowering her massive head into his lap. Why couldn't a woman be more like one of his dogs? Bela and Bilko demanded nothing; they were grateful for their food and shelter, happy merely to lie by his side or jog beside his horse. They asked only for his company and a loving touch every now and then.

The thought froze in his brain. Anika was a great deal more than a dog; perhaps his mistake lay in treating her as a pet. Frantiska, after all, had seemed content at Chlum, thrilled to sit beside him at dinner, satisfied to watch over his sons. And he had shown only as much appreciation as he dared. If he had been more open about his feelings and affection, she might have begun to make demands in that bizarre feminine language he did not understand.

Was that why he feared Anika? If he told her how much he cared, she would press him, and he would disappoint her, and she would be hurt. And if Anika were hurt, neither Novak, nor Lev, nor Svec, nor half the knights in the garrison would ever forgive him. John would never forgive himself.

"It is better this way," he whispered to Bela, his mind pulling away from his unsolvable dilemma. "She must choose. Either she remains with us as a scribe, or she leaves. But either way she is responsible for her own decision."

Sighing in contentment, Bela snorted softly.

Thirty-Four

For two days Anika did not sleep or eat. She wandered among the knights, doing routine tasks in a routine way, while her heart and mind battled one another. Her heart yearned for the man who had taken her hands, the strangely vulnerable master whose outward charm and openness masked a very private man. Her mind decried the attraction, for it was obvious enough that Lord John of Chlum cared only for Anika as a scribe. For four years they had worked together, planned together, witnessed victories and defeats. And though she did not understand why he had decided to quit the Hussite League, he was right about one thing—her knighthood had lost much of its luster.

Anika walked to the well in the courtyard and sat down on the stone rim, turning to peer into its murky depths as if she could glimpse a picture of the future forming in the dark. Why wouldn't God just tell her what to do? She had sworn to serve him, and yet he had given her no clear sign . . . only yearnings. She was twenty years old, and her heart now yearned for softness, for quiet nights and companionable suppers, for the mewling of a baby in her arms. But her brain reminded her sharply that she would not find those things with Lord John. A great social gulf stood between them, widened further by her disguise and his indifference.

Between her heart and mind, like a solid stone fence, stood her will—and the vow she had taken. She could make no choices about her future until she had kept her vow and avenged her father, her mother, Petrov, and now Jan Hus. But she could not do that if Lord John would not send his knights to the coming war.

"Kafka."

She lifted her eyes. Novak stood before her, his hands on his hips, a probing query in his gray eyes. "You were supposed to teach Svec how to toss a dagger."

"Sorry," she murmured, uncrossing her legs. She was about to rise, but Novak pressed his hand to her shoulder, stopping her.

"Welladay, what's this worried look on your face?" His clear, observant eyes studied her. "You've worn this look for two days, and I'm beginning to worry about you."

"Would that I could tell you," she murmured, resting her elbows on her knees. "But I don't understand the problem myself. I only know that I must make a decision, and God has not yet shown me what I should do."

His eyes narrowed slightly. "Has it come to that, then? Is it time for you to . . ."

His voice trailed off, and Anika knew he was afraid to finish the thought. "I don't know what I should do," she whispered miserably. "Truth to tell, I am ready to leave this armor behind, but I've a vow to fulfill and nowhere to go. And I would miss you and the others terribly, Novak, were I to leave Chlum."

"There, there, my friend." Novak sank to the stone edge next to her and clasped his hands. "The garrison won't be the same without you." He crinkled his meaty nose. " 'Twould be a lot dirtier, and that's the truth."

Anika smiled as a ripple of mirth touched her heart. "I would miss you, too, my mentor." She clapped her hand upon his broad shoulder. "And I hope that at least I have taught you not to hate women. We are not all cats like Lady Zelenka."

He laughed hoarsely. "I heard that she-wolf spent last week at Lidice, hoping to win Laco's son for a husband. Apparently she has given up on our master and thought to make that arrogant Miloslav an offer of marriage."

"They probably deserve each other."

"Aye, but I hear she didn't have enough time to win the rascal's heart. Cardinal D'Ailly and his retinue descended upon Lidice, and Zelenka's father called her home lest she spend the night under the same roof as that cursed man."

"Cardinal D'Ailly?" Her drifting thoughts hurtled back to earth at the mention of that hated name. She drew herself up, swallowing to bring her heart down from her throat, and pitched her voice below the others in the courtyard. "The cardinal is in Bohemia? Is he still at Lidice?"

Novak's brow wrinkled with contemptuous thoughts. "That son of a snake is planning something with Lord Laco. I hear they are returning to Constance within a fortnight, but they are now plotting some sort of strategy for the Catholic League."

Her answer came, not as a dazzling burst of mental illumination, but as a tiny pinhole of light. Slowly it widened, gathering strength and scope, until Anika knew exactly what she had to do. God had inspired this idea, and once her vow was fulfilled she could return to Lord John and be whatever he wanted her to be . . . if he would have her.

"Thank you, Sir Novak." Anika placed her hand on the old knight's arm, then stood.

"You still haven't told me what troubles you," Novak called as she began to walk away. "You will tell me, won't you?"

"Some day." She threw him a smile over her shoulder and kept walking. "You already know too many of my secrets."

"Kafka!" Leaping up, he dashed forward and caught her by the arm, spinning her to face him. Annoyance struggled with humor on his rugged face as he glared down at her. "You are not planning on visiting Lidice, are you? Laco is a powerful nobleman, and his knights are a fierce company." He stepped back, examining her countenance. "What is this expression on your face? You look like a fox about to do something utterly foolish."

"Foxes are never foolish, Sir Novak." She smiled in exasperation.

"You are my friend, and if I need you, I will tell you. Now let me go; Svec is waiting for me."

Novak released her arm but remained in his place, grumbling as she walked away.

———

She led Midnight out of the barn for a quiet afternoon ride. The guards saluted her without suspicion, and Anika let the horse move out at a relaxed canter until she knew she had moved beyond the tower guards' sight. Then she quietly turned the horse toward Lidice.

The answer, she saw now, was amazingly simple. Her imagination had been clouded by dreams of fighting in the coming war, but why couldn't she use Petrov's silver sword in one bold stroke? She could not single-handedly defeat the collective church council, but she could behead it. Cardinal D'Ailly was one of the council's most influential members; until they elected a pope he would probably be *the* most powerful. By killing D'Ailly she could both avenge her loved ones and make the corrupt members of the council suffer.

She rode through the day and into the twilight, studying signposts and the setting sun to find her way. Within an hour after sunset, a shining net of starlight spanned the deep vault of heaven, and in the east a silvery glow outlined the mountains behind Prague. As she rode, a new and unexpected warmth surged through her. She wasn't afraid. Novak had trained her well, and the long sojourn in the woods outside Constance had prepared her for this overland journey. Everything in her life had led up to this coming day, and Anika basked in the knowledge of her skill.

She reached one of the small villages outlying Lidice just as she noticed a hint of thinner darkness in the east. She needed to stop now and hobble the horse, for she would need at least an hour of rest.

The velvet dark, with its smells of manure and animals, seemed to enfold her like a gloved hand as she slipped off her horse and led Midnight over the soft earth of the village road. Where could she rest? She was afraid to sleep near one of the houses, for an early-rising villager might find her, or the stallion might whicker and reveal her whereabouts.

The moon peeked from behind a cloud, casting shadows and silver light upon the sleeping village, and Anika saw the church steeple rise from the patched rooftops. "Perfect," she murmured, quickening her step. "A sanctuary."

She hesitated when she reached the churchyard. She could go inside, but what if someone discovered her horse? 'Twould be better to rest outside, with Midnight hobbled nearby. Changing direction, she led Midnight to the small graveyard beside the church building. A few melancholy tombstones dotted the gray clumps of grass, looking insubstantial but faintly sinister in the dark, and one large slab of granite lay beneath a particularly imposing stone.

Anika hobbled the stallion within reach of a thick patch of grass, removed her helmet, then sank to the slab, her armor scraping against the stone. The huge headstone rose above her in the moonlight, reminding her that she was trespassing upon the eternal resting place of Pepik Tichacekov, 1386–1406. Underneath the name and date, the stonecutter had inscribed, *If revenge is sweet, why does it leave such a bitter taste?*

"Unlucky Pepik," Anika whispered, lowering herself to the chilly slab. "Only twenty years old—my age. What did you do, Pepik, to come to your grave so young?"

She stretched out on the granite block and closed her eyes, willing herself to rest, but through the embracing folds of sleep and snatches of troubled dreams her mind kept replaying the name and age of Pepik Tichacekov—born in 1386, died in 1406. Twenty years old, the sum total of his life represented by a single horizontal slash on a granite marker. As a copyist Anika had inscribed thousands of horizontal slashes; they represented sudden and dramatic breaks in thought or a sharp change in tone—just as the dash on the tombstone represented Pepik Tichacekov's short and unhappy life.

The voice of a solitary hound broke the quiet of the night, and Anika sat bolt upright, as wide awake as if someone had just poured cold water on her face. The night was dying; already the India ink sky had turned to indigo. She had to go.

"Farewell, Pepik Tichacekov," she murmured, turning to look at the granite marker one final time. The wind, steady and cool from the forest, hooted in response.

As she unhobbled the horse, she fortified herself for the task ahead by revisiting her past. She reminded herself that her flight to Chlum was precipitated by Lord Laco's evil intentions toward her, and Laco and D'Ailly were associates. A cold shiver spread over her as she remembered Cardinal D'Ailly's conduct toward Hus and his presence at her father's death. She had always dreamed of meeting D'Ailly on the field of battle, but since Lord John would not send his knights to fight, she would take her vengeance alone.

Dawn had begun to spread its gray light over the earth when Anika rode up to the quiet meadow outside Laco's castle. Midnight whinnied and shook his head, his jangling bit the only sound in the tranquillity of the woods. Staring at the castle before her, Anika pulled a sealed parchment from a leather sack at her waist. She had personally scrawled out a Latin message for the cardinal, suspecting that D'Ailly would be so alarmed to think the council might act without him that he would hasten to return to Constance. She could then confront him in the woods, without interference from Laco's knights.

Gathering her courage, she slipped on her heavy helmet, then mounted and spurred her horse forward.

"My lord."

John looked up, surprised to see Novak entering his bedchamber with a great deal more trepidation than usual. One of the knights must have committed a serious offense.

"What is it, Sir Novak?" John answered impatiently, dreading the thought of another disciplinary action. That was the problem with knights—the men were too full of themselves, and their toys were too dangerous.

Novak's smile was strained, his eyes hard and wary. "He is missing. He did not sleep in his bunk last night."

"Who?" John reached out to take a robe from his chamberlain. Demetr, who had entered to go over the household accounts, sighed loudly in exasperation.

Novak rolled his eyes pointedly at Demetr, and John knew in an instant that the captain spoke of Anika. "Sir *Kafka* is gone, my lord. He must have ridden out before sunset last night, for the black stallion is missing, and he was Kafka's favorite. No one has seen him this morning."

A sourness rose from the pit of John's stomach as he sank back onto his bed and silently considered this news. Anika had made her choice, then. He had offered her a place in his home, and she had chosen her disguise instead.

A series of terrible regrets swept over him. He should have been firmer from the beginning. He never should have allowed her to become a knight. He should have been more open in his appreciation of her skills, and less quick to let his temper rise when she upbraided him about his sons. She had been right, after all, and had probably been Lev's and Svec's truest friend.

"Kafka has joined the Hussite League, then." He stared at the floor, trying to hide his inner misery from Novak's probing stare.

"No, my lord." Novak spoke slowly, and John looked up. The captain's charcoal eyes gleamed with a message that could not be voiced before Demetr and the chamberlain. "Kafka asked me last night about Lord Laco," Novak went on, speaking slowly and distinctly. "I told him that Cardinal D'Ailly was visiting Lord Laco at Lidice. Kafka seemed excited to hear the news. I believe—no, I am positive—that Kafka has ridden to confront the cardinal."

"Lidice?" John closed his eyes as frustration and despair tore at his heart. His failings had been double. Not only had he failed to convince Anika to remain in the safety of his home, he had also failed to save her life. For if she thought she could confront Cardinal D'Ailly at Lidice, she was severely mistaken. Laco's knights were known for shooting first and later asking questions of arrow-pierced bodies.

"What should I do?" he asked, more a prayer than a direct question.

Novak didn't hesitate. "Mount up, my lord, and I'll ride with you. If we take the mountain passes, we may be able to redeem that youth from his folly."

"Yes." The hunger to go after her gnawed at John's heart. He would find the stubborn girl, he would bring her back kicking and screaming if he had to, he would *make* her understand.

If only he did not find her too late.

———

The sunrise spread across the horizon like a peacock's tail, luminous and brilliant, and a sigh of relief broke from Anika's lips as she pressed her mount forward. She was approaching Lord Laco's castle with a great deal of noise and no sign of stealth, just as a legitimate messenger would.

She sat straighter, feeling as if her dormant resolve had renewed itself. She had been lulled into a comfortable life at Chlum, but today, finally, her vow would be fulfilled. Cardinal D'Ailly would pay the blood price he had demanded of her parents and Jan Hus, and tonight the world would weep with relief that such concentrated evil had passed out of it. The council, too, would grind to a halt, for D'Ailly was the draft horse behind which that body careened over the lives and souls of men.

Half a dozen heads appeared over the ridge of the battlement as she galloped forward, guards startled by her rapid and bold approach. "Who goes there?" one of them demanded, his bow already drawn in his hand. "Halt and identify yourself!"

Anika reined in her galloping horse, knowing she looked suspicious. She had hidden her blue and gold surcoat in the woods, not knowing if she would ever be back to get it. Now she wore only her hauberk, armor, and helmet.

"I have a message," she cried, deepening her voice as best she could. "For Cardinal D'Ailly."

The knight whispered to his companion, who whispered in turn to the next man in line. Then all but two of the guards disappeared, but the two remaining had nocked arrows into their bows and stood ready to fire.

Anika could hear her own quickened breathing. Under her heavy helmet, a bead of sweat trickled down her cheek.

After a long time, another man appeared on the battlement, and Anika's heart went into sudden shock when she recognized him. The last traces of boyishness and youth had evaporated from his face, but Miloslav's arrogant, striking features had not changed.

Her fingers tightened around the reins as her temper flared. This evil boy's lechery had stolen her father's life and forced her to run for her own.

"Who are you, and why do you seek Cardinal D'Ailly?" Miloslav's voice scraped like sandpaper against her ears.

"I bring a message for the cardinal," Anika repeated, the tight knot within her begging for release. She lifted the sealed parchment and waved it slightly. "The message comes from Constance."

Miloslav seemed to pause; then his full lips lifted in a sneer. "I told him not to trust messengers from the council." His words sent an apprehensive shiver down her spine. Was some new mischief in the making?

Miloslav gestured toward a road that led off to the west. "The cardinal and my father left for Constance yesternoon. You should have met them on the road." His voice dripped now with malice. "But perchance you were sleeping in the weeds or making merry with a wench. Or perhaps you had too much ale. In any case, you are not the knight your armor says you are."

Anika lifted her chin. Miloslav had always been arrogant and obnoxious. It would be an honor and delight to challenge and beat him on his own field, with his own men watching. She had unseated Manville and even Novak a time or two. She could certainly handle this brazen fool.

Her fingers moved toward her glove, ready to remove the gauntlet and toss it to the ground in the challenge he obviously desired to provoke, but an inner voice chided her.

Who was more important, the cardinal or this loudmouthed

youth? They had both made her suffer, but Miloslav's death would affect no one. A blow struck against D'Ailly, however, would resonate throughout the civilized world. Miloslav might be a braggart and a scoundrel, but the very root of perdition rode somewhere in the woods behind her.

She glanced over her shoulder toward the road. If they had left only yesterday, they could not be far ahead. Cardinals traveled in ponderous processions; if she rode well, she could overtake them.

"I will be off, then," she called, wheeling her stallion around. Ignoring the laughter of the men on the rampart, she spurred Midnight forward and followed the rutted path that would lead her westward to her quarry.

The knights of Lidice rocked with mirth until the mysterious messenger had vanished around a turn in the road. As the dust settled, Miloslav wiped his eyes and slapped one of the knights on the back, ready to descend to his chamber.

"No courage at all in that one," the knight remarked, returning his arrow to the quiver on his back. "One word from you, my lord, and he was away like the wind."

"It may have been the urgency of the message that drove him away," another guard said, folding his arms. "Of certain he was odd, though. I have never seen a messenger from the council travel without an escort or ensign."

"Neither have I." Miloslav frowned, an ominous thought taking shape in his mind. He could not find any trace of that knight in his memory, but there was something about him, something oddly familiar. He had not seen such defiance since that fool Ernan O'Connor chose to die on a muddy street rather than bend to a nobleman's wishes.

Miloslav perched on the edge of a stone railing and scratched at his beard, thinking. There had been something peculiar in that slender knight, some passion born of experience, some *personal* hatred and grief, evidenced by the knight's quick move to remove his gauntlet. But who was this nameless knight, and when had Miloslav given him offense? In all the winding length of his memory Miloslav could not recall offending a knight who had let the offense pass—or one who survived a challenge with enough spirit to confront him yet again.

A sense of uneasiness crept into his mood like a wisp of smoke. Something was not right. Any messenger from Constance should have passed the cardinal and Miloslav's father on the road . . . and Miloslav could not ever recall seeing a messenger from the council who rode alone. The journey was too long and too dangerous to send a single knight with an important message.

Someone meant harm, either to the cardinal or Miloslav's father.

His hands were suddenly slick with sweat, yet his mind went cold and sharp, focused to a dagger's point. "Saddle my mount," he called to a groom, taking a moment to tie on his cloak. He would not need armor for an encounter with that slender knight—only a sword, a bow, and maybe a stout piece of rope to bind the traitor.

If he decided to let him live.

Thirty-Five

A faint wind breathed through the trees, and Anika leaned over the saddle and peered down at the hoofprints and carriage ruts on the path, then smiled in pleased surprise. An hour before, she had passed a clearing where several charred campfires still steamed from the previous night; Cardinal D'Ailly and his party could not be far ahead. The cardinal probably traveled with at least two carriages and several knights, and Lord Laco surely had at least that many. A procession that size would not move rapidly through the mountains.

She picked up her reins, ready to prod Midnight forward, but a sharp, insistent crack in the woods set alarm bells ringing within her. Turning in the saddle, Anika saw an arrow protruding from a tree trunk only an arm's length away from her head. The missile's shaft was still vibrating. Stiff with surprise and terror, she slid from her saddle in a heap, taking care to hold tight to the reins so Midnight could shield her.

Panic rioted within her. Who was attacking? Robbers? Hussites? Catholics? Whoever it was, she knew with pulse-pounding certainty that she would be dead now if her unknown assailant had wanted to kill her. She had been riding without her helmet, completely exposed, as relaxed as if she were sitting for a portrait. The aggressor had uttered no warning, and she had been defenseless. Why had she been singled out? And where was her enemy? The arrow had come from behind her, but he could have moved. He could be nearly upon her even now.

Standing on shaky legs, Anika held tight to her saddle, keeping Midnight's flank before her as a shield and her head beneath the curve of the horse's back. With a trembling hand she carefully reached toward the cantle where her helmet hung. Seizing the blessed hunk of metal, she thrust her head into it while absently murmuring a prayer: "Father God, who art in Heaven, blessed be your son and the one who trusts in you."

She was alone, far away from every friend, and facing an invisible enemy. Last night she had dreamed of her showdown with Cardinal D'Ailly, had mentally rehearsed every step of the fatal ballet in which she would confront, swing, and slash. But she had never imagined *this* place and time.

"Hussite knight!" The cry echoed among the hills but definitely came from the trail behind her. "Show yourself and prepare to meet your heretic friends in hell!"

Anika choked back a frightened cry. She rose on tiptoe, carefully raising her head above the horse's back. For a moment nothing moved amid the foliage and trees. Then her wide eyes spied a gleam of sunlight on a bright hauberk. One man stood there in the brush, a hooded cloak concealing his head, a bow in his hands. Who was he? A straggler from D'Ailly's caravan?

No. In an instant her anger fled and she could taste hate in her mouth—acid, foul, burning. Any man who attacked from behind and without warning was no knight. Knights were trained to fight fairly, to give largess to an enemy who asked for mercy, to model God's justice. This man was a cold-blooded and cowardly villain, probably hoping to rob her as soon as he had finished with this torturous game of cat and mouse.

"Come out and show yourself," Anika cried, breathless with rage. As her voice bounced among the trees, she tensed—in her fear and anger she had spoken in her *woman's* voice.

Her assailant lowered his bow. Even from this distance Anika saw his teeth part in a smile of overweening confidence and surprise.

Heaven above, he knows. And he thinks I am a helpless maid dressed up for disguise, a girl clad in her father's armor.

His next words proved her suspicions. "My lady," he called as he came forward from his hiding place, the lively note in his voice only incensing her more, "how sorry I am to disturb the peace of your journey. But I did not expect to come across such a rare treasure. I was told to watch for those troublesome Hussite knights who practice witchcraft and worship a dead heretic."

She felt sweat bead on her forehead and under her arms as he came close enough for her to see his face. Then prickles of cold dread crawled along her back as he pushed back the hood from his head. Miloslav!

She pressed her hand to Midnight's flank and forced herself to think. If she leaped on her horse and galloped away, he could have an arrow in her back before she'd gone twenty paces. And even if she did manage to elude him, he knew these woods. He could tear through the forest and cut her off at a bend in the road, or lie in wait for her as she blindly pursued the cardinal.

She swallowed down the taste of bile and let her head fall against her saddle. She could hear the whispers of his feet compressing the ground as he advanced. Then he stopped, barely ten feet in front of her horse. When she lifted her head, he caught her eye and gave her an exaggerated wink. "Excuse my manners," he said, his blue eyes dark and insolent, "but I forgot to ask if you are in some sort of trouble. Can I offer you a nobleman's assistance?"

Perhaps she could surprise *him*. Still holding the reins in her hands, Anika released the saddle and moved a step back, for the knave to better see her form. Thank heaven she still wore her helmet. Though he knew her a woman, he did not yet know *which* woman he faced.

"You have proved already that you do not intend to assist me," she said softly, her eyes not leaving his for an instant. "No honorable man would strike from a hiding place, and without warning."

Lord Laco's son shrugged and held out his hands. "An honest

mistake. When the land is filled with heretics, one cannot be too careful." He stepped closer, spooking the stallion. Afraid the animal would kick her, Anika dropped the reins and let Midnight trot away, leaving herself exposed and vulnerable.

Her eyes roamed over his figure. Over his hauberk he wore a sword at his waist, safely sheathed. A dagger hung from his belt. Somewhere in the woods he had discarded his cowardly bow and the quiver of arrows as well. He must have felt her appraising gaze, for he lifted his chin, revealing at close range a youthful face already seamed with deep-cut lines, a map of violent passions and unhealthy habits.

She retreated before his gaze, hunching her shoulders forward under her armor, making herself as small as possible inside it. Let him think the armor was merely a disguise; let him believe the sword hung at her waist only for show.

"Come, my girl," he said, extending a hand to her. "Cardinal D'Ailly and Lord Laco cannot be far ahead. I believe you had a message for them?"

Anika took another step backward. Let him think her afraid—she was. He had to believe she was a coward.

"Ah, I see by your eyes that you are frightened. There is no need to be frightened of me, my lady."

Again he stepped closer, but this time Anika held her ground. "Stay back, sir," she whispered, softening her voice. Slowly, awkwardly, she pulled her sword from its sheath as though it were heavy and unnatural in her grasp. Folding both hands around it, she let the tip fall to the ground. "Do not come closer, or I shall be forced to defend my honor."

"Foolish girl," Miloslav sneered, coming closer. He now wore an expression of remarkable malignity. "Drop that blade before you cut yourself. You won't be needing it today."

"No." She shook her head stubbornly.

"Woman!" A sudden thin chill hung on the edge of his words. "By all the saints, I'll make you drop that blade!"

"You will not make me do anything!" she yelled, seething with mounting rage. He rushed at her then, a thunderous scowl darkening his brow. With the ease that comes from long practice, Anika swung the blade up and across, neatly cutting the exposed area of flesh beneath his chin.

Stunned as much by her movement as by the sting of pain at his throat, Miloslav staggered backward, a soft gasp escaping him. The wound was not deep, but it bled freely. He lifted his hand to the cut, then pulled it away, studying his blood-spangled palm as if he had never seen it before. After a long moment, he gave her a mocking smile and seemed to swell as he considered her in a new light.

"You clever wee witch! Do you know who you have just cut?"

"You are Miloslav, son of the villainous Lord Laco!"

His sharp face twisted in anger. "Brave words from a girl who hides in a man's armor. Come closer, my dear, and let me see what variety of fruit I am about to pluck!"

Without hesitation, Anika charged at him, knowing she would have to inflict all the damage she could before he drew his own sword. He met her rush with a blow, slamming the heel of his hand against the side of her helmet, sending a spray of darkness across the backs of her eyes.

Her feet gave way, and she fell forward, her sword flying from her hand. The force of his blow sent her helmet tumbling off her head, and she felt gravel and stone grind into her lips as the surfaces of her front teeth scraped the ground. The gleaming hilt of her sword lay only inches away. Choking back a sob, she clawed for it as Miloslav's shadow loomed over her, his own sword now drawn and ready.

"You shall not escape me now." A smile lightened his voice. "Ah, a redhead. I'm partial to them, you know. Turn over, I want to see your lovely face."

"No!" Summoning all her strength, she pushed herself up and forward, struggling to reach her sword. But one hand, like a band of steel, wrapped around her ankle and dragged her over scree that scratched her armor and scraped her nose and lips. She heard her own voice lift in a crazy, full-throated shriek. Then suddenly that iron grip released her. But before she could move, a heavy weight landed upon her back, pinning her to the ground. Lifting her head, she saw the interplay of shadows and realized that while his heavy boot held her down, his hands were casually tugging at his gloves, his face turning toward the road ahead.

The *empty* road ahead. There was no help for her. The knights of Lidice, one of whom might have halted this brutality in the name of chivalry, had already passed. And she, like a proud fool, had left Chlum alone, ignoring Novak's advice and Lord John's gentle admonition.

"There is one thing I find very interesting." Miloslav's voice was soft, but the venom in it was clear. "You know *me*, but I don't know *you*—at least I don't recall having the pleasure of meeting you."

His glove landed in the dirt at her face with a soft puffing sound. She turned her head, and suddenly his face was bent toward hers, nearly upside down in his effort to see her.

"Do my eyes deceive me?" he blurted out. "Can it be the green-eyed beauty from Bethlehem Chapel?" He tugged the other glove from his hand, his voice filled with deadly implacable triumph. "Did you know you are the only woman I could not get? Ah, Anika, how anguish seared my heart when you would not come to Lidice!" A leering smirk passed over his face.

"Liar!"

Miloslav laughed as if sincerely amused. "Do not worry, my dear. I am a devoted lover. I have stored the memory of your lovely face like a seed in the dark and fertile soil of my imagination. And now I am delighted to find that in the bright light of this day, that memory has bloomed to flesh and blood within my grasp."

Keeping the weight on his foot upon her back, he lowered his remaining glove to her face, delicately tracing the outline of her eyes, nose, cheek, and chin. "Though your lovely face is not so pretty, today, hmmm? I do believe that cheek will have a bruise on the morrow . . . if I decide to let you live long enough to feel it." His voice went softer still, filled with a quiet menace all the more frightening for its control. "You see, Anika, you have displeased me mightily. I offered you a place in my home, and you spurned it. No one says no to me . . . and lives to enjoy the consequences of such folly."

Resisting the urge to panic or protest, Anika took a deep breath. Why was she lying here like a dove in the coils of a snake? She was not helpless; she had trained hard and long. As a knight of Chlum she had passed her test and proved her mettle. Though she might never be as strong as others, she was not a quitter. She would not let this brute hurt her. She had not come this far and suffered silently to be left broken and bruised and humiliated in an anonymous patch of forest.

After a instant in which she struggled for self-control, Anika strengthened her voice and made a solitary demand: "Release me."

"Release you?" Miloslav waved his gauntlet before her gaze, then dropped it next to her face, sending another spray of dust into her eyes. "You wanted to throw down the gauntlet before me this morning, didn't you, fair knight? 'Tis a pity you didn't. We would not have had to postpone this pleasurable encounter."

His cloak fell in the dirt, and Anika realized he was removing what little armor he wore. Why wouldn't he? He thought her as helpless as a baby.

"Perhaps," he droned on, slightly increasing the pressure of his foot upon her back, "if you are quiet and agreeable, I won't kill you now. When we are done here, I will escort you to the Council at Constance where you can explain why you wanted to find Cardinal D'Ailly. There was no message, am I right? I know you, Anika O'Connor. When you could not be found, I set out to learn all I could about you. I know you and your father were close to Hus. And now you are an enemy of the Church and a spy, else you would not be here dressed in such an unnatural fashion. Only the heresies of Jan Hus would induce a woman to surrender her womanly garb."

His sword made a distinctly metallic sound as he dropped it on the ground behind her. Anika closed her eyes, her clamped lips imprisoning an angry sob.

"Whether you wear a kirtle or armor makes no difference to me now. You are a lovely wench, Anika, especially when your eyes are flashing with fire."

She heard gravel crunch as he knelt beside her. She felt the pressure of his hands upon her hips, then he turned her as easily as if she were a sheaf of straw. Sweat and blood had soaked the hair at his neck and stained his hauberk where she'd cut him, but his mouth curved in a predatory smile.

"Little Anika," he said, his hands pinioning her arms to the ground. "So strong! Where did you learn to wield a sword like that? Who has been hiding you all these months?"

His face loomed closer, and she turned her head to avoid his noxious breath. On the ground she saw her sword, her helmet, the tools of a calling she would disgrace if she could not escape.

His eyes followed hers, and his hands left her arms as he reached out and grasped her helmet. "This basinet is marked with the ensign of Chlum," he said, studying the emblem engraved into the metal. He held the helmet to the side while he grinned down at her, his weight heavy as he leaned over her. "So Lord John has been hiding you? No doubt you have repaid him with your favors. But the time has come to share his secrets, so let *me* kiss your pretty face as well—"

Obeying an impulse that sprang from some place deep inside her, Anika lifted her hands and grasped her helmet as Miloslav prepared to toss it away. For an instant they grappled for possession, but the strength of desperation flowed through Anika's veins. In one movement she jerked it from his grasp, then swung it, hard, toward her attacker's head.

He did not cry out at the blow. He merely stared at her, his eyes wide with surprise, then crumpled sideways like a rag doll, a thin trickle of blood running from the place in his forehead where the edge of her basinet had cut him.

Sobbing in relief, Anika turned and scrambled away on her hands and knees, dirt and gravel sticking to the damp skin of her palms. "Oh, Father God," she whispered, pressing her hands to her face as she crouched behind a bush next to the road. Her thoughts whirled in tumult. "Have I killed him?"

She knew she ought to go over and check for sounds of breathing, but she could not bear to be near that body again. Miloslav would have to remain in God's hands. Rising to her feet, she gingerly retrieved her helmet and sword, then turned to whistle for Midnight. The stallion stood only a few feet away in the woods, his eyes wide and fixed upon her. At Anika's signal he cautiously emerged from the trees and trotted over.

Before mounting, she glanced again at Laco's son. Blood from the wound in his forehead had painted his visage into a glistening devil mask. With a shiver of vivid recollection, she remembered how Petrov had scolded her: *Believe me, child. If you had seen but one day of war, you would pray to Almighty God that you might never see such a thing again.*

If war was anything like this, she wanted no part of it after today, but this scoundrel was just another in a long string of reprobates firmly attached to Cardinal D'Ailly's belt. That evil man corrupted everyone he influenced.

She placed her booted foot in the stirrup and swung herself up, determined not to look back.

———

Not until sunset stretched glowing fingers across the sky did Anika find her enemies' camp. From the camouflaging safety of the woods, she saw that Laco's servants had pitched several tents inside a meadow between the fork of two roads. Anika had no trouble determining which tent housed his Eminence the cardinal. One tent, gaudy with red and purple ornamentation, sat aloof and reserved at the center of the camp. She knew she'd find Cardinal D'Ailly inside.

Tying Midnight's bridle to a nearby tree, she dismounted, rechecked her armor, and again touched the hilt of Petrov's silver sword. The weight of the blade at her side was comforting, like a rune, something to hold on to. She had come a long way in four years, and every moment of labor had pointed toward this hour.

She was grateful to have found the cardinal's caravan at the end of the day. As the other knights removed their armor and settled in for a few hours rest, she could wander into the camp in her armor and without an identifying surcoat. No one would think her appearance odd. She could walk straightway into the holy man's tent, and there confront him with his sins.

She leaned back against a tree and crossed her arms, waiting for twilight.

"So she left when you said we would not go to war?"

Numb with exhaustion, John of Chlum nodded in answer to Novak's question. They had been traveling for an entire day and had endured a cool reception at Lidice only to learn that a strange knight had appeared that morning, then promptly galloped off in the direction of Constance. Though Lord Laco's steward had been pointedly rude, John had managed to be polite.

Novak shook his head. "I would not have thought a maid would be so eager for the bloodshed of war. In truth, she is a gentle soul."

"Yes." John's back ached between his shoulder blades; he stiffened and pressed his hand to the base of his spine. The sun was sinking in the west. Soon they would have to find a place to rest for a few hours. But how could they stop when Anika was still out there, still pursuing a fool's path?

"What do you think, my lord?" Novak asked, folding his hands atop the pommel of his saddle. "Some of the men are ready to go to war. They say the Catholics aren't our Christian brothers, that we are right to fight them. They mean you no disrespect and they'll abide by your decision, but I've got to be truthful and tell you that they are wondering what you're thinking."

"I am thinking," John released a long, exhausted sigh, "that only God knows who his true children are. There are Hussites who place more faith in freedom than in Christ, and there are Catholics who have found the truth of the gospel even amid the trappings of Rome. Remember, Novak, there were sympathetic cardinals on the council at Constance. Not all of them wanted Hus executed."

"But their protestations were weak," Novak pointed out. "Or they did too little, too late."

John nodded, too drained to debate the issue. "Be that as it may,

I will not fight in a war against the Catholic League. Just as the Shepherd went out to find his wee lost lamb, I will not attack the Catholic Christian brother who seeks peace. Let the ninety-and-nine aggressors come, and I will defend my home. But I will not go out against them."

"Look, my lord—someone is in the road!"

Following Novak's pointing finger, John peered ahead through the gathering dusk to the place where a body lay sprawled across the road. Even from this distance he saw that the head and neck were mottled with dried blood, and a bruise marked the forehead. John slipped from his mount and hurried forward, half-afraid he had found Anika.

But this was a man of not more than twenty-five years. The mouth was a wide, lipless line, like a cut in dead flesh, and the sharp, hawkish face seemed disdainful even in unconsciousness.

John pressed his fingertips to the young man's neck. "He lives!" he called to Novak, who was still astride his horse. "Bring the water pouch, will you?"

Novak dismounted stiffly, then brought the pouch. John splashed a few drops of water upon the man's face. For a moment he feared the stranger would not awaken. Then the youth sputtered for a moment and thrust up his hand as if to ward off an attack.

"Have no fear." Crouching by the wounded man's side, John spoke slowly, feeling his way. "You are among friends. I am John of Chlum, and this is my captain. Were you beset by robbers?"

The youth's eyes fluttered for a moment, then opened. "Lord John of Chlum?"

"Yea."

The youth's blue eyes flashed with cold. "The knights of Chlum are cursed Hussites."

John stiffened, resisting the urge to drop the ungrateful man's head back to the hard ground. "The knights of Chlum are allied with God, the king, and peace," he said, helping the stranger sit up. "We do not believe men of God should fight one another."

"I see." The youth lifted a hand to the cut on his forehead, then winced and gave John a rueful smile, the first sign of friendliness he had exhibited. "Bandits, as you said. I'm afraid they have taken off with my money purse."

"Your sword lies yonder," Novak called, pointing to the weapon on the ground. "And your gauntlets and cloak there."

"Thank you." As the young man slowly stood and moved to retrieve his belongings, John tried to catch Novak's gaze. What sort of bandit would leave a valuable sword in the road? And why would a brigand remove his victim's gloves and cloak?

"A lying tongue leads to death, my friend," Novak suddenly drawled, leaning casually forward upon his horse. "Confess—this was no robbery; 'twas a duel. The gauntlets on the ground prove it." Novak's eagle eye stared down his heavy nose. "Whom did you fight?"

"No one, I assure you," the youth answered, his eyes snapping with malice. "Though I do not know why the bandits removed my gloves. They have doubtless scattered my belongings throughout this area, and perhaps my horse as well."

"We will give you a ride," Lord John offered, conscious of the setting sun. "But you must hurry. We should move on before darkness falls."

"By your leave then, pray give me a moment to look for my possessions." Pulling on his gloves, the young man turned and moved into the woods, seeming to search through the foliage and grasses beside the road. After a few moments he disappeared in the bushes, though John could still hear the rustling sounds of his movements.

John mounted his horse. "I am not certain I trust him," he murmured in a low voice, uncomfortable with his inability to come up with a suitable explanation for the bizarre situation. "If he were more honest, we might come to a reasonable accounting of what happened here."

"Let me confront him, then," Novak answered, lifting his reins and turning his horse. The animal moved toward the woods where the youth disappeared, and Novak called over his shoulder. "If he has nothing to hide, he won't mind riding behind my saddle. But if he proves to be a problem, I'll truss him like a sack of potatoes—"

His voice broke off in midsentence, interrupted by a soft whizzing sound. John sat motionless, horrified, as Novak fell woodenly from the saddle, an arrow protruding at a garish angle from the side of his head.

Warning spasms of alarm erupted within him, but before John could move, another arrow flew through the air, this one piercing his shoulder precisely at the junction of his breastplate and arm guards. The mesh coat of mail had been designed to withstand a sword blow, but the arrow's sharpened barb pierced it like a hot knife through butter. John clutched the arrow as his stallion pranced beneath him, then jumped at the sound of the stranger's voice.

"I could have killed you," the young man called, his tone imperious and bold in the thickening air. "And I will, if you do not obey my wishes."

Through a blur of pain, John squinted at the woods behind him. The man was stealthily stalking through the tall weeds, a drawn crossbow in his hands, an arrow cocked and ready.

"What do you want?" John called, his voice harsh and raw. "Why would you attack those who are trying to help you?"

"Because you are the enemy, John of Chlum," the man answered, a grin overtaking his bloody features as he came closer, "and my father, Lord Laco, has vowed to rid Bohemia of Hussites."

Now the youth stood only a few feet from John's horse, the point of his arrow aimed directly at John's hauberk.

"Dismount, then lie on the ground so I may bind your hands," the youth commanded in a shrill voice. "And then you shall follow your master Hus to Constance. I imagine you will be tried and burned like the other heretics."

John paused, weighing the fiend's demands. He could make a stand and die beside his valiant captain, another martyr for the cause. But how could he help Anika if he surrendered now? This monster had already killed the worthy Novak, Anika's only other hope of rescue.

Fighting his own battle of personal restraint, John stiffly dismounted and lowered himself to the ground. Every movement of the arrow in his arm sent such a brilliant pain flashing through his muscles and shoulder that he cried out in dazzled agony, but the youth ignored him, grabbing his hands and roughly tying them with rope from John's own saddle.

Across the path, John saw the frozen countenance of his beloved captain and friend.

"You will be remembered," he whispered, his mind filling with sour thoughts. "Upon my word of honor, Novak, I will make sure your sacrifice is not forgotten."

Thirty-Six

Night had spread her sable wings over the cardinal's encampment by the time Anika ventured out of the forest. Walking as slowly as she dared, she sauntered into the camp, paused at a kettle over the fire, then moved purposefully toward the ornate tent in the center of the settlement. The cardinal would be inside, ostensibly saying his prayers.

With each forward step her heart pounded harder in anticipation. Tonight she would have her vengeance. Her mother, her father, Petrov, Jan Hus, the three student martyrs, Jerome of Prague—every innocent who had ever died under the battering arm of the corrupt church would be avenged. She, a knight like no other, would do what none of the others dared do. She would strike a blow for righteousness, innocence, and truth. She would strike the dragon's head.

She slipped inside the emblazoned tent without a sound. God must have approved her plan, for the cardinal sat inside, alone. He had draped himself over a chair, a golden goblet in his hand, a book upon the table before him. A small brazier with glowing coals warmed the space; a small oil lamp on the table lit it.

It was her moment of truth, the moment she had waited and prayed for. And he would see her face, know the one who brought God's righteous vengeance to him at last. She jerked the helmet from her head and dropped it at her feet.

"Cardinal D'Ailly!" Her voice, juicy with contempt, startled the man so that he jerked upright, spilling wine over the blood-red cassock he wore.

He cursed, then glared up at her. "Why do you disturb me, boy?" he called, sponging uselessly at the wine stain with the fabric of his flowing sleeve. "Who gave you leave to enter?"

Her blood slid through her veins like cold needles. "Jan Hus gave me leave," she whispered, pulling her sword from its sheath. A silken thread of warning ran through her voice as she advanced toward him. "Ernan O'Connor gave me leave. Megan, his wife and my mother, gave me leave. Jerome of Prague gave me leave. The three student martyrs, beheaded in Prague, gave me leave. Almighty God himself has given me leave to come to you."

D'Ailly stared at her with a cold, hard-pinched expression on his face. "Who are you? What do you want?"

His stammering voice only buzzed in her ear. "For the deaths of these and many other innocent people, you are sentenced to die tonight, Cardinal D'Ailly. Article one: You have ignored the Word of God and followed your own ambition and hunger for power. Article two: You have entertained the plots of evil men, including Lord Laco of Lidice, who sleeps outside this tent. Article three: You have approved divers sorts of evil for your own profit's sake—"

The cardinal made a harsh keening sound in his throat, then gasped, "Guards!"

Within striking distance now, Anika flicked her sword at him, positioning the sharp point against D'Ailly's throat. "No—stop," he whispered, his terror like a scent on him. He swallowed, his Adam's apple doing a dance in that pale, thick neck. "Just tell me what you want. Gold? I have plenty. Position? The church can always use a brave knight."

"I want you," Anika replied firmly, her eyes impaling him. "Your life must be forfeited. As long as you live, innocent souls will perish."

"No." The cardinal swallowed again, then lifted his hands in a gesture of surrender. "I will not harm anyone. I have not harmed anyone. Look there, on the table. I have been reading the works of Jan Hus—he was one of your people, was he not? Look there, at the book I found." He gave an anxious little cough. "Master Hus would not approve of what you're doing."

Anika stared at him with deadly concentration. Either the man was a very good liar, or he thought her a complete fool. "You hated Hus!"

"No!" The cardinal trembled like a leaf. "Look there, I beg you. Upon the table."

Still holding her sword at his throat, Anika cut a look from the cardinal to the table. The book was open, its pages scrawled with a familiar handwriting. Intrigued, Anika leaned closer. The handwriting was her father's! 'Twas a book he had transcribed in Prague, during the early days of his work for Hus. The words were Hus's appeal to Christ, written shortly after the pope condemned him in 1412.

A paragraph leaped up at her. *"I was as a gentle lamb who is carried to the slaughter, and I did not know they devised their counsels against me. You, however, Lord of angelic hosts, who judges justly and tries the reins and the heart, let us see your vengeance upon them."*

"If you are studying Hus, you are only seeking to find ways to discredit him." Anika turned back to the cardinal, her eyes raking his face. "And even from the printed page, Hus's blood cries out for vengeance. I have come to obey the call."

"Who *are* you?" D'Ailly asked, his nose quivering like a root for water. "You speak like a woman, and yet—"

"It matters not. Prepare to die, Cardinal D'Ailly."

"Wait." Nervously he moistened his dry lips. "You would not send a man to meet God without saying his final confession? Even your beloved Master Hus was allowed to confess himself before he died."

Anika paused a moment, the point of her sword wavering at the prelate's throat. *A knight shows mercy to whoever asks it.* This worthless sack of skin deserved no mercy, but she could show Christian charity where he had failed.

"Confess yourself then," she murmured, lifting her chin in an abrupt gesture. She lowered the tip of her sword a few inches. "And be quick about it."

Without rising from his chair, the cardinal pressed his fleshy hands together and closed his eyes. Anika did not take her eyes off him but listened as he began his confession: "Asperges me, Domine, hyssopo, et mundabor: lavabis me, et super nivem dealbabor. Misere mei, Deus, secundum magnam misericordiam tuam." *Thou shalt sprinkle me, Lord, with hyssop and I shall be cleansed; thou shalt wash me, and I shall be made whiter than snow. Have mercy on me, O God, according to thy great mercy.*

Yes, confess yourself to God, she thought. *Be sprinkled with hyssop and washed. And pray God to have mercy on you, for great are your sins.*

Anika's heart hammered in anticipation; she breathed in ragged gasps. The adrenaline rush of her blood eased somewhat, and the chamber around her began to swirl in her peripheral vision. She felt herself trembling all over and clung tighter to her sword.

"Confiteor Deo omnipotenti, beatae Mariae semper Virgini, beato Michaeli Archangelo, beato Joanni Baptistae, sanctis Apostolis Petro et Paulo, omnibus Sanctis, et tibi Pater: quia peccavi nimis cogitatione verbo, et opere: mea culpa, mea culpa, mea maxima culpa." *I confess to Almighty God, to Blessed Mary ever Virgin, to Blessed Michael the Archangel, to Blessed John the Baptist, to the Holy Apostles Peter and Paul, to all the angels and saints, and to you my brothers and sisters, that I have sinned exceedingly in thought, word, and deed, through my fault, through my fault, through my most grievous fault.* The cardinal struck his breast three times, then went on. "Ideo precor beatam Mariam semper Virginem . . ." *I ask Blessed Mary ever Virgin . . .*

In Anika's inner ear her father's voice kept mingling with the cardinal's. *"I would prefer the most unfair peace to the most righteous war,"* she heard her father saying. *"There should be no war in a God-directed world."*

The sound muffled and changed; now she heard Lord John speaking, his voice velvet edged and strong. *"Between Christ and war there is unalterable opposition; there cannot possibly be harmony. The day of war is nothing but a harvest for the devil."*

Petrov's face, deeply seamed yet shining with love, momentarily superimposed itself over the cardinal's flushed countenance. *"Anika, little bird, in disarming Peter, Christ disarmed every knight. Peace is not an absence of war; it is a virtue we all must cultivate."*

Her father's voice rang through the tumult in her brain: *"Revenge is the poorest victory in all the world, me lass. To kill a hornet after it has stung you does not make the wound heal any faster, does it?"*

In another round of painful memories, Jan Hus appeared. *"There will come a time when you will want to lay down your sword, Anika. When that time comes, do not resist the impulse. God speaks in a quiet voice, too. And his will lies in surrender."*

"If revenge is sweet, why does it leave such a bitter taste?"

"In disarming Peter, Christ disarmed every knight."

"Turn the other cheek."

Anika dropped her sword and pressed her hands over her ears, clenching her eyes tight. Was she losing her mind? She had come so far, accomplished so much, and yet these meddlesome memories would not let her continue! Was she weak? Or had she misinterpreted the signs that led her to this place?

" . . . beatum Michaelem Archangelum, beatum Joannem Baptistam . . ." *Blessed Michael the Archangel, Blessed John the Baptist . . .*

She could not kill the cardinal. Anika opened her eyes, dredging that admission from a place beyond logic and reason. No matter how hard she trained, she was not and could never be a cold-blooded murderer. But now that she had boldly entered and threatened this man's life, how could she escape certain death?

"Father God, give me light!" she begged, slipping to her knees on the cardinal's thick carpet. Ignoring the suddenly silent prelate, she clasped her hands and lifted her eyes to heaven.

The answer, when it came, was not audible, but more real than anything Anika had ever experienced. A presence filled the tent and a new kind of reverential fear shook Anika's body from toe to hair, lighting her face and quieting her heart.

I, the God of your fathers, will defend myself.

Despite her fears and confusion, Anika felt a hot and awful joy flood her soul. God had heard her; this voice was his!

Who are you, daughter of dust, to defend and avenge the Almighty God? Do not take revenge, but leave room for God's wrath, for it is mine to avenge; I will repay. You have looked upon this man of sin and striven to make yourself virtuous, but you have only created yourself in his image. The opposite of sin is not virtue; it is faith.

Anika trembled as a rush of comprehension, love, and compassion flooded her soul. Knowledge too deep for words and emotions too powerful for description lifted her heart and mind from her heavy vow. She opened her hands to heaven and breathed deeply of the celestial air that seemed to have filled the tent.

In a blinding instant she realized that revenge is a sword that wounds the one who wields it. If she killed the cardinal, she would be as corrupt and hate filled as the council that had executed Master Hus.

She had thought that by obeying the rules of knighthood and chivalry she could please God and slake her own thirst for vengeance. But Lord John and Sir Petrov were right. Christ did not want her to wield a sword on his behalf. He didn't want her to *do* anything. He wanted her to have faith in his plan for her life.

Men like Cardinal D'Ailly took great pride in their outward righteousness, just as she had taken pride in her knighthood. She had become as self-centered as the cardinal, thinking that the truth lay in *her* rather than in God. She had been certain that her work and the fulfillment of her vow would set things to right, but faith required that she surrender her will, her desires, her hurts to God. She was more than a knight—she was whatever God wanted her to be. And if that included being a woman, a wife, or a chambermaid, Anika was willing.

The light, the glory, lasted only a moment, but it was enough. As the mighty rushing sound faded, Anika sank back on the carpet beneath her, tears of relief coming in a rush so strong it shook her body.

Cardinal D'Ailly stopped speaking and stared, astounded, at the young knight swaying on his knees. 'Twas probably a Hussite boy whose zeal had caused him to attempt this bit of butchery, but the

Hussites should have known better than to send a boy to do a man's job. The youth was quaking now, his face lifted toward the ceiling of the tent, his eyes closed, his hands clasped in prayer.

D'Ailly opened his mouth to shout for the guards, then thought better of it. This gutless boy was no danger, not anymore, and if he handled the situation himself, he might bring a bit of embarrassment to Laco's pompous knights. They deserved to be humiliated for whatever egregious blunder had allowed this boy to enter the camp.

Quietly, smoothly, he drew his own dagger from a belt under the folds of his cassock. This blade would pierce the boy's mesh hauberk, and he would strike right through the heart, putting an end to this foolish youth.

He lifted the dagger and paused for a moment, distracted by the purity of the boy's delicate face. What was the youth thinking? He had undoubtedly been caught up in that intellectual sweep of comprehension known only to adolescents and university scholars like Hus. Well, in the morning the Hussites would realize the dangers of allowing their zealous and misguided youngsters to wander the woods at night. He would order this boy's body to be left upon a rock, covered in the white and gold banner of the Catholic League.

He smiled, thinking about it.

Open your eyes, Anika.

Her eyes flew open. D'Ailly was leaning forward in his chair, a dagger gleaming in his hand like the tooth of a monstrous serpent. A satanic smile wreathed his face as he moved resolutely forward, his sweeping sleeves fluttering over the table as he rounded toward her—

"No!" she cried, scrambling backward to avoid the blow. The cardinal grimaced and rose from his chair, but his sleeve passed over the open oil lamp. Red-orange flames licked the fabric of his robe, leaping up the cardinal's arm with fiendish exuberance.

A scream clawed in his throat.

Anika rushed toward him, trying to beat the flames out with her gloved hands, but the cardinal resisted her help. For a few moments the two struggled against each other. In a dance of death they circled around the tent, until the flames ran down the cardinal's cassock and the man became a human torch.

With an inhuman, eternal bellow the cardinal stumbled from the tent, startling the knights outside. A blizzard of anxious commands filled the air as Anika coiled back into the flickering shadows, her mind paralyzed with terror and surprise.

She had to get away. Delay could cost her life.

As a hard fist of fear grew in her stomach, she turned toward the dark forest, then followed her heart into the night.

Intense exhaustion bore down on her with an irresistible warm and delicious weight. Tired of running, Anika stopped in the forest and curled up on a large boulder beneath a tree. As tides of weariness and despair engulfed her body, she pressed her hand over her eyes and thanked God that the cardinal still lived.

She had barely managed to escape, for as soon as Lord Laco's knights doused the flames, they spread into the woods to search for the young man the cardinal insisted had tried to kill him.

Hiding in the brush only a few feet away from her horse, Anika heard Midnight's whinny and a knight's triumphant cry. She crouched in a hollowed-out spot in the earth, too frightened to move, as the knights of Lidice led Midnight away.

For hours she shivered there, occasionally lifting her head to catch voices that brushed past her on the wind: "He'll live, thank God." "Who do you suppose could have done it?" "He was never a handsome man, but nobody deserves the face he'll have after this." Finally the woods grew quiet, and the only sounds Anika heard were fluttering leaves and the quiet sigh of the night.

She rose to her unsteady feet and turned so that the cardinal's camp lay behind her. She knew she would have to be miles away by the time the sun rose or Laco's knights would be able to track her. And so she ran and walked and ran again, trying to follow the stars, hoping that she ran toward Chlum, toward *home*.

The first tangerine tints of the rising sun had lit the forest when she awoke the next morning. She climbed down from her rock, grateful for the silence of the moist black earth and wet parchment texture of the leaves beneath her feet. The woods vibrated softly with insect life, and a few feet away a road pointed a curving finger through the trees.

That road led home—to Chlum, and to Lord John, if he still cared for her. Though she had spurned his offer of protection and flown in the face of his convictions, she knew she could stand before him now as a woman and as a knight and say she had been wrong.

If only Lord John would forgive and receive her again.

———

The morning had nearly died when she spied another pair of riders on the road. Two men were coming her way on horseback, both horses walking at a slow and steady pace. The man on the biggest horse carried the reins of the second rider, and even from this distance Anika could see that the second rider's head was bent forward as if he'd had too much to drink.

The fool. A sour grin twisted the corners of her mouth. Someone's master would be terribly displeased. She grimaced and kept walking, determined to ask for water or a bit of bread, but stopped when one of the horses lifted his head in a broken whinny. Lord John's favorite stallion had always trumpeted in just that way.

She took a deep breath, resisting the sudden bands of tightness in her chest. The horses wore blue and gold livery like that of Chlum, but neither rider wore a knight's surcoat. The horses moved closer, and Anika felt the wings of tragedy brush lightly past her, stirring the air and raising the hair on her forearms.

"Greetings!" she heard the first rider call, his voice high-pitched, reedy, and horribly familiar. Her breath caught in her lungs. Miloslav! He seemed not at all surprised to see her and lifted his hand in a casual gesture. "I am glad to see you again, my dear. Your lord is wounded and needs attention."

As the horses drew nearer, a cold lump grew in her stomach, spreading chilly tendrils of apprehension through her body. A frightened glance at the second rider confirmed what she feared—Lord John was wounded, and Miloslav's prisoner.

Was her ordeal not over? Had God spared her yesterday only to kill both her and Lord John today?

Lifting his head, Lord John met her eyes. His gaze held no rancor or blame, but a familiar softness settled around his mouth, the way he always looked just before he smiled. "Sir Kafka," he called, his voice breaking with huskiness. "Faith, it is good to see you."

"My lord," she began, eager to explain, but Miloslav stopped her with a cold glance.

"If you are loyal to this man, you will do as I say," he said, grinning at her with cruel confidence. "I have no loyalty to him, so I care not whether he lives or dies. And since he is wounded, it may be a mercy to place a dagger in his heart and ease his pain."

Anika knew hurt and longing lay naked in her eyes. "Don't," she replied in a low, tormented voice. "Don't hurt him . . . any more. Tell me what you want."

"That's much better." Miloslav eyed her with a calculating expression. "Much more cooperative today, aren't you? That's good." His dark gaze traveled from her helmet to her shoes. "You are walking today. Where is your horse?"

Anika shook her head. "Lost. In the woods."

"And that sharp sword of yours?"

She shook her head again. "Lost."

He winked at her broadly. "Ah, the trials of knighthood. Not what you expected, is it, little woman?"

She licked her lower lip and stared at him, managing to quell her anger. She would need all her wits about her this time.

Miloslav jerked his head toward a stand of trees a few feet away from the path. "Go there," he said, untying the knot of his cloak. He pulled the garment from his shoulders, then gathered it into a bundle and tossed it toward her. "Take off that hallowed armor; you do not deserve to wear it. Put on the cloak and wait for me . . . or he dies."

Catching the cloak in her arms, Anika shot one look toward Lord John. His eyes were large and fierce with pain and something else—worry? For her?

She cast her eyes downward and turned toward the woods, not wanting him to share her shame.

"Well, Lord John, we have found the bird that flew from your coop," Miloslav taunted, drawing his thin lips into a tight smile. "Surely you didn't expect to keep her all to yourself?"

Clamping his jaw tight, John strained uselessly at his bonds and stared into the shrubbery where Anika had disappeared. Was he to blame for the tragedy that would occur here today? Hiding a homeless, hopeless girl had not seemed such a bad idea . . . until she worked her way into his heart. Perhaps if he had shared his feelings, if he had been honest, she would not have insisted upon leaving.

What a fool he had been. His aloof pride was the seismic fault of his life, driving away all those who ought to be precious to him. He had been reared to be conscious of his position, his title, his responsibilities, and that consciousness had kept him at arms' length from his parents, his wife, even his children. He had only dared share his heart with Novak, his captain, and Jan Hus, his friend, but all the safeguards in the world could not protect him from hurt and anguish. *For what is your life?* the Scriptures reminded him. *It is even a vapor that appears for a little time and then vanishes away.*

He would not let the rest of his life evade him. If he lived another hour or another thirty years, he would live it to the fullest and in the light of God's love.

Almighty God, release me, allow me to escape, and I will never hold myself aloof again. I am not a tower of strength. I am not above needing someone to love. Forgive me, God, for I have shunned the good you sent my way.

With his remaining strength he flexed and jerked against the ropes that held him. As his body sang with pain, he locked a scream behind his teeth. Useless. The suffering of the last twelve hours had left him drained, hollow, lifeless. He might as well be lying with Novak on the forest road, for he could not help Anika now.

"I hope you have said your farewells to the girl," Miloslav said, withdrawing his dagger from his belt, "because I cannot risk leaving you here while I take my pleasure with her. Even in your weakened condition, you might ride off and carry this story to someone who will believe it."

"You, sir," John answered, forcing dignity in his voice, "will not live long enough to enjoy the pleasures of your sin. And then you will rot in hell."

The insolent young man contradicted him with a smile that set John's teeth on edge. "Ah, but you are the one appointed to die today." He yanked the reins of John's horse until the animal stepped closer, bringing John within striking range. The rebellious youth lifted the dagger, and John closed his eyes, bracing himself for the blow.

Amid the chatter of birdsong he heard Miloslav's quick intake of breath, then a cry. John opened his eyes in time to see the young man slowly topple from his horse, a blade buried to the hilt in his chest.

John sat motionless as wave after wave of shock slapped at him. Turning toward the woods, he saw Anika standing in a clearing, her arm still extended from her throw, her lovely face locked with anxiety.

Anika watched the dagger hit its target, then held her breath until the son of perdition fell from his saddle and lay unmoving in the soft grass by the path. She had nearly forgotten about the blade Petrov instructed her to carry always in her boot, but the slender dagger had proved quite efficient.

Slowly she made her way out of the woods, her eyes intent upon the body. Miloslav had risen up once before to challenge her and hurt someone she loved; she did not want to meet him yet again.

"He is dead," Lord John called from his horse.

She stiffened at something she heard in his voice, something jagged and sharp, like words torn by the blade of a knife. He was looking at her, not with eyes of love and gratitude, but with a melancholy and weary expression, like one who has spent too much time with an active child. He sighed heavily, his voice filled with anguish. "Novak is dead, too. I am sorry, Anika."

She stood in lonely silence, biting her lip until it throbbed like her pulse. Her teeth chattered, and against her will her body began to tremble. "It is my fault, isn't it?" she asked, not daring to meet her master's eyes. "Was he with you? Were you looking for me?"

"Yes." John spoke softly as if to spare her feelings. "But do not blame yourself. He was a knight, and he died doing what he loved to do. He died defending someone he loved."

Her emotions bobbed and spun like a piece of flotsam caught in a roaring river. "This one," she whispered, pointing to the fallen Miloslav, "never did believe I was a knight. He thought this armor, my sword, were only a disguise. And they would have been, if not for Novak. He taught me everything—how to use a sword, pull an arrow, throw a dagger—" Her gaze clouded with tears. "Though he always claimed to hate women, with me he was as gentle as a father, as understanding as a friend."

"I suppose I should thank God Novak tolerated you," Lord John answered, a faint smile upon his face. "If he had not taught you how to toss a dagger, this hour would have ended far differently." He winced in pain as he turned slightly in the saddle. "We will have to go back and fetch his body home to Chlum, where he belongs."

Lord John's usually lively eyes were ringed with dark circles. Suddenly aware of her master's pain, Anika wiped her tears and hurried forward to untie his bonds. His body was obviously hot with fever. The arrow shaft still protruded from his arm, yet he sat upon his horse in a pose of weary dignity.

"What is your choice, then, Anika?" he asked as she used his dagger to cut the ropes.

Her mind whirled at his dry response. "My choice?" His implacable expression unnerved her, and she paused, choosing her words carefully as she looked up into his eyes. "My choice, my lord, is to serve you. To join your household, to honor you in any way I can. I do not recant my vows of fealty, my lord, but with your blessing I would recant my vow of knighthood."

She glanced away, feeling herself flush, rattled by the pressure of his gentle eyes. She cut upward with his knife until the rope broke and his arms fell stiffly to his side. Anika knew each movement brought her master great pain, but he said nothing as she slipped his dagger into her own belt.

"Anika—what do you *want* to do?" He made a credible attempt at coolness, marred only by the thickness in his voice.

Placing her hands on his foot in the stirrup, she lifted her gaze and searched his face, reaching into his thoughts. She thought she saw a faint flicker of doubt in the depths of his soft dark eyes. "Employ me as a maid or a servant, my lord, but do not cast me off." Tears blinded her eyes and choked her voice, but she pressed on, unwilling to consider the future apart from him. "You are all I have. You are my life . . . my home. Whatever I do, I would like to do it for you."

With a grimace of pain he slid from the saddle and stood beside her. His dark eyes flashed a gentle but firm warning. "I have no need of maids or servants," he said, lifting his good hand to her shoulder. Slowly his palm opened, and he cupped her cheek. "What my castle needs is a wife, a position I should have offered you long ago."

Anika felt the touch of his gaze, as gentle as the surf on a sandy shore. "I was wrong, Anika, not to let you know the depths of my feelings for you. You are a friend, you are a delight, you are the love I never dreamed could exist."

She felt a trembling thrill as his voice echoed her own longings, but her senses reeled in confusion. "Yet you are a nobleman, and I am only a merchant's daughter."

"You are more noble than any woman I have ever met." The warm wave of his breath reached her ear as his voice softened. "Anika, I need you at my side. My sons need you. I need you to teach me how to be a father."

She pressed her hand over his as a tremor caught in her throat. What would *The Art of Courtly Love* advise her to do now? Surely there was some formula, some set of words she was supposed to use in response . . .

But she had never done anything by the book. "I love you, my lord John," she whispered, reveling in the heartrending tenderness of his gaze. "I can think of nothing I would rather do than spend my life by your side."

He extended his arm and bent toward her, and she was powerless to resist the silent invitation. She moved into his embrace, fully aware of his strength and his need for her.

"We must get you to a physician," she said, afraid to hold him too tightly. "That arrow must come out, and the wound be cleansed."

"There will be time enough for that," he answered, and before she could protest further, his lips brushed against hers. Anika gently wrapped her arms about his neck as her pulse pounded in her ears and the song of the wind whispered among the trees.

"Time enough," she promised. Then her lips caressed his with exquisite tenderness.

Epilogue

Dr. Henry Howard
Professor of Medieval European History
New York City College

Dear Dr. Howard:

I don't know if you'll remember me—we met in the college library about six months ago. You told me about Cahira O'Connor and suggested—none too subtly, as I recall—that because I had red hair marked with a white streak I might be connected to the legendary O'Connors of Ireland.

It's probably impolite for me to say what I thought of you and your story that afternoon. Let's just say I was a little *skeptical,* shall we? But after I began to investigate a bit, I found I couldn't let the story go. The manuscript you've just read is the first fruit of my efforts. I worked on Anika's story for my semester English project and plan to research Aidan and Flanna next year. (If you have any professor friends in the English Department, you might want to take them to tea this summer and tell them to fortify themselves for next term. I expect they might find me a wee bit long-winded.)

Why am I so interested in these women? I don't know. Maybe it's because I'm afraid World War III will break out after the millennium, and the president will issue a call for red-haired piebalds to fly B-52s or something. Seriously, I've been having nightmares about what might happen . . . if I'm really one of Cahira's chosen few. But at least Anika's story had a happy ending.

As you probably know, the war Anika anticipated did break out in 1419. In that year the new pope, Martin V, with the support and urging of Holy Roman Emperor Sigismund, declared a crusade against the Hussites. To the emperor's surprise, the Hussite army handed the invading Crusaders several stunning defeats, then took the offensive, attacking Catholic strongholds in Slovakia, Silesia, and Lusatia. Anika herself did not fight in the war but worked as a copyist, sending copies of Hus's letters to those who fought for the Hussite cause. She and her husband, Lord John, did much to keep the flames of reformation alive. Together they had four children, none of whom was known for having red hair *or* any sort of piebaldism.

Baldasarre Cossa, formerly Pope John XXIII, *was* eventually reinstated as a cardinal. Unlucky pennies do always turn up, hmm?

The Hussites celebrated a partial victory in 1431 when another church council convened to settle the dispute. As a concession to the Hussites, the Catholics agreed to allow the celebration of Communion of bread and wine in Bohemia. This satisfied the Ultraquists, a moderate group who limited their demands to the four articles cited by the Hussite League, but a more radical faction, the Taborites, refused to compromise. This group, drawn mostly from the rural peasantry, called for the complete abolition of clerical vestments and the Latin liturgy. They also attacked the monarchy and the feudal system. (The Powers That Be weren't too thrilled with the Taborites' demands. I'm afraid they were doomed to fail.)

Finally, at the Battle of Lipany in 1434, a combined force of Ultraquists and Catholics defeated the Taborites, effectively ending the Hussite wars. Sadly, over the next two hundred years, the concessions won by the Ultraquists were eliminated.

Despite the setbacks, however, Jan Hus did not die in vain. Over one hundred years later, the great reformer Martin Luther found a volume of Hus's sermons preserved in a library at Erfurt. "I was seized with a curiosity to know what doctrines this great heretic had taught," Luther wrote. "The reading filled me with incredible surprise. I could not comprehend why they should have burned a man who explained Scripture with so much discernment and wisdom. But the very name of Hus was such an abomination that I imagined that the heavens would be darkened and the sun would fall at the mere mention of it. So I shut the book with a sad heart, consoling myself with the possibility that it was written before he fell into heresy."

Later, in 1529, Luther wrote to a friend, "I have hitherto taught and held all the opinions of Hus without knowing it. With a like unconsciousness has Staupitz taught them. We are all of us Hussites without knowing it."

So, Professor Howard, I must thank you for spurring me forward. I have just discovered that not only may I be a direct descendant from Cahira O'Connor, but I have been a Hussite for many years . . . and had no idea.

I stopped by your office one afternoon, hoping to find some information on the Ultraquists, but your assistant, Mr. Taylor Morgan, said you were out. He was very helpful, though . . . and I'd like to call upon him again sometime, if you don't mind. (Did you discover him in the library, too? Maybe I should spend more time there!)

If you have some free time during the summer, please give me a call. I'll begin my work on Aidan O'Connor soon and could use some information about the seventeenth century.

Sincerely,

Kathleen O'Connor

P.S. If Mr. Morgan is available, perhaps I could take you both to lunch! It would be my pleasure.

The information regarding Pope John XXIII, also known as Baldasarre Cossa, is historical and was found in Dr. W. N. Schwarze's book *John Hus, the Martyr of Bohemia*. Cossa, now regarded as an antipope, was "given to every form of vice," and the historian Gibbon called him "the most profligate of mankind." According to Dr. Schwarze, Cossa is charged "with good reason, of having poisoned his predecessor to make room for himself. In his own person he typified the evils and disease of the times."

The historical portrayal of Baldasarre Cossa is in no way intended to reflect upon contemporary Catholics. Baldasarre Cossa's papacy was later invalidated by the Catholic Church, and on October 28, 1958, Angelo Guiseppe Roncalli took the name the antipope Baldasarre had used: John XXIII.

No work stands alone, and I must thank the following authors for their fine books. The wealth of information in each volume made it possible for me to delve deeply and authentically into the worlds of chivalry and fifteenth-century Bohemia.

Bartak, Joseph Paul. *John Hus at Constance.* Nashville: Cokesbury Press, 1935.

Andreas Capellanus. *The Art of Courtly Love.* New York: Columbia University Press, 1990. (John Jay Parry's translation of the work originally written between 1182 and 1186).

Edge, David and John Miles Paddock. *Arms and Armor of the Medieval Knight.* New York: Crescent Books, 1988.

Gies, Joseph and Frances. *Life in a Medieval Castle*. New York: Harper & Row, 1974.

Gies, Joseph and Frances. *Life in a Medieval City*. New York: Harper Perennial, 1969.

Riley-Smith, Jonathan. *The Oxford Illustrated History of the Crusades*. New York: Oxford University Press, 1995.

Schwarze, W. N. *John Hus, the Martyr of Bohemia*. New York: Fleming H. Revell Company, 1915.

Spinka, Matthew. *John Hus at the Council of Constance*. New York: Columbia University Press, 1965.

Spinka, Matthew. *John Hus, A Biography*. Princeton, New Jersey: Princeton University Press, 1968.

The Heirs of Cahira O'Connor
Book 2

◆◆◆

The Golden Cross

AVAILABLE IN STORES OCTOBER 1998

Prologue

The phone rang again, the fourth time, and I skidded on the slippery tile as I rounded the corner, then nearly tripped over my mastiff, Barkly, who had decided to carpet the cool kitchen floor with his two-hundred-pound carcass. Reaching over Barkly for the phone, I accidentally knocked over the chipped mug that held my collection of kitchen implements.

Amid a clattering of spatulas and wooden spoons, I lifted the phone to my ear. "Hello?"

"Miss O'Connor?"

Grimacing, I hopped over Barkly and bent to pick up a wooden spoon before he decided to chew it. Only telephone solicitors call me "Miss O'Connor," so I'd just destroyed my kitchen and nearly broken my neck for the chance to subscribe to *Southern Fly-Fishing* or some such thing.

"Yes?" I frowned into the phone. "Listen, I'm really very busy—"

"I won't take much of your time, Miss O'Connor." The man

sounded slightly apologetic. "But I've just finished reading your work, and I must say it surpasses anything I ever expected."

My breath caught in my lungs as I recognized the voice. "Professor Howard? You read *The Silver Sword?*"

"But of course, my dear." I could hear a smile in his voice. "And I was most impressed by your scholarship and attention to detail. Your work seemed very precise, quite well-documented."

I clutched the telephone cord and leaned back against the counter, momentarily forgetting about Barkly, about the book I'd been reading, about everything. Professor Henry Howard liked my work!

"Thank you, sir," I stammered.

"I had no idea similar women had descended from Cahira O'Connor," he went on. "How on earth did you find them?"

"I just typed the words 'O'Connor' and 'piebaldism' into an Internet search engine," I muttered, stating the obvious. "And there they were, all four—Cahira, Anika, Aidan, and Flanna. Suddenly Cahira's deathbed prayer made sense. She had begged heaven that her descendants might break out of the courses to which they were bound and restore right in a murderous world of men."

"Incredible," he murmured, surprise and respect apparent in his voice. "I was very impressed. If you had been my student, I would have given you the highest possible mark."

"Well," I shifted my weight, "my English professor was a little daunted by the length of my paper. She was expecting one hundred pages; I gave her four hundred. But I did pass her class."

"You mentioned in your letter that you plan to continue your research. Might we meet for lunch one day this month to discuss what else you've discovered? You also mentioned my assistant, Mr. Taylor Morgan," the professor went on, a teasing note in his voice now. "He has read your work as well and would be happy to join us."

A blush burned my cheek at the mention of Taylor Morgan, and I was glad the professor couldn't see me at that moment. Flush with the joy of completing a gigantic task, I'd felt a little bold when I wrote the note I left with the manuscript of *The Silver Sword*—and I had strongly hinted that Mr. Taylor Morgan was exactly my type . . . of research assistant.

"Um, sure," I answered, wrapping the phone cord around my wrist. "I'm working part-time at the Tattered Leaves bookstore down on Sixth Street this summer. There's a little coffee shop nearby."

"I know the place. Shall we say Friday, at 1:00? I'd like to avoid the crowds if at all possible. And Mr. Morgan teaches until 12:30."

"Friday." I felt a foolish smile spread over my face. "Fine. And in case you've forgotten what I look like, I'll be the redhead—"

"Miss O'Connor,"—I could hear the professor's grin in his voice—"I could never forget what you look like. Your red hair led me to you in the first place."

They were waiting for me when I panted my way through the coffee shop doorway at five minutes after one. The professor rose and pulled out a chair for me, and Taylor Morgan stood, too, his blue eyes smiling at me from behind a pair of chic wire-rimmed glasses. He was wearing a cotton shirt and khakis, looking completely cool and elegant even in the city heat, and as I slid into my chair, my mind stuttered and almost went completely blank. The sight of Taylor Morgan at close range could do that to any girl, I suspected, but he wasn't about to be impressed by my scholarship if I sat there and stammered like a star-struck schoolgirl.

So I looked at the professor instead. Middle-aged, soft, and infinitely respectable. He certainly didn't give me the tingles—except for the fact that he liked my work.

We exchanged polite hellos; then the professor asked again how I'd found the other descendants of Cahira O'Connor. "The Internet search engine I used picked up four references to 'O'Connor' and 'piebaldism,'" I said, scanning the menu. I decided on my usual tuna sandwich, then dropped it back on the table. "And each woman followed her predecessor by two hundred years, give or take. Cahira lived in the thirteenth century, Anika in the fifteenth, Aidan in the seventeenth, and Flanna in the nineteenth. All of them were O'Connors, and all had red hair and a white streak above the left temple."

The professor's gaze darted toward the streak of white hair that marked my own temple. I sipped from my water glass, waiting for some kind of response.

"Do you plan to investigate these other two women?" Taylor asked, his voice husky and golden and as warm as the sun outside. "Will that work fit into your current studies?"

"I've already done most of my research on Aidan O'Connor," I answered, shrugging, "and I'm an English major, so I'll find a way to use everything I've learned. Or maybe I can talk to my adviser about setting up some sort of independent study."

"It would be a shame," Taylor answered, capturing my gaze with his, "to let such scholarship and hard work go unrewarded. And I'm eager to hear about the other women."

"What I want to know, Miss O'Connor," the professor said, lowering his menu and folding his arms on the table, "is what you intend to do about your own involvement in the lineage. You are an O'Connor: You have the same physical characteristic that marked the others—"

"I have to admit that I've wondered about that," I answered, a sense of unease creeping into my mood like a wisp of smoke. "I think I am supposed to be the chronicler, nothing more. If God did answer Cahira's prayer and her descendants are linked to me, then I am the only one with the resources to tell their story. I have access to the Internet, I have a computer, and such technology was completely unimaginable until this century . . . "

"For your sake, I hope you're right," Professor Howard answered, his hazel eyes registering concern. "Because if you're not—well, didn't they all fight in a war? I'd hate to think that armed conflict lies around the corner of the millennium—"

I held up my hand, cutting him off. "That's not quite right, Professor. Cahira didn't say that her descendants would fight in wars, only that they would fight for right in a man's world. Aidan

O'Connor, for instance, didn't go to war. In 1642 she was living in Batavia, a Dutch colony on the island of Java in Indonesia, and the islands were at peace."

"How in the world did the descendant of an Irish princess end up in Indonesia?" Taylor's blue eyes flashed with curiosity.

I took a deep breath as my gaze moved into his. At that moment Mel Gibson could have walked into the coffee shop and I wouldn't have even glanced his way. "It's a long story. If you have to rush off to another appointment, I probably shouldn't even begin it."

Taylor leaned forward on the table and clasped his hands. "I cleared my calendar for you," he said, looking at me with a smile in his eyes.

From somewhere on the other side of the table I heard Professor Howard say something about having a 3:00 dentist appointment, but his words barely registered. If Taylor Morgan was willing to sit and listen, I'd talk all day and into the night . . . if he wanted me to. Such a sacrifice. Still, the man wanted to know . . .

"Okay." I smiled at him. "But first I'd like a Coke and a tuna sandwich. Let's order now, 'cause I don't take kindly to interruptions."

Taylor lifted his hand, signaling the waitress, and I pulled my notebook from my purse. While he and the professor ordered sandwiches and soft drinks, I studied my outline.

"Okay, Miss O'Connor," Taylor said, an easy smile playing at the corners of his mouth. "We're ready. Tell us how an O'Connor descendant ended up in the middle of the Pacific."

"Aidan O'Connor wasn't born in Indonesia," I answered, setting my notebook on the table. "Her parents, Cory and Lili O'Connor, were as Irish as shamrocks, but they were living in England when Aidan was born. In 1632, when Aidan turned fourteen, her parents risked everything to escape the plague. Over twelve thousand Londoners died that summer."

"The O'Connors emigrated?" Professor Howard asked.

I nodded. "Yes, to Batavia, capital of the Dutch colony in the Spice Islands. Many Englishmen fled London for the Caribbean,

New England, and Virginia, but Aidan's father longed for something different."

"Wise move on his part," Taylor answered, shifting in his chair.

"Not really," I answered, lifting my brow. "He died on the voyage. Upon their arrival in Batavia, Aidan and Lili found themselves destitute. They had no patron, no resources, and no social welfare system in a colony that prided itself on industry and social order. Lili had to turn to the world's oldest profession just to survive."

"Prostitution?" the professor whispered, his face twisting in dismay.

"She guarded her daughter," I whispered back. "But Lili became what the Dutch called a *procuress*—she procured whatever, ah, entertainment a visiting sailor might need in the port city."

"Hold that thought," Taylor said, pausing as the waitress placed a sweating soft drink in front of him. "You just said the Dutch were known for industry and social order. I can't imagine them tolerating such a practice."

"Batavia was like most other large cities; two very different worlds existed within it," I answered, nodding my thanks at the waitress. "There was the civilized world where respectable folk lived and worked, and a darker world they largely ignored. Oh, every once in a while they'd send the sheriff's constabulary to round up the beggars, cutpurses, and drunks, but for the most part they enjoyed pretending that the notorious flophouses, musicos, and taverns did not exist."

"So our Aidan lived in the underworld?" Professor Howard's forehead crinkled in concern.

"Yes, and she might have remained there unnoticed," I answered, "but everything changed one afternoon when Schuyler Van Dyck and his family went for a carriage ride along the waterfront."

One

---◆---

Aidan O'Connor lifted her eyes to the green mountains in the distance and wished for a moment that she could lose herself in their velvet shadows. Surely she could find a cool breath beneath the gigantic trees that soared above the ridges. She knew the natives had built their thatched houses beneath the towering trees, secure in the cathedral-like stillness and shade.

But she was a child of Europe and therefore relegated to the "civilized" areas of Batavia—the squalid, crowded area near the wharf in general, and one crowded corner near the intersection of Straight and Broad Streets in particular. Here the air smelled of ale and open sewers, occasionally punctuated by a particularly strong whiff of a prostitute's perfume. Crowds of sailors and merchants clogged the alleys; wagons and horses jammed the cobbled streets. Drunken seamen looped their arms about each other's necks and sang sea chanties in a sweaty shove and jostle; women squealed in pretended protest as whiskey-logged lips pressed against theirs even in the revealing light of day.

Aidan glanced down the sloping length of Broad Street to the place where the cobbled road spilled into the harbor. A tall, three-masted ship was sailing into the harbor, her sails fluttering as the eager seamen gathered them in. Soon the ship's crew would come ashore, thirsty, hungry, and eager to experience all they'd been denied in the strict discipline aboard ship.

Sinking to a stone bench outside the tavern, Aidan pressed the damp fabric of her bodice to her chest, wiping away the pearls of sweat that dotted her skin. Bram or Lili would come looking for her in a moment, demanding to know why she'd run out again. They didn't mind the noise, scents, and ribald atmosphere of the tavern, but Aidan did—terribly. One of these days she would completely tire of the stale odors of frying oil, shag tobacco, and unwashed beer mugs. She'd get up and walk out forever. Perhaps she'd stroll all the way to one of the native villages. And while the Javanese stared at her in wonder, she'd kneel in front of one of their sacred Banyan trees, close her eyes, and lift her hand in a solemn vow never to return to the tavern again.

God wouldn't like it, some inner voice warned. The Almighty didn't approve of his children kneeling to pagan totems. But God had done nothing for her except take her father and blight her hopes, so perhaps he wouldn't even care if she ran away.

She lifted her petticoat for an instant, tempted to forsake all modesty in exchange for the touch of fresh air upon her bare legs. But no lady exposed her feet in public, not even brassy barmaids of the Broad Street Tavern.

A handsome coach-and-four pulled out of the traffic on Market Street and turned onto Broad, the horses' hooves clacking almost merrily upon the cobblestones as the coach moved toward her. Aidan paused, spellbound by the unusual sight. These were people of quality, that much was obvious from the uniformed driver who held the reins. So what were they doing on Broad Street?

The coach gleamed bright in the morning sun, and through the open windows Aidan could see three men and a young woman who wore the contented, slightly superior look of a newly married lady. Her gaze caught Aidan's as the carriage passed, and the superior look intensified as a small, smug smile quirked the corners of her mouth.

"Aidan! Lili's calling for you."

Orabel's familiar voice cut into Aidan's thoughts, and she looked toward her friend, removing the rich woman from her sight. "I'll be in soon, Orabel. Tell Lili I need a moment alone."

"You're an odd one, Aidan." Orabel sank to Aidan's side on the stone bench, then leaned forward to stare at the departing coach. "My goodness, did you see that woman's gown? Yellow satin! So pretty! I've always wanted a yellow dress. 'Tis such a happy color, don't you think? The color of the sun, of morning, of flowers—"

"She didn't look like a happy woman," Aidan answered, gazing down the road again. The carriage had moved away; only the bright brim of the woman's feathered hat was still visible. "I think red would be a better color for that one. Or maybe purple. She seemed a little high and mighty."

"Of course she did," Orabel answered, straightening. "Don't you know whose carriage that is?"

Aidan shook her head. "I can't say that I care."

"You should!" Orabel lifted her hand in a regal gesture and pointed toward the departing coach. "The gentleman who just passed was Schuyler Van Dyck, the cartographer. He's quite famous, you know, for his maps. The seamen all talk about him. They say he's employed by the Dutch East India Company—"

"Who isn't?" Aidan looked at her hands, idly musing that all of Batavia might be said to be in the employ of the Verenigde Oost In-dische Compagnie, more commonly referred to as the V.O.C. Even she and Orabel spent their lives serving whiskey and ale to seamen who sailed on the company's ships. Without the V.O.C. there would be no Batavia, no spice industry, no reason for the natives to resent the Europeans who had flooded this lovely island and defiled a nat-ural paradise.

"He's an artist." Orabel spoke slowly, verbally underlining the word. "Like you, Aidan. You ought to stop him one day and offer to draw for him."

"Of course." A smile tugged at Aidan's lips. "And he will be so astounded at my talent he will be forced to take me under his wing and teach me all he knows. He'll write the crowned heads of Europe to alert them of his grand discovery. And then I shall be famous! King Charles of England, or perhaps Louis of France, will invite me to become artist-in-residence at one of their grand palaces. And then

I will send for you, dear Orabel, and together we shall sit in a gilded room and eat four meals a day, all the sweet cakes and pudding we like. We'll have clean slippers for our feet and all the yellow dresses we could ever wish for, of silk brighter than the sun!"

"You don't have to make fun of me." Orabel glared at her with burning, reproachful eyes. "I only thought you should meet him. You are a very good artist, Aidan. I only wanted to make you feel better."

"What is there to feel better about?" Aidan clasped her hands together and stared at them. "I'll never be an artist, Orabel, no more than you will be the governor's wife."

"I might be the governor's wife." Orabel spoke lightly, but pain flickered in her eyes, and her voice trembled as she continued. "You never know what could happen in a day, Aidan. And things have to get better than this. If I thought this was the best we'll ever know— well, I couldn't bear it."

Stricken with sudden guilt, Aidan slipped an arm around Orabel's slender shoulders. "Of course things will be better. You're going to meet someone one day. Some nice man in the tavern will take a fancy to you and ask you to marry him."

"Just like Lili says," Orabel murmured, her hands rising to her cheeks.

"Just like Lili says," Aidan answered, stroking her friend's pale blond hair. Orabel was young, probably no older than sixteen, and more fragile than most of the others. Hope was all she had, and Aidan had been thoughtless.

"You see?" Orabel pulled away and looked at Aidan with suddenly bright eyes. "If I can find a husband, you can be an artist, just like you've always wanted to be. You could find this Heer Van Dyck and draw a picture for him." A coaxing note lined her voice. "He will like it, I know he will."

"Sure I can." A shadow loomed over the huddled girls then, and Aidan cringed as Lili's sharp voice cut through the muddled sounds of the morning. "Aidan! Orabel! What are you doing out here when there's work to be done inside?"

"Coming, Lili," Orabel sighed. She caught Aidan's eye and grinned as she stood up. "If we're going to catch rich husbands, I guess we'd better go back inside where the men are."

"I'm right behind you," Aidan answered, standing. She turned to go, then paused for a moment of silent speculation. She was no more likely to arouse Schuyler Van Dyck's interest than Orabel was to catch a decent husband in the tavern, but if Orabel wouldn't give up, why couldn't Aidan at least try to meet Heer Van Dyck?

The thought was so absurd that she laughed aloud.

Struggling to conceal her anger, Lili swallowed hard as Orabel and Aidan sashayed back into the tavern and moved toward the bar. Bram thrust a tray of pewter mugs at each of them and gestured toward a group of rowdy seamen who sat at a table in the far corner.

Lili pressed her hands against her apron and bit her lip, glad that this time, at least, the girls were of a mind to obey. Orabel had never been much trouble—the girl had a pliant spirit and a gentle one; she was as easily bent as a young twig. But Aidan was twenty, well past youth, and as stubborn as a stuck door. She was more than old enough to be married, but she turned her pert little nose up at every lad Lili pushed her way.

"Honey, can I come see you later?" A slobbering sailor leered up at Lili and reached out to tug on her sleeve.

"Not today, love," Lili answered, smiling without humor. "I've got me hands full here, can't you see? But perhaps I can get one of the other lasses to bring you a drink. No sense in dyin' of thirst in a strange port, is there?"

The sodden fool nodded his head, blindly agreeing, and Lili gave him her brightest smile. "What's your pleasure, sir? Would you like to drink with the blonde, or perhaps the redhead?"

His red-rimmed gaze swung over the room, and a smile ruffled his mouth as he focused on Aidan's flaming hair. "I'faith, she'd do," he answered, his hand wavering as he tried to follow her slender form moving through the room. "She'd do for later, too, if you can get her for me."

"Och, no, sir!" Lili shivered in pretended horror. "Sure, don't I know she's a fair lass, but I wouldn't wish her on me own worst enemy. She's cursed, that one, and bad luck to any man who as much as touches her."

"Truly?" The sailor's eyes bulged in fear, and Lili felt a small fierce surge of satisfaction as she nodded.

"Truly." She leaned forward, placing a trusting hand upon the sailor's arm. "See that white streak of hair over her left ear?" She waited until the breathless sailor nodded, then went on in a broken whisper: "That's the sign. The white springs from her heart, only a few inches below her ear, don't you see? Any man who touches her will feel the white-cold touch of death upon him before morning dawns unless he's been properly married to her first."

"Blimey," the sailor whispered, his voice fading away to a hushed stillness.

Lili straightened. "I'll have her bring you a drink, sir, and you'll enjoy her company. But mind that you heed my warning. 'Tis a terrible fate that awaits the man who is overly familiar with that young lass."

Leaving the man to ponder the dangers that awaited a roving hand, Lili snapped her fingers in Aidan's direction. The coppery head turned, and Aidan's eyes met Lili's for a moment before Lili gestured toward the man seated next to her.

A swift shadow of annoyance flitted across Aidan's face; then she resolutely tucked her empty tray under her arm and painted on a wide smile. "Come talk to this one, Aidan, me girl," Lili said, forcing a light note into her voice as her daughter approached. "Just in port from Ireland, he is, and 'twill do you good to hear a bit of the brogue. Bring him a fresh pint, lass, and let the man talk."

Lili moved away, feeling the pressure of Aidan's hot eyes upon her. Aidan hated talking to the men, she hated serving them, she hated smiling and pretending to be interested their ships and their mothers and their dreams of God, gold, and glory. But it was a decent life, the best a penniless girl could hope for, and Lili was grateful that she'd been able to offer it to her daughter . . . whether or not her daughter appreciated it.

Lili pushed past a pair of arguing men and another barmaid, then leaned against the wall, inhaling deeply of air that had been breathed far too many times. Shifting her weight from her tired feet, she folded her arms across her chest and lowered her head for a rare moment of silence.

"Well, Cory, 'tis not what you had in mind when you took us from England," she murmured, lifting her eyes long enough to see Aidan smother a yawn as she struggled to pay attention to the petrified sailor, "but I've kept her pure and reasonably virtuous. She'll make somebody a good wife, you mark me words."

Even now, after all these years, her eyes misted as she turned her thoughts toward the husband who lay somewhere at the bottom of the sea. "If you've an audience with the Almighty, put in a word for me and the girl, will you, laddie? We could use a bit of help now and again. Aidan's getting older, too old by many standards, and if I don't get her married soon, she'll spend all her days here at the tavern . . . just like me." She paused to dash a tear from the corner of her eye. "Not that I mind, Cory, me love. But you left us with nothing. Bram offered this wee bit of help, and he's kept us out of the workhouse . . . most times." Her eyes focused on Aidan's gleaming red hair. "I've been left with nothing, Cory, and I wouldn't wish my lot upon another soul. So, if you'll beg the Almighty to overlook me sins, I won't hold your departing this life against you."

"Lili!"

Bram's roar shattered her momentary serenity. Lili pulled herself off the wall and began threading her way through the milling crowd, feeling as much in control of her life and destiny as any woman had a right to feel.